About the Author

Elizabeth Kelly is a historical fiction author best known for The Tudors Series. She is a former teacher with a degree in Ancient History and Archaeology and is fascinated by historical research. She enjoys travelling to see places of historical interest including the Pyramids, the Great Wall of China and the medieval abbeys of England. She was inspired to start writing historical fiction after taking several online courses in creative writing during the lockdown. She is a highly imaginative writer who loves to create an escape into the alternative reality of creative fiction. She lives in Yorkshire.

The Tudors Series

(1) The Tudor Maid (the story of the seamstress Margery Hallows).
(2) The Tudor Lady in Waiting (the story of Lady Margaret de la Roche).
(3) The Tudor Fool: My Life with Henry VIII (the story of Will Somers).
(4) The Dark Lady: The Rise and Fall of Queen Anne Boleyn.

This book is

dedicated to my brother Richard.

THE TUDOR LADY IN WAITING

AUTHOR: ELIZABETH KELLY

ILLUSTRATOR: JULIA BAI

Copyright © 2023 by Elizabeth Kelly

Illustrator: Julia Bai

All rights reserved. No part of this publication may be reproduced, distributed or transmitted in any form or by any means, including photocopying, recording, or other electronic or mechanical methods, without the prior written permission of the publisher, except in the case of brief quotations embodied in critical reviews and certain other noncommercial uses permitted by copyright law.

List of Principal Characters: Fictional

Lady Margaret de la Roche.
Sir Thomas de la Roche (her father).
Margaret Pennington (her mother).
Lady Agnes da la Roche (her grandmother).
Sir Robert Fairley (her husband).
Lady Catherine Fairley (her daughter).
Don Pedro Dávila y Córdoba, the Marquis of Las Navas (her son-in-law).

List of Principal Characters: Historical

King Henry VIII (1509-1547).
Queen Catherine of Aragon (1509-1533).
Queen Anne Boleyn (1533-1536).
Queen Jane Seymour (1536-1537).
Queen Anne of Cleves (January 1540 – July 1540).
Queen Catherine Howard (1540-1542).
Queen Catherine Parr (1543-1547).

King Edward VI (1547-1553).
Queen Mary I (1553-1558).
Prince Philip of Spain (1554 – 1558).
Queen Elizabeth I (1558-1603).

Lady Margaret Douglas, the king's niece.
Lady Jane Grey, the king's niece (10th July 1553 – 19th July 1553).

Pope Clement VII.
Cardinal Lorenzo Campeggio.
Cardinal Thomas Wolsey.
Cardinal Reginal Pole.

Archbishop Thomas Cranmer.
Bishop Steven Gardiner.

Edward Stafford, Duke of Buckingham.
Thomas Howard, Duke of Norfolk.
Edward Seymour, Duke of Somerset.
Thomas Seymour, Lord Admiral.
John Dudley, Duke of Northumberland.

Seigneur Eustace Chapuys, Spanish Ambassador.

Chancellor Thomas More.
Chancellor Thomas Cromwell.
Chancellor Thomas Wriothesley.

Sir William Compton, Groom of the Stool.
Sir William Paget, Secretary.
Master Andrew Windsor, Keeper of the Wardrobe.
Sir Henry Guildford, Comptroller of the Household 1522 – 1532.
Sir William Paulet, Comptroller of the Household 1532-1537 and Lord Chamberlain of the Household 1543-1555.
Sir William Norris.
Sir Francis Weston.
Sir Nicholas Carew.
Sir Anthony Denny.
Sir William Herbert.

Dr Thomas Wendy.
Dr William Butts.
Master Hans Holbein, the king's painter.
Master Robert Amadas, the king's goldsmith.
Master John Penn, the king's barber.

Ladies in Waiting

Lady Margaret de la Pole, Countess of Salisbury.
Lady Elizabeth Stafford, Duchess of Norfolk.
Lady Anne Stafford, Countess of Huntingdon.
Lady Gertrude Courtenay, Marchioness of Exeter.
Lady Mary Say.
Lady Maud Parr.
Lady Maria de Eresby.
Lady Isabel de Vargas.
Lady Blanche de Vargas.

Maids of Honour

Mrs Stoner, the Mother of the Maids.

Lady Anne Stanhope.
Lady Jane Rochford.
Lady Elizabeth Blount.
Lady Mary Boleyn.
Lady Anne Boleyn.
Lady Anne Gainsford.
Lady Margery Horsman.
Lady Mary Shelton.
Lady Anne Parr "Nan."
Lady Mary Zouche.
Lady Jane Seymour.
Lady Elizabeth Darrell.
Lady Anne Basset.
Lady Catherine Howard.

Ladies in Waiting to Queen Mary

Mrs Susan Clarencieux
Lady Jane Dormer
Frances Neville
Magdalen Dacre
Lady Margaret Douglas
Lady Catherine Grey
Lady Mary Grey.

Historical Notes on Henry VIII and His Six Wives

Henry VIII married Catherine of Aragon on 11 June 1509. He was 17 and she was 23. They were crowned king and queen on 24th June 1509. Catherine had six pregnancies but only one child survived. Their daughter Mary was born on 18th February 1516. On 9th November 1518 she bore a stillborn daughter but had no more children. Her motto was "*Humble and Loyal.*"

Henry married Anne Boleyn on 25 January 1533. He was 42 and she was 31. Their daughter Elizabeth was born on 7th September 1533. Catherine died on 7th January 1536 aged 51. Anne Boleyn was executed on 19 May 1536 aged 34. Her motto was "*The Most Happy.*"

Henry married Jane Seymour on 30 May 1536. He was 45 and she was 28. Their son Edward was born on 12 October 1537. She died on 24th October 1537 aged 29. Her motto was "*Bound to Obey and Serve.*"

Henry married Anne of Cleves on 6 January 1540. He was 48 and she was 24. Their marriage was annulled on 9th July 1540. Her motto was "*God Send me Well to Keep.*"

Henry married Catherine Howard on 28th July 1540. He was 49 and she was 19. She was stripped of her title of queen on 23rd November 1541 and executed on 13th February 1542 aged 21. Her motto was "*No Other Will But His.*"

Henry married Catherine Parr on 12 July 1543. He was 52 and she was 30. Her motto was "*To Be Useful In All I Do.*"

Henry died on 28 January 1547 aged 55. He had reigned 36 years (1509-1547). Catherine Parr married Thomas Seymour in May 1547. She died on 5th September 1548 aged 36. Anne of Cleves died on 16th July 1557 aged 41.

King Edward VI reigned from 1547 to 1553. He died on 6th July 1553 aged 15.

Queen Jane I the "Nine Days' Queen" reigned from 10 July to 19th July 1553. She died on 12th February 1554 aged 16 or 17.

Queen Mary I reigned from 1553 to 1558. She died on 17th November 1558 aged 42.

Queen Elizabeth I reigned from 1558 to 1603. She died on 24th March 1603 aged 69.

Historical Notes on the Text

(1) Some ladies in waiting served all six wives of Henry VIII including Lady Anne Herbert (nee Parr), Countess of Pembroke (Nan); Lady Anne Seymour (nee Stanhope), Duchess of Somerset and Mrs Elizabeth Stoner, the Mother of the Maids. Lady Jane Rochford (nee Parker) served the first five wives but was executed for her complicity in the adultery of Queen Catherine Howard in 1542. Lady Eleanor Manners (nee Paston), Countess of Rutland maintained her post throughout the reigns of four queens from Anne Boleyn to Catherine Howard.

(2) The remarkable discovery of the gold heart-shaped pendant in 2019 gives an insight into the style of Tudor jewellery from the early sixteenth century. It is marked with the emblems and initials of Henry VIII and Catherine of Aragon and the motto "*Toujours.*" It also illustrates the king's predilection for giving personal love-tokens to the ladies he admired. A likely occasion for such a gift was the birth of Prince Henry in 1511. Henry celebrated with a joust in which he competed as Sir Loyal Heart. The Westminster Tournament Roll of 1511 shows him tilting before the queen on a horse bearing their initials and the device of a gold heart. In 1526 Henry competed in the Shrovetide joust on a horse bearing the motto: "*Declare I dare not,*" and the device of a flaming heart in tribute to his love for Anne Boleyn. His accounts for the spring of 1526 list four gold brooches commissioned from his goldsmith which were probably gifts to her. One of them represented a lady holding a heart in her hand. His love letters to Anne Boleyn in 1527 mention the gift of a bracelet with his picture. In return, she sent him a jewel depicting a storm-tossed maiden on a ship. Thomas Fuller refers to a jewel pendant with his likeness which he gave to Jane Seymour which a furious Queen Anne tore off her neck (The Worthies of England (1662).

(3) Sir William Paulet, Marquess of Winchester served as Comptroller of the Household 1532-1537 and Lord Chamberlain of the Household 1543-1555. He had a successful career as a courtier throughout the reigns of four Tudor monarchs and famously said, "I am sprung from the willow and not from the oak."

(4) Maria de Salinas came from Spain to serve Queen Catherine of Aragon in

1503. By 1514 she was Queen Catherine's closest friend "whom she loves more than any other mortal." In 1516 she married William Willoughby, Baron Willoughby of Eresby. Henry gave her a dowry of 1100 gold marks and Grimsthorpe Castle in Lincolnshire. He also named a warship after her. In August 1532 she was ordered to leave Queen Catherine's service and not to communicate with her. In January 1536 she visited Queen Catherine on her deathbed and is said to have been buried beside her in Peterborough Cathedral.

(5) Margaret Pennington and Mabel Clifford served as chamberers of Queen Catherine of Aragon. She gave them gowns of crimson velvet and russet satin in October 1511 and May 1512. Margaret was the daughter of William Pennington of Hunsdon. She married John Cooke of Gidea Park in 1512.

(6) Elizabeth Stafford, Duchess of Norfolk became a lady in waiting to Queen Catherine of Aragon in 1509 and served her for sixteen years. In 1516 Elizabeth carried the Princess Mary to the font during her christening. In 1530 Elizabeth brought letters concealed in oranges from the papal emissary in Italy to Queen Catherine which she then passed on to the Spanish Ambassador Eustace Chapuys. When Anne Boleyn was crowned on 1 June 1533, Elizabeth refused to attend the coronation "from the love she bore to the previous Queen."

(7) Gertrude Courtenay, Marchioness of Exeter was another of the court informants of the Spanish Ambassador. In November 1534 she warned him that Catherine of Aragon and her daughter Mary were in danger because Henry had said that "he would no longer remain in the trouble, fear, and suspense he had so long endured on account of the Queen and Princess." In January 1536 she reported that Henry had said of Queen Anne Boleyn that "he had made this marriage constrained and seduced by sortileges and for this reason he considered it null."

(8) Anne Gainsford witnessed the book of prophecy found in the chamber of Queen Anne Boleyn which she dismissed as a bauble.

(9) Mary Zouche came to court to escape from the misery of her life with her stepmother Susan Welby.

(10) Henry VIII had a liaison with an unknown lady between September and December of 1534. According to the Spanish ambassador Eustace Chapuys she was "a very beautiful maid-of-honour of the court." Queen Anne Boleyn wanted to send her from court, but Henry refused.

(11) Anne Basset was appointed as a Maid of Honour following Lady Lisle's campaign of gift-giving to Queen Anne Boleyn and Queen Jane Seymour.

(12) "Some godly person" found the dropped arrest warrant signed by the king and brought it to Queen Catherine Parr. Henry VIII's physician Dr Wendy warned Catherine Parr of her danger and advised her to "conform herself unto the king's mind, saying, he did not doubt but, if she would so do, and show her humble submission unto him, she should find him gracious and favourable unto her" (John Foxe, 1563, Book of Martyrs).

(13) Jane Dormer joined the household of Lady Mary at the age of nine. She became a lady in waiting to Queen Mary at the age of sixteen. She was such a favourite that she carved her meat at meals and often slept in her chamber. After the death of Queen Mary in 1558 she married the Duke of Feria and went to live in Spain. She was trusted to deliver her jewels to Queen Elizabeth in 1559. Her secretary, Henry Clifford, wrote her biography c.1610.

(14) Bridget Manners was presented by her father as a New Year's Day gift to Queen Elizabeth in 1595 at the age of fourteen.

(15) Mary Fitton came to court as a maid of honour to Queen Elizabeth in 1595 aged seventeen. Her father asked his old friend Sir William Knollys to keep a protective eye on her. He promised to "defend the innocent lamb from the wolfish cruelty and fox-like subtlety of the tame beasts of this place."

Contents

Introduction: My Father's Household (1505 -1519) 1

Part 1: The Household of Queen Catherine of Aragon (1519 – 1532) 7

Part 2: The Household of Queen Anne Boleyn (1532 – 1536) 51

Part 3: The Household of Queen Jane Seymour (1536 – 1537) 147

Part 4: In the Household of Queen Anne of Cleves (1539 – 1540) 181

Part 5: In the Household of Queen Catherine Howard (1540 – 1542) 189

Part 6: In the Household of Queen Catherine Parr (1543-1547) 203

Part 7: The Household of Dowager Queen Catherine Parr (1547 – 1548) 225

Part 8: The Household of Lady Mary Tudor (1548 – 1553) 235

Part 9: In the Household of Queen Mary I (1553 – 1554) 249

Epilogue 269

Bibliography 271

Introduction: My Father's Household (1505 -1519)

"Devote yourself completely to acquiring virtue. Behave so that your reputation may be worthy of perpetual memory. Whatever you do, above all, be truly honest, humble, courageous and loyal"

(Anne de Beaujeu, Lessons for my Daughter 1497).

My name is Lady Margaret de la Roche and I am the only child of Sir Thomas de la Roche. Our family is old and honourable for our family line dates back to the Norman Conquest. As does our ancestral manor-house which is known as Ravenseat. The symbol of our house is a raven, but the reason for the choice is lost in time. My father told me that it is because the raven was a symbol of faithfulness. But the servants said that the ravens have nested in the trees beside our house for centuries. No-one was allowed to disturb them and their raucous cawing was a familiar sound at sunrise and sunset.

We are not a wealthy family, but we are distinguished for our history of loyal service at the royal court. I bear the honour of having served all six wives of King Henry VIII. Four of them fell disastrously out of favour, but I never did. And for that I give credit to my father who brought me up as a perfect courtier from my childhood. By the age of ten I could converse in French, perform all the fashionable dances and embroider with the skill of a grown woman. I had also mastered all the popular card games and was familiar with all the noble houses of the land and their lineages. Naturally, I could ride well and my deportment was impeccable. These skills were my birthright. They were the qualities by which I was recognised as a lady of noble birth.

Introduction: My Father's Household (1505 -1519)

My father boasted that I took after his mother Agnes in looks. And truly, her youthful portrait was the very image of me with large dark eyes and abundant brown hair. But there were no portraits of my mother and my father never spoke of her. I assumed that she had died young. But my grandmother once confided to me that against her wishes my father had married a low-born girl who was the local beauty. After my birth she had broken her marriage vows and deserted us. They had never heard of her again.

"You must never speak of her, Margaret," she counselled me. "It would only bring pain to your father. As her fate is unknown, he cannot remarry and has no son to inherit. You are all that he has and his entire hopes rest in you." It saddened me to think that my mother was an unworthy woman and I wondered what she was like and what had become of her. I did not even know her name. But I could not ask any questions. My father had destroyed every memory of her. I resolved that I would make him proud of me and restore the honour of our family.

My grandmother knew the entire history of our family and took great pride in being a De Roche. She told me many stories about my noble forebears and the lives of the kings and queens they had served. Her father had fought at the battle of Agincourt in 1415 in the army of King Henry V. And her husband had fallen at the battle of Bosworth in 1485 fighting for King Henry VII. She was adamant that my future lay in being prepared for a life at court. One night, I overheard her discussing the matter with my father.

"Margaret has fine looks, a good mind and an aristocratic name. But we are a poor house and there is no-one suitable for her to marry hereabouts. She would end up being thrown away upon some merchant or banker with deep pockets. But if she goes to court suitably educated and attired, then she will show to advantage like a pearl in its setting. There she will meet the pick of the gentry and attract the offers that are worthy of her."

"But she is so young to go to court on her own. Who would care for her there?" objected my father.

"I do not speak of her going there now, but in a few years' time she will be ready," she insisted. "She must be introduced into the queen's household as a maid of honour. There she will associate with accomplished women of rank and learn the social graces of the court. It will be the duty of the queen to find her a suitable husband of birth and means. As a young lady of her circle, she will be eligible for alliance into the best families in the land."

Poor grandmother did not realise that noble families did not match their sons to impoverished brides. They sent them to court to make their fortunes by taking up a position in royal service or making a wealthy alliance. But ever afterwards I secretly fantasised about my future life at the court. I imagined it to be like the knightly tales of King Arthur's Camelot. I would serve the queen faithfully and virtuously. Troubadours would sing songs in praise of my beauty, but I would not even look at them. Knights would request my favours to joust in tournaments, but I would refuse. And then a visiting prince would come to court and see me. He would fall in love with me at first sight and the queen would reluctantly part with me. She would give me a ring as a sign of her affection and I would be married and live happily ever after. These happy dreams inspired me through many long hours of practice at reading French, embroidering cushions and playing on my lute. I was determined to be worthy of my future at the court and to renew the fortunes of the family.

I first came to court in 1519 at the tender age of fourteen. I well remember the day of my presentation on New Year's Day. I was dressed in a stiff new dress of black satin. It was a bitterly cold day and my feet were freezing in my thin leather shoes. My father and I had waited for hours for our turn to enter the Great Hall and greet the king and queen. After several hours had passed, I had grown very weary and gave my father imploring looks. However, he was determined not to give up. "Take courage, Margaret," he urged me. "This is your great chance." Finally, he had the presence of mind to hand a gold mark to the chamberlain and we were quickly escorted through the doors. King Henry and Queen Catherine of Aragon were seated upon a raised dais beneath a huge crimson canopy of state. The walls of the hall were covered with huge tapestries depicting scenes from the life of King Solomon and the Nine Worthies of Chivalry. And along the length of the hall was a trestle table lined with gleaming gold and silver objects of every kind imaginable. There were finely chased cups and goblets, fantastically shaped salt cellars, encased clocks, quantities of plate and fat velvet purses of coins. It seemed a fortune greater than all the treasures of the Temple in Jerusalem. These were the New Year's gifts to the king.

My father's name was announced and he grabbed my hand and pulled me forward to stand before the king and queen. I could hardly keep up with his long strides. "Make your curtsey, Margaret," he prompted as he swept into a deep court bow. I made my reverence with modest grace just as I had been taught.

King Henry was in a splendid humour and greeted him kindly, "Welcome to court, Sir Thomas. We are glad to see you and we wish you a good New Year!"

My father seized the opportunity. "Your Majesty, this is my daughter Margaret. She is my only child and my most precious possession. But I willingly present her as my New Year's day gift to you!"

The room fell quiet as the courtiers took in this unexpected departure from custom. They were ready to be affronted by his impertinence. But the king was amused and forestalled their reaction. "I declare that she is the fairest gift I have been offered this day. Is that not so, Catherine?"

"Indeed, she is Henry," affirmed the queen. "And I would be pleased to accept her as one of my maids of honour here at court."

"You are fortunate, Lady Margaret," said the king. "Many young ladies would be honoured to have the chance to serve the queen."

I curtsied again. "I am most grateful to your Majesties and I promise to serve you well."

"Then it is settled, Sir Thomas," said the king. "You may bring her to us at our Easter court. My chamberlain will advise you how to prepare your daughter for the queen's service."

The chamberlain stepped forward with alacrity and ushered us out of the door again. My father turned to me with a beaming smile. "Well done, Margaret. You have made me very proud this day." To have pleased my father was all the reward

I needed. I forgot about my aching legs and throbbing feet. The chamberlain instructed my father to send two sets of clothes with me, one of satin and one of damask silk. Then he turned his attention to the other eager petitioners who were waiting to pay their respects. My father took me home in triumph to tell my grandmother of our success. She was certain that this stroke of good fortune meant that my future was secure.

On the night before my departure my father took me to stand in front of the family roll of honour beside the fireplace in the great hall. It recorded all the names of our De La Roche ancestors.

"You see this, Margaret," he said tapping it.

"Yes, father," I replied, thinking that he meant to tell me a story about one of my forebears.

"This is made of oak which is solid and enduring," he said gravely. "The De Roches are like oaks in their upright loyalty. Indeed, we are as constant as a rock which is the meaning of our name. We stand firm in our convictions and do not yield to storms. We have been loyal servants of the Crown for centuries and we hold fast through tribulations and are constant to the end. Always remember the faithfulness of your ancestors and be worthy of it."

"Yes father," I replied dutifully.

"You are a young girl, so you have everything to learn," he admonished me. "Spend your time in listening rather than chattering. Show yourself to be modest, diligent and trustworthy in every way. Study your mistress so that you can anticipate her wishes and be ready for whatever she needs. Every night look to your dress for the following day so that your appearance is faultless. And rise early in the morning so that you are prepared to serve well. It is not enough to be handsome, clever and talented. In order to succeed at court, you must gain the favour of your mistress and the court officials. Those who are foolish are sent away, but those who are wise will prosper. The queen is known to be considerate of the future of her ladies and takes care that they are placed in good marriages."

The following day, my father saw my trunk of clothes safely stowed upon the cart. He reminded me to say my prayers and write to him and he gave me his blessing. I was a pretty little maid and I felt proud to wear my new silk dress. In my hands I held a black Latin missal as evidence of my piety. I was nervous about beginning my new life at court but also excited by the prospect of so great an adventure. I had high hopes of my future in the service of the queen. There was no telling where my life at court might take me. My happy daydreams occupied me throughout the long journey to Greenwich Palace.

Part 1: The Household of Queen Catherine of Aragon (1519 – 1532)

"Place yourself in the service of a lady who is well regarded, who is constant and has good judgement."

(Anne de Beaujeu, Lessons for my Daughter, 1497).

We had journeyed far from sunrise and the chill air of the April morning had gradually thawed into a pleasant spring breeze. I sat on the jolting cart wrapped tightly in a thick woollen mantle. Along the grassy banks and budding hedgerows of the winding trackway I could see patches of primroses, clusters of violets and tall clumps of cow parsley. Finally, we arrived at the splendid redbrick palace beside the river Thames. It was a vast building with tall octagonal towers and high mullioned windows. The bright afternoon sun made the walls glow and the panes sparkle. A row of barges lay tied up against the riverside where a group of waiting boatmen sat on barrels. My nose wrinkled as I caught the stench from the water lapping against the banks. It didn't seem to bother the boatmen who were smoking their clay pipes and laughing amongst themselves. The wheels of the cart came to a juddering halt at the gatehouse. I stumbled down from the cart and thankfully stretched my numbed legs. The gatekeeper took me to a side door of the palace where I was received by a tall, imposing woman dressed in an impeccable black silk gown.

"So you are the new addition to the queen's household?" she enquired doubtfully. Her voice was just as formidable as the rest of her.

My heart pounded in my chest as I made my best curtsey. "Yes, Madam. My name is Lady Margaret."

"I am Mrs Stoner, the mother of the maids." She looked down at me with a disapproving frown. "You know there is a waiting list of candidates to serve Her Majesty. How did you contrive to be selected?"

I considered telling her that my father had presented me as a New Year's Day gift. But I was afraid that she would consider it impertinent. "It was the wish of His Majesty," I replied.

I did not know it but it was the perfect answer. She looked displeased, but asked me no more questions. "You will live in the dormitory of the maids of honour of which I am in charge," she informed me. "I expect you to be tidy, punctual and respectful. Every morning you will attend Her Majesty in her Privy Chamber. You will accompany her to mass in her chapel and then you will stand beside her table while she has her breakfast. You will provide pleasant company for Her Majesty, assist with her sewing for the poor and see that she is entertained. You will observe absolute discretion in your role as a maid of honour. It is a great honour and a privilege for a young girl to serve the queen."

I curtsied again as I tried to retain this catalogue of instructions. "Yes, Mrs Stoner." I hoped that I would be able to meet the expectations of this daunting lady. It would be dreadful to fail and be sent back home. My father and my grandmother would be so disappointed.

"This evening you shall be introduced to Her Majesty and swear your oath of service to her," she continued. "Now you may go to the dormitory. If you have brought a servant then she may unpack your garments and store them in your chest."

"I do not have a servant, Mrs Stoner." I knew that my father could not meet the expense of providing a servant. I was determined that I would manage on my own.

She raised her eyebrows slightly. "In that case, you must attend to your wardrobe by yourself. You will find that you must meet the highest standards as a lady of the court. You must reflect the honour and dignity of the queen at all times and it is a great responsibility."

"Yes, indeed Mrs Stoner," I replied. My heart sank as I wondered how I would compare with the other ladies of the court. But I reminded myself that I was a De Roche. And I had brought two new dresses to wear just as the chamberlain had instructed my father.

"I will send a page to carry your things to the dormitory," she concluded. "There you will meet the other maids of honour. They will tell you what to do."

It seemed I was dismissed. "Thank you, Mrs Stoner," I replied. She walked away down the corridor and left me with the page. My mind was in a whirl as I followed him to the dormitory. He deposited the chest at the door. "I ain't allowed to go inside there, my lady," he whispered. Then he disappeared into the gloom of the long stone corridor. I summoned up my courage and knocked on the door. A young servant girl opened it.

"I am Lady Margaret de la Roche. I have just arrived at court," I said.

"Please come in, my lady," she replied.

Inside the room I saw two rows of beds with chests standing at the end of them. The walls were hung with plain drapes and the fire was unlit in the stone fireplace. There was nothing very grand about my surroundings. My chamber at home was far more comfortable. I felt a pang of disappointment.

"Which one is my bed?" I asked her.

She led me to the end of the row. "This bed has not been taken yet, my lady. And you can put your chest at the end of it."

"Please bring in it and help me to dress. Where are the other ladies?" I enquired.

"They are all attending Her Majesty in her Privy Chamber, my lady," she explained. "But they will return here this evening once the queen has retired."

I put on my best gown of blue silk and was relieved to find it in perfect condition. It made me feel more confident in these strange new surroundings. I arranged my belongings as best I could and locked the chest. Then I put the key in my pocket. I wondered what I should do until the others returned.

"When do we dine?" I asked for I felt very hungry after the long journey. I wished that I had thought to bring a supply of wafers.

The girl gave me a sympathetic smile. "Her Majesty dines at six o'clock in the evening. Her ladies attend her and then they dine afterwards."

I did not feel that I should wander around the palace on my own. I was afraid that I might get lost. So I sat on my bed in the dreary room and waited for the other maids of honour to appear. Finally, a young lady with blonde hair and cold grey eyes entered the dormitory. I guessed that she was about my age. She was dressed very finely in a gown of green satin with wide velvet sleeves.

"I am Lady Anne Stanhope," she said unsmilingly. "I have come to bring you to Her Majesty."

"Thank you, Lady Anne. I am quite ready," I replied promptly. She looked me up and down and smirked. "Follow me, Lady Margaret. We must not keep Her Majesty waiting."

I trailed after Lady Anne wondering if all the queen's ladies would be so distant. I tried to keep track of the way, but it was all that I could do to keep up. Now that the moment of presentation had come, my heart was beginning to thump and my palms were moist with sweat. We passed through the Great Hall and came to a door guarded by two tall Yeomen of the Guard in scarlet livery bearing great halberds. She nodded to them and they allowed us to enter into the queen's Privy Chamber. Lady Anne led me straight to where the queen was sitting with her ladies and swept into a deep curtsey. I took a deep breath and did my best to imitate her.

"Your Majesty, this is Lady Margaret de la Roche who has newly come to court," announced Lady Anne with serene composure. I envied her perfect self-confidence in the midst of this dignified assembly.

Queen Catherine of Aragon was a stately woman with plump cheeks and a gracious smile. She was dressed very richly in a gown of crimson velvet with cloth of gold sleeves. Her bodice and head-dress were bordered with great rubies and lustrous pearls. She wore a gold Jesus pendant set with diamonds and three pendant pearls and a golden girdle with roses and pomegranates. She sat very straight upon a chair of patterned gold satin beneath a purple cloth of state. Her feet rested on a black velvet footstool embroidered with the king's arms.

"We welcome you to our service, little Lady Margaret," she said with a kind expression. "I recall that your father brought you here as a New Year's Day gift. It was a gallant gesture to give us his most precious possession."

"I am honoured to be here, your Majesty," I replied in a steady voice. "I am your most humble servant."

"You are a delightful addition to my household," she declared. "Mrs Stoner, please bring my Bible and we shall swear Lady Margaret to our service."

Mrs Stoner stepped forward and placed the great black Bible in my hands. "Hold it up straight, Lady Margaret and say these words after me. They are your oath of service to Her Majesty."

I clutched the heavy book tight in my hands, took a deep breath and made my vow in a firm voice. "I swear to be true and faithful to my sovereign lord, King Henry VIII and to my lady Queen Catherine of Aragon. I shall be loyal, humble and diligent in my service. I shall give good advice and counsel. And I will do and say nothing that is contrary to their honour. So help me God and the holy contents of this book." I handed the Bible back to Mrs Stoner who bore it away. Now it was done and I felt elated. I wished that my father could have been here to witness this moment. I stood up straight and smiled like a true lady of the court.

"Bravo, Lady Margaret," said Queen Catherine approvingly. "Now you are one of us entirely. I hope that you will be happy here at court. It is good to have young people among us. And now we shall have some music to make ourselves merry. Let us hear the ballad of Lady Alda's Dream."

A minstrel stepped forward holding his lute and bowed to the queen. "It would give me great pleasure to play for your Majesty," he declared as he began:

"In Paris sits Lady Alda, the betrothed of Rondale.
Six hundred ladies are with her; all are of high degree.
Three hundred are playing drums, three hundred are weaving silk."

I recognised the song as the tale of the French warrior Roland who died at the battle of Roncevaux in Spain. But I had never heard such great artistry before. The queen applauded graciously and he continued by singing more Spanish ballads recounting the adventures of the famous hero, El Cid. I was entranced and the tense knot in my stomach relaxed. Life at the court would be a wonderful thing, I thought. The queen was the kindest of ladies and her musicians were surely the finest in the world. Afterwards, Queen Catherine of Aragon read to us from the lives of the saints. It was one of her favourite stories about St Agatha who refused to marry a pagan and was martyred for her faith.

I sat on a joint-stool of polished walnut to listen to the tale of the holy martyr. But that first evening my attention was drawn away to admire the beautiful furnishings of the queen's apartments. The great stone fireplace was carved with the initials of the king and queen and her own device of a pomegranate. On the mantelpiece stood a pair of gold candlesticks and a clock in a silver case engraved with a rose and crown. One either side of the fireplace stood tall cupboards filled with gold and silver plate of the finest quality. The walls were hung with tapestries depicting Jupiter and Juno and the Passion of Christ. The floors were covered with coloured Turkey carpets and the cushions were embroidered with Tudor roses and the arms of England and Spain. I surreptitiously pressed my feet into the soft silk rugs and brushed my fingers against the velvet cushions. *Life at court is even more splendid than the tales of Camelot,* I thought.

I soon became familiar with the routine of life as a maid of honour. The queen rose at dawn and attended mass which was followed by a light breakfast. Then she went to her Presence Chamber where she sat beneath the canopy of state and gave audience. I was amazed at the constant stream of visitors that came to see her. I saw that some visitors brought her gifts to gain favour such as orange marmalade and confits. There were foreign merchants who brought fine goods to sell such as imported silks and satins from Antwerp and Venice. And there were travelling minstrels who sought permission to entertain the queen with their singing or playing. The queen was gracious and attentive to all her visitors, no matter how humble. Watching her was a masterclass in how to be a great lady. Lady Maria de Eresby stood ready with a great purse of coins to give whatever reward the queen chose to bestow upon her visitor. Queen Catherine gave gifts and alms every day as it was expected that a great lady would be generous. Afterwards, the queen took the time to review the day's accounts with Lady Maria.

"How much did we lay out today in rewards, Lady Maria?" asked the queen. She was always most conscientious in examining her personal expenses.

"Your Grace, we have made payment of twenty-two pounds to Master William Locke, the mercer of London, for certain silks and five shillings to Master John, the hardware man, for making two pairs of sleeves," said Lady Maria. "We gave six shillings to a servant of my Lady Sidney for bringing a present of suckets and marmalade and ten shillings to a Spanish woman in reward for bringing salt lampreys. We gave sixteen shillings to a monk that brought a gift of a lyre and eleven shillings to a servant of Lady Burkeley for bringing a tame deer. We gave a reward of ten shillings to Petty John the minstrel and twenty-six shillings in alms for a poor woman to obtain her husband's freedom in London."

"Is there anything else?" she enquired.

"There is the sum of thirty shillings which your Grace lost in play at Primero and Imperial with your ladies."

"Let it be paid," she said decisively. "And we must not forget to send some of the lampreys to the king's table, Lady Maria. They are his favourite dish."

At ten in the morning, Queen Catherine would take a meal in her Privy Chamber. But on formal occasions she would dine in her Presence Chamber at a high covered table. Her thirty maids of honour would stand around the table as she ate while the ladies in waiting attended upon her according to their rank. The astringent scent of orange flowers surrounded her. She washed her hands in it before and after every meal. The king preferred rosewater for his ablutions. Lady Margaret Pole held the ornate gold finger bowl, Lady Elizabeth Stafford presented the fine linen towel and Lady Anne Stafford kept the assay cup for tasting the wine served to the queen. A procession of marvellous dishes was presented and served at the table. They included the queen's particular favourites of baked lampreys and orange marmalade. I stared at this outlandish fare in astonishment until Mrs Stoner pointedly cleared her throat and glared at me. She had given me strict instructions on how to deport myself.

"As a maid of honour, you must remember that you represent the honour and glory of the queen's majesty. You are to stand up as straight as a doorpost and keep silent. On no account are you to look at the queen or distract her by your foolish fidgeting. On public occasions the queen's ladies form a guard of honour around her in the same way as the king's own yeomen."

I was amazed by the richness of the queen's table so early in the year. At home we were dining largely on pickled mutton and kale. For the first course there was pottage, roasted swan, and fritters followed by dishes of stewed cranes and venison served with white manchet bread. The second course included quince pies and cream of almonds accompanied by a selection of oranges, pomegranates and figs served upon gilded spice plates. The sight of these strange fruits served for desert fascinated me. The most exotic ones that I knew were damsons and medlars.

"Where do they come from?" I whispered to Lady Anne Stanhope when Mrs Stoner's eyes had turned elsewhere. She smiled at my ignorance, but condescended to answer me. "The court is supplied by the royal gardeners who send fruit and lettuce in season and the park keepers who supply the venison and wild boar. And a number of merchants bring the exotic fruit from Spain and Portugal. Master Robert Hobart provides the sweet oranges, lemons and dates that the queen loves best, but every consignment costs twenty shillings. The king and queen often receive special dishes from members of the court who know their fondness for lampreys, cheese and quince jellies. And during the summer progresses many of their subjects present them with gifts of chickens, apples and hazelnuts and are rewarded with a few shillings in return."

At the end of the meal, the queen retired to her private apartments and we took our own repast in the Great Hall. Each of us was entitled to an allowance of bread, meat and ale every day. In the afternoons the maids of honour attended the queen in her apartments. On fine days she might go out for a ride or take a walk in the palace gardens. Often there would be plans for a court masque to rehearse or sewing for the poor to complete. The main meal of the day was served at six o'clock in the evening. Afterwards, there would be entertainments including gambling with cards and dice, music and dancing. Some nights in the queen's privy chamber we listened to the queen's minstrels playing on the lute or the virginals, or the royal choristers would come to sing a new composition. Sometimes the queen's jesters performed and made merry in the chamber. At other times visiting entertainers provided some novelty such as a blind harper or a man with a dancing dog. On special occasions, there would be entertainments in the Great Hall attended by the king and queen and the entire court. The Master of the Revels would prepare a masque on a topic such a debate between married love and chastity as to which of them was the greatest. But more often there would be masques on martial themes and courtly romances which the king preferred.

It was known that my mother had died which won me the sympathy of my new mistress. Queen Catherine asked her ladies to care for me and this favour admitted me into her inner circle of attendants. My small stature, dark eyes and black hair gave me a Spanish appearance and the Spanish ladies readily accepted me as one of them.

"Look, the little one, she is a Spaniard!" said Lady Isabel de Vargas.

"Indeed, she has the look of a true hidalga," agreed her sister Lady Blanche.

"But not these clothes," said Lady Maris de Eresby fingering the costly dark blue silk with distaste. "Her people, did they not know to dress her for court? We shall dress her as befits a hidalga of her age."

The ladies made a project of my debut and brought me to the queen's own dressmaker insisting, "It is the queen's command!" An intense debate took place as a selection of splendid materials were inspected and then rejected in turn. Finally, a choice was approved. Another discussion took place over the proper style of the dress and the correct accoutrements. A few days later I was robed in the completed dress of fine russet velvet with a blackwork collar and cuffs and a Spanish head dress and fan. When the Spanish ladies brought me to the queen, she laughed, and said that no Infante had been better dressed. And indeed, the style had been modelled upon her own garments.

"A true daughter of Spain!" she declared. "I shall present you to His Majesty later."

And so, after mass in the Chapel Royal, she called me forward. "Make your curtsey to the king, my child," she said. I did my best to oblige her. King Henry was a giant of a man whose size and presence dominated the room. He wore a doublet of white satin striped with gold, a massive gold collar set with diamonds and pearls and a cap of black velvet set with jewelled brooches. When he gazed down at me, the sheer magnetic force of his personality held me captivated. I craned my neck to look up at him and he looked amused by my expression of awe.

"Do you remember this little one?" she asked the king.

"Of course, I do," he replied. King Henry prided himself on his memory for names and faces. "She is my New Year's gift from Sir Thomas de la Roche. Welcome to court, my dear."

"Thank you, your Majesty," I replied.

"Perhaps we should send her over to your father, King Ferdinand," he suggested as he surveyed my elegant costume.

"He has enough hidalgas at his court already. I shall make of her a fine young lady."

"I have no doubt of it," said Henry. "She has only to follow your example, my dear."

The Spanish ladies were satisfied with their efforts and took care that I should always appear well in the queen's apartments. And appearance was the most essential quality for a lady at court. In fact, my unusual costume was something of a curiosity at court and I was often taken for a foreign visitor. In addition to dressing in the stately Spanish fashions, I set myself to read the poetry of Castile. The queen's musicians taught me to sing the ballads of *Count Arnaldos* and *Good King Sancho*. The queen and her ladies were delighted by my efforts. They showed me the Spanish manner of dancing, using a fan and playing at cards. I learned the new-fangled art of Spanish blackwork embroidery which the queen had made fashionable and I sent my father an embroidered shirt to demonstrate my skill. Lady Maria de Eresby advised me that the best way to please Queen Catherine was to attend every service with her in the chapel. She assured me that I would make an ideal consort for a Spanish grandee for they valued the qualities of piety, charm and grace. I did my best to behave with the same dignity as the Spanish ladies and it always stood me in good stead at the court.

Mrs Stoner, the mother of the maids, seemed rather displeased that I had been adopted in this way. But the queen's Spanish ladies were such favourites that she dared not object. My relationship with them also aroused the envy of some of the other maids of honour.

"You are not a real Spaniard," said Lady Anne Stafford spitefully. "You have never been to Spain and you don't even speak the language. You are no more of a Spaniard that I am!"

"I have never said that I was, Lady Anne," I retorted. "But if the queen and her ladies like my company then I am pleased to content them."

The queen was served by the greatest English ladies in the realm. Over time, Lady Maria de Eresby told me their stories. "You have no mother or relation here at court, so I shall acquaint with the ladies in waiting of the queen's household. You must learn their titles and their order of precedence for that is vital to know in a court. The king's sisters have the highest rank of the ladies at court. His older sister Margaret Tudor was married to the King James IV of Scotland and had a son named Prince James. After he died, she was remarried to Archibald Douglas, the earl of Angus. They have a daughter called Margaret Douglas who is the king's niece. The king's younger sister, Mary Tudor, was married to King Louis XII of France. After he died, she was remarried to Charles Brandon, the duke of Suffolk. They have two daughters named Frances and Eleanor. Her title ought to be that of the duchess of Suffolk, but everyone at court still refers to her as the Queen of France. She has the greatest regard for Queen Catherine. They are just as close as sisters. The royal ladies are to be addressed as "Your Highness" or "Your Grace." Do you understand?"

"Yes, Lady Maria," I answered respectfully.

"After the ladies of the king's family, Lady Margaret Pole is the most noble lady in the kingdom and that is why the king chose her to be the Lady Governor of the Princess Mary. She has Plantagenet royal blood for she is the daughter of the Duke of Clarence. But she has lived a tragic life as a consequence. Her father was drowned in a vat of Malmsey wine on the orders of his brother, King Edward IV. You will notice that she always wears a bracelet with a vat on it as a memorial of him. When King Henry VII took the throne her brother Edward, the duke of Warwick, was imprisoned in the Tower and then executed. And she was married to Sir Richard Pole, who was a mere gentleman, for the king feared her pretensions. Of course, these are matters which are never to be mentioned. She has five children and the king has created her to be the Countess of Salisbury in recognition of her status."

I listened with growing fascination to this incredible tale. "Does that mean that she has a claim to the throne in her own right?"

"Hush, child!" exclaimed Lady Maria in alarm. "Never say such things. It is treason even to speak of it. It is the Princess Mary who is the heir to the throne. But you should know why the king is wary of the Pole family. They stand too close to the throne. And they have too many boys when he has none."

I realised that there were dangers in the court of which I was unaware. My father had told me nothing about the last of the Plantagenets. I was grateful to Lady Maria for enlightening me.

"Besides the Poles, the other great houses in the land are the Staffords, the Howards and the Percys. Lady Elizabeth Stafford, the Duchess of Norfolk is one of the closest friends of the queen. And Lady Gertrude Courtenay, the Marchioness of Exeter is another loyal friend to Her Majesty. You will soon learn to recognise them for they attend the queen whenever they are at court."

My first impressions of court were dazzling. It seemed to me that I had tumbled into an earthly paradise and I blessed my father for sending me here. I loved to witness the daily ceremony of the dressing of the queen. The royal wardrobe was a sight to behold. Her dresses were made of the most wonderful fabrics including cloth of silver, blue cloth of gold and tawny cloth of gold. The honour of dressing the queen was the privilege of the highest ladies in the land. They alone had the right to take the precious garments into their hands. Queen Catherine possessed a marvellous collection of jewellery including gold spangles set with glowing gems which were carefully sewn onto the bodice of her dress each day. The king and queen presided over a court which was renowned for its magnificence. They both enjoyed music and the courtiers were encouraged to play the lute and sing. It seemed that almost every day there was hunting and picnics and every evening there were masques and dances. I was glad that I had been taught how to sing and dance and ride a horse. But there was much that was new to me. I had never taken part in any pageants, but the king was very fond of them. If you had asked me, I would have said that the king and queen were the happiest couple in the land. They always addressed each other with the greatest courtesy. But that was for the benefit of the court and the foreign ambassadors. It was not long before I discovered that the queen was an unhappy woman and the king was a discontented man. She sought solace in her devotion to spiritual practices. And he found distraction in his romances with her maids of honour.

It would sound absurd to say that a life of a lady in waiting was exhausting. I did not have any heavy work to do like the chamberers or launderers. And yet the life of an attendant was full of continual watching and waiting. Some nights my eyes would be heavy as I waited for the king and queen to take their fill of pleasure. As the long hours passed, I would struggle to remain alert and maintain my cheerful demeanour. The senior attendants took little interest in the endless court masques and spent their time reviewing the dress of the nobles and courtiers. They would have lengthy discussions about who had purchased new costumes, what they had cost, who were trying to set new fashions and who had altered their previously worn gowns and were trying to pass them off as new. But some aspiring courtiers would ruin themselves in their desire to impress. The costliest outfits were the price of a house and only the royal family and the greatest nobles could afford to dress with such extravagance.

I had arrived in time to witness the Easter celebrations at court which were marked with a succession of splendid banquets and entertainments. But I watched in dismay one evening in the Great Hall as the king singled out Mistress Elizabeth Blount for his partner. The queen ought to have received the honour of the first dance. Bessie Blount was a lively young girl with golden hair who excelled at singing and dancing. Queen Catherine was forced to watch as her husband openly paraded her maid of honour before the court. However, she maintained her gracious air throughout the evening. But it was a great relief to me when we could finally retire to the queen's apartments.

Lady Mary Say lost no time in expressing her indignation to the queen. "Mistress Blount is a disgrace to all women. She should be sent from court, your Grace."

The queen did not betray a flicker of concern. "If the lady pleases His Majesty, then she also pleases me. Let us have some music to inspire our thoughts."

A lute-player struck up a Spanish ballad telling the story of Count Fernán González, the founder of Castile. It was a very lengthy tale. After a dozen verses, I sidled closer to Lady Maria de Eresby.

"I agree with Lady Say," I confided to her. "Why does the queen say that Mistress Blount pleases her?"

"Oh my dear, you are so young!" she replied. "Lady Say may be an informer who only pretends to sympathise with the queen. Her enemies would like to trap her into saying something disloyal about the king. But that is something that she will never do. You might as well know that the young woman has been the favourite of the king for the past two years. The king is deceived by these courtiers who flaunt their pretty daughters before his eyes. They intend only to promote themselves and gain estates and titles from him."

Lady Maria's words opened my eyes to the true nature of the court. Its outward magnificence dazzled all those who came to visit the king and queen. But for those who lived there it was a hazardous place. The minor courtiers looked for powerful patrons who would protect them. And the leading nobles competed for power and influence. And so the court was dominated by rival factions. An experienced courtier like Lady Maria was constantly on her guard to avoid their schemes. She shared her true thoughts with very few. And she taught me many useful lessons.

"The court is a battlefield, my child," she warned me. "You cannot learn this lesson too soon. Those who are royal are taught this from childhood. Do your best not to cause offence and to remain on good terms with everyone. A smile is your best defence and good manners will take you far. Beware of those who are too friendly. And especially be on your guard against those who would share confidences. If you reveal your secrets to another then you will put yourself forever into their power. Make it your rule to refuse gifts. If you are pressed, then say that you are greatly obliged and you will be sure to tell the queen of their kindness. This will gain you a reputation for virtue and you will secure the trust of your mistress. In my time I have been offered countless bribes, but I have refused them all. And so I can serve the queen with a clear conscience."

Mistress Blount rose even higher in favour when she bore the king a son. He was named Henry Fitzroy according to the custom with illegitimate royal children. The king doted on him and provided him with his own household. Mistress Blount received her reward two years later when she married Sir Gilbert Tailboys of Kyme. But by then, the king's attention had already shifted to another maid of honour named Mary Boleyn. She was much admired at court for her fine blonde hair and stylish French gowns. She had served in the French court where it was said that she had gained the attention of King Francis I. Her family lost no time in marrying her to William Carey who was a favourite courtier of the king.

King Henry first signalled his interest in her at the Shrovetide Day joust in 1522. He rode out with the motto, *"Elle mon coeur a navera"* emblazoned on the trappings of his horse. When he tied the blue silk scarf of Mary Boleyn around his lance then we understood who it was who had wounded his heart. Two days later, he singled her out for attention in the Chateau Vert masque. Her radiant youth and charm was remarkable and she was the undisputed star of the evening. On this occasion her younger sister Anne made her first appearance at court. She was dark haired and reserved and not so ready with her smiles. The two sisters appeared among a group of virtuous damsels in gold bonnets who were imprisoned in a castle. Its walls were defended by a number of disdainful ladies in black bonnets who vowed that they would hold the fortress. The king dressed in crimson satin led his gallant knights in cloth of gold to their rescue. A Battle of the Sweets took place in which the strange ladies threw rosewater and confits and the gentlemen returned dates and oranges until they were driven out. Then the gentlemen took the ladies of honour by the hand and brought them down to safety. Mary Boleyn outshone them all and the king eagerly carried her away as his prize. They danced together very gracefully and then they took off their masks and made themselves known.

It was clear that Henry was captivated by the drama of these masques. They aroused his deepest romantic fantasies of himself as the triumphant victor in love and war. It was at the masques that the king selected his favourites from the most beautiful and sophisticated ladies at the court. But over time the attraction would inevitably dwindle and fade. And then his restless eyes would seek out a new lady-love to begin the adventure again.

The queen was the first to express her admiration of the performance saying, "Very charming indeed, most delightful." And the proud parents of the Boleyn girls hovered in the background applauding loudly. I looked on with envy for I would have loved to have worn a costume of white satin and taken part in the festivities. But Lady Maria counselled me to be patient.

"You are much too young, my dear. It is not the custom in Spain for well-born damsels to consort with gentlemen. It is an Italian fashion and the queen does not like it. She fears that these masques turn the girl's heads and make them bold. They dance themselves to their ruin. She does not want that for you. But it is the king's pleasure and she cannot gainsay it."

I wondered if the queen was thinking of the time when the king honoured her as the lady of the masques. But there was no sign that she felt any disappointment. *She is a truly loyal wife*, I thought. *She shares her husband's pleasure even when it is to her own dishonour.*

In return for the favours of Mary Boleyn, the king rewarded her family with manors and lands. And the following year he named a new ship "*The Mary Boleyn*" in her honour. The oldest Boleyn girl was now the established favourite. She bore a daughter named Catherine and then a son named Henry but neither of them were acknowledged by the king.

Queen Catherine affected not to be aware of her husband's paramours, but on one occasion I overheard her confiding to Lady Maria de Eresby. "It is the way of many men and kings are no exception. Even my own dear mother had to suffer it. And yet she was a great queen and deeply loved my father."

The queen's ladies were outraged on her behalf. They said nothing to the king's favourites. But behind their backs they heaped scorn upon them and prophesied disaster for their futures.

"One day they will regret having traded their virtue for a few baubles," predicted Lady Maria. "Even if they marry, how can any man respect them? They will have to live with their shame for the rest of their lives. They are foolish girls to prize themselves so lightly. Undoubtedly the duke of Norfolk is behind this latest affair. He would govern the whole realm if he could."

"What does he have to do with it, Lady Maria?" I asked.

"Why he is the lady's uncle, of course," she informed me. "It is in his interest for the king to favour his family. You must have noticed that she has acquired a wardrobe that is worthy of a duchess. It looks ridiculous on such a young girl. And it shows such disrespect to the queen. In Spain no mere knight's daughter would display herself before the court in such a manner."

"Why doesn't the queen send her away?" I queried. I had no idea that it was not as simple as I imagined or that the queen had no power to countermand the king's wishes.

"Such trifling matters are beneath the notice of a great lady," declared Lady Maria resolutely. "The wise Roman Seneca reminds us that to bear trials with a calm mind robs misfortune of its strength. And you will come to understand how well the queen lives out this precept. She is an example to us all."

Lady Maria had served a long time in the court and knew the queen's mind better than anyone. She could tell the truly loyal from the time-servers. And so did the queen, but she was gracious to all and gave no excuse for jealousy. She took notice of the least of her servants and slighted no-one. It was no wonder that she was so greatly loved and admired.

I wondered how the king had come to marry a Spanish princess. "How did you come to serve the queen here in England?" I asked out of curiosity. Lady Maria was only too pleased to tell me the story.

"In the beginning there were more of us ladies of Spain attending Princess Catherine." Her eyes took on a distant look as she recalled the past. "I was known then as Maria de Salinas and I was the same age as you. When we left Spain Queen Isabella charged us to take care of her daughter and serve her faithfully. I promised in the name of the Holy Virgin that I would not fail her. The princess came to England in 1501 to marry Prince Arthur who was the oldest son of King Henry VII. After their marriage many of the Spaniards were sent back for the king did not wish to be burdened with them. But the following year Prince Arthur died of a fever at Ludlow Castle. The whole nation mourned his loss. It was a disaster for his parents and a tragedy for his young widow who was now only the Dowager Princess. More of her household were sent away and she went to live at Durham House. And there she stayed for the next eight years in great misery. There were only six of us Spanish ladies left and we did our best to cheer her. But they were weary days for we had no visitors and no entertainment. The king did not invite us to come to court for any of the festivities. We sold our jewellery; our clothes grew ragged and we dined on bean soup and stale fish."

"Why didn't you return to Spain?" I said indignantly. I could not understand a foreign princess being treated so shabbily. But I was impressed by her courageous spirit in the face of such adversity.

"Every day I expected that the princess would be recalled by her parents so that another marriage could be arranged," said Lady Maria. Her face took on a grave look and she clutched the crucifix around her neck as she remembered that painful time. "But King Henry VII was reluctant to return her dowry. In 1503 his wife died in childbirth. And the following year, Queen Isabella of Spain died too. It was a time of great misfortune. There was no hope of any of us making a suitable match for we had no dowries. Princess Catherine could not even afford to pay us our wages. One of the maids of honour called Francesca de Caceres grew impatient. She eloped with a rich Genoese banker because she despaired of her future. But the rest of us were steadfast and loyal. We swore to remain with the princess in every difficulty. And then suddenly everything changed. In April 1509 the old king died and Prince Henry succeeded to the throne. The first thing he did was announce his marriage to Princess Catherine. I was present at their marriage and their coronation. As the Queen Consort she now had a household of a hundred and sixty people including eight ladies in waiting and thirty-three maids of honour to attend her."

"What was life like for you then?" I asked eagerly. This was more like the grand story I had expected to hear.

"It was like something out of a fairy tale." Her eyes grew warm and she regained her customary smile. "In those first years there was constant festivity. In the daytime they would ride out together for hunting and picnics. In the evenings they would partner together for dancing. No other couple could compare with them for grace and skill. It was the delight of the king to ride in jousts where he wore the queen's favours. And it was the pleasure of the queen to take part in his masques. Every day he would send her gifts. He wrote love-poems for her and had them sung by his musicians. It was one long romance and I thought that it would always be that way. You have only to look around you in the palaces and you will see their initials displayed everywhere. He was proud to have such a queen. When the king went to war in France, he appointed her as his Regent. The Scots invaded England, so she gave orders to raise an army. She rode north to address the troops and they defeated the Scots at the Battle of Flodden Fields. She showed herself to be a true daughter of Queen Isabella."

"And when did you get married, Lady Maria?" I wanted to hear more pleasant tales.

"The king and queen were eager to see their servants were well-matched." She looked down at her hand and surveyed her ring proudly. "I married Baron William Willoughby de Eresby and the king gave us a dowry of a thousand gold marks and the residence of Grimsthorpe Castle in Lincolnshire. But I returned to court to continue to serve the queen. I was her closest friend and she could not do without me. We both shared the grief of losing our firstborn sons. But then I had a daughter named Catherine and the queen had a daughter called Mary. My husband accepted the lack of a son as the will of God and it did not diminish his regard for me. But the king grew increasingly frustrated that he had no male heir. Queen Catherine persuaded him to educated the Princess Mary like a prince. She reminded him that her mother Queen Isabella was a great Spanish queen. But the king was unsatisfied. He said that it was not the custom in England. We hope that he will make a great match for his daughter so that her sons may be his heirs. Only then will he feel secure. For his father claimed the throne in battle and even now there are those who would contest his right to rule. I tell you this so that you will understand the situation. It is no easy thing to be a queen. She has known great sorrows and her greatest consolation is her daughter Mary."

"Has the king always cast his eyes upon the ladies of the court?" I wondered how he be so fickle when he had been blessed with such a long and happy marriage.

"No, my dear, it was not always so." She paused to consider her thoughts. "When he first married the queen, he had eyes only for her. He was then a young man of seventeen and she was only twenty-three. But her beauty was such that she appeared to be much younger. In those days, he would have done anything to please her. I remember how he and his men disguised themselves as Robin Hood and his Merry Men. They came into the queen's apartments wearing hoods and took the queen and her ladies by surprise. She made a play of not recognising these strangers, but invited them to dance with them. Finally, the king removed his hood and revealed his true identity to the ladies. He delighted in their applause and admiration. They were like the sun and the moon to each other."

"Why has he changed? Everyone says she is an admirable queen." It grieved me to think how hurt she must feel at his selfish behaviour.

She sighed deeply. "It is a sad tale, my child. It is because she cannot give the king a son. Six times she has borne children. But only the Princess Mary lived. The queen bears her disappointment bravely. But not the king. His discontent has turned into a grievance. I do not know how it will all end. And I fear for Her Majesty. Who will take her part?"

Queen Catherine pinned all her hopes for the future on her daughter. Princess

Mary was a pretty child with the characteristic red-gold hair of the Tudors. She shared her parent's love of music and their quick intelligence. Queen Catherine was determined that she should be educated as befitted a future queen and invited the famous Spanish humanist Juan Luis Vives to take up the post of her tutor. He advised that the princess should read the Bible every day and study the works of Plato, Cicero, and Seneca. However, romances were forbidden for fear of corrupting her mind. Fortunately, the Princess Mary was a natural scholar and excelled in all her studies. By the age of nine she was able to write a letter in Latin. But despite her accomplishments King Henry was unsatisfied with the prospect of a female successor. He appointed the six-year-old Henry Fitzroy as the duke of Richmond and Somerset, which made him the highest ranking noble in the kingdom. He also granted him landed estates which were worth a fortune. These honours caused speculation that the king intended to make the boy his heir. Queen Catherine protested that an illegitimate child should not to be exalted above her daughter and his income was far more than Princess Mary received. King Henry took offence and dismissed three of her Spanish ladies from court. But shortly afterwards, he sent the Princess Mary to preside over the Council in Wales and established her own court at Ludlow Castle.

"It is a hard thing to part with her so young," said Queen Catherine to Lady Maria. "She is only nine years old and still needs her mother's care. And yet it is right that she should have her own household as a princess and the heir to the throne. I must put my trust in her governess, Lady Margaret de la Pole, and her tutors. They will continue her education in languages, history and music and make an accomplished woman of her. The king will be proud of his daughter and see that she is fit to rule."

In December 1524 a delegation of ambassadors from King James of Scotland came to court and in their honour the great pageant of the Chateau Blanc was staged at Greenwich Palace. On St Thomas's Day, a herald came to the queen's Presence Chamber. He wore a coat of arms of red silk emblazoned with a castle with four silver turrets. He sounded his trumpet and proclaimed that the king had given the keeping of the castle to four fair maidens of the court. They had given the custody of the castle to a captain and fifteen gentlemen who vowed to defend the castle against all comers. The four damsels appeared in gowns of cloth of silver with long trailing sleeves and jewelled hairnets. The fortunate ladies included the king's sister Mary Tudor, Lady Gertrude Courtenay, Mistress Jane Parker and Mistress Anne Boleyn. They were the envy of the rest of the ladies of the court. They bore shields of different colours which they presented before the king. The herald declared that the white shield signified the tilt, the red shield denoted the tournay, the yellow shield stood for swordplay and the blue shield represented the assault. The ladies stood on either side of the herald and held their shields aloft. I noticed that this time Mistress Anne was not so reserved as before. She tossed her head and smiled as she displayed her shield to the king and her large black eyes flashed invitingly as she stood before the assembled courtiers. There was not a man present who could keep his eyes off her.

The following day, a solemn joust was held and two ancient knights entered the field. They presented themselves before the queen and asked her permission to enter the lists. The queen and her ladies praised their courage and then they threw off their cloaks and revealed themselves as the king and the duke of Suffolk. The king ran eight courses and broke seven spears against his opponents so that all the onlookers marvelled at the king's strength. When the courses were run the knights took off their armour and went to supper. After they had dined the king brought the ambassadors to the queen's chamber where they danced with the ladies of the court. And then two masked men appeared dressed in cloth of gold and crimson velvet with caps and shoes of gold. They danced with Mary Tudor and Mistress Anne Boleyn and the company applauded their grace and skill. Finally, they unmasked to reveal themselves as the king and the duke of Suffolk. The ladies feigned great astonishment when they beheld their faces, but especially Anne Boleyn. And then wine and spices were served and the company made merry together. The Scottish ambassadors praised the king for his joyous pastime, but he barely acknowledged their compliments. He only had eyes for his bewitching partner who had turned the evening into her own triumph.

In February 1526 the court assembled at Greenwich for the annual Shrovetide joust. On this occasion King Henry rode to the tiltyard in a fine costume of cloth of gold emblazoned with a flaming heart and the significant words, *"Declare*

I dare not." The mystery was not hard to solve for Mistress Anne Boleyn made her appearance in the queen's party wearing a dress of bright red silk and a gold pendant in the shape of a heart. When the knights approached to pay their respects to the queen, she had the effrontery to smile and nod at them. The queen ignored her impertinence but her chief ladies in waiting were outraged. However, Mistress Anne was quite unabashed and spent the afternoon fingering her pendant and looking pleased with herself. The men at arms ran their courses for over two hours and broke at least a hundred spears. The king defeated all challengers and celebrated his victory by drawing out a red silk scarf from his bosom and winding it prominently around his arm. Mistress Anne flushed pink with satisfaction at the sight. Finally, the knights disarmed and retired to the court for a splendid banquet to mark the beginning of Lent.

Lady Maria did not fail to note the implications of this display and took me aside. "My dear Margaret, you have no mother to advise you. I wonder at these noble families who send their daughters here to make a good match. In truth, service at court is like walking into a den of lions. I have seen well-born girls seduced and abandoned by deceitful men who only care for their own pleasure. You will find that you must uphold your honour like a shield around you. Only then will you be respected. And do not let your head get turned by flattery. Tell your suitors to write to your father for permission to court you and that will cool the ardour of the insincere."

I was keen to please Lady Maria, but I thought little of such admonitions. I wanted to enjoy the pleasures of life at court, not guard myself against its dangers. Later, I wished that I had paid more attention to her warnings. I soon discovered the truth of her words. Truly, those who served at court were tempted as much as the Lady Eve in the garden of Eden. Since I was so young, I affected not to understand the compliments of certain gentlemen of the court or pretended they were made in jest. But Lady Maria had neglected the question of how to respond when the king made overtures. I had seen both Bessie Blount and Mary Boleyn become favourites in their turn. And now it seemed that Anne Boleyn would be another. Suppose the king made me the object of his favour one day? How should I respond?

"How does the queen tolerate these false-hearted ladies?" I asked Lady Maria. Her mouth became a thin line.

"Indeed, the queen is so good that she pities them and prays for their forgiveness," she sighed. "She is the soul of honour and grieves that her example failed to keep them from the path of folly. Truly they are lost souls. After the king has tired of them, what future will they face? Someone will be found to match with them, but it will not be a union founded upon respect. They will live lives of bitter regret."

"Why does the king dally with such fools when he has such a great lady as his wife?" I said contemptuously.

"Hush!" reproved Lady Maria. "It is not your place to question the king. Such things are not to be discussed. The queen does not even notice them. They are too far beneath her. Never once has she reproached the king for his lack of fidelity. She knows that even the greatest kings may commit indiscretions from time to time."

From this time, it was evident that the king had chosen a new favourite. And it became increasingly difficult for the queen to maintain her usual polite indifference. This affair was different. The aloof Mistress Anne Boleyn seemed determined to prove that she was no easy conquest and the king was becoming obsessed with her. Bessie Blount and Mary Boleyn had behaved modestly in their roles as the king's mistress. But Anne Boleyn gloried in her success without any sign of shame. The king danced with her more frequently than anyone else. She displayed a succession of expensive gold brooches which were clearly royal gifts. And every time she appeared at court she wore a fine new dress in the latest French style. She often wore a French hood edged with pearls and a pearl necklace with a gold initial B. Soon other noblewomen were copying her and she set a new fashion for French hoods. However, the queen and her ladies in waiting retained their preference for wearing English hoods. It became a means of judging who was a supporter of the queen and who was courting the favour of the rising Boleyn faction.

In May 1527 Queen Catherine was encouraged by the arrival of an embassy of French ambassadors at Greenwich. They had come to conclude a marriage alliance between the Duke of Orleans and the Princess Mary. King Henry had ordered the construction of a grand banqueting house in the tiltyard. There he prepared an extravagant spectacle to impress his future allies with his power and magnificence. The centrepiece was a splendid pageant featuring his daughter which was intended to win the hearts of the ambassadors. At the end of the hall eight beautiful ladies appeared in the guise of classical goddesses. They were dressed in cloth of gold with their hair gathered into jewelled nets. The Princess Mary was adorned with so many precious stones that their splendour and radiance was dazzling. She led the ladies before the king and they performed an elegant dance for the company. Then eight youths bearing torches appeared and performed a dance. Each one of them took a lady by the hand and they danced in couples with stately glides. Then eight noblemen appeared disguised in masks. They wore black satin gowns, gold doublets and caps of tawny velvet. They each chose a lady as their partner and danced an elegant Pavane followed by a lively Galliard. I was entranced by the sight of the splendid pageantry. *How fortunate I am to witness what was designed for the eyes of foreign dignitaries*, I thought.

At the end of the dance the partners unmasked themselves. When the king was revealed, it was seen that his partner was Mistress Anne Boleyn. I saw Queen Catherine's look of pride turn into dismay. The whole occasion had been planned to focus upon the future of the Princess Mary. But the king could not resist putting his own desires first. He did not care if it gave offence to his guests. It was deeply painful for the queen to see King Henry display his paramour before the eyes of the French embassy. After the grand pageant, the ambassadors returned to the supper hall where the tables were spread with every sort of confection and choice wine. They were visibly impressed by the magnificence of the occasion. The king gave them extravagant gifts to encourage them to write enthusiastic reports to the king of France about the courtly dress and accomplishments of the Princess Mary. But they did not fail to observe that the young girl of eleven was thin, spare and small. She was far from ripe for marriage. King Henry had to set aside the idea of a foreign alliance for his daughter. Queen Catherine was greatly disappointed by this unexpected setback.

Not long after this occasion we had a surprising visitor. Lady Mary Carey came to see the queen. She no longer looked like the belle of the court. She was not attired as finely as before and her hair was not so carefully dressed. Her rosy glow had departed and she looked wasted and pale. She curtsied and stood before the queen demurely, but both her hands were clenched tightly into fists. When she looked up, I saw that her eyes were red-rimmed and bore a defiant look. "To what do we owe the pleasure of your company, Lady Carey?" asked the queen with an ironic smile.

Lady Mary blushed, for it was a long time since she had waited upon the queen. "I have come here to warn your Majesty. The king has fallen in love with my sister Anne and has offered to make her his mistress. But she has refused to consider it. She hoped to impress him with her exceptional virtue and she has succeeded. He has vowed to marry her as soon as it may be done. But your Majesty should not be concerned. As you know, His Majesty's relationship with my family would make such a marriage impossible by the laws of the church. The king will not deny it and I will assert it publicly."

The queen's face betrayed no emotion at this extraordinary declaration. "You have my thanks, Lady Carey. For my own part I am resolved that everything that I say and do will be done under the direction of my lawyers. And now you may leave us."

She curtsied, "I am at your Majesty's service." Then she departed leaving us to ponder her warning.

"What do you think of that Maria?" asked the queen, raising her brows.

Lady Maria came to stand close to the queen so that her words would not be overheard. "Her family are no longer dressing her for effect, that is clear. She has been cast aside by them just as decidedly as the king has done. She has nothing to show for her brief moment of glory. It must be painful to be usurped by her own sister."

"Still, it is surprising that she would reveal her family secrets to me," replied the queen. "Yet she did not ask for anything. Can her words be trusted or is it just a play?"

"It seems these Boleyns are not even loyal to each other, your Majesty," remarked

Lady Maria with satisfaction. "I fancy that she does not relish being set aside and this is her revenge upon her sister."

"Could it be true that he has promised her marriage?" said the queen. She looked troubled at the idea.

"It cannot be so. It is simply wishful thinking," insisted Lady Maria. "Soon the king will tire of this Anne just as he tired of her sister."

"I fancy that she is cast in a sterner mould," she said thoughtfully. "She is not one to be satisfied with a fine wardrobe and a few jewels. She will set her sights higher."

"What more can she expect?" said Lady Maria with contempt. "She is a nobody with a few French mannerisms. She may be more subtle than her sister, but she will not intrigue the king for long."

"Pray for her, Maria," she replied compassionately. "For I am sure that you will have reason to pity her in the end."

"You are my concern, your Majesty," she declared. "From what I can see, this Anne can look after herself."

"Even so, I fear that one day she will regret this affair just as much as her sister has done."

"You are too good, your Majesty," she replied stoutly. "They will reap what they have sown. There will doubtless be another mistress to come and then they will both be left forlorn and friendless."

"Hush, Maria! Do not speak of his Majesty in that way," said the queen reproachfully. "He is surrounded by bad counsellors and they have led him astray. But I believe that he will repent of falling into temptation and return to his rightful self again."

"Yes, your Majesty," she agreed.

"Come, Maria," said the queen resolutely. "Let us go to the chapel and pray together for guidance and strength. We must remember that true faith is always tested. We shall not yield to despair but persevere in hope."

The queen's loyalty to her husband was steadfast and I hoped that it would prove to be justified. Unfortunately, the affair was far more serious than she had realised. In June 1527 King Henry came to visit the queen in her Privy Chamber.

"Welcome, Henry," she exclaimed in delight as she set aside her sewing. "It seems so long since I last saw you here. Come and sit down next to me."

He took his place on the crimson chair of state but his face was sombre. "We must talk Catherine. I cannot keep silent on this matter any longer. It has become clear to me that we must separate. I have sent a messenger to Rome to ask for an annulment."

"What are you saying, Henry?" exclaimed the queen. "You cannot be in earnest!"

"Our marriage may have been acceptable in the eyes of the world, but it was morally wrong," he burst out. "It was done for reasons of state and because I pitied you as a forlorn lady. But now my conscience is no longer at peace."

"Henry, we have been married these past eighteen years," she declared in dismay. "How can you doubt our marriage? Our parents agreed to it and the Pope gave us a dispensation."

"It is true that we were legally married, but you were my brother's wife," he said looking discomfited. "It was an abomination in the sight of God and this is why we have no sons."

"It was no sin, Henry. Arthur never knew me. I came to you a true maid and this you know yourself."

Henry stood up and folded his arms. "I am the king and I must have an heir. I ought to have a houseful of children by now but I only have a daughter. And you are too old for more childbearing. I have no choice but to take another wife and have sons. You must retire into private life or enter a convent. There is no other way to secure the succession."

"I will never consent to such a proposal. I will live and die as your wife and the queen." The queen's implacable calm was like a peak without a fissure. It was impossible to gain a foothold on it, let alone scale the heights. The king's pent-up sense of grievance erupted.

"Madam, I declare you are selfish!" he snapped. "Yes, you are entirely self-regarding. You think only of your own position and prestige. But I have to think of the good of the nation."

Catherine continued to sit serenely in her chair. "Husband, you can command me in all that is right. I wish only to please you. But to contradict our marriage is to contradict Holy Writ. It cannot be!"

Henry began pacing around the room in his agitation. "It has been done many times and it will be done again, I say. There have been many occasions when popes have dissolved marriages. There is good cause when it is a barren match. I would spare you all this unpleasantness and make everything easy for you, Catherine. You may choose your own house of retirement. I would treat you most generously. But I must be free. I must have a son. It is a necessity."

"Our marriage is good, Henry," she insisted. "Pope Julius II granted us a dispensation. And it will be upheld by the Holy Father Pope Clement. Or else he will issue a new one to satisfy your concerns. But our marriage was made before God. It cannot be dissolved!"

Henry stood in front of Queen Catherine and glared at her. "It can and it will! I say that it can! You are no longer the daughter of the rulers of Spain. A new monarch sits upon the Spanish throne. Any king would do the same as I do in order to get himself an heir."

"You already have an heir, Henry," she asserted. "We have a fine daughter, Mary. She has been educated like a prince. And she can be married to your choice of a husband. She is young enough to bear many sons."

"A woman cannot bear rule in England," he retorted. "It is different here from Spain. There would be civil war. I have kept the peace of the kingdom all these years. And I intend to pass the kingdom to my own son in peace. You must agree to end our marriage, Catherine. You must be reasonable for everyone's sake."

"I will never agree to such a sacrilege," she protested. "I will remain your wife until my death. And I will never betray myself nor our daughter by denying it."

"You will agree in the end, Catherine. There is no other way. I will leave you to think on the matter."

He left in great dudgeon leaving the queen shocked and grieved. She sent at once for the Spanish ambassador Mendoza and asked him to write at once to her nephew, the emperor Charles.

"I am a lone woman in this land," she lamented. "I must have advice. I fear that the king's obsession with the Lady Anne is the cause."

"Do not distress yourself, your Majesty," he replied. "I shall ask His Imperial Highness to write to the Pope. Such a proposal will never be permitted. It is an offense against God and an insult to the royal house of Spain."

"I will never agree to separate from the king," declared the queen. "I was destined to be married and to be queen of England ever since my childhood. How can I say that my life was a lie? How could I betray my own child?"

"Your Majesty, I am sure that the Pope will uphold your dispensation and assure the king that his marriage is good. This is just a temporary obsession and I am sure that it will pass in time."

And so began the terrible crisis of the King's Great Matter which was to cause great suffering to Queen Catherine and trouble to the nation. The queen continued to fulfil her public duties and dressed herself even more regally as before. She could not imagine that a mistress could ever displace the rightful queen. But as the rivalry at court increased between the queen and Lady Anne, I became distressed on her behalf. Rumours swept the court that the queen would soon be exiled, imprisoned or sent to a convent.

"Your Majesty, can we not leave this place and go to live in Spain?" I urged, for our life here seemed unbearable.

"Should a knight depart from the battlefield during the heat of combat?" said the queen resolutely. "Rather he should prevail against his enemies or suffer an honourable death. It is rightly said that a castle that is never assailed is not to be praised and nor is a knight who has never proven himself in battle. My mother, Queen Isabella, overcame many obstacles in order to unite Spain under her rule. I must be worthy of her example. A true princess does not abandon her place but prays for the strength to persevere in it. Do not be afraid, Lady Margaret, for the angels are on our side."

And so I prayed, but our trials continued. In the bitter chill of January 1528 my father wrote to tell me of the death of my beloved grandmother:

"My dear daughter, I am sorry to have to tell you of the death of your grandmother Agnes. She passed away peacefully from this life at the age of seventy-eight and has been buried in our parish church. I have no doubt of her receiving her due reward as a faithful servant. Although I miss you more than ever, you must remain at court. Make yourself indispensable to the queen. It is the key to your future. Your affectionate father, Thomas de la Roche."

I was deeply grieved at this sad news. She had seen herself as the guardian of our family honour and represented a proud and indestructible force in our lives. She had stood in the place of a mother to me and I knew that she regarded me as the daughter she had always wanted. I had looked forward to sharing my own stories of the king and queen when we were together. She would have enjoyed them so much. Now she would never hear them. I consoled myself by paying for ten masses to be said for the repose of her soul.

Every day it became clearer that Mistress Anne had the favour of the king and the courtiers became more marked in their attentions to her. They sought her favour with presents of sweet oranges and rosewater. Her star was in the ascent and it seemed that nothing was too good for her. King Henry delighted in making the most extravagant gifts such as clocks in gold cases, printed books garnished with gold and rare talking popingays. Almost every day he sent her costly love tokens from his goldsmiths such as gold brooches in the shape of roses and love-knots, a gold cup with a falcon design and a gold tablet with the letters H and A set with emeralds, pearls and diamonds. He ordered Flemish silk tapestries and Turkish carpets to adorn the walls and floors of her apartments. And he bought her fine horses and saddles for riding and hawks and greyhounds for hunting. Consequently, she grew very proud and dressed herself in the richest clothes and the finest jewels. It was regarded as scandalous among the nobility for Mistress Anne to wear gowns of purple velvet and crimson satin as if she were a member of the royal family. But since it was the king's pleasure, no-one at court was bold enough to make any objection.

I watched as the king lavished these precious gifts upon Mistress Anne. But I did not think that she deserved them. She was not even a loving companion to him. She was just a ruthless schemer who cared only for herself. It made my heart burn within me when I saw how the true queen was neglected for her false rival. Queen Catherine refrained from making any complaint or comment. She was aware that any remark would be reported at once by the spies in her household. I felt increasingly torn between loyalty to Queen Catherine and my duty to my family. Accordingly, I sought advice from Sir William Paulet who was Comptroller of the Royal Household and my father's friend:

"Sir William, I wish you would advise me on my situation," I asked. "I wish to be a true servant of Queen Catherine who has been very good to me. But everyone is saying that Mistress Anne has the king's heart and soon the queen will be sent away from court and her ladies exiled with her or else dismissed to their homes. What should I do?"

Sir William listened to me gravely and gave a wry smile at my predicament. "My dear Margaret, the whole court is asking the same question. The greatest virtue of a courtier is to prefer the king's opinion to your own. Always agree with the king's views and you cannot go wrong. Those who would rather follow their own conscience end up losing favour and are sent from court."

"But I am the servant of the queen," I protested. "Surely, my loyalty is due to her above all."

"Listen to me, Lady Margaret," he advised. "Queen Catherine is a noble and virtuous lady and everyone pities her very much. But it is unwise to champion her cause against the king's wishes. Those who fall out of favour are unlikely to regain it again. And so you see that the highborn and the ambitious are paying their court to Mistress Anne to show their loyalty to the king. As a maid of honour to the queen I counsel you to take a middle path. Continue to serve the queen faithfully, but take care to show every courtesy to Mistress Anne. Keep your counsel about the king's affairs and do not get drawn into gossip. As you know, spies are present everywhere in the court. A good courtier is respectful, but does not take sides. Remember that if you wish to remain long at court. A courtier seeks to bend with the prevailing wind. I myself make it a rule to imitate the willow rather than the oak."

I thanked Sir William and returned to my dormitory. However, spending my days in the company of the queen it was hard not to feel the unkindness and humiliation that was her daily fare. Queen Catherine maintained her regal dignity and virtuous conduct in the face of constant provocation and her loyal ladies seethed with anger on her behalf.

"Her Grace is a saint," declared Lady Maria de Eresby. "Every day she returns good for evil in this court of vipers. She has no friend here but the Spanish ambassador. Her only solace is in prayer and the blessed sacrament. If it were not for her daughter, the Princess Mary, I truly believe that she would die of a broken heart. May the good Lord open the eyes of the king so he may repent of his ill-usage of her."

The other ladies were quick to agree. "It was an ill day when we came here to the English court. Better we had stayed in Spain where her Majesty would have been honoured for her qualities."

But Queen Catherine would not encourage their complaints. She was as brave as a lion and as proud as a peacock. However, she now took the precaution of speaking Spanish whenever she had anything confidential to say to the Spanish ambassador or one of her ladies. It was unlikely that the court spies would be able to understand.

"Queen Catherine is the descendant of ancient line of kings and queens," Lady

Maria asserted proudly. "Her mother, Queen Isabella, never allowed herself to be discouraged by challenges, no matter how great. She regarded them as tests of her faith and she prevailed. She would never have relinquished her position as queen to any rival. This Nan Bullen is a mere commoner. She has nothing to recommend her other than the king's favour. Her sister once had it and what is she now? Queen Catherine is revered by the people for her goodness and kindness. She is older now and the king has grown fickle but she has never faltered in her loyalty, not once. And she is greatly respected by everyone at court."

"And by all her ladies and her servants, Lady Maria," I agreed.

"This is a dangerous topic, you understand? Merely to talk about it could be regarded as treason. Morally, the queen is in the right and her marriage is sacrosanct. However, at the end of the day it is the king who decides what is the law in his own realm."

"Then what will happen to Her Majesty?" I asked in trepidation.

"I fear that the king will seek to set her aside and take a new wife," she sighed. "There is a risk that this matter could lead to war. The Pope could excommunicate him and encourage other Christian nations to invade. The queen is of Spanish royal blood and has powerful relations. The emperor Charles is her own nephew and he might take up her cause. And of course, the queen and her daughter Mary are greatly loved by the people of England. They might rise up on their behalf and set the Princess Mary on the throne. So the king is beset by dangers in forsaking his wife and daughter. He does not dare to go to extremes whatever the rumours may say. He cannot imprison or execute them without endangering himself."

"Surely he would not put his own wife and child to death!" I protested.

"The queen will not believe it of him," said Lady Maria. "But he has put himself into a most difficult position. The sensible option would be to set aside the notion of annulling his marriage. But he will not hear of it. Indeed, he is beyond reason in the matter. And so he is at an impasse and is becoming increasingly frustrated."

"What does the queen intend to do?"

"She will not agree to enter a convent of her own free will and he cannot force her. The Holy Father will never agree to annul his marriage and he cannot compel him either. There are no proper grounds for dissolving their union. A dispensation was provided for their marriage so that settles the matter in the eyes of the Pope. It is true that other kings have annulled their marriages. But in this case, the Pope is unwilling to offend the emperor Charles. Even the wisest advisers of the king are at a loss. It is said that Cardinal Wolsey went down on his knees and begged the king to think no more of it. But to no avail."

Things became worse. The king granted Mistress Anne her own apartments and her own retinue to serve her. She appointed a circle of ladies from her own family and friends. Life at court became a martyrdom of pinpricks. The court entertainments became focussed upon the preferences of Mistress Anne. The masques and the pageants were chosen by her and featured her ladies in waiting. At tournaments the king displayed her colours and the knights sought the favours of her ladies. None of them were bold enough to acknowledge the rightful claims of the queen although Queen Catherine continued to preside over the contests. When the king was declared the winner, he barely acknowledged the queen's applause and turned to smile at Mistress Anne instead.

Lady Maria did not fail to note the implications of this display. "There was a time when these knights vied to win the queen's favour at the joust," she remarked bitterly. "She awarded the prizes and the king presented her with a garland of silk roses as a token of his love. How soon he forgets these things! But she remains as constant as the day."

The king left the field followed by his train of knights who followed his example in saluting Mistress Anne. The queen's smile did not falter despite their shameful behaviour. She took her seat with dignity and slowly unfurled her fan as though nothing were amiss.

Lady Maria turned pale with anger at the sight. "Knights of straw, false varlets! May their lances break and their chargers throw them down into the dust where they belong!" she muttered. "It is truly said that in a time of need friends will be as rare as a horse with white feet."

"Do not say so, Lady Maria," I protested. "The queen has many faithful servants who will never abandon her."

"Even our Lord was deserted by all at His time of trial," she reminded me. "So do not boast like St Peter. Be watchful and do not speak your thoughts aloud where any fool may hear them."

The King's Great Matter came to a climax with the arrival of Cardinal Campeggio, the Papal Legate from Rome. On 31st May 1529, the legatine court opened in the great hall of the Blackfriars in London. It was intended to make a judgement about the lawfulness of the king's marriage. Queen Catherine was summoned to the court and appeared in a regal dress of crimson velvet edged with sable. But rather than taking her seat, she fell upon her knees before King Henry and made an eloquent plea:

"I take God and all the world to witness, that I have been to you a true and humble wife, ever conformable to your will and pleasure, being always well pleased and contented with all things in which you had any delight. I never grudged in word or countenance, or showed a visage or spark of discontent. I loved all those whom you loved for your sake, whether I had cause or no; and whether they were my friends or my enemies. When you married me, I was a virgin without touch of man. And whether it be true or no, I put it to your conscience."

The discomforted king made no reply to her appeal. Queen Catherine rose and departed from the court ignoring the calls for her to return. The trial proceeded without her. Only the upright Bishop Fisher testified on behalf of the queen and insisted that, "The marriage of the king and queen can be dissolved by no power, human or divine." Finally, the Papal Legate, Cardinal Campeggio, revoked the case to Rome for a ruling. The king was left defeated and furious.

After the collapse of the Blackfriars trial there was great rejoicing in the queen's apartments. Our mistress had been vindicated and her rights had been upheld. It was inevitable that the Pope would find in favour of the queen and the sanctity of Christian marriage. The tables were now turned upon the king. Instead of bringing the queen to trial, he himself would be called to trial in Rome. He would be the one to face humiliation and dishonour. The queen looked more relaxed than she had done for months and her ladies-in-waiting chattered together in excitement. For once they threw all caution to the winds and spoke their minds.

"My husband says that this will be the finish of Cardinal Wolsey," asserted Lady Gertrude Courtenay. "And a good thing too. It was a scandal to have such a worldly man wearing the robes of a Cardinal."

"This will be the end of the annulment," agreed Lady Margaret Pole. "The king will be forced to give up his concubine, that shameless woman."

But we rejoiced too soon. Although, the failure of the trial did prove to be the finish of Cardinal Wolsey, it did not mark the end of Mistress Anne Boleyn. The king became all the more determined to uphold her and find another means to achieve his desire. In the absence of Cardinal Wolsey, other voices made themselves heard. Master Thomas Cranmer, the chaplain of the Boleyns, and Master Thomas Cromwell, the former lawyer to the Cardinal, suggested canvassing the universities of Europe for theological opinions on the annulment. They reported back that the majority of theologians favoured the argument for annulment.

Buoyed by their support, King Henry tried again to convince Queen Catherine to end their marriage. But she stayed resolute in her refusal. "You know yourself, without the help of any doctors that your case has no foundation! I will never agree to end our marriage." And so, the stalemate continued and the tensions at court increased. Every day, Mistress Anne conducted herself more like the centre of power and influence. It made our lives as ladies in waiting increasingly difficult for we could neither diminish our service to Queen Catherine nor risk offending the rising star of the king's unofficial consort.

In August 1529 the Spanish ambassador, Eustace Chapuys, arrived at court. He was a man of medium height with shrewd eyes and a charming smile. He was dressed in the subdued fashion of a Spanish gentleman with a black satin doublet and a dark mantle of marten fur. He presented himself to Queen Catherine and advised her that he had been sent by the emperor Charles to give her support over the King's Great Matter. He was to prove himself a fearless champion of the queen and a most able diplomat.

"My good Seigneur Chapuys, you are most welcome here," she said with a gracious smile. "Your arrival has been expected for my nephew wrote to tell me that he was sending his most capable envoy to assist me."

"His Majesty is too kind, your Majesty," he replied with a gallant bow. "I come from Savoy and I can speak French, Spanish and Latin. I fear that my English is not so good but I will try to remedy it."

"You would seem to be eminently qualified to defend my case. I hear that you are not only a qualified canon lawyer, but a former judge."

"That is so, your Majesty. I counsel you to try to remain on good terms with the king in the hope that his infatuation will run its course. In the meantime, I will maintain a regular correspondence with the emperor on your behalf."

Queen Catherine respected his advice and thanked God for providing such a counsellor in her time of need. She maintained her self-control and never showed any sign of displeasure towards Mistress Anne or the king. However, there were times when the strain of having two rival consorts in one court became too much. On St Andrew's Day in November 1529 King Henry condescended for once to dine with the queen. After his third cup of wine had been poured, he became quite jovial.

"I declare this is very pleasant, is it not my dear?" he said affably.

The queen put down her cup and pushed back her chair. "How can you talk of your pleasure Henry when I have been suffering the pains of Purgatory these past months? You have left me to dine by myself and you have completely neglected to visit me. It is more than flesh and blood can stand!"

The king could never bear to be confronted with his failings. Immediately, he began to bluster. "You are your own mistress, Madam, and you are quite free to do as you please in your household. Whereas I have to bear the burdens of the state. I am so hampered with the business of government that I have to work night and day and I scarcely have time to dine."

Queen Catherine was unconvinced by his protests as she knew quite well where he was spending his time and with whom he was dining. "You have treated me very badly Henry and you know it."

The king was taken aback by her reproaches. He had expected the queen to be grateful for his attention. "You cannot expect me to visit you in your apartments anymore, Madam," he replied indignantly. "You know quite well that I am not your legitimate husband so it would not be right for me to do so. My almoner, Doctor Lee, has proved this to me beyond a doubt. And many other theologians are of the same opinion."

Queen Catherine was tired of this nonsense and spoke her mind for once. "I do not care a straw for your almoner's opinion, Henry. It is for the Pope alone to decide. And I have no doubt that for every lawyer who might find in your favour, I could find a thousand to declare that our marriage is good and indissoluble."

King Henry was mortified at being taken to account. "If the Pope does not declare our marriage to be null and void then I will denounce him as a heretic and marry whom I please."

The queen was stung by his expressed intention to marry again. "You know yourself that there is no ground to seek a divorce, Henry. And you do not need the help of the Pope or lawyers to tell you so."

The king was entirely at a loss to know what to say. "It seems that your dining table has turned into a courtroom, Madam. So I shall leave you to dine in peace and I bid you goodnight." He left her Privy Chamber in high dudgeon and went in search of Mistress Anne. But when he confided his troubles to her, he met with no sympathy.

"Haven't I told you that it does no good to discuss the matter with the queen?" she reproached him. "I see that one day you will give in to her arguments and cast me off. It makes me weep to think that I have wasted my youth in useless waiting when I might have made a good marriage elsewhere by now."

"Don't talk that way, sweetheart," he pleaded. "I promise you shall lose nothing by it. I will see that you are raised up to a higher rank in the court so that everyone will esteem you just as much as I do."

Accordingly, on 8th December 1529 Sir Thomas Boleyn was created Earl of Wiltshire by the king. Her brother George became Viscount Rochford and Mistress Anne was now known as the Lady Anne Rochford. Her new title only increased her arrogance. The Boleyn faction were now in the ascent at court and the king could not do enough to honour them. The following day he held a banquet to celebrate the occasion. Queen Catherine did not attend and the Lady Anne took the place next to the king instead. This presumption did not fail to give offence to the other great ladies who were present including the king's sister Mary Tudor, the Duchess and Dowager Duchess of Norfolk and the Marchioness of Exeter. They came to pay their respects to the queen and to share their indignation.

"Who are these Boleyns that the court should bow down to them?" demanded Lady Gertrude Courtenay. "And what is to be done about this insolent woman who thinks that she outranks us all? Can no-one reason with the king?"

"I fear not," replied Mary Tudor. "He is quite besotted with her. He has even quarrelled with my husband Charles Brandon for her sake. I am sorry to see the king forget what honour is due to his wife and sister. But I shall not attend the court in future if I am to be slighted by this shameless creature."

"We must be patient, dear sister," said Queen Catherine. "It is true that she is the is the scandal of the court, but he will not tolerate any criticism of her. Only the Spanish ambassador dares to speak on my behalf now. We must put all our hopes in him."

My heart burned within me as I saw my blameless mistress denigrated every day. I wished that I could defend her honour but I was powerless. I wondered that the king did not see Mistress Anne for the vain and selfish creature that she was. She had learned all the arts of attraction at the French court but underneath her alluring exterior she was cold and heartless. I doubted that she genuinely cared for the king at all. Whereas the poor queen deeply loved her husband and it grieved me to see how little he valued her regard. *He is unworthy of her*, I thought.

The following year, there was another quarrel. The king had sent one of his gentlemen of the Privy Chamber to Queen Catherine with some linen and asked her to have it made into shirts for him. King Henry was most particular about his clothes and the queen was an expert at making his shirts and embellishing them with blackwork embroidery. It was a long-established custom between them for Queen Catherine recalled how her own mother Queen Isabella of Spain had taken pride in making shirts for King Ferdinand. When Lady Anne heard about the matter, she was furious.

"Why on earth would you ask the queen to make your shirts, Henry?" she demanded. "Why didn't you give the linen to me?"

"It is a trivial matter, sweetheart," he protested. "She has been making them for years. It means nothing."

"You mean that you prefer that she should make them instead of me?" she bridled.

"Not at all, my love," he asserted in dismay. "It is only that she knows just how I like them."

"Do you think that she is better at sewing than I am? she declared. "Everyone knows that I am an accomplished needlewoman but you are completely disregarding me. Do you think that you can have two wives at the same time?"

"Do not upset yourself, my dear," he implored her. "It was just that I did not wish to trouble you. I would be only too pleased for you to make me a shirt with your own fair hands. I shall have a supply of my linen sent to your apartments at once."

Lady Anne was placated and she did complete a shirt for the king in order to demonstrate her skill. But she soon tired of the drudgery of the task and arranged that one of the courtier's wives should take it over on her behalf.

In July 1531 King Henry finally cut the Gordian knot of his domestic difficulties. He set out on his summer progress in the company of Lady Anne Boleyn and left the queen behind at Windsor. Queen Catherine was bitterly hurt to be left without a word. She sent a messenger to the king to express her regret that she had not been able to bid farewell to him before his departure. But King Henry bluntly replied that he cared not for her adieux. And he forbade her to send him any further messages.

"This is not him, Maria," she insisted loyally. "He is so good. It is that woman who has poisoned his heart against his own wife and child."

She spent the summer alone at Windsor for most of the nobles deserted the court. Meanwhile the king and his favourite spent their time in the parks surrounding the great forest of Windsor and being entertained at the houses of his friends. King Henry was determined to gain the support of the nobility for the annulment of his marriage. Queen Catherine clung to the hope that on his return he would regain his senses. Soon the Pope would make a ruling and command him to return to his wife. She would be ready to welcome him back and forget this unpleasantness. Then all would be as before.

But instead, the king sent a messenger commanding her to remove her household from Windsor and go to live at The More. Her royal apartments were given to Lady Anne Boleyn, the de facto queen. Queen Catherine wrote to her nephew Charles V saying, *"My tribulations are so great that it is enough to shorten ten lives."*

Lady Maria was stoical in the face of the king's vengeance. "Be of good cheer, your Majesty. We have lived through hard times before."

"Yes, indeed, Lady Maria," replied Queen Catherine courageously. "None get to God but through trouble. Give orders to the household officials to pack up and carry our things to The More. Do not alarm the ladies or the servants. We shall treat this as if it were a summer progress."

"Very good, your Grace," said Lady Maria and departed to make the arrangements. That evening I sat and packed up my chest along with all the other maids of honour. Our mood was universally gloomy. Would we be exiled from court for good? What would become of us? The following day we put our belongings onto carts and set out for the former house of Cardinal Wolsey. It was a sad journey that felt more like an exile. We arrived to find the apartments were bare, the kitchen unstocked and the gardens neglected. We wondered how long we would have to stay in this forsaken place.

"It is a shabby way to treat a queen," said Lady Maria fiercely. "A royal daughter of Spain and he treats her like a beggar. Why send her to this dilapidated and drafty place? Why not a suitable residence like Richmond or Eltham where she would have the comforts due to her station?"

She bustled about seeing that the fires were laid, that hot wine and wafers were brought to the queen and her sheets were properly aired. The servants unpacked the fine tapestries, the plate and the linen and furnished the queen's apartments. Her officials raised the canopy of state in the main hall and set up the queen's court for the winter season. We still received visits from foreign ambassadors who were uncertain if the queen's banishment was permanent or temporary. Queen Catherine made them welcome and always had a smile on her face. She presided over her court at Christmas with as much cheer as she could muster. She waited for a sign of reconciliation from the king, but none came.

At New Year she hoped that Henry might be disposed to relent from his anger. She sent him a gift of a fine gold cup as a sign of her continued regard. But her courier returned white and shaking. The king was furious that she had disobeyed his order. He refused to accept the cup. It was inappropriate to exchange gifts when they were no longer man and wife. But I heard the messenger whispering to Lady Maria that the king had given Lady Anne fine drapes of cloth of gold and crimson satin. And she sat beside him under the royal canopy as if she were his true wife and consort.

The queen had no heart for any further entertainment that season. She devoted herself to prayer instead. And she bravely told her household to take heart for surely this was a trial sent by God. But they should not despair for the One who turned the heart of St Paul could surely perform the same miracle for the king. They must earnestly pray for it. She was convinced that soon he would come to his right mind and send for her.

"The queen will be vindicated," muttered Lady Maria. "The Holy Father will uphold her right against the concubine. And the emperor will not allow his own blood to be shamed before the world."

In May 1532 Queen Catherine was told to leave The More and remove with her household to Hatfield Palace. The house was a beautiful place in the springtime. I wandered through the bluebell woods and tried to find some consolation in the glory of nature renewing itself. I brought some flowers to the queen in the hope that they would cheer her spirits. But life was becoming increasingly harder. We felt like exiles in our own land. Some of the ladies began to grumble that we had been forgotten by everyone. But Lady Maria remained stalwart in her support for the queen and maintained the household in proper order in spite of the circumstances. Undoubtedly, her loyal endeavours were reported by spies. In August 1532 Lady Maria received an order to leave the queen's household and not to communicate with her in the future.

"Send for me if you are in need, your Majesty," she urged. "I will come to you through fire and water."

The queen gave a sad smile as she bade her farewell. "No, my dearest friend, you must not put yourself in danger for my sake. I have committed my cause to God and I am at peace with the world."

Shortly afterwards another message arrived. It commanded that the young English ladies in the queen's retinue should be sent to join the household of Lady Anne Boleyn. I had to pack my chest and make myself ready for departure. I went to take my leave of Queen Catherine most reluctantly. The good lady had tears in her eyes. She gave me a rosary with beads of lignum set in gold as a remembrance of her and asked me to keep her in my prayers. I took one last look at my beloved mistress and saw that her face had become thin and aged from her many troubles. However, she maintained her gracious smile and indomitable strength. I promised myself that I would remain faithful to her example, but I bitterly regretted the loss of my dearest friends.

Part 2: The Household of Queen Anne Boleyn (1532 – 1536)

"Nothing is firm or lasting in the gift of Fortune; today you see those raised high by Fortune who, two days later, are brought down hard."

(Anne de Beaujeu, Lessons for my Daughter, 1497).

On my return to court, I found that things were greatly changed. There were no more Spanish ladies to be seen at court. They had either returned to their homeland or remained with the entourage of Queen Catherine. Lady Anne had declared that she wished all Spaniards were at the bottom of the sea. She would only be served by English ladies and preferred that they could speak French and had courtly accomplishments. In my despondency I sought out Sir William Paulet again and asked for his advice. He listened to me soberly.

"Sir William, I do so much want to remain in service to the queen. Do you think I can ask to be allowed to return to her household?"

He shook his head vigorously. "Lady Margaret, I speak to you as I would to my own daughter. Do not quarrel with your fortune. The Dowager Princess has an uncertain future and her household could be disbanded at any time. You are most fortunate to have been chosen to remain here at court. So I counsel you not to display any sign of displeasure but to be grateful for the opportunity to serve the new queen. Do your utmost to be pleasing and helpful to her. Show a merry countenance and take great care how you speak. The court is no place for the careless and there are many daughters of the nobility who would be glad to have your place. Even if you do not like the new queen, you must dissemble your feelings and give her no cause to complain about you. It will now be her responsibility to choose a suitable husband for you when the time comes. You have a duty to your family and you do not want to find yourself married off to a fool, a pauper or a commoner. You have made a good beginning and now you must set yourself to please your new mistress. I counsel you to change your dress from these Spanish clothes to the new French fashions. It will be an outward sign of your loyalty. It is not always easy to be a courtier but remember that the path of wisdom and safety is found in following the wishes of the king rather than your own inclinations."

Sir William must have written to my father for I soon received a letter from him.

"My dear Margaret, I am pleased to hear of your good fortune in being taken into the retinue of the Lady Anne. I have provided funds for you to purchase French headdresses and have your dresses remade in the latest fashion. I hope that you are doing your utmost to give satisfaction and look to hear good reports about you. I remain your loving father, Thomas de la Roche."

In obedience to my father, I did my best to conform myself to please the Lady Anne Boleyn, although I resolved never to forget my former allegiance. I made a careful study of her tastes. She was a highly accomplished lady who had been trained in the sophisticated pastimes of the French court. She would have stood out in any company. She liked reading French books and embroidered beautifully. She had a passion for new dresses and fine jewellery. She was skilled in playing the lute and composing songs. She participated in court masques with the greatest confidence. She had a witty tongue and enjoyed clever conversation. The king was plainly enchanted by her and sent her splendid gifts every day.

It was at this time that I gained a new neighbour in the dormitory. Her name was Mistress Anne Parr and she was the daughter of Lady Maud Parr. Her mother had ensured that she was very well educated and carefully prepared for life at court. She was not only remarkably attractive with blue eyes and auburn hair, but unusually stylish for such a young maid of honour. Her wardrobe was exemplary as Lady Maud had served Queen Catherine for many years and had often been rewarded with gifts of fine clothing and expensive pieces of fabric. For once, Mrs Stoner had nothing to say in reproach.

Part 2: The Household of Queen Anne Boleyn (1532 – 1536) | 53

"Please call me Nan like everyone at home," she said as she perched on the thin pallet of her bed. "My brother William and my sister Catherine are already married so it will be my turn next. My mother wanted me to serve at court in order to have the best chance of making a good match."

"It is the same with me," I told her as I tried to firm up my bolster. "My family have great hopes that I will make my fortune here. But everyone who comes to court has got the same idea."

"I'm sure you will soon make a match," she said reassuringly. "You are so pretty that you are bound to attract suitors."

Nan had none of the competitive spirit that characterised so many of the maids of honour. I felt quite at my ease with her. "There are lots of pretty girls here. The fashion now is for everything to be in the French style."

"Yes, I know." She tugged her sleeves into place. "My mother went to great lengths to discover the latest fashions in the French court so that I would make a good appearance."

I smiled and placed a hand against my skirts. The silk felt deliciously cool against my fingers. It had been a hot day and I welcomed the opportunity to rest in the peace of the dormitory. "Is your sister here at court?"

"No, she is married to Sir Edward Burgh but his health is so poor that she has to stay in Lincolnshire and seldom comes to court," she explained. "I was brought up from my cradle to be a courtier. My mother was widowed young and became a resident lady in waiting to Queen Catherine. So my sister Catherine, my brother William and I were brought up in the household of my uncle. As soon as I was old enough, I became a maid of honour myself. I have known nothing else but the life of court. My sister Catherine had a different fate to mine because mother arranged a match for her."

"She was more fortunate than us then," I remarked. I could see that Nan's situation was very similar to mine. Both our families had sent us to court to make our fortunes.

"In some ways," agreed Nan. "But then her husband is sickly and she is forced to live the whole year round in the countryside. I would like to find a dashing young husband of my own age. But it is rare to find a match who is young, rich and titled. My mother is determined to marry us as well as possible. She wants us to have a good future and not suffer as she did when she was left as a young widow with children but no means to provide for them."

I realised then that other maids of honour were faced with difficult circumstances at home and seeking to make their fortunes at court. Not all of them were from wealthy families as I had supposed. A newly arrived maid of honour named Mary Zouche told Nan and I a pitiful tale of her life at home.

"I am so glad to be here at court and away from the troubles at home." Her tears rolled down her cheeks faster than she could wipe them away. "When my lady mother died, there were six of us children, three girls and three boys. My father promised to take care of us. But when he remarried, he forgot his promise. His new wife made no pretence to be a mother. Indeed, she complained that six step-children were a monstrous burden and expense. She said that our father could not afford to provide for so many children and we would have to marry whoever would take us. She soon came to detest the very sight of us. Our father looked upon us so coldly that we felt like foundlings. My younger sisters were in tears every day. Finally, I told them that we should turn to our mother's family for help."

"What did you do?" I asked feeling quite amazed by her courage and resourcefulness.

She drew out a grubby handkerchief and blew her nose. "I wrote a letter to my cousin Sir John Arundel at court. I asked him to plead our case to Cardinal Wolsey and find us places in service. I knew that it was our only hope of making suitable matches. He succeeded in finding a place for me as the oldest girl and persuaded my father to consent. My stepmother was greatly displeased by such an extravagant plan. But my father did not like to offend our relations and he thought that it might provide for my future. And so I came here in the hope that the queen will find me a good match. If I marry well then it will benefit my poor sisters. They can hardly endure the misery of our father's house. For we are certain that if our mother had lived then our lives would have been vastly different." She paused and wiped her eyes again.

I was astounded by her tale of misery and realised that I was fortunate that my own father had not remarried. Her story could easily have been my story too. It was terrible to think that she had no consolation in her own home. I hoped that Lady Anne would find her a good husband so that she might be happy at last.

"I am sure that Sir John will do his best to find a suitable husband for you," said Nan compassionately. "And perhaps your sisters will be able to come to join you here at court. But you must not let the sadness of the past weigh upon you. The role of a courtier is to make good cheer. A merry lady will make a match far sooner than one who is forlorn. Do your best to gain the queen's favour and then you will have a happy future."

Nan was wise beyond her age due to her mother's guidance. It was a great solace to have a trusted companion at court. Now I had someone to unburden my thoughts and share the rare times of leisure. The life of a lady in waiting was one of constant occupation. It was difficult even to spare the time to write a letter home. Nan was the best-educated maid of honour at court and she often regretted that she had so little opportunity to read.

"If we are not invited on the next summer progress then I would be glad to stay here in the palace and read to my heart's content," she confided to me. "In fact, I would steal into the king's apartments and explore his library. It is said that he owns the greatest collection of books in the kingdom. He has all the newest books and all the ones which have been forbidden as well."

"If we are not invited to go on progress then we will be expected to go home for the summer. I would enjoy the peaceful life of the country," I said longingly. "I would not have to worry about the style of my hair or the fashion of my gowns or who is spreading gossip."

"You imagine that you would, but you have forgotten the boredom and drudgery of life in the country," said Nan teasingly. "You would spend all your time mending the household linen and making fruit preserves."

"When you are married then you will have to do the same," I reminded her. "You will have no time to spare for idle reading."

"Oh yes, I shall!" she retorted. "I will rise early every morning and read in peace before the household stirs. That is when the mind is most retentive. And I shall have maids to attend to the household sewing. I am resolved that I will never pick up a needle again!"

"Then you will have to marry a great nobleman who can afford to keep a household of servants to wait upon you," I advised her. "In the meantime, it is our duty to wait upon the queen."

"I shouldn't think that Queen Anne will want us in her entourage when she goes on progress," predicted Nan. "She prefers to surround herself with as many Boleyn cronies as possible."

"She will want to make as great a show as possible so that won't matter," I observed. "I can't abide the way she performs whenever the king brings visitors to see her. She shows off her French at the slightest opportunity and shamelessly fishes for compliments. She hasn't the least dignity but only a vast self-conceit. I cannot understand why the king is so besotted with her."

"Yes, for she doesn't even have the good looks of her sister Mary," remarked Nan. "It is a great pity that she did not stay in France."

My relationship with Nan consoled me for the loss of Queen Catherine and Lady Maria. We soon became the closest of friends and I felt that I had always known her. Even Lady Anne Stanhope was civil to Nan when she learned that she was from a noble family with good connections at court. Nan's mother had served Queen Catherine for many years and was highly respected. Lady Anne Stanhope's family had recently arranged a match for her to Edward Seymour. He was an Esquire of the Body to King Henry which only increased her sense of importance. Surprisingly, Lady Anne respected her glacial self-possession and never singled her out for ridicule.

To our relief, Mrs Stoner directed her vigilant eyes towards the newcomers at court. And Lady Anne focussed her attention upon the family and friends who formed her inner circle such as Lady Mary Boleyn, Lady Jane Rochford, Lady Mary Shelton and Lady Anne Gainsford. They were the ones who were invited to attend her in her privy chamber, who accompanied her on walks in the palace gardens and joined her on riding expeditions. Lady Anne was wary of any ladies who had shared her time of service to Queen Catherine and relegated them to the background. However, since Nan and I were among the best dressed maids of honour we avoided being singled out for criticism. We excelled in the skills of music, dancing and languages which were her particular talents. And we were quick to learn the pastimes and dances from France which the Lady Anne favoured. She insisted on regular masques and entertainments to impress the king. We were often kept busy sewing costumes for the latest diversion. However, it was the Lady Anne's favourites that took the best roles regardless of their talent for dancing. This was a source of constant irritation for myself and Nan.

Lady Anne preferred to forget about her time as a maid of honour and acted as though she had been born to the nobility. Indeed, she began to usurp the privileges reserved only to royalty. At Easter she performed the ceremony of blessing cramp rings which was the prerogative of anointed queens. But the clergy raised no objections as she had the countenance of the king. It seemed that Lady Anne was above all constraints at court. However, the king's sister, Mary Tudor, made it known that she refused to attend court while "that shameless hussy was flaunting herself there." Few others were prepared to risk the king's displeasure. One who did was Lady Elizabeth Howard, the Duchess of Norfolk, who was a great friend of Queen Catherine. She was openly critical of Lady Anne and declared that she would be the ruin of her family. When she was discovered to be smuggling letters to the queen concealed in oranges, the king lost patience and banished her from court. Bishop Fisher and Sir Thomas More were both sent to the Tower for taking her side. That left the Spanish ambassador, Seigneur Chapuys, as a lone voice in her favour at court. Since he was not a subject he could afford to speak out on behalf of Queen Catherine and Princess Mary. It was the common people who were the most vociferous in demonstrating their loyalty to the former queen. King Henry was mortified to hear shouts in her favour when he rode out hunting or went on progress with Lady Anne. He had always prided himself on his popularity with his subjects.

It was well known that there were spies employed at court. There had been a huge uproar when Queen Anne discovered that the love letters which King Henry had written to her had been stolen. She kept them in a locked coffer beside her bed. But somehow an audacious thief had managed to pick the lock and substitute a set of empty scrolls for the precious letters. It was assumed that a sympathiser with the former queen had committed the crime. Queen Anne was enraged by the loss and insisted that the yeomen guards search the dormitories and possessions of all the royal servants. Some discoveries were made and several servants were dismissed for theft, but there was no sign of the letters. A great reward was offered for their return, but it went unclaimed. Queen Anne was convinced that the thief must have had an accomplice in her household who advised where to find them and when to take them. She complained to the king that the guards must have been bribed and he should also search their belongings. But the king refused to take action against his yeomen lest it alienated their loyalty.

"Our lives depend upon their vigilance, and I will do nothing to compromise it," he insisted. "Nor can we replace our entire household with new staff. The only remedy against such occurrences is to keep old and trusted servants about us at all times."

Queen Anne had to reconcile herself to her loss, but she railed bitterly against the dishonesty and ingratitude of those who had wronged her. She also reproached her servants for failing to prevent the intrusion.

"My ladies should be ashamed that such a foul deed was perpetrated without their knowledge," she declared. "Where was your duty, your attention and your care for your mistress? Not even a fly should be able to enter my bedchamber, let alone a thief! I do not know how you can hold their heads up and I can hardly sleep at night."

For several weeks she insisted that the ladies who served on night duty should not lie on their pallets waiting to be called, but stay awake all night in chairs. Finally, she relented but the incident increased her suspicion of her household and our discontent with such a mistress.

King Henry decided to seek the support of the French king for his divorce. So he planned to make a state visit to France together with Lady Anne. In order to give her sufficient rank to meet the French royal family and their nobility he resolved to appoint her as Lady Marquis of Pembroke. A special ceremony was held at Windsor on 1st September 1532. Lady Anne wore a dress of crimson velvet and the finest jewels and was attended by the highest nobles in the realm. The king invested her with a mantle and coronet and granted her a thousand pounds a year to maintain her dignity. As a result of her increased status her household was enlarged even further. On 13th September 1532 the Dowager Princess Catherine was told to leave Hatfield and sent to reside at Elsying Palace in Enfield with a much-reduced household. Most of her remaining English ladies were sent to serve Lady Anne.

Not everyone welcomed the elevation of Lady Anne Boleyn as a Marquess. Some resented her on behalf of Queen Catherine and others objected to her arrogance. At all events, someone sent her a strange warning. She came into her bedchamber one day and discovered that a drawing had been left on the counterpane of her bed. It showed a male figure labelled with an "H" and two female figures labelled "K" and "A". The "A" figure was missing her head. The meaning was quite clear. Queen Anne passed it to her attendant, Anne Gainsford.

"Look at this nonsense," she remarked. "Some varlet has sent me a prophecy. They think to alarm me but I am not so easily frightened."

But Mistress Anne Gainsford was shaken by the discovery. "If I thought it true, I would not marry him even though he were an emperor."

Lady Anne dismissed it, saying "I think the thing a bauble and I am resolved to have him whatever might become of me."

Naturally all her servants and ladies were questioned on the matter and naturally no-one knew anything about it.

King Henry and Lady Anne could talk of nothing but their forthcoming state visit to France. The king was determined that it should be a great success and establish Lady Anne as his official royal consort. He had already given her the rank of the highest lady in the land. Now she should have the finest clothes, the richest plate and the most valuable jewels. In preparing her wardrobe for the state visit the king sent word to all his merchants and jewellers to bring their finest wares to court for their perusal. They made their fortunes from the vast quantities of goods he purchased from them. Lady Anne's seamstresses outdid themselves making costly state gowns of cloth of gold with diamond spangles and velvet embroidered with gold. They also made an elaborate nightgown of black satin lined with taffeta and trimmed with velvet. This led to rumours that their marriage would take place very soon regardless of the Pope's consent.

"But really, Henry," she pouted. "How can you expect the French to take me seriously unless I am wearing the jewels of the Queen of England? Otherwise, they are bound to look down on me and take me for your mistress!"

"Never fear, Nan," he replied stolidly. "You shall have them to wear. I will send Norfolk to The More to fetch them here at once."

Lady Anne's pout turned into a smug smile. My heart burned for the poor Dowager Princess Catherine. Had she not lost enough already? I remembered the occasion when Lady Maria had showed me the queen's jewels. In pride of place was a gold pendant in the shape of a heart. Emblazoned upon it in red enamel were the initials of the king and queen and the inscription, "*Toujours*."

"The queen prizes her jewels for every piece tells its own story. This is the queen's most treasured possession," she told me reverently. "It contains a lock of the king's hair and she wears it constantly as a reminder of his love. It was his gift to her to celebrate the birth of Prince Henry in 1511. He held a joust in which he competed as Sir Loyal Heart and defeated all challengers. His horse bore the device of a golden heart in tribute to the queen. He wanted the whole court to know of his devotion to her."

"It is beautiful, Lady Maria," I said with admiration. She turned it over and showed me the reverse side which bore the emblems of a Tudor rose entwined with a Spanish pomegranate.

"A lady's jewels show her honour and standing in the eyes of the world," said Lady Maria proudly. "And a queen's jewels demonstrate her power and majesty.

There is an art to wearing them. The great stones show to their best effect when worn around the neckline of a gown, upon the girdle or around the head-dress. In this way, the queen is surrounded by signs of her royalty and wealth." By taking them away, the king was diminishing her position in society. A queen without her royal dress and jewels was hardly a queen any more.

Later that day, the duke of Norfolk was announced. He entered and paid his respects most punctiliously. But his face looked far more grim than usual.

"You are most welcome, my good Norfolk," said King Henry eagerly. "And what tidings do you bring us?"

"Your Grace, I regret that my visit was not successful," he reported. "The Dowager Princess refused to give up her jewels as she claimed that they are the property of the rightful Queen. And she declared that it was against her conscience to adorn someone who is the scandal of Christendom and a disgrace to the king."

My heart rejoiced to hear her bold reply. But Henry's eyebrows drew together and a dark flush appeared on his cheeks.

"Did you hear that, Henry!" shrieked Lady Anne. "She insults us both! How could you allow her to deny the king's expressed wishes? You let her make a laughing-stock of you!"

"Your Grace," the mortified duke replied. "The Dowager Princess said if you commanded her then she would obey him in this as in other things."

"Indeed, I will," growled King Henry. "I will write to her this very night. You need not trouble yourself any further in the matter, Norfolk. I shall send a messenger to her tomorrow to bring them back. You may leave us."

The duke bowed and departed without another word. "You see how they sympathise with her behind our backs, Henry," she complained petulantly. "Not even my own uncle can be depended on!"

"Do not distress yourself, sweetheart," said King Henry soothingly. "'Tis but a short delay. I promise that you shall have them very soon."

"I am only asking for what is my due," she insisted. "They are not her property and she should have surrendered them already." She tossed her head and pouted.

"She will not refuse my stated command," he assured her. "It is merely a token protest."

"She has no right to deny your wishes. She is your subject and you are providing for her whole household. She is an ingrate and my uncle is a fool!" She scowled and turned away.

The following day she shut herself up in her apartments as a sign of her annoyance. But in the evening King Henry arrived beaming from ear to ear followed by a stout yeoman bearing a brass-bound chest.

"Keep up, man," he urged him. "Put it down where the Lady Anne can see it. You see, my dear, I have brought you the jewels as I said I would."

"I did not sleep all night from this dreadful commotion, Henry. I am quite exhausted by this affair," she grumbled, but her eyes were fixed greedily upon the casket.

"Now open it up. Quickly man, the Lady Anne has been waiting to see them."

The lid swung back revealing an array of neatly stacked black velvet bags. "We shall open them on your bed, my love, and you shall see what it means to be the Queen of England."

Lady Anne forgot her complaints in the pleasure of unwrapping the regalia of the queen. I saw the familiar pieces spread out across the counterpane and sighed to see the velvet bags carelessly thrown aside. It would take ages to match them up correctly again. But I dared not interfere with the king's moment of triumph. He was bursting with pride in himself. He picked up a fine pearl collar with a superb diamond cross with fumbling hands and held it out to her. Lady Anne could hardly conceal her delight as she picked up the necklaces one by one and tried them around her neck. But she could not bring herself to admit her satisfaction in obtaining such a prize.

"There is hardly time to get them cleaned in time for the visit, Henry," she complained. "And who knows how long it has been since these pearls were last re-strung?"

King Henry looked crestfallen. "Look, my dear, you have not seen the best of them yet. There is a great store of brooches and bracelets of colours that will match any gowns. They include all the pieces that my father bought for my mother Queen Elizabeth."

Lady Anne examined a gold bracelet set with four table rubies. "These stones are quite exceptional. It is a shame that they are spoiled by these old-fashioned settings."

"All these great jewels can be reset according to your taste," he said deferentially. "I will send for my goldsmith and he will remake them just as you wish."

"It is a huge task to undertake, Henry," she protested as she put the bracelet down. "My wardrobe is not even finished yet. It is too much to expect me to have to manage at the last minute."

"Just pick out the pieces that you like the best, my love," he urged her. "The others can be remade after our return."

"I can hardly adorn myself with jewels which bear her initials, Henry," she objected with a frown. "You had better send for your goldsmith right away. He will have to work around the clock to get these ready."

What a shrew, I thought. I could foresee days of tiresome labour lay ahead. I almost felt sorry for the king as his romantic dreams crumbled to the ground. He had envisaged a scene of loving gratitude as his sweetheart beheld his fabulous gift of jewels. Instead, he had not received a word of thanks and even more demands were being made of him. He was not known for his restraint or patience, but he said not a word in reproach. *He must be besotted by her*, I thought. *Whatever does he see in her?* I held my breath when I spotted the heart-shaped pendant tossed upon the counterpane. Lady Anne picked it up and snapped open the locket suspiciously, but finding it empty she cast it aside. Queen Catherine must have kept the lock of hair as a last remembrance of the king's love.

"Really Henry, didn't it occur to you to have these jewels sorted before giving them to me? All these pieces with Spanish devices should have been removed," she asserted.

"They are the queen's jewels so they are all rightly yours," said Henry looking deflated.

Lady Anne pouted. She was not yet ready to be mollified. "They are no use to me and it wounds me to see them. I think you might have given some thought to my feelings if you love me as much as you say."

Henry turned pale and tried his best to placate her. "It is no matter, my dear," he assured her. "They can all be remade. The goldsmith will set aside all his other work to complete them. And you will meet the French looking like an empress."

She stopped frowning as she considered the idea. "I will have to have all my new gowns brought in here so that I can make matched sets for them," she demanded. "I shall have to dine here in my apartments to get through all the work. So don't expect to see me until it is done." And so the gold pendant was forgotten by them both. But I thought of how much it had meant to Queen Catherine - and still meant even now. *They deprive her even of the solace of her past memories,* I thought to myself.

The following days were a flurry of activity as the Lady Anne sent for her costumes and planned a set of jewels to match each one. She wanted a complete parure of rubies to complement her dress of crimson cloth of gold and another parure of emeralds for her dress of green damask silk.

"The settings must be entirely remade," she declared. "I cannot wear such ill-assorted pieces."

Master Amadas, the king's goldsmith, looked appalled by her demand. "My lady, it will take weeks of careful work to accomplish so great a task."

Lady Anne took umbrage at his reluctance. "You have only days so you must find other skilled craftsmen to assist you in the work. I will give you clear written instructions for each set of jewels and you shall have a sample piece of fabric from each gown." It was clear that her mind was made up.

Soon all of her household officials and servants were looking strained and harried by her endless commands. It seemed that nothing was good enough to please her – not her newly-made gowns nor her fine linen undergarments nor even the shoes made by the king's own shoemaker. "The king shall hear of this!" was her constant refrain. Nan and I did our best to keep busy with errands. Between ourselves we named her, "My Lady Disdain."

King Henry visited her every evening after dinner only to be met by a litany of complaints. "My ladies have no idea how to dress a queen according to her station. The French are going to laugh at my ensemble. My officials are hopeless and can get nothing done. I have to see to everything myself!" The king would have to spend his time soothing her in order to avoid a full-blown tantrum.

"It will all be worth it, sweetheart. King Francis and his nobles will be enchanted when they see you. They will be ashamed of their poor costumes when they see how regal you look. You will be the centre of attention and their minstrels will sing your praises!"

However, their ambitions were dealt a fatal blow by the latest news from France. King Francis regretted that neither his wife, Queen Eleanor, nor his sister Marguerite were willing to receive the Lady Anne. In fact, no French lady of rank could be persuaded to welcome her to court. Lady Anne flew into all the fury of a woman scorned.

"I might have known that it would end this way!" she raged. "The French are determined to humiliate me. And you are allowing them to do it. It has been a complete waste of time, Henry. I have spent hours planning these dresses and it is all for nothing. I will not go to France at all!"

King Henry spent hours reconciling Lady Anne to the disappointment of not attending the French court. It was finally agreed that she would remain in Calais where King Francis would make a visit without the royal ladies.

Serves her right! I thought to myself. *The French are not fooled. For all her fine feathers and title she is still only a former maid of honour. And she is not even the true wife of the King for he is still married to Queen Catherine. Why should the French Queen recognise her?*

Part 2: The Household of Queen Anne Boleyn (1532 – 1536)

Finally, on 7th October 1532 King Henry and Lady Anne set out from Greenwich. The king was accompanied by the dukes of Norfolk and Suffolk, his son Richmond and his gentlemen of the Privy Chamber. Lady Anne was attended by a retinue of thirty ladies in waiting. Four days later they boarded *The Swallow* and set sail from Dover. On arrival at Calais, they were welcomed by the Mayor and escorted to their mansion at the Exchequer. King Henry went to spend four days with King Francis and his court at the Abbey of Notre Dame in Boulogne. He wore a splendid gown of white velvet embroidered in gold and a crimson satin doublet set with pearls which King Francis had given him. In return, Henry made gifts of horses, mastiffs and falcons to Francis. Then King Francis made a return visit to Calais where King Henry hosted a banquet in his honour at the Staple Inn. That evening Lady Anne and seven other ladies made a sensational appearance dressed as Greek goddesses in gowns of cloth of gold and crimson tinsel with gold laces. After performing a dance before the two kings the ladies partnered with the gentlemen. And when the ladies took off their masks it was revealed that Lady Anne was dancing with King Francis. The two monarchs bade each other farewell and on 12th November 1532 King Henry and Lady Anne sailed back to Dover. It was there that they finally consummated their love. King Francis had promised to support their marriage and Lady Anne was convinced that her position was secure. She put on her splendid black nightgown and swore her ladies to secrecy. But by January she was boasting that she had a particular craving for apples. Soon rumours began to circulate in the court that she was expecting the king's child.

On 24th January 1533 Anne Gainsford came to tell me that at six o'clock the following morning I must put on my best dress and go to wait on Lady Anne in her apartments. And I must say nothing whatever to anyone. To my great astonishment I found that I had been selected to witness the secret marriage of King Henry to Lady Anne. The ceremony was performed by the king's chaplain, Rowland Lee, in the presence of just a few attendants. The king told his chaplain that he had been sent a dispensation from the Pope to marry again, but to avoid any trouble he had decided to hold the ceremony in secret. In fact, he had not received any permission but he was determined to be lawfully married so that their child would be born in wedlock. I wondered why I had been chosen to attend such an important occasion, but Anne Gainsford was ready to enlighten me. The king had insisted that he wanted no tattlers to be present and Lady Anne had replied in jest that I was the most close-mouthed of all her ladies. After the ceremony she sternly reminded us not to speak a word or we would be dismissed from her service immediately. But the king was in the best of good humours. He gave each one of us a purse of ten gold marks as a reward. I was bursting to tell Nan of this extraordinary event, but I dared not take the risk. The following month, Queen Catherine was sent to Ampthill Castle and her household was reduced to just ten ladies.

At Easter 1533 Anne Boleyn appeared in public as Queen for the first time. She attended mass in the Chapel Royal wearing a dress of cloth of gold adorned with diamonds. Lady Mary Howard carried her train and she was attended by sixty ladies. After the service the king invited his nobles to make their court to the new queen. The duke of Norfolk was sent to inform Queen Catherine that she need not trouble any more about the king, for he had taken another wife. She was told that she had to renounce her title of queen. In future, she would be regarded as the widow of Prince Arthur with the rank of Princess Dowager of Wales. Queen Catherine drew herself up and retorted that as long as she lived, she would call herself Queen of England. She ordered new livery for her household embroidered with the joint initials of the king and herself.

After his marriage to Queen Anne, the king made arrangements for a spectacular coronation to present his wife to the people as the new Queen of England. On Thursday 29th May 1533, Queen Anne appeared at her reception by the lords of England which took the form of a spectacular water-pageant. She was dressed in a gown of cloth of gold and she travelled in her royal barge from Greenwich to the Tower of London. A flotilla of fifty barges had assembled in her honour displaying the emblems of the mayor, aldermen and city guilds of London. They escorted her on the journey accompanied by the sound of musicians playing and minstrels singing. As the barge arrived at the Tower of London a thousand guns were fired to salute her arrival. Master Kingston, the Constable of the Tower, was waiting to receive her and he escorted her to the royal apartments which had been newly prepared and sumptuously furnished.

On the last day of May, I arose early and dressed in my new gown of crimson velvet with a border of red cloth of gold. It was by far the most opulent dress that

I had ever worn. The highest ladies in the land dressed the queen in her gown of white cloth of gold and her mantle edged with ermine. Her black hair hung loose about her shoulders and she wore a circlet of gold set with sapphires, diamonds and pearls on her head. Then I joined the rest of the queen's ladies to board the waiting chariots for the formal city reception. The procession was led by the peers of the realm in order of precedence. Queen Anne rode in a rich chariot of white cloth of gold and a canopy of cloth of silver was held over her head by the four Lords of the Ports. I rode in the fourth chariot together with Nan, Mary Zouche, Margery Horsman and Jane Seymour. We drove through the streets of London which were newly laid with gravel and decked with rich hangings of scarlet and gold in celebration. We saw the city guilds in their bright liveries lining the streets. Behind them stood the citizens who had come out of curiosity to witness the spectacle. But few of them cheered or doffed their caps as the queen passed by. Some of them mocked the banners bearing the combined initials of the king and queen with shouts of "HA – HA!" There were even some cries of "God save Queen Catherine!" We were welcomed by a series of pageants in which speeches were made in praise of the queen. Finally, we arrived at Cheapside where the mayor and aldermen were waiting to greet the queen. The mayor gave her a purse with a thousand gold marks as a gift from the whole of the city. Queen Anne reproached the mayor for the lack of enthusiasm from the crowds, but he protested that he could not command men's hearts. Then we arrived at the palace of Westminster which was hung with fine tapestries of Fame and Honour and the Life of King David where we stayed for the night.

On the first day of June Queen Anne was crowned at Westminster Abbey. She wore a robe of purple and crimson velvet edged with ermine and a gold coronet with a cap of pearls. The clergy and lords of the realm preceded her dressed in their robes of state. The crown was borne before her by the High Chamberlain and the dowager duchess of Norfolk carried her train. She was followed by the peeresses of the realm wearing robes of scarlet trimmed with ermine and coronets on their heads. Then came the queen's maids dressed in gowns of scarlet edged with white Baltic fur. The queen took her place on the throne before the altar and a canopy of cloth of gold was held over her head. And there she was anointed queen of England by the archbishop of Canterbury and the *Te Deum* was sung in thanksgiving. And after the mass she proceeded to Westminster Hall for the coronation banquet. A wonderful feast was served of countless dishes and each course was announced by the sound of trumpets. Finally, a gold plate of sweetmeats and a gold cup of wine were presented to Queen Anne to signify the end of the festivities. Then the ladies escorted the triumphant queen from the hall and assured her that it had been the most splendid feast that was ever seen.

On our return to Greenwich, Queen Anne celebrated the occasion by hearing the oath of her new household. She stood before us looking as grand and imposing as if she had never been a mere maid of honour herself. King Henry hovered protectively in the background like her guardian angel. I lowered my eyes at the sight of him. *Brute!* I thought to myself. *All this show for your concubine when your true wife is left abandoned and forlorn in the countryside!* I felt sick at heart. How could I serve such a pair as my master and mistress? But what choice did I have? They were the king and queen. I dutifully mouthed the words of allegiance. Queen Anne could not resist the opportunity to lecture us.

"You are to be honourable, discreet and thrifty in your conduct. I would have you set a godly spectacle to others by your virtuous demeanour and by attending mass every day. You shall not swear nor quarrel on pain of instant dismissal from the court. Remember that it is an honour to serve in this household. That is all."

Her eyes shone in triumph as she gave the dismissal. The courtiers scurried away to their dinner. I lingered by the door as I had no appetite. King Henry came forward with a smile to compliment her and she preened like a vain young peacock displaying its feathers. I knew that I would either have to find a way to please the new queen or else keep well out of her way. This was easier than I expected as the queen immediately surrounded herself with her favourites and kept the rest of her ladies at a distance. My first contact with her came the following Sunday. After the morning mass she summoned us to her Presence Chamber and gave each one of us a small book of prayers and psalms to wear at our girdles. We all curtsied to the queen and expressed our thanks for her kindness. She gave a satisfied nod and held up her own copy for us to see.

"I expect all my ladies to be above reproach," she reminded us. "I am giving you the precious gift of the Word of God so that you made read it in your leisure time and profit from it. I wish to see my ladies engaged in virtuous pursuits and not wasting their time in idle pastimes. And now you may go to my Privy Chambers and spend the next hour in devotional reading before you continue with your sewing."

Queen Anne furnished her apartments to emphasise her royal status. The king had given her everything she could possibly desire. She had cupboards lined with gold and silver plate and a coffer full of jewels. She sat in a chair of state under a canopy of cloth of gold and velvet embroidered with Tudor roses. The floors were lined with silk carpets and the walls were spread with tapestries depicting Arthur and Guinevere and the meeting of Solomon with the Queen of Sheba. Her bed was hung with crimson satin and covered with sarcenet quilts. Her cushions were embroidered with the crowned initials H and A and fruitful symbols of honeysuckles and acorns. Her emblem was a white falcon with a sceptre in its talons which I thought was entirely fitting for someone of her rapacious nature. Her falcon and initials were soon to be seen everywhere in the palaces. They proclaimed her victory over people as well as possessions for her servants bore her livery and badge. She took as her motto, "*The Most Happy.*" And why would she not be? She had taken the place of the rightful queen and there was no-one to contest her.

In the summer of 1533 Queen Anne was unable to go on a progress with the king for the birth of her child was too near. She was confined to her chamber to rest and her mother, Lady Wiltshire, her sister Lady Mary Carey, Lady Jane Rochford and Madge Shelton were in constant attendance on her. The king came to visit her in the evenings but it ranked with her that he could go out every day and take his pleasure in riding and hunting. She pouted when he told her of his successes in archery contests and tennis games when she was restricted to reading, music and playing cards. The boredom told on her and her temper grew worse every day. She consoled herself by making grand plans for the future of her royal child.

"Mother, I have decided that if the child is a boy, we will call him Henry. And if it is a girl then she will be Mary. His other daughter will have to be known as Mary the Bastard," she laughed.

"Your Grace, you should not joke about such things. The king has consulted a number of soothsayers and they have all foretold the birth of a son," said Lady Wiltshire.

"Except one of them," muttered Lady Mary Carey. "William Glover said it would be a girl."

"He got no reward for his false telling," snapped Queen Anne. "Of course, it will be a boy. The royal midwives have all said the same thing. Do you think you know better than them?"

"Your Grace, do not distress yourself. You must use the time to rest," counselled Lady Wiltshire.

"I do nothing but rest, mother," she observed irritably. "It is becoming unendurable. I would much rather take a walk in the palace gardens. It is July and this room is boiling hot."

"You could still take a chill, your Grace. You must not risk yourself. We are the one who would take the blame. Lady Margaret, fetch the queen's fan and bring it here."

I stood beside the queen's bed and fanned her diligently. "Don't blow my hair around that way. Can't you even use a fan properly?" she grumbled.

"Shall I read to you, your Grace?" asked Lady Jane Rochford solicitously.

"No, not now," she said dismissively. "Mother, I have decided that Lady Bryan shall take care of the child's governance as she did before. I must give orders for napkins of the finest linen to be prepared for the baby. And Master Cornelius shall make a gold teething ring set with coral."

"There is already an entire chest full of napkins, your Grace," Lady Wiltshire assured her. "I have looked them over myself and they are quite new and unused. And you need not worry about gifts for the child. They will be provided by the guests at the christening. You will have far more than you need from what I remember of past events."

"You must tell me everything you remember, mother. I am determined that my child's christening will be a far more splendid occasion than anything that has happened before."

"Of course, your Grace. I am certain that the king would wish it to be so."

"I shall have Archbishop Cranmer to preside and all the foreign diplomats will attend. The godparents shall be the highest nobility in the land."

"It would be advisable to have the Duke and Duchess of Norfolk as the godparents, your Grace," recommended Lady Wiltshire. "They will carry the child into the church behind a great procession of gentlemen, squires and chaplains, the mayor and aldermen of London, the members of the King's Privy Council and the Chapel Royal and finally the barons, bishops and earls in order of precedence. There is a font of silver which is used for the christening of royal children. The highest nobles have the honour of carrying the wax candle, the salt, the oil of chrism and the covered gilt basins. The others hold a canopy over the child who is wrapped in a rich gold cloth. After the christening, the trumpets will be blown and the Garter Herald will make the proclamation and then the christening gifts will be presented. And then in going out the gifts will be carried in precession before the child for everyone to see."

"I shall discuss the godparents with His Majesty, mother," said Queen Anne decisively. Her eyes were glittering and she had quite recovered her spirits. "It is a pity that we cannot attend the occasion ourselves. But I am determined that it will all be conducted as befits the true heir of His Majesty. Where is this gold cloth for the christening? Let it be brought to me so that I can judge if it is worthy."

"All the regalia for the christening is stored in the Chapel Royal and the Jewel Tower," said Lady Wiltshire. "But as I remember, the christening cloth was kept in Her Majesty's wardrobe. I mean, that of the Dowager Princess. It was a special piece of cloth of gold which was very finely woven."

"Then it must be sent back to the palace. What use is it for her to keep it? Why was this not thought of before? Why is everything left to me to order?" complained Queen Anne.

Queen Anne demanded that the royal christening cloth should be sent for at once. The king was so anxious to please her that he sent a message to Queen Catherine asking her to give it up. However, she refused to consider the idea. She protested that the christening cloth was her own property brought from Spain. Moreover, it was a present from her own mother Queen Isabella. King Henry was reluctant to press the matter any further. But he signalled his displeasure by ordering Queen Catherine to move her household to Buckden Towers. So on this occasion, Queen Anne did not get her wish. She compensated by ordering a fine mantle of purple velvet to be made with a long train furred with ermine.

King Henry had made plans for splendid jousts, masques and banquets to celebrate the birth of his son. But on 7th September 1533 a red-haired girl was born instead. The king was disappointed, but insisted that sons would follow in time. He cancelled the planned entertainments. Three days later Princess Elizabeth was christened on the church of the Observant Friars at Greenwich. The church was hung with tapestries and a silver font was placed in the middle of the church beneath a crimson canopy fringed with gold. A procession of the highest nobles in the realm bore the gold basins, the candle, the salt and the chrism oil into the church for the ceremony. The Dowager Duchess of Norfolk carried the child in the newly-made mantle and her grandfather, the earl of Wiltshire, held the train. The Bishop of London performed the baptism and the Garter King of Arms proclaimed her as the Princess of England and the heralds blew their trumpets. Then the guests presented their gifts to the infant princess and were served with refreshments of wafers, confits and hypocras wine. The christening gifts were carried out of the church in procession for everyone to see and brought to the queen's chamber.

When Princess Elizabeth was three months old, she was assigned her own household and sent to live at Hatfield House. Lady Margaret Bryan was appointed as her governess. Princess Mary was told that she must no longer style herself as a princess. In future she would be known as Lady Mary, the king's daughter. Queen Anne demanded that her jewels and plate should be confiscated since she was now unworthy of such honours. Her loyal governess, Lady Margaret Pole, refused to hand them over and was dismissed from her service. She asked to remain with Lady Mary and serve her without pay, but her request was refused. Lady Mary's household was disbanded and she was sent to wait upon her sister at Hatfield.

Part 2: The Household of Queen Anne Boleyn (1532 – 1536)

In March 1534 Pope Clement VII finally announced that the king's marriage to Queen Catherine of Aragon stood firm and canonical. King Henry was ordered to live with her as his lawful wife and queen and maintain her with love and princely honour. Queen Catherine was vindicated, but the judgement came too late to make any difference to her situation. The king ignored the Pope's verdict and sent her to live at Kimbolton Castle where she was served by a physician, a confessor and three women servants. Sir Edmund Bedingfield and Sir Edward Chamberlain were appointed as her Steward and Chamberlain. She was forbidden to receive any visitors unless they held a special license from the king. I wondered why the king continued to treat the poor lady so vengefully and suspected that it was due to the influence of Queen Anne. She could barely tolerate the existence of his rival wife and daughter. She told the king that she would not conceive a son while Catherine and Mary lived. They were traitors who deserved death.

The sole ally that the displaced queen could rely on was the Spanish ambassador, Eustace Chapuys. He was the only person at court who dared to protest to the king about his treatment of her. The king blandly replied that God and his conscience were on good terms and his family matters were none of the emperor's concern. But the ambassador was determined to do his utmost to protect the former queen and her daughter. One day I received a note asking me to meet him secretly at his house for the sake of our mutual friends. I was startled by his ability to send messages to members of the queen's household, but I supposed that the ambassadors had connections throughout the court. I decided to take the risk and go there. His servants were expecting me and admitted me straightaway to see the ambassador. He greeted me with his usual charming smile.

"Seigneur Chapuys, I am honoured to meet you," I said as I made my curtsey.

"The honour is mine, Lady Margaret," he replied, kissing my hand. "I am most grateful that you accepted my invitation."

"What can I do for you, Seigneur?" I asked.

He motioned me to sit down. "It is a delicate matter, Lady Margaret," he said. "I have come here to assist Queen Catherine and Princess Mary in their difficulties.

But in order to advise them well I need information. Especially from their friends here at the court."

I sat up straight and looked him in the eye. "Seigneur Chapuys, I think that you are asking me to become an informer. I do not think that is a role which is suited to a lady of honour. It is true that I am a friend of Queen Catherine. But I have sworn an oath to serve Queen Anne faithfully."

He signalled to his servant to bring us wine. "Your scruples do you credit, Lady Margaret. I do not ask this lightly. I am concerned for the safety of Queen Catherine and her daughter. Their lives could be in danger in this matter. I seek information only to protect them. And did you not also swear an oath to serve Queen Catherine loyally?"

I took the wine cup and waited until the servant had left the room. "That is so, Seigneur. And she was a most kind and worthy mistress. But Lady Maria de Eresby warned me most particularly against becoming a spy at court. I do not think that the queen would approve."

He smiled reassuringly at me and took a delicate sip of the wine. "Ah, the queen and her ladies are a most superior class of women. They would never think of asking for your help. It is I that ask on their behalf. All I wish is for you to report any conversations that you hear concerning them. I know that Queen Anne is not their friend and she plots against them. But there are still many here at court who support Queen Catherine and I believe that you are one of them."

I tasted the wine and enjoyed its pleasant warmth. "Yes, Seigneur, I do support her. And I account her as the true queen and my true mistress. So I promise to tell you if I hear of any danger to her or the princess. But how shall I warn you?"

He put down his cup and leaned forward. "It is better that you do not write anything, Lady Margaret. And we should avoid meeting again in person in case we are observed. But I have a trusted servant who acts as my go-between. His name is Master Rodrigues Gonzales and he sells trifles such as buttons, ribbons and laces to the ladies and gentlemen of the court. I shall describe you to him and you shall ask him if he has any matched sets of mother-of-pearl buttons to sell.

That will be the sign that you are one of my friends. He comes to the court every afternoon between noon and three o'clock. So if you have something to relate you must choose a moment when he is alone and you can speak privately."

It seemed a sensible arrangement. "I have seen the gentleman and I understand what I am to do."

He beamed at me. "I thank you on behalf of Queen Catherine for your willingness to undertake this service. Do not speak of it to anyone else. It must be a complete secret between us. I do not even tell the queen my sources of information. In that way I keep everyone safe from harm."

And so I became a spy for Ambassador Chapuys in the apartments of Queen Anne. I told no-one of my commission, not even Nan. I wondered how many others at court were reporting to him. But I would never know. Most of what I heard was unimportant gossip. But there were occasions when the frustrated Queen Anne voiced her complaints and threats against her predecessor and her daughter. I did not think that it was wrong to warn Queen Catherine of what was said. I was sure that in my place Lady Maria de Eresby would do just the same.

In passing information to Ambassador Chapuys, I felt that I had embarked upon a valiant enterprise which would assist Queen Catherine in her distress. The next day I sought out Master Rodrigues' stall and enquired about the mother-of-pearl buttons. He nodded at me gravely in response.

"I was told to expect you, my lady," he whispered. "I do not need to know your name. Simply come to me when you have anything to tell my master. I will report it faithfully to him."

And so once a week or a fortnight I would visit the Spanish peddlar's stall to pass on whatever I had heard. On each occasion, I felt that I was striking a blow on behalf of the true queen.

"Choose whatever you wish, my lady," urged Master Rodrigues. "There is no charge for so great a friend of Her Majesty."

Little by little, I acquired a fine collection of lace, silver buttons and coloured ribbons. Ambassador Chapuys was as discreet as he had promised and never paid the slightest attention to me in public. In this way, I felt that I was still acting as a loyal servant of Queen Catherine. And at New Year, the ambassador sent me a purse of gold nobles as a token of his gratitude.

Following Queen Anne's coronation, the king increased her household again and there were many newcomers at court. However, life in service to Queen Anne was a very different affair to that of Queen Catherine of Aragon. The Boleyns were seen as an inconsequential family. Sir Thomas Boleyn had been a mere knight before he was raised up to be the earl of Wiltshire. Queen Anne knew that she was being compared with her predecessor and was determined to excel her in every way. She laid down sterner rules of conduct for her household, she gave greater alms and dressed herself more flamboyantly. But no-one was deceived by her outward performance for her desire to impress was only too apparent. Her arrogant behaviour served as a mask for her insecurity but it failed to win her many friends. I could not avoid comparing her with the majestic Queen Catherine of Aragon who had taken pride in the harmony and sophistication of her household. She had taken care to share her favours fairly among her attendants to avoid any feelings of envy. All of us had treasured Books of Hours and valuable items of clothing from the royal wardrobe as signs of her regard for us. I had felt proud to serve such a mistress. Many felt just the same and muttered their discontent against the arrogance of "that upstart Nan Bullen" behind doors and below stairs.

Queen Anne liked to boast of her superior education in the French courts. She had an enviable collection of books in English, French and Latin in her apartments. It pleased her to read aloud virtuous precepts in French from *"Lessons for my Daughter"* by Queen Anne de Beaujeu and *"The Book of Three Virtues"* by Christine de Pisan. Then she would amuse herself by asking one of her maids of honour to render it into English. When she realised that both Nan and I could speak fluent French she rarely called upon us. But she often asked Lady Jane Seymour to translate and enjoyed her evident dismay. The Seymour family were only minor nobility and Lady Jane had unremarkable looks and limited conversation or knowledge of the world. She seemed lonely at court and spent much of her time working on her embroidery. Her parents did not believe in educating their daughters and she could barely read and write her own name. So she was frequently at a loss whenever poems were recited or works of literature were discussed.

Queen Anne enjoyed ridiculing those who lacked her courtly accomplishments. One day she decided to make an object lesson of Lady Jane's retiring nature. "In the French court the maids of honour were trained in the art of profitable conversation. Indeed, the wise Queen Anne de Beaujeu admonished her daughter upon this very subject with the words: *"Ne soyez pas comme ces femmes stupides qui, en compagnie, n'ont ni présence ni port, qui ne savent pas quoi dire et ne peuvent pas répondre d'un seul mot quand quelqu'un leur parle."* Lady Jane, I know how much you value such virtuous precepts. Please translate it for our benefit."

"Please excuse me, your Grace, but I am not familiar with the French tongue," replied Lady Jane timidly.

"How extraordinary! And yet it is an indispensable skill for any lady at court. Lady Anne Parr, perhaps you would be willing to oblige us instead."

Nan's face flushed red. "Queen Anne de Beaujeu said, "Do not be like those foolish women who in company have no presence or bearing, who do not know what to say and cannot reply with even one word when someone speaks to them."

"Exactly so, Lady Anne. For it is a most necessary accomplishment in any lady of worth to take part in pleasant conversation. And it is a burden to the rest of the company to have to endure the tiresome reticence of those who have nothing of interest to say. Really Lady Jane, you have been here six years but you haven't profited one jot from the example of the ladies here. I don't know how such dullards were chosen to serve at court. You might as well have stayed at home."

Jane invariably bowed her head meekly and accepted the criticism. There was no fight in her and she never answered back. In the end, Queen Anne grew tired of belittling her ignorance. I found that I despised them both: Queen Anne for parading her accomplishments and Jane for submitting to her bullying. I wondered why she didn't take lessons in reading, writing and French conversation to improve herself. *Does she make a virtue of her ignorance?* I thought. Her skill with a needle was remarkable and she seemed to be content to spend her days laboriously embroidering cushions for the queen's apartments. The designs were invariably Biblical scenes of David and Goliath or the Salutation of the Lady Mary. Queen Anne could find no fault with her stitches although she would denigrate her old-fashioned choice of images. She preferred the classical themes of Paris and Helen or The Three Fates. The continual disparagement led us to look down on Jane. She was well-born, but had neither outstanding looks, fortune nor accomplishments. Her sister-in-law, Lady Anne Stanhope Seymour, was a forceful character who derided her as a weak fool.

"I declare she is an embarrassment to me," she told us. "She is becoming too old to serve as a maid of honour. It was her father who arranged for her to come to court in the hope of making a good marriage. But she doesn't like it here, poor fool. She says she preferred living at home in the country and helping her mother. Her brother Edward is hoping to persuade his father to send another of his sisters here in her place. She will end her days as a nursemaid or seamstress. But not in my household. One of her sisters must take her. She is not my own kin, after all!"

A born spinster, we agreed. She would have been better placed in a nunnery sewing for the poor all day long. She will surely end up as a drudge in the household of one of her brothers or sisters. A fate which all noblewomen secretly dreaded. So Jane became increasingly lonely and isolated among the maids of honour. But she never showed resentment and remained demure and humble. Finally, her fortunes unexpectedly turned. Queen Anne's spiteful remarks about "that insipid little ninny" aroused the sympathy of the king who was moved to defend her on one occasion.

"The girl is well enough," he pronounced. "Some men prefer wives who are more diligent in sewing than reading. And it is virtue that is the chief ornament of a woman. As the Book of Proverbs reminds us, "A virtuous woman is far above rubies.""

"So you would prefer it if I sat in a corner sewing all day and had nothing to say for myself?" bridled Anne.

"Nay, sweetheart," he assured her. "I said that some men would prefer it. I did not say that I would prefer it."

"I should hope not," rejoined Anne tartly. "Or else the court would be as dull as ditchwater."

But something about Jane's quiet peaceability drew the king's notice. His mother, Elizabeth of York, had had a reputation as a peacemaker and the young Henry had grown up in the atmosphere of her gentle kindness. Queen Anne was the ideal fascinating mistress. But a wife should have the qualities which his mother had exemplified. The contrast was emphasised by Queen Anne's unkind mockery of Jane.

"She has the intellect of a milkmaid and the temperament of a dairy cow," she observed. "We shall have to marry her to a farmer for no gentleman would want such a goose."

"She is well enough," persisted the king. "It is a good example to the court to have such gentle maidens among us. I would that more of the ladies devoted themselves to sewing rather than gossip and intrigue."

Queen Anne's eyebrows drew together. "My laundress can sew even better than her. But noble ladies should have more spirit. In the French court she would be regarded as a stupid little mouse and sent back home to her parents."

"Her father was one of my best captains in France and I would not so offend him," he replied. "As long as she conducts herself virtuously, I would not reproach her for her lack of education. She does not need to be a clerk, but a good wife."

"It is a pity that one of the other girls was not chosen instead," shrugged Queen Anne. "There are so many ladies seeking a place at court. The opportunity is wasted on her. She has no capacity to learn and no ambition to improve herself. I cannot undertake to find a husband for her – unless any of your gentlemen happens to be a complete fool."

"None of my gentlemen are fools," said Henry smugly. "I pride myself on choosing only the best for my service."

"Well, I didn't get to choose all my ladies," retorted Queen Anne petulantly. "I had to find places for my predecessor's sewing circle. She is by far the worst, but some of the others have the sullen manners and indolence of the Spanish contingent. They are as merry as a set of tombstones and just as apt at dancing."

Henry smiled complacently. "You cannot expect your ladies to compare with you, sweetheart. Neither can my gentlemen compare with me."

"But they should have some mark of quality about them," she complained. "It reflects poorly upon me to have such ninnies about me. They haven't the least idea how to entertain or amuse. They are only able to play endless games of cards. I should think that they would bore any man of sense to death within a month. They cannot dress themselves with any style and even a Spaniard would tire of their sombre looks and dull conversation. In future, I will have no more milksops about me. I shall insist that any new candidates should be handsome, intelligent and witty. I must have something with which to work!"

"As you say, my dear. They must be fit for the court." Henry agreed with his forceful wife, but from that time he gained an impression of Jane as a gentle maid who reminded him of his beloved mother.

Fortunately, for Jane some of the ladies in waiting were far kinder than the young maids of honour. They had served the regal Queen Catherine and disapproved of Queen Anne's unkindness. Lady Maud Parr came to talk to Jane about her inability to read and write.

"Indeed, my dear, in the time of our mothers and grandmothers it was common for ladies to be illiterate. But nowadays it is considered advantageous for girls to be educated. I taught both my daughters in the same manner as my son. And now Anne can read, write and make conversation in both English and French. Would you not like to do the same?"

Poor Jane was flustered by this unexpected kindness. "I am most grateful for your interest, Lady Parr. But my dear mother was convinced that it is undesirable to educate women. She feared that it would make them proud and stubborn. She always reminded me that the Virgin Mary could neither read nor write but she found favour with God for her virtue. And so I should take her as my model and imitate her piety, her modesty and her industry."

"That would be well enough if you had stayed at home to help your mother in the household," said Lady Maud patiently. "But here at court you will face a great disadvantage as an uninformed lady. If you learned to read then you could occupy yourself with devotional works. And if you were able to write then you could send news to your friends and oversee your accounts. Do you not think that would be beneficial?"

"I would not wish to contradict your better knowledge of such things, Lady Parr," said the flustered Lady Jane. "I can only say that my lady mother believes that ladies do not need to be clerks. And their chaplains can read aloud to them from such good works as tend to virtue. She is convinced that the highest calling of any lady is to bear children and care for them. So I would not dare to defy her opinions."

At this reply, Lady Parr admitted defeat. It was not her place to set a daughter against her mother. However, she took counsel with another lady who sent for Lady Jane to try to resolve matters. This was none other than Lady Gertrude Courtenay, one of the highest aristocrats in the court. She was a devoted friend of Queen Catherine and despised Queen Anne as her usurper. She readily agreed to act as the patroness of Jane and alleviate her misery.

"I am most honoured that you asked to see me, Lady Courtenay," murmured Lady Jane as she made her curtsey.

Lady Courtenay gave her an appraising look. "I understand that your mother has a prejudice against learned women. However, there are many other accomplishments which well become a lady of the court. A maid of honour may be distinguished for her piety and devotion, for the correctness of her deportment and dress, for her skill at dancing and riding and for her talent at sewing and lacemaking. I hear from Lady Parr that you are a fine needlewoman."

Lady Jane blushed and hung her head. "Lady Parr is a most gracious lady. But I fear that my skill with a needle is nothing out of the ordinary."

Lady Courtenay smiled graciously. "Modesty is a great virtue, my dear. But it must not be overdone. Lady Parr is a woman of sound good sense and her judgement can always be trusted. Beside your talent at embroidery, what else can you do? Can you sing or play on an instrument?"

"I regret that I cannot, my lady," she demurred.

"No matter, there are many other good qualities. How did you occupy yourself at home?"

"I assisted my mother with the care of the younger children, my lady. I supervised the cleaning of the plate and the linen. And I made simple receipts, perfumes and household remedies in the stillroom. I had the charge of the kitchen garden and herb plot for the household. My mother thought that every country lady should have a good knowledge of wholesome plants."

Lady Courtenay nodded her head thoughtfully. "I see that your mother believed in a practical education for her daughters. Here at court, there is good training in the spiritual life, in social skills and the art of good conversation. I propose that you shall come to my chambers every afternoon and I shall inform the queen that you are undertaking some fine sewing for me. My attendants shall advise you how to dress and comport yourself and practice the conversational arts. We shall pay attention to reading good works and discussing poetry. We will begin tomorrow."

Jane was so overcome by this decisive plan that she dared not make any protest. And before long she began to cut a different figure in the court. The kind interest of her benefactress raised her spirits and her carriage became more confident. She no longer appeared as a figure of pity. Queen Anne ceased to torment her apart from decrying her preference for English styles of dress. But in fact, they became Jane very well and made her look intriguing. Since her conversational abilities were much improved it did not matter so much that she could not compose a poem nor cap a French quotation. Few ladies could compete with Queen Anne on that level. And the ones who could were prudent enough to allow her to excel their skills. And so Jane settled down in her role as a lady of the court. Neither Nan nor I took much interest in cultivating her society but we were glad that she was no longer the target of the queen's barbed wit.

Queen Anne often vented her temper upon her retinue and we grew adept at reading the signs and making ourselves inconspicuous. But none of us escaped the lash of her tongue. One day it was my turn. The king had sent his excuse for not being able to go out riding. The weather was too cold to permit a walk or picnic in the palace gardens. And a long-awaited consignment of rich fabrics from Antwerp was delayed yet again. Thwarted of her anticipated pleasures she lashed out at us.

"It seems that I have to see to everything myself! she scolded. "What use are the lot of you? Nothing but drones sitting around and taking your leisure. You fancy that you will make fine matches just because you serve in court. But none of you are fit to run a household. You are just a pack of tattling gossips with no concern for your mistress and I am sick of the sight of you!"

"There, there, your Grace," said her old nanny Mrs Orchard in an effort to calm her down. "Do not lose your composure. You will be able to go out riding tomorrow, I daresay."

The queen's face turned dark and her temper spilled over into venom. "You, Lady Anne Parr. How long have you served at court? You were not much help to your former mistress, were you? And you are no more so to me."

"And you, Mistress Shelton," she snapped. "You are my cousin but you think of nothing but your clothes and your admirers. When was the last time you opened a book to improve your mind?"

"And you, Lady Margaret. It is not sufficient to be an ornament in my bedchamber. You must strive to be useful and entertaining. Bring a pack of cards and send for a musician to play for me. If you had any regard for me then you would have suggested it yourself."

We all bowed our heads in the face of this senseless rage for it was useless to protest. But inside we burned with resentment. I could not respect such a queen as my mistress. She scolded like a lowborn housewife. I thought back longingly to regal Queen Catherine who never raised her voice to her servants. She rarely needed to utter a rebuke for her household were eager to serve her well. Queen Anne finally ended her tirade.

"I shall speak to the mother of the maids about your dilatory attitudes," she announced pointedly. "From now on I expect to see you all usefully employed in my rooms."

The following day, a great bundle of canvas appeared in the Privy Chamber and we were directed to sew shirts for the queen to distribute to the poor. Queen Anne smiled complaisantly to see us sitting there hour after hour sewing in silence. She did not even call a musician to play for us. Instead, she arranged for her chaplain, William Latimer, to read homilies to us on the virtues of duty, service and humility. He was renowned for his piety and had no taste for worldly frivolity.

"Her Grace desires that her ladies should use themselves according to their calling with modesty and chastity. You should act as if you were always in her presence and your conduct should be beyond reproach," he reminded us gravely.

Fortunately, we were all skilled at sewing and by the time the shirts were finished she had grown tired of the dull atmosphere.

"It amazes me that my ladies should be as dreary as a company of laundry maids on a wet afternoon," she complained to us. "I see that I shall have to send for some of the gentlemen of the court to amuse me."

Once again, card games, dancing and poetry were the order of the day. The courtiers vied with each other to pay her flattering compliments and her ill-humour was superseded by vivacious charm. When the order from Antwerp finally arrived, she was eager to claim our services in order to plan a collection of new costumes for herself. She took her role as the leader of court fashion extremely seriously. Nan was adept at discussing different styles and trims with the queen and the next fortnight was spent in commissioning each outfit from the court dressmakers. She waited with mounting impatience for them to be completed and then planned a number of suitable occasions to show them off to the king and court. She was in her most contented mood whenever she was the centre of attention and her retinue breathed a sigh of relief. The king was equally vain about his appearance and extravagant in his dress, so in that sense they were a well-matched couple. However, she was far more temperamental and demanding than the king. Her retinue often became exhausted trying to live up to the expectation that her rooms should always be distinguished by witty conversation and sophisticated entertainment. The queen often invited some of the king's gentlemen to enliven the company but they did not always succeed in pleasing her.

One evening, Queen Anne wore a dress of green damask silk which was her favourite colour. She knew how well it complimented her dark hair and brilliant black eyes. She paused and looked in the mirror and smiled with satisfaction. She was in a mood to be admired and praised for her appearance. But when no compliments were forthcoming, she grew exasperated and took them to task. "I declare that you gentlemen are just as indolent as my ladies. You need some good occupation to liven you up. Tomorrow night you must each present a poem for our entertainment."

"And what theme would you prefer, your Grace," asked Sir Henry Norris. "Shall it be love or fortune, pastime or the tranquil mind?" He was pleased for he was a renowned poet. However, some of the other courtiers looked rather dismayed at the idea.

"You may take your inspiration from the theme of ladies. There are plenty here to stimulate your thoughts." Clearly the queen was anticipating some flattering verses.

The following evening, the gentlemen arrived with their scrolls of verse and I looked forward to an entertaining interlude.

"Who shall be one to open the lists for our battle of words?" asked the queen. "What did you make of our theme, Weston?"

Sir Francis Weston stepped forward and bowed. He was dressed very elegantly in a doublet of crimson taffeta lined with yellow sarcenet, scarlet hose and a crimson cap with red and yellow feathers. He unfolded his paper and gave a mischievous smile.

"These women all
Both great and small

Are wavering to and fro,
Now here, now there,
Now everywhere;
But I will not say so.

So they love to range,
Their minds doth change
And make their friend their foe;
As lovers true
Each day they choose new;
But I will not say so.

They laugh, they smile,
They do beguile
As dice that men doth throw.
Who useth them much
Shall never be rich;
But I will not say so.

Some hot, some cold,
There is no hold
But as the wind doth blow;
When all is done,
They change like the moon;
But I will not say so.

So thus one and other
Taketh after their mother,
As cock by kind doth crow.
My song is ended,
The best may be amended;
But I will not say so."

The maids of honour giggled at this sally. Queen Anne looked rather vexed. "You are not very complimentary about the ladies, Weston. Perhaps you have been recently disappointed in the field of love. Norris, I hope that you have something more gallant to offer us."

Norris was looking no less elegant in a doublet of dark green satin and yellow hose and a black velvet cap. "With your permission, your Grace, I will do my poor best," he replied. "These lines are on *How to Obtain Her*:

"The more ye desire her, the sooner ye miss;
The more ye require her, the stranger she is.
The more ye pursue her, the faster she flyeth;
The more ye eschew her, the sooner she plyeth.
But if ye refrain her, and use not to crave her,
So shall ye obtain her if ever ye have her."

The maids of honour whispered together indignantly. Queen Anne raised her eyebrows at Norris. "That is hardly what I would call gallant. I would pity any lady who was wooed in such a manner. George, I hope you will oblige us with something more encouraging."

Lord Rochford stepped forward with look of self-satisfaction. He wore a doublet of tawny velvet and black satin with gold buttons, black satin hose and a tawny cap. He unfurled his scroll and began to read with a mock-solemn expression.

"If women could be fair, and yet not fond,
Or that their love were firm, not fickle still,
I would not marvel that they make men bond
By service long to purchase their goodwill;
But when I see how frail those creatures are,
I muse that men forget themselves so far.

To mark the choice they make, and how they change,
How oft from Phoebus they do flee to Pan;
Unsettled still, like haggards wild they range,
These gentle birds that fly from man to man;
Who would not scorn and shake them from the fist,
And let them fly, fair fools, which way they list?

Yet for disport we fawn and flatter both,
To pass the time when nothing else can please,
And train them to our lure with subtle oath,
Till, weary of their wiles, ourselves we ease;
And then we say when we their fancy try,
To play with fools, O what a fool was I!

"Worse and worse!" exclaimed the queen, "What kinds of ladies are these that you describe? Fickle, frail and fond! My ladies will be sadly disappointed if that is the best praise that you can offer. Brereton, I hope that you can make amends for your fellows."

He bowed and drew a paper out of his sleeve. He wore a doublet of russet satin and brown silk hose with a russet cap. "If it please your Grace, I shall read these lines on *The Gift*:

Some do long for pretty knacks,
And some for strange devices:
God send me that my Lady lacks,
I care not what the price is.

I walk the town and tread the street,
In every corner seeking
The pretty thing I cannot meet,
That's for my Lady's liking:

The mercers pull me, going by,
The silk-wives say 'What lack ye?'
'The thing you have not,' then say I:
'Ye foolish knaves, go pack ye!'

It is not all the silk in Cheap,
Nor all the golden treasure;
Nor twenty bushels on a heap
Can do my Lady pleasure.

But were it in the wit of man
By any means to make it,
I could for money buy it than,
And say, 'Fair Lady, take it!'"

"It seems that you pay your court to strange and contrary ladies, Brereton!" she observed. "You were my last hope of hearing a courtly sentiment. I see that you gentlemen have put your heads together to make a game and mockery of the matter. I ought to have set the theme as the praise of faithful ladies. Are all of you so jaded on the subject of true love? Perhaps the ladies whom you admire can tell that you are fickle-hearted gentlemen!"

Sir William Brereton saw that their jest had fallen flat and tried his best to retrieve the situation. "The truth is, your Grace, that all other ladies are sadly lacking in comparison to your Majesty."

"Do not try to cozen me, Brereton," she admonished him. "It would be more truthful to admit that the gentlemen of this court are sadly lacking in gallantry. No lady would be won by any of your verses."

Lord Rochford realised that they had displeased the queen. "They may not have been very gallant, your Grace. But surely you found them amusing?"

"They were neither amusing nor entertaining. It is a great pity that there are no poets of note among you," remarked the queen. "I enjoyed many delightful evenings listening to contests of verse during my time in the French court. Perhaps I should invite some of their gentlemen to pay a visit over here and demonstrate the true spirit of courtly romance. However, it is possible that you may perform somewhat better tomorrow. And so I bid you all goodnight!"

The gentlemen withdrew looking rather abashed. They took the hint and the following evening they returned with their new compositions in hand. Queen Anne had dressed in a gown of crimson satin trimmed with gold lace and pearls. She looked every inch the great lady. She smiled and caressed her pearl necklace as the gentlemen took it in turns to read their poems to her. This time the verses were as agreeable as she could have wished and she was pleased with her entertainment.

She pronounced young Weston as the winner of the contest and gave him a purse of gold. The others received gracious smiles and compliments as they took their leave. Her brother, Lord Rochford, lingered behind and picked up a scroll lying on her bedside table.

"What is this, Anne?" he asked.

"Oh, that," she remarked with complete indifference. "It's a poem from Henry. I shall have to write a reply to it."

"He should ask Wyatt or Surrey to pen his verses," he said dismissively. "Look he compares your lips to a gillyflower. How commonplace! Even I can do better than that!"

"So why don't you compose a reply and save me the trouble?" she challenged him.

"Very well," he replied mischievously. "You can send this verse to His Grace:

"My love for thee is infinite, O high and mighty lord.
I rejoice that we have wed at last and shout the news abroad.
If only I had words to spare to frame to your great parts.
The greatest cod in Christendom – 'tis greater than your heart!"

"Hush George, for heaven's sake!" hissed the queen looking around uneasily. But she could not help giggling.

Her dropped to one knee like a lovesick swain. "Alas, my sweet lady, I have been stricken too long with the dart of love. Your eyes, your lips, your sweet voice are incomparable! Behold your poor servant and grant me the favour of kissing your fair hands or else I shall die of longing!"

"Stop it, George! You go too far," snapped Queen Anne, her eyes flashing fire. "It has been no joke to play the coy mistress for years on end. If the king had been given good counsel I should have been married and crowned long ago."

"As lovers go, you might have done a lot worse," he replied imperturbably. "After all, he is generous enough so what does it matter if his verses are foolish things and his taste in dress is appalling. It is a pity he does not take some points from us on how to dress in the French style."

"That is the fault of his tailor, John Malt," she grumbled. "He persuades him to wear the most expensive cloth of gold so that he will look magnificent. So of course, we always clash and he never notices."

"What a shame that I am not the king," he sympathised. "I would always dress to do you credit. I tell you Anne, the man gets vainer as he gets older. His morning levees take longer and longer because he is determined to look the same as he did in his youth. If you were to meet him at a public day at Hever, you would think him a poor fellow."

"Hush, George! Someone could report you!" she chided.

"They'd never dare!" he asserted confidently.

"Have you no discretion, George? Don't you care who might be listening?" she said petulantly.

"Who would be listening to us?" he said carelessly. "Only your maids are here and they don't count."

"All the same, it is folly to talk as you do. If you have no care for your own reputation then you might at least have some care for mine." She unfastened her pearl necklace and laid it on the table.

"Your reputation is safe enough," he replied as he eyed the pearls enviously. "The king adores you. Here is the proof of it in this scroll. How are you going to answer him?"

"I shall show the deference and flattery that he expects. Then he will send me a fine jewel as a token of his devotion. See if he doesn't!" she boasted.

"You have a great chest of jewels already," he reminded her. "What need have you for more?"

"A queen must always look the part," she said smugly. "There are those who are ready to decry me or outshine me if I gave them the chance. But I shall make very sure that they do not get it."

"Never fear, there are none here to outshine you," he stated. "They have no understanding of how to dress for effect."

"And sadly, there are very few who can frame their minds to compose a verse," she declared. "I am doing my best to raise the standard, but it is an uphill struggle. Most of my ladies can hardly tell the difference between a good poem and a bad one. I have it in mind to make a collection of the best love-poetry in the court. My ladies can write them down in a book and add to it whenever I judge a new piece to be worthy."

"It is an excellent plan," he replied enthusiastically. "You must include Wyatt, of course. "*My Lute Awake*" is one of his finest poems."

"And we must not forget Surrey," she resolved. "I shall certainly include "*O Happy Dames*."

"And I hope that you will not find my humble efforts to be entirely without merit," he proposed.

"Perhaps. I shall have to think about it," she said looking away with a provocative smile.

He tapped the scroll against his chin. "Are you planning to include any of Henry's ballads? He will be offended if he is left out. He believes he sets the standard among the court poets."

"He won't know anything about it," said Queen Anne with finality.

But of course, there are no secrets in a court. Ambassador Chapuys and Master Cromwell had informers in both the royal households. None of the three Boleyn children had the least discretion and they did not survive the tempests of the court. Lady Mary Carey was the first to suffer for her imprudence. She secretly married a soldier named William Stafford and was banished from court. And Lord Rochford's foolish tongue proved to be his undoing in the end. King Henry was far too proud and sensitive to endure anyone's mockery. Queen Anne and Lord Rochford courted their own downfall with their careless words.

It was not very long afterwards that one of the royal pages brought me a poem addressed to myself. His name was Master James Gage and he was well known in the court for his ready smile and obliging attitude.

"Like to a ring without a finger,
Or a bell without a ringer,
Like a horse was never ridden,
Or a feast and no guest bidden,
Like a well without a bucket,
Or a rose if no man pluck it,
Just such as these may she be said
That lives, not loves, but dies a maid."

"What do you have there?" asked Nan. I threw it across to her and she caught it deftly.

"I cannot tell. A verse from an anonymous poet, but it is not much of a tribute." It was not exactly a declaration of love nor was it particularly flattering. I wondered if it was someone's idea of a jest.

"No, not at all," agreed Nan. "We shall have to bribe the page boy and find out who has had the audacity to write it." But Master James would not be persuaded by our shillings. "I cannot say, my lady. But if it pleases you, I can take back an answer. You may call on me whenever you wish."

"A strange admirer indeed, declared Nan. "Perhaps it is his way of trying to pique your interest."

The following day another verse arrived tied with a scarlet ribbon. The page presented it to me with a knowing look in his eye.

"Like a cage without a bird,
Or a thing too long deferred,
Like the gold was never tried,

Or the ground unoccupied,
Like a house that's not possessed,
Or the book was never pressed,
Just such as these may she be said
That lives, ne'er loves, but dies a maid."

"The author is challenging you," said Nan. "I think you should reply in the same vein." We duly put our heads together to compose a counter-verse.

"The bird in cage doth sweetly sing;
Due season proffers everything;
The gold that's tried from dross is pured;
There's profit in the ground manured;
The house is by possession graced;
The book, when pressed, is then embraced:
Such is the virgin in mine eyes
That lives, loves, marries ere she dies."

The fatal word marriage must have discouraged my would-be gallant, for there was no sequel. "It was probably some old married man or practiced seducer seeking to test your virtue," said Nan dismissively. "One with a close purse for he sent you no gift. And one without courage for he shrinks from declaring himself. He is no suitor to waste your thoughts upon. He probably sends that poem to every maid at court."

"I am sure you are right, Nan." I was relieved and yet a little disappointed that so little should result from the exchange.

"For all we know it was penned by another page who dares not reveal that he has been casting his eyes upon the queen's ladies," she mused. "It may even have been the work of the page who brought it."

I smiled at the idea. That would be a possibility. A page could only presume to send such verses in secret.

"After all, the widowed Queen Catherine of Valois married her servant, Owen

Tudor," she observed. "And he was the ancestor of the Tudor kings. It must give hope to all love-lorn pages."

Suddenly, the poem seemed romantic after all. After all, a humble suitor was a very different matter from a craven one.

"Leave it to me," said Nan. "I'll get the truth out of him." She turned from her errand looking satisfied. "It was just as I thought," she declared. "Master James has confessed everything to me. He has conceived a great admiration for you. But since he is too poor to buy you any gifts or tokens, he thought that he would write a love-poem. He has often heard the gentlemen of the court reading their verses in the royal apartments and was so bold as to compose one of his own."

I felt rather flattered by his attentions even if he was an admirer of low station.

"Naturally, I told him that he was far too young to be paying his court to anyone," said Nan. "I warned him that if Mrs Stoner discovered that he was sending poems to the maids of honour then he would be dismissed from court at once. And so he begs your forgiveness and promises that he will never annoy you again. Actually, I felt rather sorry for him. His verse is not so bad for a young boy."

"Are we so very different, Nan?" I asked. "We are also here at court to make our fortunes. And we live in dread of failing in our service and being sent home empty-handed."

Nan dismissed the comparison. "Nonsense, Margaret. It is entirely different. He is born to servitude, but we are of noble stock."

"And so my little romance has come to nothing," I sighed. "I fear that I shall never find a suitable match."

"Do not be afraid, Margaret," she consoled me. "You are too pretty and good-natured to remain on the shelf."

And yet I could not help but see how many other maids of honour had been matched already. And even the new arrivals at the court were confidently discussing their suitors in the dormitory. There were dozens of well-born ladies at the court and many of them had the advantages of property or family connections. I had no fortune or powerful relations to negotiate on my behalf. I knew now that it was not enough to be young, attractive and accomplished to succeed at court.

"What are your hopes for the future, Nan?" I asked her. She sat down on her bed and adjusted the loose ties on her sleeve.

"Like all the other maids of honour, I suppose," she replied. "I want to live up to my mother's hopes for me. She has sacrificed so much for her children. And she is so well respected at court. You know, the Parrs were an old family with a respectable fortune when she married my father. But the king's father imposed fines upon all the nobility to increase his wealth. My parents were left with crushing debts on their estates and the worry of it killed my father. If it had not been for my mother's career at court then we would have been left as the poor relations of my uncle. I would like to make a good match which will please her and set her mind at rest. I am the last one to be married now."

I nodded. It was the same with me. I was supposed to revive the standing of the De Roches with a good alliance. But it was not as easy as my family had imagined it would be. "But don't you want to please yourself as well?"

"Yes, of course," she said. "I dream of a handsome young suitor with a fortune or at least a promising future. I want to be the mistress of my own household with servants and the income to dress well without worrying about the cost. I have had enough of struggling to manage a way of life that I cannot afford to live. And I want my children to grow up without the need to make their own way at court. I would like them to be desirable matches who will not have to try to win favour and fortune as we have to do. My sister Catherine has done well enough for herself. I hope to make a match which will be worthy of my mother's efforts to educate and provide for me."

"I have almost given up on such a hope, Nan," I sighed. "I have spent ten years at court but I have never had a suitor. But I think that Queen Catherine would have found me a match if only I had remained in her service."

"Listen Margaret, many ladies who are well-born, attractive and dowered are still refused matches," she reminded me. "Even Queen Anne was rejected by the Percy family when she first came to court. She was not considered noble or wealthy enough to match with young Lord Henry Percy. She was heartbroken and had to leave the court for a time. But you must never speak of it. It is a great secret. She pretends that the king was her only true-love. There are even rumours that she had a romance with Sir Thomas Wyatt before she came to court. It is common knowledge that he wrote a number of poems to her in the hope of winning her affection. But when she refused to become his mistress, he became her bitter enemy."

"I think she was very wise," I replied. "Why should she compromise herself with a married man for the sake of a few poems?"

"I think so too," said Nan. "But he was offended that she rejected his deep passion for her. The report even reached the ear of the king and he sent Wyatt abroad on a diplomatic mission. He couldn't bear to think that he had an rivals in his court."

I was intrigued by the story of the queen's romance. "And what became of Henry Percy?" I asked her.

"He was married to the wealthy Lady Mary Talbot," she informed me. "But it is said that they are most unhappy together. He could never forget his great love for Queen Anne. Courtship is a hazardous venture. A lady cannot be too careful. Her reputation can be ruined by a few unkind rumours. It makes no difference if they are true or false."

I remembered that Lady Maria de Eresby had said much the same thing. A virtuous maid must guard her reputation as fiercely as a tigress guards her cubs. She should ignore vain compliments and seek an honourable match. Those who fell through frailty were to be pitied and despised. In Spain it was the business of the parents to make arrangements. Here at court, it was a matter for the queen. So I should guard my eyes and my heart, she had advised. Be polite and courteous, but discourage worthless flattery.

"Do not be over-ready with your smiles nor show availability in your eyes," she had counselled. "It will only attract the worst sort of men in the court to test your virtue. They will imagine you to be an easy conquest of whom they can boast later. Do not be quick to laugh at idle words and a proper man will think more highly of you." I knew the Spanish were strict and believed in seclusion for well-born young ladies. They were scandalised by the easy ways of the English nobility.

My secret involvement with Seigneur Chapuys had seemed quite an adventure in the beginning. However, as the atmosphere at court grew increasingly tense, I became more fearful of playing the informer. My visits to Master Rodrigues became much rarer. I saw him only once a month and then not at all. I decided that it was too dangerous a venture to continue. Suppose the courier was suspected and interrogated? He would surely reveal the identities of his informants. Seigneur Chapuys had immunity as an ambassador, but I had no protection. I blamed myself for getting involved in an intrigue. I should never have taken sides in a dispute between the king and queen. If my part was discovered then I would be disgraced and perhaps my family would be ruined with me. I resolved not to see the courier again.

But the Spanish ambassador was not minded to lose his informants so easily. I received a message inviting me to meet with him. When the dormitory was quite empty, I burned it on the fire. But then another came and I was afraid that I would be discovered. And so I came to see the ambassador on a quiet Sunday afternoon.

He welcomed me with his usual charming smile. "Greetings, Lady Margaret. It has been long since we met, has it not? Indeed, it has been too long. And our mutual friend tells me that he has not seen you these several months past. I began to fear that you might be ill."

"I am not ill, Seigneur Chapuys, but I am fearful of the mood at court," I confessed. "I can no longer take the risk of being involved in matters which are so high above me. When even the great stand in danger, then what will become of the lowly?"

"It is true what you say about the great being in danger," he heartily agreed. "Perhaps you do not know what has become of our dear queen. She is most hardly used, poor lady. Most of her friends have been taken from her so that she is left quite alone and unsupported. She lives a miserable life of poverty without even the comforts that a lady like yourself enjoys. I do my best to cheer her spirits and assure her that she still has steadfast friends here at the court. Surely you are still among their number?"

"I have the greatest respect and affection for the queen," I protested. "But I do not think she would want to see me in danger for her sake. She has the heart of a proud and valiant warrior and she has no fear of martyrdom. But I am only a humble maid and in these times it is necessary to act with great prudence. There are watchers everywhere in court seeking to denounce others for a profit."

"Take courage, Lady Margaret," he urged me." I assure you that your reputation is quite safe."

"I have come to beg you, Seigneur, to write me no more letters," I pleaded desperately. "If they were discovered then I would be quite undone. And if I were seen burning them then I would be suspected. I keep no writings in my chest and I have sent all my books and letters home. These days it is safer for a maid to content herself with her embroidery."

"Indeed, that is wise," he conceded. "All I ask is that you keep your ears open for any threat to the queen. You know where to find Master Rodrigues and it may be that you will save her from great harm."

"I must go now, Seigneur Chapuys," I answered firmly. "I ask you as a man of honour not to seek me out again or contact me in any way for my peace of mind."

"Very well, Lady Margaret," he replied sadly. "And do not forget to pray from the queen who is so beset by perils on every side."

I made my way back to the dormitory with my heart hammering in my chest and lay down on my bed. I wondered whether I had been observed. And I hoped that the ambassador would keep his word and this would be an end of the matter. I recalled the wise words of Queen Anne of Beaujeu to her daughter: "Those who have their secrets hidden have them imprisoned, but if they tell their secrets then they themselves are in prison." I had meant it for the best, but I had put myself in the power of another and lost my safety. How difficult it was to live at court and how easy it was to make mistakes. I resolved that this was one mistake that I would never repeat. But foolishly, I did not keep my resolution.

Queen Anne's maids of honour were kept busy sewing garments for the poor for her to distribute when she went on progress. She was determined to out-do Queen Catherine's reputation for works of charity. However, the ladies of her inner circle occupied themselves by making costumes for the court masques in her bedchamber. When they grew tired of their labour, they would amuse themselves by practicing the dances with Queen Anne. She could never resist an opportunity to demonstrate her superior skills. In every pageant she took care to take the leading role dressed in an exquisite new costume. It was even said that she composed the masques herself. She was Diana the Huntress surrounded by her attendant nymphs, Athena among the Nine Muses and Venus at the Judgement of Paris. On these occasions King Henry naturally played the part of her triumphant lover. "He must not be familiar with the story of Diana and Actaeon," Nan whispered to me gleefully. "I think he prefers the courtly romances of King Arthur and his knights," I whispered back. But we were galled to be excluded from our share of the gaiety. We knew that our dancing, singing and playing was far superior to that of the queen's favourites and we longed for the opportunity to wear a fine costume and take part in the entertainment.

But we should not have repined about the masques. True, they were a mark of status, but they were also a source of danger. They drew too much attention to the charming maids of honour. Bessie Blount, Mary Boleyn and Anne Boleyn had all attracted the king's eye at court masques. It so happened that an entertainment called "*The Masque of Beauty*" was planned but one of the chosen ladies became too unwell to take part. Master John Farlyon, the Yeoman of the Revels decided that Nan would be a good fit for her costume and would master the dances competently. The following evening, she was a great success and I was proud of my friend. But there was a sequel. The king sent for Master John to congratulate him and enquired about the talented dancer.

"Who is that lady?" enquired King Henry. "I haven't seen her in any of the masques before. From now on, she is to appear at all my court entertainments. When is the next masque taking place?"

"There is one planned for next week called "*The Masque of Queens,*" your Majesty, but the parts have already been chosen."

"Nonsense, man! We would see her dance again. You will arrange it for us."

And so Nan, to her great delight, was summoned again by the testy officer. "Mistress Parr, you have been granted a role as the Queen of Sheba in the next masque. This is an important part so you must not disappoint me. You will wear a special costume to perform an exotic dance. Then you will conclude the entertainment by giving a speech to the king in praise of the wisdom of King Solomon. I will give you the words which you are to learn by heart."

The following week Nan was an even greater success. The king rewarded her with a purse of gold and requested that the Queen of Sheba would condescend to be his dance partner. Throughout the evening he referred to her as *"Mistress Sheba"* and told his courtiers to pay their respects. Naturally, everyone took it as a witty jest. But the following day, Sir Henry Norris, the Groom of the Stool, sent for Nan and told her to dress herself in her best gown and be ready to attend the king that evening. He wished to enjoy the pleasure of her company. Could she sing and play music as well as dance? Was she skilled at playing games of chance? From then on, King Henry began to marked attentions to Nan. She was nineteen years old and extremely lovely, most accomplished and high spirited. I tried to ignore my growing sense of disquiet and told myself that he simply admired her looks and enjoyed her company. The king invited her to partner him in the court dances in spite of the claims of ladies of higher rank. He requested her to sing and play for him and complimented her abilities. She played chess, Primero and dice with him using a supply of coins which Sir Henry Norris had given her. He tactfully advised her to allow the king to win.

The king's favour meant that Nan became the centre of attention and prominent nobles vied for her attention. Lady Maud Parr was congratulated on all sides for her daughter's accomplishments. She thought that Nan's fortune was made and hoped that an offer of marriage would soon be made. But the king lost no time in making his intentions clear. A succession of gifts and notes made their way to the dormitory. The king's own page requested her to send for him when she had composed a reply. Nan showed the letters to me in alarm and my heart sank at the implication. *He sees her as another Bessie Blount*, I thought. *But she is too good for him!* Before long the court became aware that the king had chosen a new favourite.

"What am I to do, Margaret?" she asked me.

"Speak to your mother," I urged her. Lady Maud was a formidable character whom everyone respected.

But even she had no answers. "It is the king's habit to amuse himself with the queen's ladies," she said with tears in her eyes. "My dear, this is not what I wanted for you. I brought you to court to make a respectable alliance. The Parrs are not like the Boleyns or the Blounts. They think nothing of casting away their daughter's virtue for the sake of gaining royal favour. And yet we cannot afford to offend him. If your father were alive this would never have happened!"

"I don't want to be his mistress, mother," wept Nan. "I know that the queen suspects something for she has turned very cold towards me. I am sure that someone has told her about the king's behaviour. But it is not my fault. I never looked for his favour. Not in that way."

"I have no doubt about it, my child. But it is very injurious to your reputation and it will ruin all my hopes for a good match. To be a king's mistress is a worthless game. The benefit is all on his side and neither Bessie Blount nor Mary Boleyn got much to show for it. We could say that you were sick and send you away but I fear that he would see through the ruse. He would send his doctors to treat you and have you brought back to court."

But Queen Anne pre-empted Lady Maud in taking action. Lady Rochford came to tell Nan that the Queen wanted her to come to her bedchamber and read to her. This seemed so unlikely a tale that Nan and I exchanged doubtful looks. However, I could not accompany her without being summoned. When she did not appear at dinner, I went to look for her in the dormitory and found her weeping upon her bed.

"What is the matter, Nan?" I asked. But I had already guessed the cause.

"As soon as I entered the queen's chamber, she started to berate me," Nan sobbed. "She called me terrible names and said that I was a wicked jezebel and a sneaking snake. She said that a whore like me belonged in the gutter and she would not have me in her service any longer. She told me to pack my things and leave the court right away. She would not let me say a word. And her favourites stood around and sneered at me as a shameless hussy. I do not know what is to become of me!"

I was filled with anger at the selfishness of the king and the queen. We were mere pawns to them. "She cannot send you away against the king's wishes. We will tell your mother what has happened and she will set things to rights. If you are the king's favourite then you can rely on his protection."

As I was speaking, Lady Maud came into the dormitory. She was flushed and agitated which was quite unlike her usual unruffled manner. "My dear, I know what has happened. A terrible scene has occurred between the king and the queen. It is the last thing I would have wished to have happened!"

"Is it going to cause a scandal, Mother?" asked poor Nan.

"I fear that it will for the news is all around the court. The king is in a rare temper and the queen is weeping tears of rage. She confronted the king and demanded that he send you from court at once. She claimed that you showed no regard for her as your mistress and failed to attend her in her confinement. And that he ought to show a better consideration for her at such a time and respect her as his wife. The king insisted that you would not leave the court for it was not his wish. She must close her eyes and bear it like her betters had done before her. A fine time for him to start to appreciate Queen Catherine!"

Henry hated emotional scenes and the queen's objection only made him more determined to have his way. Consequently, he showed even greater favour to Nan and sent her fine presents every day which she placed in her chest.

"I now have his likeness on a gold chain, a brooch in the shape of a love-knot and a gold bracelet," she sighed. "A pair of gloves and a pair of sleeves. He wants to send his shoemaker to measure me for new shoes. He thinks that these fine things will serve to nourish love between us. But I take no pleasure in them for all they do is tally my price."

It was clear that the king had no intention of giving her up. I grew anxious for my friend as her spirits sank and she became ever more subdued and dejected.

"He wants me to leave the dormitory and move into my own set of private rooms," she confided. "Or if I wish, I can leave the court and live as a guest at the house of Sir Nicholas Carew and his wife. I would have my own apartments there and servants to look after me."

"That might be preferable, Nan, for you wouldn't have to see the queen," I advised.

"If he does send me to live in a house, I shall insist that you and my mother come with me. He says that I can ask for whatever I please. I suppose I could have my own lute, my own spaniel or even my own horse."

"Why don't you ask for the complete works of Cicero? That would take him a while."

That made her laugh. "Yes, that would be a better choice. I know I ought to be flattered by all these presents, but I feel like a hunted deer, Margaret."

I felt vexed on behalf of my friend. The gifts were pretty but of no great value. They didn't compare to the settlement that Nan could expect to receive as a bride of good birth. And they were trivial in comparison with the rewards he had lavished upon Queen Anne. He had sent her ropes of pearls, rings set with diamonds and great gold cups as tokens of his love. He had bought her entire wardrobes of fine clothes and furs, chests of jewels and stables of horses. It was clear that he took Nan for a simple maid who would be dazzled by the sight of a few trinkets of her own. But Mistress Anne Boleyn had not been content to prize herself so little and neither should Nan.

"I wouldn't make any concessions to him yet, Nan," I counselled. "He is living out a courtly romance with you. He imagines himself as a chivalric knight with you as his lady-love. Send him a poem and that will please him."

"What sort of a poem?" she asked.

"One that shows that you understand the game of courtly love."

"You will have to write it for me, Margaret. I can't think of a thing to say."

"I will compose it and you can write it out in your fine Italian hand. How about this:

'The lady in the tower saw the knight on the road.
He bid her good-day and she sent him a cup.
"O valiant knight, you have journeyed far.
I know not your name and you know not mine.
If you would be worthy to knock on my door.
Defend my poor honour and so win my heart!"'

"Are you sure that is what he wants?" asked Nan.

"It is a game for him to win your favour. He has already begun the siege of the tower. You must hold out hope and he must prove his worth."

It seemed that the king had a literal mind for he responded by sending Nan a fine chased cup which she gave into her mother's keeping.

"Now write an acrostic of your name – you know the sort of thing," I prompted.

"No, you will have to write one, Margaret. I really can't do it."

"It is quite simple: '*Never swerving aside, Always faithful and true, Now you know my name. NAN.*' He will be bound to write one back that spells out HENRY. Then you can set him a challenge to prove his love."

"Have you prepared one already?" she asked,

"Something like this I think:

"You send me your name and I send you mine.
I know not your country, you come from afar.
If an unknown knight will send me his pledge.
His lady will wear it close to her heart."

"These poems are utter nonsense," complained Nan.

"Of course!" I said with my best imitation of a coy smile. "The very idea of courtly love between a king and his wife's maid of honour is nonsense. That is why he prefers the fantasy of the unknown knight and his fair lady. Remember how much he likes disguisings. These are just the same."

Sure enough, the king responded by sending an acrostic poem of his own to Nan. And he followed it with another verse in praise of a kind lady. "He does seem to like them," admitted Nan. "And he sends a token every time."

"Your role is to intrigue and encourage but remain unattainable for as long as you can."

"And what has made you such an expert on matters of the heart?" she enquired.

"I have read "*The Romance of the Rose*," but clearly you have not."

"My mother preferred me to study the classics," she retorted.

"Then you have got some catching up to do. He will be expecting his next poem. Are you going to write one?"

"Why should I when you are so much better at them?" said Nan. "Have you thought of another?"

"O faithful knight I bid you tarry,
My face is fair but my castle is guarded.
Only true love can open the door.
Only loyal service will conquer the fortress."

"What stuff, Margaret!" protested Nan. "Any lady who wrote that would be a complete ninny."

"That is because you have no sense of romance," I observed. "The king wants to fulfil his dream of love with the ideal lady. He is looking for mystery and challenge. It is for the knight to prove his love and win his lady. This is how Mistress Anne became his obsession."

"Well, I don't want to be like her," she objected.

"You are not like her, Nan," I assured her. "He sees you as a pure young maiden. All you have to do is offer hope and promise."

"It is a great pity that he is not courting you instead of me. You would enjoy it so much more!"

"I am saying that this is the point of writing the poems. They feed his fantasy of courtly love. You are the Guinevere to his Lancelot."

"He will be getting tired of composing these poems by now," said Nan.

"Not at all. You must not give your favours too soon. Let him dream about them for a time. He must brave the trials of the joust and the hunt before he achieves the prize."

The king sent more gifts to his unattainable lady and a poem on the theme of unrequited love. "It is just as I said, Margaret. He is growing impatient with me."

"No, he is becoming more interested because you are not an easy conquest. Remember that he waited six years when he courted Mistress Anne. You must set him a challenge."

"What do you mean?" asked Nan.

"You are not to be won by sadness, but with pleasure. Send him a gentle rebuke."

"Do you have something in mind, Margaret?"

"O valiant knight, the days are long!
I wait in my chamber and play on my lute.
My songs are sad and my soul is forlorn,
Send me a verse to cheer my heart!"

The king sent over a troop of minstrels to play ballads for Nan and invited her to go on a picnic with him the following day. I felt that the poems had done their work. The king was impressed that Nan was a lady of mettle. I was sure that her beauty and grace would do the rest. Before long, Nan was known as the established favourite of the king and had moved into a set of private apartments with her own servants and a pet spaniel. The court was convinced that Nan was already the king's mistress and a number of courtiers were making overtures to her to encourage the affair. They knew that Queen Anne and her circle were constantly inciting the king against Queen Catherine and Lady Mary. They hoped that the breach with Queen Anne would become final and he would be reconciled with his former wife and his estranged daughter.

Lady Maud felt that after the drama with the queen the die was now cast. And as a loyal friend of Queen Catherine, she was susceptible to the arguments in support of her and her daughter. She persuaded Nan to write a letter to Lady Mary. It counselled her to take heart because she had true friends at court and her troubles would soon come to an end. And Lady Maud encouraged Nan to speak to the king on behalf of the Lady Mary and ask him to show her favour. She thought it was the very least that they could do for her. I thought it was a dangerous ploy to involve Nan in court politics. These courtiers were eager to make use of Nan, but if things went badly they would turn away. If Nan had to please the king, then she should have the proper recompense of a pension, an estate and a husband of her own rank to take care of her. However, none of these rewards were forthcoming. I started to hear whispers around the court that Nan was being unfaithful to the king. It was said that she was meeting with a young gallant in her private apartments. I came to warn her immediately.

"Someone is making trouble for you, Nan," I informed her. "The king is a suspicious man and if he hears these rumours you are lost."

"We know who is making the trouble and why. She is spreading these tales to discredit me."

"You must tell the king at once," I advised. "Let him speak to your servants. He chose them himself and they will exonerate you."

And so the servants were questioned. They were loyal to Nan and revealed that they had been offered bribes by a lady to testify against her. She was Lady Jane Rochford, the sister-in-law of the queen. Further investigation discovered that she was the source of the false rumours. The king was furious and had her banished from the court. There were no more plots against Nan after that.

However, the denouement came when Lady Anne Shelton intercepted one of Nan's messages to Lady Mary and reported it to the king. Fortunately, it merely expressed her good will and contained nothing incriminating. But it still caused a rift with the king who was morbidly suspicious where his daughter was concerned. He said that Nan was a foolish girl to interfere. Lady Mary had brought her troubles on herself by her stubborn pride. He alone would decide what was best for his daughter and his kingdom. The romance was over and soon Nan was back living in the dormitory. The king and queen were reconciled. She received Nan back into her service without comment and was too relieved to make any objections.

"We must make the best of it," sighed Lady Maud. "These are the fortunes of the court. There is still hope of making a match for you. After all, being the king's mistress is an entirely different matter." She was putting a brave face on things for Nan had nothing to show for it. She sold the horse and her mother kept the spaniel.

"All I have left is the lute," said Nan. "Perhaps I should try my fortune as a lady minstrel at the court of France."

"Don't blame yourself, Nan," I consoled her. "You could hardly refuse the king. It would have meant leaving the court for good."

Queen Anne immediately revenged herself by excluding Nan from the court entertainments. In her stead the pretty Madge Shelton was chosen as the principal maid of honour to perform in the masques. She was a cousin of the queen and part of her inner circle. She was now the toast of all the courtiers and Nan was entirely forgotten.

Naturally Nan was disconsolate. "He wasn't serious about me, Margaret. I was just a temporary amusement for him like Bessie Blount and Mary Boleyn. I despised them both as weak and foolish girls, but look at me. I am no better." The disappointment and disgrace took its toll upon the upright Lady Maud. Her health took a turn for the worse and she died the following year.

Lady Jane Seymour was feeling equally downcast at this time. Her family had arranged a fine match for her with Sir William Dormer. She was delighted at the prospect and was eagerly preparing her trousseau for the wedding. But at the last minute her betrothal had been broken off. Her prospective mother-in-law didn't consider her good enough for her son. She made another match for him with Lady Mary Sidney. Jane had been looking forward to leaving court and leading a quiet domestic life. She wanted to be the mother of a large family just like her own mother. Now she was forced to remain at court and endure her humiliation like poor Nan. She was then aged twenty-five and was no great beauty. The charitable called her a pleasant lady but I found her company to be insipid and tiresome. I thought it doubtful that she would ever make another match.

As it happened, Queen Anne soon had cause to regret favouring her cousin Madge so highly. When she became pregnant again, she withdrew from her demanding role in the court entertainments. Mistress Shelton's prominent role in all the pageants soon drew the king's eye. And soon King Henry found the lively young Madge to be delightful company in the evenings. They partnered in all the dances and played cards together. Of course, it was not long before the rumours reached the queen's ears. Naturally, she was furious with her cousin. But her family persuaded her that it was better for one of her own relations to amuse the king than a lady of another house. She was renowned among the ladies for her love of poetry. I wondered how long she would manage to sustain an exchange of romantic verses with the king. But after six months, the king grew tired of her and the whole court wondered who would be the next favourite.

In the summer of 1535, the reconciled king and queen set out on their annual progress together. In September they arrived at Wulf Hall in Wiltshire, the family home of the Seymours. There King Henry met Lady Jane Seymour who had been tasked with ensuring his comfort. This gave her the opportunity to appear before the king without being overshadowed. She was devoted in her attentions and her quiet manner pleased him. I wondered if part of her charm lay in her inability to pen a verse. A month after the royal couple returned to court the queen announced that she was pregnant again. It was not long before the king began to show tokens of his favour to Lady Jane. Her family had taken note that the king had commended her on his visit to their home. They had taken care to invest in a new wardrobe for their hitherto neglected daughter. The king also sent her gifts of fine clothes and expensive bolts of fabric so that she appeared as splendid as a nobleman's daughter. Naturally, this did not go unnoticed by the queen. Then the king started to send her presents of jewellery as love-tokens. Things came to a head when Lady Jane appeared in the queen's privy chamber proudly wearing a new jewelled pendant around her neck. It was apparent from the quality that this could only be the work of the royal goldsmith.

"What is that you are wearing? Show it to me," demanded Queen Anne.

"Indeed, it is nothing, your Majesty," said Lady Jane with her eyes lowered. "It is only a gift from my mother."

"Do you take me for a fool, girl?" snapped the queen. "Do as I say!"

"Pray do not be angry with me, your Grace," said Lady Jane. "It is just an old family heirloom."

Queen Anne was so provoked that she snatched the chain and tore it off her neck. She examined the necklace and saw that it held a picture of the king in a diamond frame. She threw it back at her in a rage. "How dare you flaunt that in my presence! You are nothing but a slut. Stay out of my rooms in future, for I don't want to see your devious little face."

Lady Jane turned and fled. Queen Anne collapsed on her bed sobbing. But worse was to come. The following week the queen went to visit the king in his apartments and discovered Lady Jane sitting on his lap.

"Get out of here, you shameless creature! How dare you be so familiar with the king. Get out I say!"

Lady Jane gave the king an imploring look, but he was mortified with embarrassment and so she scurried away.

"How can you treat me like this Henry? At such a time? I love you so much that it breaks my heart to see that you love others. I cannot bear it!" she wept.

"You must close your eyes and endure as your betters have done before you," he said mulishly.

"Do you refer to that barren old woman? The one who had nothing to give you?" she taunted him.

"What more do you give me? he snapped. "I still have no son! After all this time, there is still no heir for England! It is as well that you have your place, Madam, for I would not give it to you again."

"I was the one who enabled you to break the chains that bound you to Catherine and Rome," she reminded him. "Wolsey had no intention of empowering you to reign as a true king. He was the servant of the Pope of Rome and not of the King of England. I gave you the book on Christian Obedience which opened your eyes to see what a king should be. You owe everything to me."

"You forget, Madam, that I am the one who raised you up from nothing. And I can put you back there again if I choose."

"I am your wife and your queen, Henry," she protested. "I freed you from the tyranny of the Pope who would have tied you to a barren wife forever."

"I freed myself, Madam. And I still have no son. Where is the son that you promised me? How long must I wait for my heir?"

"The Princess Elizabeth is your heir. She will be a great queen!" she declared. But her words had no effect.

"A woman cannot rule this kingdom," he contended. "I must have a son. Before God, I believe that I have taken another barren wife."

"I will give you a son, Henry, I swear it on my love for you. There is still time."

But her time was running out. Queen Anne began to fear that what she herself had done to Catherine of Aragon, Jane Seymour was about to do to her. It was a bitter moment. She had always been so sure of her power over the king. What woman had ever known such a courtship as hers? King Henry had wooed her with protestations of passionate love, daily gifts of silks and jewels and the deference of the foreign dignitaries. The honour of the court had been hers for the asking so she had never troubled herself to win friends and allies. But her whole position was based upon the insubstantial regard of the king. She had been standing on a precipice without knowing it. She was no foreign princess like Queen Catherine of Aragon. Her family's position depended on the king's favour as much as hers. There was nowhere for her to turn. And the more she raged, the more the king withdrew from her. He had never been able to abide emotional scenes. He liked for everything to be pleasant and just as he wished them to be.

Lady Elizabeth Boleyn, the Countess of Wiltshire, tried in vain to moderate her daughter's headstrong behaviour. "My dear, do try to be more conciliatory to the king. A wife is expected to defer to her husband. The king has been complaining that Catherine never spoke harshly to him."

Queen Anne bridled at the suggestion. "I have no wish to emulate her, mother. It did her no good to acquiesce to the king. He tired of her in the same way that he tired of my milksop sister Mary. Henry knows that I am not afraid to speak my mind."

But the countess was right. Queen Anne expected the king to continue his devoted courtship. But her sharp tongue had begun to rankle. It made him wish that his wife was more compliant. It also made him susceptible to the company of ladies who were gracious and respectful. He had always yearned for admiration and he found solace in their attention. Naturally, this led to passionate tears and tantrums from the queen. But the king could not abide scenes and became increasingly irritated. What more did she want of him? Had he not made her the queen?

The fateful year of 1536 began with the news of the death of Queen Catherine. For a brief time, Henry and Anne rejoiced that the shadow of the past no longer threatened them. There was no more cause to fear a Spanish invasion and a rising in favour of Catherine and Mary. The king confiscated the Dowager Princess' goods to pay her funeral expenses and she was laid to rest in Peterborough Cathedral. When I heard of the death of Queen Catherine, I felt a deep shame and remorse. She had died alone and comfortless while I enjoyed the pleasures of the court. But the king and queen rejoiced to hear the news. Queen Anne gave the messenger a rich reward and they dressed themselves in yellow to celebrate. King Henry proudly showed off the Princess Elizabeth to his courtiers at a great banquet and there was as much merriment as if it were Twelfth Night. I could not manage to keep a smile on my face as I stood beside the table and watched them. Nan gave my hand a sympathetic squeeze while I pretended that I had a headache.

I blamed Queen Anne for stoking the king's vengeance against her. She was nothing more than a petty-minded shrew! And she was not content with having taken the king and hounding Queen Catherine out of her palaces. No, she would have every mark of status. She would have her state barge to travel on and her chest of jewels to wear. She would have her royal christening robe. She would have her daughter Mary to serve her daughter. And she would have her initials and insignia chiselled off the walls as if she could obliterate every memory of her. How much the poor lady had endured at her hands! My heart burned within me as I prayed for the downfall of Queen Anne. *May she suffer as that good lady suffered. May she die abandoned and wretched! She is unworthy of that good lady's place. She is no true queen and all the court knows it. I shall never name her as queen in my thoughts but only as Nan Bullen the Concubine.* In the end, the chance came my way to settle the score on behalf of good Queen Catherine.

When Master Secretary Cromwell summoned me to see him, I was convinced that my sympathies for the exiled Queen Catherine had come to light. But it seemed that ambassador Chapuys had been as discreet as he had promised. And it was apparent that Master Secretary Cromwell had a similar interest in the affairs of Queen Anne.

"Lady Margaret, I trust that you are happy here at court?" he asked me. I wondered where this was leading. Master Cromwell was gaining a reputation as a man on the rise. But he dressed unobtrusively in the modest attire of a lawyer.

"Yes indeed, Master Secretary," I assured him.

"And yet I have the impression that your service is not greatly valued by your mistress," he remarked casually. "You are not among the ladies whom she praises."

My heart began to pound. Had I given offense? Was I about to be dismissed? "I am content to serve however it may please their Majesties."

"That is a prudent answer, Lady Margaret," he acknowledged with penetrating look. "You conduct yourself as a lady of discretion and that is an admirable quality. I want you to take heed of her Grace's conversations and report them to me. You are alone here at court and in need of good friends. I will take care of you and make sure that there is always a place for you in service. And I will provide better for you than your mistress. You need not dress so modestly in the future. Consider what I have said and report anything of interest that you hear. I assure you that it will be entirely confidential. And the king will consider it a service to him."

What a dilemma! I remembered the counsel of Lady Maria never to spy on my mistress for then I would fall into the power of my recruiter. And yet, this was the perfect way for me to take revenge for the treatment of Queen Catherine. *Let Queen Anne's own words condemn her*, I decided. It was true that she had done nothing for me. Why should I not take care of myself? I realised that I was no longer the innocent girl who had come to the palace so anxious to please. I was now wise in the ways of the court. If I did not marry, then I must make my own fortune somehow. I resolved that I would keep my eyes open and my mouth shut and ensure that I was never suspected.

"Yes, Master Secretary," I agreed. But he sensed my reluctance.

"You need not pity yourself, Lady Margaret" remarked Master Cromwell irritably. "We must all make sacrifices in the service of the king. I myself enjoy not a moment of leisure. I am besieged by endless petty requests which deprive me of the time to rest or eat."

Just then there was a knock at the door and a servant entered carrying a basket and a letter. "Your honour, I bring you a gift from my master Sir William FitzWilliam. And I have a message for the attention of your honour."

"Give my thanks to your master and assure him that I will give every consideration to his request," Master Cromwell suavely replied. "If you go to the kitchens, they will give you a drink of ale."

"Thank you, your honour," said the servant and scurried away.

Master Cromwell broke the seal on the letter and read it with a sigh. "Sir William writes that his wife sends me a dish of fowl of her own fatting. And by Sunday night he will send me a piece of red deer. He has a suit to make to me which he trusts that he can disclose at our next meeting. My work is constantly interrupted by these petty demands."

I was surprised to be taken into his confidence in this way. Perhaps the formidable Cromwell had a human weakness after all. I wondered if he was disheartened by the arrogance and complacency that typified the court. "How weary you look, Master Cromwell," I commiserated. "I know that you spare the king from many burdens. Why don't you take a moment of respite from your labour? If you send your servant to fetch a trencher and some wine, I would be pleased to serve you this dish."

Master Cromwell gave me a look of genuine gratitude. He was accustomed to dealing with contempt on one side and servility on the other. I wondered how long it had been since he had last enjoyed the company of a lady while he dined. "As you wish, Lady Margaret," he replied warmly. "You may give your commands to my servant outside the door."

I took charge without hesitation. "Bring refreshments for your master. He requires a loaf of manchet bread, a flagon of Rhenish wine and a custard tart. And get a service of silver and fine linen." I returned to Master Cromwell and gestured at his cluttered desk. "All these letters must be removed if you are to dine in here." I saw a look of regret pass across Master Cromwell's face. "I promise not to disarrange them. If you will permit me, I will place them safely on this chest."

"As you please, Lady Margaret," he replied as if he were conferring a favour upon me.

When the servant returned, I set out the service on the desk and laid out the dishes as meticulously as if I were attending on the queen. "You are to stand behind your master's chair and pour his wine," I instructed the servant. "And before I serve him this dish you shall taste it." I turned to Master Cromwell. "It is a normal precaution, I assure you. Your servant should insist upon it. I pray you sit so that I may serve you." I could see that he was flattered to be treated like a nobleman. He rapidly disposed of the dishes and watched attentively as I directed the servant to remove the service to the scullery and replaced his precious letters in their exact places again.

"I am beholden to you for your efforts, Lady Margaret," he said courteously. "You would make an admirable secretary if you were a man."

"You should be better served, Master Cromwell," I advised him. "There is no reason why you should not have a page to attend you. I am sure that His Majesty would be pleased to arrange it for your comfort."

"It is a good thought, Lady Margaret. And now I shall not detain you any further." He was once more his usual imperturbable self.

I gave the matter no further thought, but evidently Master Cromwell did. The following week his servant brought a message requesting me to visit his chambers. When I arrived, I was surprised to find a merchant there with an assortment of fine bolts of coloured silk laid out upon the desk. There was no sign of any documents so I supposed that they were locked away inside the chest.

"I am Master Thomas Osbourne of London, my lady," he informed me. "Master Cromwell has an audience with the King this morning. But he asked me to bring a selection of my best silk wares for your perusal. He wishes you to choose one as a personal gift."

I had seen mercers show their wares at court on many occasions. But always in the service of my mistresses. I had never expected that it would be my good fortune to choose a costly silk for myself. I was accustomed to having my gowns provided by the court wardrobe which were always second rate in their quality and style. It took all my expertise to embellish them.

"You must advise me, Sir," I said to the merchant.

He beamed at me. "These are genuine silks of Genoa, my lady. They are fit for the Queen. I have only just unloaded my ship. For a lady of your colouring, I would recommend the brighter colours to draw attention to your eyes and hair. The dark blue, the nut-brown and the tawny are all good matches."

I noticed that there was no red or black in his collection, but they were the most expensive colours. Nor were there any pieces with silver or gold thread. Queen Anne had a preference for black, green and cloth of gold. Many of her maids of honour wore white or tawny in order not to stand out. Finally, I settled on a dove grey silk which would be elegant but unobtrusive. The mercer complimented me upon my taste and folded it into a parcel so that it would not attract attention. I placed it carefully at the bottom of my chest. I decided that I would save it for a special occasion.

The following day, I saw Master Osbourne again as he presented his stock for the inspection of the queen. This time he brought a more extensive selection of silks and satins which included the royal colours of purple, crimson and cloth of gold. There were also rare shades of aquamarine, pearl and emerald. Queen Anne's astute eyes quickly picked out the most expensive pieces and she signalled her Mistress of the Robes to put them away into storage. I did not repine at the sight of these flamboyant pieces for I could not have worn them. Instead, I revelled in the knowledge that I had been offered a choice before the queen. How vexed she would have been if she had known! Master Cromwell could easily have arranged the meeting after allowing the queen her prerogative. But instead, he paid me the compliment of being the first client. I admired the subtle manner in which he had requited my favour. In the world of the court, we were both held in little account. But it was sweet, just for once, to taste the privileges of the nobility which our royal masters took for granted.

On the day of Queen Catherine's funeral, Queen Anne lost her child. Her enemies predicted that this would increase her estrangement from the king. "She has miscarried of her Saviour," it was said. We were attending to the distraught queen when the arrival of the king was announced. I had expected that they would console one another in their loss. But the king was in no mood to give any comfort. He had lost too many children and he was angry. He did not even ask the exhausted queen how she fared.

"I see that God does not intend to give me male children," he said flatly. He viewed the queen's pallid face with distaste. She had not kept her promises to him. He was no better off than before.

"Henry, please," whispered the queen. "You must not blame me for this. It was not my fault."

"I shall speak to you later when you are up," he replied with finality. Then he turned on his heel and left the queen to her bitter tears.

But Queen Anne was spared the king's reproaches for he was disillusioned with his contentious queen. Instead, he renewed his attentions to Lady Jane Seymour. She had been advised by the enemies of the queen that she should on no account comply with the king's wishes except by way of marriage. A story circulated that the king had sent Lady Jane a purse full of sovereigns and a letter. She had kissed the letter and then returned it unopened to the messenger. She begged him to inform the king that she was a gentlewoman of good and honourable parents. She had no greater riches in the world than her honour which meant more to her than her life. And if he wished to make her a gift of money, she begged it might be when God enabled her to make an honourable match.

When I heard this extraordinary tale, I wondered who had coached her in those eloquent phrases. Her expert performance proved to be a masterstroke. The king could never resist the attractions of an unattainable lady. His desire for her was increased tenfold. He considered that she had behaved most virtuously. In order to prove that his love was honourable he vowed that he would speak to her only in the presence of her family. Consequently, Master Cromwell vacated his palace apartments near to the king. Edward Seymour and his wife Anne moved in there to act as the chaperones of the modest Lady Jane. The king had recently appointed him as one of his gentlemen of the Privy Chamber. It was a great triumph for the Seymour family. Lady Jane was now the king's acknowledged mistress but at the same time her reputation was unassailable.

While the king continued to show his favour to Lady Jane, he entirely neglected the queen and barely even spoke to her. She was miserable and had no heart for any of her usual amusements. Her only solace was to order fine new outfits for her young daughter, the Princess Elizabeth.

A decision had been made in that room. The king was determined to end his fruitless marriage and take a new wife. And how did I know? Because Master Cromwell sent for me to meet him in private. His face was lined with fatigue but his eyes were as sharp as ever.

"Lady Margaret, I am going to trust you with a great secret," he said gravely. "The king has tired of his marriage. He will have no more disappointments. All that remains is the grounds to end the marriage. As one of the queen's attendants you are ideally placed to report upon her activities. Who are her favourites among the gentlemen of the court?"

I thought for a moment. "I would say they were Sir Henry Norris, Sir William Brereton and young Sir Francis Weston. They are the ones who visit her most frequently."

"Is that all?" he demanded.

"There is also the lute-player, Mark Smeaton," I added. "She often sends for him to play for her and gives him gifts."

"And which one visits her the most?"

"That would be her brother, Lord Rochford." He was the one person in the court in whom she confided.

He twisted the ring around his finger. I noticed it was set with a fine aquamarine. "Does he go into her bedchamber?"

"Yes, Master Secretary."

"And what do they talk about there," he enquired.

"Mostly the gossip of the court. He tells her jokes and makes her laugh."

"Have you ever heard them discussing the king?" he pounced.

I hesitated for a moment. "I have heard them talking about the king's taste in dress and poetry."

"What do they say?" he demanded.

"That his clothes are gaudy and fanciful and his verse is poor."

"That is most interesting," he said, surveying me keenly. "I want you to keep your eyes and ears open, Lady Margaret. Watch closely who comes to visit the queen. Pay careful attention to their conversations and report them to me immediately. The king wants a speedy conclusion to this matter. He does not want a lengthy battle over it as with his first wife." He picked up his pen and signalled to me to leave.

The annual May Day jousts took place at Greenwich Palace and I attended the queen as usual. She wore a gown of tawny velvet lined with black sarsenet and edged with black lambs' fur. Queen Anne was in good spirits as her brother Lord Rochford was leading the challenge against Sir Henry Norris. On this occasion the king was not taking part. He had given up the sport since his accident earlier in the year. At the end of the joust the victorious knight approached the royal box, raised his visor and saluted. It was Sir Henry Norris. The queen smiled graciously and threw him her scarf which he deftly caught and tied around his arm. The crowd erupted with enthusiastic applause. But the king got up without a word and left the tiltyard with a party of his attendants. The queen was as much at a loss as the rest of us. "Is he ill?" we wondered. "Is there some sudden emergency? Why has he not come to bid farewell to the queen?" It was said that the king's sudden departure was prompted by a letter, but no-one knew what it was about.

The following day, Queen Anne returned to the festivities dressed in a gown of cloth of silver with sleeves of carnation silk. She wore her gold heart-shaped pendant set with a ruby like a great drop of blood. She was in a merry mood as she watched her champion play at a tennis match. "I wish that I had placed a bet," she declared. "He is sure to win the match." But her enjoyment was interrupted by the appearance of a messenger.

He handed her a document. "Your Majesty, by order of the king you must present yourself before the Privy Council at once."

The queen's face turned pale with fear, but she maintained her composure. "Attend me," she murmured as she arose. Nan and I quickly followed her as she accompanied the messenger to the council chamber. Inside, the duke of Norfolk, Sir William FitzWilliam and Sir William Paulet were waiting. Their faces looked grim. Only Sir William Paulet took off his cap as the queen entered.

"What means this, my lords?" asked the queen unflinchingly.

"I am here to inform you that you are accused of committing adultery with three men including Sir Henry Norris and Mark Smeaton," said the duke unsympathetically. "They have already confessed their guilt. You are under arrest for the crimes of adultery and treason. And you will be conducted to the Tower as soon as the tide has turned."

"You cannot do this, Uncle Norfolk," insisted the queen. "These are all lies concocted by my enemies. You must let me speak to the king. Do not send me to the Tower without a hearing."

"It is too late for plead for mercy," said the duke without a sign of emotion. "He will not see you." I wondered at his indifference to his niece. *Is this his revenge for being slighted?*

"For the love of God, Uncle," said the queen desperately. "You must do something. Think of my daughter. If I go to the Tower I will never come back."

"This is the king's own command," said the duke implacably. "I can do nothing for you. You should pray to God for only He can help you now."

Sir William Paulet had tears in his eyes but the others were stony faced at the queen's distress. *Fine noble lords!* I thought to myself.

Queen Anne drew a deep breath. "I charge you to take care of the Princess Elizabeth, Uncle Norfolk. She is the rightful heir to the throne. You must do your utmost to protect her."

"You may rest assured that I will do my duty," he replied coldly. "Now you may go to your apartments and change your clothes. A messenger will be sent to escort you to your barge. You may bring these two attendants with you."

Queen Anne said not a word until we reached her apartments. "Bring me a cup of wine," she directed Nan as she sank into a chair. Even at such a drastic moment, she kept her presence of mind. "Bring me my black velvet dress with furred sleeves and my sable mantle," she instructed. "It will be cold in the Tower. Help me to dress. And then bring me writing materials."

"Will your Grace take something to eat?" asked Nan.

"Not now," she snapped. "Hurry and fetch cushions and blankets. Find a page to pack them in a basket. There is no time to lose."

I dressed the queen in her warmest things and she took care that her appearance was as distinguished as if she about to preside at a banquet. I noticed that she put on her favourite jewels and her best pair of shoes. She was not prepared to submit to adversity without a struggle. Nan found a page to pack up the bedding. She even had the foresight to find plain dresses and nightgowns for us to wear. When the Captain of the Guard came to the door, he looked disconcerted at the sight of all the queen's baggage. Clearly, no thought had been given to providing for her requirements.

"My orders are to escort your Majesty and two ladies," he said respectfully. "Your things will all be sent after you."

"Indeed, they will not, Captain," insisted the queen with a flash of temper. "I do not intend to lie upon bare boards when I arrive."

He hesitated at the thought of such an undignified procession. It was clear that he had been told to conduct the queen as discreetly as possible. "Boy," he barked at the page. "Find two servants to convey this gear to the landing point. One of my men will show you the way. Do not follow us through the palace. And do not speak a word of this to anyone."

"I am quite ready, Captain," said the queen with a toss of her head. We followed in her wake and the Yeomen guard kept close behind us. When we arrived at the barge she firmly declined to step aboard until the baggage had been loaded. The Captain plainly had no desire to manhandle her. We took the swelling tide from

Greenwich to the Court Gate of the Tower. During that terrible journey none of us could speak a word. We wondered what trials lay ahead and our spirits sank within us. The Lieutenant of the Tower was waiting to meet us there.

"Your Grace, I am Sir Edward Walsingham and I am here to escort you to the keeping of Sir William Kingston, the Constable of the Tower."

The queen wrapped her mantle closely around her. "Lead on, Sir Edward," she said bravely. "I entered with more ceremony the last time I came here." We followed him across the stone flagged yard beneath the looming height of the ancient white tower. We were brought to Sir William Kingston who regarded the queen gravely.

"Madam, I must ask you to accompany me to your lodging," he informed her.

Nan and I were both in tears. And the queen's courage had finally deserted her.

"Master Kingston, shall I go into a dungeon?" she implored him.

"No, Madam," he assured her. "You shall go into the apartments you stayed in at your coronation."

And indeed, he brought us to the same chambers that she had last used three years ago. Queen Anne looked about her with some surprise. "It is too good for me," she said. "Lord, have mercy upon me." She sank down on a chair and burst into tears. Master Kingston looked most abashed.

"Madam, here is my wife Lady Kingston who will attend you in this place. Your ladies must not have any speech with you unless she is present." She was a tall, thin woman with hard eyes set in a pinched face. Her very presence was unnerving. The thought crossed my mind that King Henry would never have passed her as fit for his rooms.

"Master Kingston, do you know why I am here?" she asked.

"No, Madam," he replied.

"I swear to you that I am the king's true wedded wife," she declared. "And I am as clear from the company of other men as I am clear from you. I request that you ask the King's Highness for permission to have the blessed sacrament brought to the closet by my chamber so that I might pray for mercy to Almighty God."

"Yes, Madam."

"Master Kingston, do you know where my father is?" she asked him.

"He is at court, Madam," he replied courteously.

"And where is my dear brother?" she said, fighting back her tears.

"He is at York Place, Madam."

"My poor mother will die of sorrow," she declared, wringing her hands. "I heard that I would be accused with three men but indeed I know no more. Is it Norris who has accused me? Is he also kept here in the Tower and shall we both die together? And is Mark here too?"

"I cannot say, Madam."

"Master Kingston, shall I die without justice?" she exclaimed piteously.

"The poorest servant of the king has justice, Madam," he assured her.

The queen laughed aloud at his words, but not with any mirth. She said no more and the Constable withdrew and locked the door behind him.

The chamber was brightly painted but it was unaired and sparsely furnished. When the baggage finally arrived, Nan and I silently occupied ourselves with unpacking the queen's wardrobe and preparing a comfortable bed. Lady Kingston looked on with raised eyebrows at this singular display of luxury for a prisoner in the Tower. We avoided her gaze for we did not wish to speak to her unless it was strictly necessary. It was quite clear to all of us that she had been placed there as a spy.

Nan busied herself in building up the fire. I did my best to remove the dust from the window with my handkerchief and wished that I had had the foresight to bring a flask of hippocras and some sweet wafers. I had no idea where Nan and I were to sleep that night. The same thought must have occurred to Lady Kingston for she rapped on the door and ordered three pallets to be brought in. The blankets were damp and musty from long storage and there was nowhere to dry them. The disapproving Lady Kingston knocked on the door again and had them taken away. Fresh bedding was brought which she informed us was from her own stock. We duly thanked her although we were aware that these efforts were not for our benefit.

The queen signalled to Nan to bring her box of writing materials. But Lady Kingston quickly forestalled her. "You may not write anything, Madam. You may only dictate your words to a scribe."

Queen Anne frowned and gestured to Nan to sit at the table "Take this down," she directed her.

"Your Grace's displeasure and my imprisonment are things so strange to me as that I am altogether ignorant what to write. But do not imagine that your poor wife will ever confess a fault which she never even imagined. Never had prince a more dutiful wife than you have in Anne Boleyn, with which name and place I could willingly have contented myself if God and your Grace's pleasure had so been pleased. You chose me from a low estate, and I beg you not to let an unworthy stain of disloyalty cast a blot on me and the infant Princess your daughter.

Try me, good king, but let me have a lawful trial, and let not my enemies be my judges. Let me receive an open trial, and you shall see either my innocence cleared or my guilt openly proved. But if you have already determined that my death and an infamous slander will bring you the enjoyment of your desired happiness, then I pray that God will pardon your great sin and not call you to a strait account for your unprincely and cruel usage of me. My innocence will be known at the Day of Judgment.

My last request is that I alone may bear the burden of your displeasure, and not those poor gentlemen, who, I understand, are likewise imprisoned for my sake. If ever I have found favour in your sight, if ever the name of Anne Boleyn has been pleasing in your ears, let me obtain this request, and so I will leave to trouble your Grace any further.

From my doleful prison in the Tower. Anne the Queen."

Queen Anne seemed calmer once she had finished it. "Please give this letter to Master Kingston and ask him to send it to the king."

Lady Kingston looked scandalised by such temerity. "Very well, Madam," she replied ungraciously.

"And I will require more attendants to serve me," the queen stated firmly. "I shall need at least two more ladies and two chamberers."

"I do not think that will be permitted, Madam," she objected.

"And I would like to have my supper now," she announced. "Be so kind as to arrange it, Lady Kingston."

She pursed her lips and departed to hammer at the door. Soon we could hear a vigorous discussion taking place. I wished that Lady Kingston shared the kindly disposition of her husband. She was not going to be a pleasant companion in this place.

The queen closed her eyes and leaned back in her chair. She looked exhausted and no wonder after such a tempestuous day. Finally, her supper was provided but she could eat almost none of it. Nan and I managed to heat some water on the fire for her to wash in. Then we helped her to undress and change into her nightgown. She ignored the presence of the obnoxious Lady Kingston who had placed her bed in front of the door. At last, I lay down gratefully on my pallet but my mind was too oppressed to let me sleep. I wondered how long we would have to stay in this place.

The following morning five more attendants arrived including her aunts Lady Elizabeth Boleyn and Lady Anne Shelton, Mistress Coffin, Mistress Stoner and old Mrs Orchard who was the queen's former nurse. Queen Anne broke down at the sight of them and it was not long before she was unburdening her mind of its troubles.

"Alas, my good ladies I was cruelly handled at Greenwich," she lamented. "Indeed, it is quite shocking to treat a queen in such a way. My own uncle gave me no comfort but said, "Tut, tut," and shook his head at me. But I think the king is only seeking to test me. Sir Norris said that he would swear that I was a good woman."

"Why should he need to say so, Madam?" asked Mrs Coffin.

"I told him to do it, for I asked him why he did not go ahead with his marriage to Mary Shelton," she explained. "And he said that he would tarry for a time. And then I said that he looked for dead men's shoes for if anything came to the king but good, he would look to have me. And he said that if he had any such thought then he would that his head were off. And I said that I could undo him if I would. But perhaps it was not Norris who betrayed me, but Weston."

"For what cause, Madam?" she enquired.

"I remember saying to him that he loved Mary Shelton better than his wife. And he said that there was one that he loved more than both. I asked who it was. And he said it is yourself. And I defied him."

"Quite right, Madam."

She wrung her hands together in her distress. "It could even be on account of the musician, Mark Smeaton, but he was never in my chamber except once at Winchester when I sent for him to play on the virginals. I spoke to him just before May Day when he was standing in the round window in my Presence Chamber. I asked him why he was so sad and he said it was no matter. And I said that he should not look to have me speak to him like a nobleman because he was none. And he replied, "No, no, Madam, a look sufficed me.""

I noticed how avidly Lady Kingston was listening to their conversation. *The queen is being far too indiscreet,* I thought. *They will use this information against her. In her position I would trust no-one around me. The only one who truly cares for her is her old nurse.*

Our life in the Tower settled into a tedious routine. The queen's meals were served with the minimum of ceremony. The queen's requests to Lady Kingston were opposed with the greatest vigour. She regretted not having brought any books for there was nothing to pass the time. Our only solace was found in reading the prayer books which were attached to our girdles.

That evening after supper the unhappy queen sent for Sir William Kingston.

"Where have you been all day, Master Kingston?"

"I have been visiting the prisoners in the Tower, Madam," he explained.

"I have been cruelly handled, Master Kingston. But I shall have justice," she declared.

"There is no doubt about it, Madam."

"If any man accuses me, I can only deny it, and they can bring no witnesses against me," she burst out in frustration. "I think that most of the people will pray for me. And I hope that my good bishops will go to the king for me. And if I die then I shall be in heaven, for I have done many good deeds in my time. But I count it a great unkindness in the king to put those about me that I never loved."

"The king takes them to be good and honest women, Madam," he assured her.

"But I would rather have those of my circle whom I hold most dear."

Even though I had pitied good Queen Catherine and wished for the downfall of her supplanter, I found I took no pleasure in witnessing the disgrace of Queen Anne. Her misery only moved me to curse the king as the cause of their suffering. His petty vengeance was unworthy of him. He had taken everything from the woman whom he had once professed to adore. And in her last days he even denied her the solace of a true friend.

The next day Lady Kingston complained that the rooms were too crowded. It was decided that Nan and I would be given leave to return to the palace. We were strictly warned not to discuss the queen's affairs with anyone. "Farewell, Madam," I said as I curtsied to the queen for one last time, conscious of the vigilant Lady Kingston. "Pray for me," she replied with a half-hearted smile. And that was all. A guard escorted us back to the Court Gate to await the departure of the next barge to Greenwich. It was fine May weather and the bright sunshine sparkled upon the ripples of the water as we were rowed along the river Thames. We thought of the queen and how she would not have the pleasure of going out of her apartments until her day of her trial.

But Greenwich Palace was no haven of peace. The queen's household were in the midst of being interviewed on behalf of the Privy Council. We heard disquieting stories that bribes had been offered to her porter and serving men and that promises had been made to the ladies of her bedchamber. Nan and I sat in the dormitory waiting our turn to be summoned. We had no duties with which to occupy ourselves. I passed the time repairing my wardrobe while Nan read her beloved Cicero. The page boy, Master James Gage, brought us the news each day for there were many rumours abroad in the court.

The next day, the expected summons finally came. Nan and I were both questioned separately. In my case, it turned out to be a mere formality since I had already told Master Cromwell everything I knew. However, I was concerned on behalf of my dear friend Nan. I waited until she returned to the dormitory and proposed a walk to take advantage of the fine weather. Then I headed for a secluded place in the palace grounds which was far away from any spies. We sat upon a wooden bench under a budding chestnut tree.

"You were sent for by Master Baynton. What happened to you?" I asked.

Nan shrugged, but she looked uncomfortable. "The same as you. He told me that the queen's guilt was known to all her ladies. And unless I was completely honest and truthful, I would end up in the Tower with her. He wanted to know about her recent conversations with the gentlemen of the court."

"Did you tell him?" I asked her.

"What else could I do?" Nan muttered, looking down at her hands. "He already knew about Smeaton and Norris and Weston and would not allow me to plead my ignorance. He said that my loyalty to the king was at stake. And Queen Anne is already doomed. She has lost the favour of the king and there is nothing that I can say or do to save her."

I agreed with my friend. We were mere pawns on the chess board and could not resist being manoeuvred. But I still felt a sense of guilt and shame. None of Queen Catherine's inner circle had betrayed her. I had not been as faithful and courageous as them. But Queen Anne had not inspired the same degree of loyalty.

Although the court was shocked by her sudden downfall, she had few supporters or sympathisers.

"What other questions did he ask you?" I wondered if Master Cromwell had been comparing my answers against those of the other ladies.

"The usual ones, I suppose," she said, shifting uncomfortably. "About which courtiers came to the queen's apartments and did she ever give them any money or tokens?"

"What did you answer?" I pressed her.

"I only told him what he already knew," protested Nan. "That Norris and Weston visited the queen most frequently and she sometimes gave them presents of money. And she did the same with Master Smeaton when he had performed well on the lute and I thought it did no harm."

"Did he ask about anyone else?" I persisted.

"He wanted to know how often her brother George came to visit her and if they were ever alone in her chamber together. He asked if the queen ever discussed her marriage to the king? And did she ever speak mockingly of him?"

"Lord, have mercy!" I exclaimed. "What did you say?"

Nan drew a deep breath. "I told him that Lord Rochford would come to see her alone at night and they had laughed at the king's gaudy dress and mocked his poems as foolish things. And he told me that he knew all this already and what more did I know? Had I ever heard the queen and her brother discuss her intimate life with the king and had they ever doubted the paternity of Princess Elizabeth?"

I was astonished. This was a matter of treason. "Did you answer him?"

She shook her head. "I said that I knew nothing whatever of such matters and he told me that the queen had informed one of her ladies that the king was impotent. Whom do you suppose would say such a thing?" she wondered.

"I can only suppose that it was Lady Rochford," I concluded. "The queen and her brother would not confide in anyone else," I said.

"So I thought too," admitted Nan. "I didn't say anything more and he let me go. But Margaret, you have not said a word about how you fared with them."

"It was just the same," I lied. How could I tell my friend that I was a miserable spy, one of Cromwell's creatures? She would never trust me again. I vowed that I would break free of him at the first opportunity.

"What do you think will come of it?" asked Nan miserably.

"It seems to me that the king is seeking grounds to end his marriage to Queen Anne. But these are petty matters."

"They are not so petty as they might seem," objected Nan. "I think they suspect the queen of having liaisons with some of the courtiers who visited her apartments."

"But they were never alone together," I reminded her. "Except for her brother George. And he doesn't count." Or so we both thought. But we were wrong.

On Saturday 12th May the pageboy, Master Gage, told us that four men accused of adultery with the queen had been tried at Westminster Hall. They were named as three gentlemen of the privy chamber Norris, Weston and Brereton and the musician Mark Smeaton. They had all been found guilty and sentenced to death. But only Mark Smeaton had confessed to the crime. Things looked very bad for the unfortunate queen. I wondered how she was faring in her chamber in the Tower.

"It's nonsense," hissed Nan once the boy had left us. "It's quite impossible for four men to have lain with the queen. We would have seen it. Or at the very least it would have been known."

"The charges are based on mere gossip," I agreed. "The queen admitted that she had conversations in which she teased three of the men. But what is Brereton supposed to have done?"

"Norris and Weston were favourites of the king," said Nan. "I am surprised that he would allow them to be condemned on such flimsy pretexts."

"I doubt that any of them were guilty," I said. "But perhaps they were singled out for being too popular. I have heard that their families are petitioning the king to pardon them."

"What about Mark Smeaton, the one who confessed?" asked Nan.

"It is rumoured that he was forced to confess. It is said they used torture on him because he was not a gentleman. But no-one knows for certain."

"It is said that a number of courtiers are already making suits for the offices and lands of the condemned men," said Nan in a hushed voice. "Their goods are now forfeit to the Crown. What will become of their wives and children?"

What neither of us of dared to mention was what would become of us? If Queen Anne was condemned then her household would be dismissed. And what would we do then? And what if they decided to charge the queen's ladies as her accomplices? We could hardly sleep for fear of what might happen next. I wished that I was back at home in Ravenseat and far away from this treacherous court.

On Monday 14th May 1536 we heard that Lady Jane Seymour had been taken to stay at Chelsea Old Manor where she was splendidly entertained and served by cooks of the royal household. The king visited her there to dine every day and the royal barge was filled with minstrels and musicians and the sound of merry making. He did not want her to be present at court during the trial of the queen. There seemed no doubt that he would soon make her his new wife. Some people believed that the marriage settlements had already been drawn up and the lady had already ordered her wedding dress.

On Tuesday 15th May Master Gage reported that Queen Anne was taken to trial at the King's Hall in the Tower accompanied by Lady Boleyn and Lady Kingston. He related the details of the occasion to us with great relish. The tribunal was composed of the principal lords of the realm with the duke of Norfolk presiding over it. She took care to dress herself in her best for the occasion. She came to court dressed impeccably in a black velvet gown with a scarlet kirtle and a feathered cap. She entered the hall with great dignity and surveyed her judges without any sign of fear. She was accused of committing adultery out of frail and carnal lust, of despising her marriage and entertaining malice against the king. She was also charged with having ridiculed the king and laughed at his manner of dressing which showed that she did not love him and was tired of married life with him.

The jury found her guilty of treason and deprived of her crown and titles. The duke of Norfolk sentenced her to be burned or beheaded at the king's pleasure. He was said to be weeping as he pronounced the verdict, but Nan and I found that hard to believe. Then the former queen, Anne Boleyn, rose to address the court. She said that if she was being condemned then it must be for reasons other than those which had been produced in court. She declared that she had always been a faithful and loyal wife to the king, although she had not always shown him the humility which he deserved. And God was her witness that she had not done him any other wrong. She said that she was prepared to die, but sorry that others who were innocent should share her fate and die for her sake. It was reported that the Lord Mayor of London had said that he could observe nothing in the proceedings against her.

Her brother, Lord Rochford, was charged with incest on the grounds that he had been seen visiting the queen's bedchamber dressed in his night clothes. He denied the charge and said that he went to speak with her because she was unwell. He was also accused of having doubted that the Princess Elizabeth was the king's daughter. To this he made no answer. He was also condemned to death. We gave Master Gage his customary penny, but he insisted that such grave tidings deserved a groat at least. We paid him and he rushed away to share the news elsewhere.

On Wednesday we heard that Archbishop Cranmer had gone to visit the queen to hear her last confession. It was said that she had sworn upon the sacrament that she had never been unfaithful to the king. It was also rumoured that the king might allow her to retire to a convent in Antwerp. But the rumour proved to be false. The king's idea of mercy was to send for a swordsman from France to perform the execution. He was said to be unwilling to condemn her to the flames out of pity.

The following day, Master Gage sensationally announced that the sentence had been carried out upon the five condemned men. All of them were beheaded in the precincts of the Tower and in sight of the Queen's apartments. Lord Rochford had made a moving speech to the crowd saying, "I pray that from my mishap you may learn not to set your thoughts upon the vanities of this world and least of all on the flatteries of the court and the favours and treacheries of fortune." Then he knelt down at the block and his head was struck off. Poor Lord Rochford! He recognised too late that the honours of the court could cost him his life. At least he made peace with his conscience before he died. No-one believed the absurd charges made against him. He was condemned because the king did not want anyone defending Anne. According to one rumour, Mary Stafford had come to court to plead with the king to spare her sister's life. But he had sent her away and warned her not to meddle in such matters.

On Friday we expected to hear the news of the death of the former queen. But it was postponed due to the executioner from France being delayed upon the road. Her execution took place the following morning within the Tower walls and the king allowed four of the queen's favourite ladies to accompany her. One of the attendants was her cousin, Mary Shelton, and she told us the whole story that very evening in the dormitory.

"Master Kingston led Anne Boleyn up to the scaffold but we saw that she looked behind her from time to time. Even then, she still hoped that the king might relent and send a pardon. A great murmur arose from the crowd at the sight of her. She wore a robe of black damask with a red damask skirt which was covered by a royal cape of white ermine. We took off the cape and she gave away her prayer book. Then she removed the coif from her head and put on a little cap of linen. Her countenance was serene and she had never looked more beautiful. She asked permission to speak to the crowd and it was granted. All the great nobles were assembled there to witness her death including her uncle, the duke of Norfolk.

She said, "Do not think, good people, that I have done anything to deserve the death. My fault has been my great pride and the crime I committed in getting the king to leave Queen Catherine for my sake. I say that everything they have accused me of is false and the principal reason I am to die is Jane Seymour."

Then she turned and spoke to us, for she saw how we were weeping for her. "And you, my good damsels, who ever showed yourselves diligent in my service. I cannot reward you for your true service but I pray you to take comfort for my loss.

Be faithful to the King's Grace and to her whom with happier fortune you may have as your queen and mistress. And esteem your honour far beyond your life and forget not to pray for me."

Mary broke off and wiped her streaming eyes. "How did she die?" Nan asked her.

"She knelt down and said, "O Lord God, have pity on my soul." And the swordsman dispatched her with one swift stroke. I heard the shouts of the crowd and the cry of the executioner as he held up her severed head. It was a dreadful sight. Then the cannons on the walls of the Tower fired to announce her death. The sound of it was deafening and my poor head is still ringing."

"How terrible for you," I commiserated. "What did you do then?"

Mary drew a deep breath. "We attended the queen for the last time. It was our duty to take care of her. We would not allow any of the guardsmen to touch her. We took her head and her body and wrapped them in white linen cloth. And then we realised how carelessly the execution had been planned. No coffin had been provided for her burial. We were almost fainting with grief but we contrived to carry her in a sheet into the Chapel of St Peter ad Vincula in the Tower. And there we found an empty arrow chest to lay her body in. It was most unworthy of a royal lady and it pains me to think of it. Afterwards, we returned to the royal apartments to pack up the queen's wardrobe. But her fine clothing had already gone. Lady Kingston told us that the clothes of condemned prisoners belonged the Constable. There were only our only bundles to take back to the palace."

"Did the queen say anything to you before she died?" I asked.

"Yes," said Mary looking sad and weary. "I managed to have a private conversation with her that morning. By then she was perfectly resigned to her death. "I would it was over, Mary," she said. "I am tired of waiting. I have never wronged the king, but I know that he is tired of me as he was before of the good lady Catherine. It has all been done because he has fallen in love with Jane Seymour and does not know how to get rid of me. But I do not care for all the harm he can do me now for nobody can deny that I was a crowned queen." I know that the queen was innocent and so do all her ladies. But she died most courageously. Everyone there in the crowd said so. She wore her finest clothes on the scaffold so that she would die as a queen." I remembered the prophetic words of Queen Catherine that one day we would pity Anne Boleyn. And I did pity her. What was she but one more victim of an insatiable king?

The following day it was rumoured in the court that the king had gone to see Lady Jane Seymour and they were celebrating their betrothal together. It seemed that King Henry had already forgotten about his second wife in his haste to marry the third. The king's choice of Lady Jane Seymour was not greatly admired. But neither was it highly resented. She was a quiet person who would not set the court at odds. We hoped that we could now look forward to a peaceful life as courtiers.

But then another thunderbolt struck the court. It was announced that the household of the late queen was now dismissed. Her banners and badges were ordered to be torn down. All of her attendants and servants would have to leave the palace at once to make room for the household of the new queen. I resigned myself to returning home for good. Perhaps it was all for the best since I was disgusted with the atmosphere of the court and the behaviour of the king. Naturally, all the relatives of the Boleyn family were obliged to leave the court including Lady Rochford. I wondered what would become of her as a widow without any property.

However, Master Cromwell sent for me again. He looked like a man released from a great strain. "I am pleased to see you, Lady Margaret. It was not my intention that you should accompany the late queen to the Tower. As soon as I was notified of the mistake, I had you replaced by the four ladies selected by His Majesty. Of course, the Constable and his wife were both entirely in my confidence and faithfully reported all the late queen's words to me. I trust you are quite recovered from the ordeal?"

It seemed that he was in an expansive mood. "Indeed, Master Cromwell. And I am most obliged for your consideration of me."

He inclined his head to me with a slight smile. "You may sit down, Lady Margaret. I have taken a great deal of trouble managing this tiresome affair over the past few weeks. But I spare no effort in the service of the king. Since you were no more the queen's friend than myself, I can tell you that I went to considerable trouble to prosecute her trial. The king was impatient to remarry and wanted no more prolonged divorces. So the charge had to be treason and the sentence was death. But I have no sympathy for her since she was my resolute enemy. The king has naturally dismissed her father from court and has appointed me as the next Lord Privy Seal. In future, I shall be known as Lord Cromwell."

I took the hint. "Yes, my Lord. I congratulate you on your good fortune."

"It is not a matter of fortune, Lady Margaret," he pointed out. "It is the reward for my good service. It has been a most arduous business, but the king is free to remarry without any shadow of scandal. In managing this matter, I have succeeded where the Lord Cardinal failed. There is no question of bigamy this time for he is a widower. Lady Jane will be his undoubted lawful wife and their children will be his legitimate heirs. So the king is most content and is prepared to be magnanimous. He is willing to retain those ladies who are not related to the Boleyn family. You will be permitted to remain at court and serve the new queen. I expect that you will be thankful for the opportunity."

What could I say? "It is most gracious of His Majesty," I replied. It seemed Lord Cromwell was just as satisfied as the king. In one stroke he had contrived to rid the court of the troublesome Boleyns and their powerful faction.

"You can be grateful to me, Lady Margaret," emphasised Lord Cromwell. "It is a capital crime not to report treason. But I have protected you from the consequences of your folly. None of the late queen's ladies suffered the penalty with her." I shuddered inwardly at the veiled threat. It was true. Only the accused men had been tried and executed. But none of the queen's ladies had been named as her accomplices. I realised that I had survived a great danger.

"I am indebted to you, Lord Cromwell," I said numbly.

"Yes, Lady Margaret, you are. It is something you should keep in mind. For only those who are loyal deserve a place in court." The smile had left his face and his eyes had turned cold. "I have much work to do in making appointments to fill the vacancies left in the royal households. But I shall send for you in due course. Now you may go."

I curtsied as best I could on my trembling legs and hurried back to the dormitory. I was glad to get away from the scrutiny of those pitiless eyes. I had not guessed at the ruthless ambition that had guided this plot. I had blamed Queen Anne for causing the deaths of the accused men by babbling their names in the Tower. At the time of their trials, I could not see how any of them had offended the king and thought that they had been the victims of misfortune. But in the days to come I saw how they were all replaced by Cromwell's men. I realised that they had been his rivals in the inner circle. And he had made use of the queen's disgrace to remove them. Truly, *circa Regna tonat!*

Ten days later King Henry married Lady Jane Seymour in the Queen's Closet at Whitehall Palace. And shortly afterwards, she was proclaimed Queen at Greenwich. Their triumph was complete. However, they did not have everything their own way. Satirical ballads were sung in the streets in mockery of the king and Jane Seymour. They circulated throughout London to the mirth of the common people.

> *"All hail the new Herod and the Lady Salome,*
> *She danced for him and she asked a reward.*
> *She was not to be had for the price of a purse,*
> *For only a head on a platter would do!*
> *She danced in his bed and he made her his queen,*
> *All hail King Harry and his Lady Jane!"*

The king was enraged by the disparagement of his new love. He vowed that he would find the culprit and make a dreadful example of him. An investigation was duly conducted but no-one knew anything of the matter. His mistake was to assume that it was the work of a disaffected male courtier. To my mind, the talented Lady Mary Shelton was a far more likely candidate. I silently applauded her for her subtle revenge on behalf of her cousin. By then, she had already left the court and was safely back at home.

The hasty marriage of the king to Lady Jane Seymour caused considerable comment at court. I overheard a conversation between Lady Maud Parr and Mrs Stoner, the mother of the maids which quite astonished me. Mother Stoner was usually the soul of discretion, but on this occasion she was most indignant. "Indeed, he has overturned the whole court for her sake. And yet she has no family connections worth mentioning. She is neither young nor handsome. What recommendation does she have to be chosen as queen?"

"I suspect that her supreme virtue is that she is so English," replied the astute Lady Parr. "The king is in no mood for French or Spanish ladies. So Jane stands out as the quintessentially fair English lady."

"What on earth does he see in her?" complained Mrs Stoner. "He could have chosen far better from among the other ladies in waiting."

"They remind him too much of his former wives," she said knowledgeably. "And being lately come to court she has no associations."

"But she is so colourless," objected Mrs Stoner. "She can hardly say two words. She is neither stylish in dressing nor accomplished at dancing."

"He has had all that already in his wives," observed Lady Parr. "And now he wants something different. A demure lady who will bow to his opinions and minister to his comfort. Only consider the motto she has chosen: *Bound to obey and serve*."

I agreed with them, but diplomatically held my tongue. The whole court was rife with speculation about the match, but she would be our new mistress and I could not risk offending her. Instead, I took the question discreetly to my fathers' friend, Sir William Paulet. He was as renowned for his insight as he was for his discretion. He thought that her very lack of talent commended her most to the king. It made the complete opposite of Queen Anne. In his opinion, Jane Seymour reminded him of his long-lost mother, Elizabeth of York. She had been praised as an ideal wife and mother.

"In Lady Jane he has found a wife who is humble, pious, virtuous and obedient," he remarked judiciously. "It is precisely what he wants. He will not tolerate a wife who might challenge him. Her retiring nature is her greatest asset. And he knows that her mother bore ten children. He is convinced that she will be able to bear him a son."

The foreign ambassadors were equally perplexed at the king's choice of so modest a wife, but concealed their true opinions under extravagant compliments. Ambassador Chapuys was prepared to be gracious about the choice of Lady Jane since he was so gratified by the downfall of Queen Anne. He was quite certain that I shared his view of the affair.

"One may rightly say that the judgements of God are marvellous and just and reward everyone according to his works," he concluded with satisfaction. "As this Anne supplanted Queen Catherine, so the Lady Jane has supplanted Anne. I feel that Queen Catherine, who was a much-wronged lady, has finally been vindicated. And the Lady Mary has been preserved from a very great danger for the concubine was constantly urging the king to have her put to death."

His observations were all very true. But when the cannons had fired for her death, I had felt nothing but sorrow and despised myself as a Judas. Lord Cromwell had kept his promise to pay me well, but now his gold marks weighed upon me like thirty pieces of silver. *The ends don't justify the means*, I reflected. *The ends and the means are the same thing*. A quiet conscience is a priceless thing, but how many courtiers had one? I realised that the whole court who struggled with these issues, and not just myself. But nobody dared to speak of them in public for fear of displeasing the king. It was the wisest course to act prudently. You kept silent and avoided joining in gossip lest you were denounced. I longed to return to the peace of my home, but I was no longer my own person. I was a servant of the queen and in the service of Lord Cromwell. There was also the cost of the journey to consider which would fall hard on my father. And I feared that if I returned, he would see how far I had fallen away from his moral standards. I no longer felt worthy of his teaching.

I thought that I might at least write a letter to share some of the momentous news from court. But in the end I had to give it up. My words were no longer sincere. I could say nothing that was real or true about my life. The truth was that

I was irretrievably compromised. I did not blame myself for swearing the oath of supremacy for, after all, I was a subject of the king. But I bitterly regretted having involved myself with the two most notorious spymasters of the court. I feared that I had learned to play the hypocrite only too well, not only to mislead the observers at court but also to deceive my own family and friends. I hardly knew who I was any more and did not know how to regain my self-respect. It was unthinkable to leave court and yet it was increasingly perilous to remain there. I had no-one to protect me from the unspeakable Cromwell. He was the dark angel of the court who would stop at nothing to do the king's bidding. He was known to be ready at all things, good or evil. He had no moral scruples and thought nothing of using lies, threats or manipulation to gain his ends. Now I was in his power and there was no way to break free.

I wondered how those moral paragons Anne de Beaujeu and Christian de Pisan would have fared if they served at this court. Would they have left, would they have maintained their principles in the face of danger or would they have maintained a prudent silence and ignored the corruption around them? I had seen how those who held to their principles had suffered. Thomas More had been imprisoned and executed. And Queen Catherine had suffered sorrow, humiliation and persecution which had shortened her life. Few of us were the stuff of martyrs. And the worldly-wise at court felt that it was wrong for a subject to set up their own conscience against that of the king. For was he not divinely appointed to govern the nation? And it was needful to consider one's duty to one's family. Was it justifiable to allow them to suffer poverty and loss of status in your downfall as the family of Thomas More had done? And so I remained with only my faithful friend Nan to console and encourage me. I had hoped that I might find a worthy match to remove me from the temptations of this court, but the atmosphere was too fevered to encourage courtship. But I resolved that never again would I act the spy. I would forget the sad story of Queen Anne, serve faithfully and regain my self-respect.

However, my good resolutions availed me nothing. It was not long before Lord Cromwell sent for me. I noticed he was dressed in an expensive fur-lined coat and a black velvet cap. "I have good news for you, Lady Margaret," he congratulated me. "You have been selected as one of the ladies in waiting to Queen Jane. Not all of your associates have been so fortunate. The king has ordered that all the supporters of the late Queen Anne are to be sent from court immediately."

"I am most grateful, Lord Cromwell," I said with a respectful curtsey.

"Of course, you will continue your good services of keeping me informed of all the queen's conversations," he continued. "And this will also serve your interests, Lady Margaret."

"But Lord Cromwell, Queen Jane is known as a virtuous lady," I protested. "There is no need to report on her."

He contradicted me sharply. "There is always a need to report on the queen's affairs. I have found you a place by recommending you to Queen Jane as a good and faithful servant. But if she ever discovered that you had been an informer then I doubt that she would wish you to remain in her household. So I advise you to make yourself useful and act with discretion. You will not be the loser for it. Remember that we are all servants of the king and our highest loyalty is to him."

"Of course, Lord Cromwell." I was so agitated that I went straight to the maid's dormitory to think. Fortunately, it was deserted at that time of day. I realised that Lady Maria de Eresby had been quite right. I had put myself entirely in the power of an unscrupulous man and my only options were to agree to his terms or to leave the court. What should I do? It was useless to seek advice. Lord Cromwell was the most important man at court and no-one could protect me from him. But I realised that I could choose what I decided to report. I would repeat only the most innocuous conversations and say that Queen Jane was a lady of no ambitions. He would have to be satisfied with that.

He was not. "Is that all you have to tell me, Lady Margaret?" he frowned. "You are clearly a clever woman and I expect intelligent service from you.

"I am not in her close confidence, Lord Cromwell," I explained. "The queen is wary of those who served her predecessor. She prefers to take counsel from her own family."

"Then I advise you to get yourself into her confidence, Lady Margaret," he demanded. "There is much competition for places at court. You see this pile of letters on my desk? Half of them come from hopeful parents soliciting places for their daughters and offering great rewards in return. You could easily be replaced for you have no strong family connections. Your best security lies in your good service to me."

"With respect, Lord Cromwell, I was appointed to provide good service to the queen," I countered.

"The time to make that argument is long past, Lady Margaret," he replied with disdain. "I need to know what the Seymours are plotting amongst themselves and I look forward to hearing a more interesting report from you soon."

What more could I say? I realised that I would have to provide more concrete information next time. Fortunately, the queen's brother, Thomas Seymour, was a vain man of no discretion. He thought nothing of airing his expectations before the entire Privy Council despite the efforts of the Queen Jane and his older brother Edward to restrain him. Soon Lord Cromwell had a whole dossier on Thomas Seymour's views. It was fortunate for him that he enjoyed the king's favour. Lord Cromwell bided his time and said nothing against him. I reproached myself for landing in such a quagmire. My father was so proud of me. What would he think if he knew the truth? I was nothing more than the creature of a baseborn official. I had none of the virtues he had commended me to cultivate. I was unworthy of the blood of my de la Roche ancestors.

Part 3: The Household of Queen Jane Seymour (1536 – 1537)

"I am therefore of this advice, that it is not mete nor convenient for a Maiden to be taught or trained up in learning of humane arts… how far more convenient the Distaff, and Spindle, Needle and Thimble were for them with a good and honest reputation, than the skill of well using a pen or writing a lofty verse with defame and dishonour"

(Giovanni Michele Bruto, The Mirror of Modestie, 1555).

Queen Jane accepted Nan and I graciously into her service. But I don't think that she ever really forgave us for slighting her when she was a fellow maid of honour. She was far above us now and that was her triumph. She never sought any familiarities nor shared any reminiscences about our past times together in service. She was determined to forget the humiliation of the past and reinvent herself as a great lady. Queen Jane took Queen Catherine for her role model. She set herself to be just as kind, gentle and pious and endeavoured to gain a reputation for dignity and peace-making. But never again would she let herself be despised. She was now the greatest lady in the realm with a household of two hundred people to serve her. The king gave her a hundred manors for her jointure and lavish gifts of jewels, furs and regal gowns.

The king's artist Hans Holbein was commissioned to make a great gold standing cup garnished with diamonds and pearls as a celebration of their marriage. It bore her motto *"Bound to obey and serve,"* and the initials H and J knit together. Other splendid jewels soon followed including a great pomander of gold with a crown and a gold tablet with the king's picture on it and a rose of diamonds and rubies.

She dressed herself ostentatiously in her favourite colours of purple, crimson, blue and white with long court trains and was accompanied everywhere by her little pet poodle. She took care to conduct herself with propriety and enjoyed listening to music and playing card games. But she was good-natured enough to overlook the former conduct of Lady Anne Stanhope Seymour. Her sister-in-law was now only too ready to assert their close relationship and claim precedence over all the other ladies including the queen's own sister, Lady Elizabeth Ughtred. Queen Jane's circle was dominated by notable flatterers such as Margery Horsman, Mary Norris and Mary Arundell. Her favourite ladies wore costly girdles, jewelled pomanders and gold tablets as signs of her favour.

As a lady in waiting to Queen Jane I would have to conform to her tastes and preferences. I wondered what they would be. Did she, in fact, have any? It turned out that she did. She rejected the French caps and dresses made fashionable by Queen Anne. Her ladies must wear English head dresses edged with gold and silver embroidery. The trains of their gowns must be three yards long. And most importantly they must adorn themselves with pearls. She made a point of wearing headdresses, necklaces and girdles richly set with pearls. She ordered a new kirtle from the king's embroiderer ornamented with over a thousand pearls. The king indulged her preference by commissioning a necklace of six ropes of the finest pearls for her. He also gave her a girdle of large pearls from which hung a splendid gold medallion set with a ruby. She wore them at every opportunity.

"Pearls are the only gems suitable for young women to wear," she pronounced and congratulated herself on setting a new fashion at court.

"You are quite correct, your Majesty," replied Mrs Stoner on our behalf. But all the ladies in waiting were appalled by this decree.

"She has neither taste nor breeding," we agreed amongst ourselves. "She is just as colourless as her precious pearls. But what else could be expected from the daughter of a country knight?"

I resented having to remake my stylish gowns into plain English fashions with insipid pearl edgings. But the queen required that her ladies should wear no less than two hundred pearls in her presence. She showed no concern that such a demand might cause considerable hardship. The maids of honour frantically wrote home asking for their family's pearl heirlooms to be sent to them. Rather than burden my father I sold my few ornaments to buy myself a pearl collar and girdle. The noblewomen were aggrieved at having to substitute simple pearl ornaments for their best jewels. They complained that the gentlemen now outshone the ladies at court festivities.

It was apparent that beneath Queen Jane's demure exterior lurked a stubborn determination to have her own way. She insisted on plenty of sewing for good causes while we listened to pious readings. Soon our fingers and backs grew sore and our tempers became frayed. Since Queen Jane lacked the education of Queen Catherine of Aragon, she allowed her chaplains to select suitable readings for her ladies. Nan lamented the disappearance of the open Bible from the queen's apartments. As Queen Jane could not read herself, it was not something of which she approved. And so we were condemned to listen to tiresome daily homilies. I noticed that a favourite theme was the duty of obedience. A daughter owed obedience to her father, a wife to her husband and a subject to their king. It fitted very neatly with Queen Jane's personal motto, "*Bound to obey and serve.*"

Queen Jane resolved to set a good example of industry to us. She took pleasure in embroidering the letter H in gold thread on pairs of coloured sleeves. Her favourite ladies made a set of rich hangings for her bed embroidered with golden crowns to emphasise her royal status. The rest of us laboriously stitched vast quantities of shirts and caps for the poor. Lady Anne Seymour made sure that she was constantly at the queen's side and they would often enjoy a pleasant walk and gossip in galleries and gardens of the palace accompanied by a few select favourites. In the evenings the musicians would be summoned to play and sing the simple English folksongs that she preferred. The king's own verses featured on a daily basis to demonstrate the queen's loyalty. Life in Queen Jane's household settled into a steady monotony. The king had no objection for he maintained a lively routine of sports and gambling with the gentlemen of his own apartments.

King Henry did not seem to mind the simple tastes of his new wife. He had grown tired of competing with the sparking wit of the Boleyn family. Queen Jane was comfortably inferior to him and provided a soothing presence at his side. There was no danger that she would ever decry his taste in dress or verse. On the contrary, she would invariably compliment him on every occasion as a loyal wife should. The older ladies applauded her good sense in knowing how to keep the king so well contented. The glittering interlude of Queen Anne was gone like the brief appearance of a blazing comet in the night which leaves nothing behind it but the dim memory of a brief glory. By contrast, Queen Jane was like the pale light of the early morning sun whose beams were steady and dependable. Her very sameness was reassuring after so much instability. After all, it was far better to thrive in a dull court than to fall in an unpredictable one.

"Queen Jane is a prim ignoramus," I complained to Nan. "Her household is no more cultured than her country home at Wolf Hall."

"At least she is not as temperamental as Queen Anne," she reminded me. "She does not make scenes and she is a good influence on the king. The court is a much safer place to be these days."

And so I did my best to reconcile myself to the new regime. The only fly in the ointment was Lady Anne Stanhope Seymour. She had become insufferably proud since her marriage to Edward Seymour and the elevation of Queen Jane. She was always to be seen in her company. The king had made her husband the Viscount Beauchamp of Hache and she was now Lady Beauchamp. She never deigned to speak to me now. She felt that as a married lady and sister-in-law to the queen she was far above the humble maids of honour. She was civil to Nan, since her mother Lady Maud Parr was well regarded among the great ladies at court. But she made no secret of her disdain for me. One day her spite got the better of her when she found me sitting in the queen's chapel with my rosary in my hands. I was thinking of Queen Catherine and wishing that she was still at court.

"There you are, Lady Margaret," she said scornfully. "You are always so demure! Butter wouldn't melt in your mouth, would it? I wonder if you are really as pious as you pretend to be?"

I concealed my rosary in my sleeve. I did not want her to see Queen Catherine's gift. "I couldn't say, Lady Beauchamp. I am sure that your knowledge of pretence far exceeds mine."

"How dare you be so saucy!" she raged. "You are nothing at this court. Your family are a broken staff and you are their last feeble twig. No gentleman would ever make you a serious proposal. You would do better to go to a nunnery. You were only accepted here out of charity, you know. Queen Jane has no interest in your company. It would be better for you to return home for she will never make a match for you. She thinks that there are far more deserving ladies in her service who are younger, prettier and wealthier."

Her words stabbed at me like knives. I knew that she was busy dripping poison in the ear of the queen. I bit my tongue for I could not afford to make an enemy of a Seymour. Someone like Lady Anne always had to have a victim and it seemed that I was hers. However, I realised that I had the perfect means of revenge to hand. I would report all her conversations to Lord Cromwell.

"How kind you are to take an interest in my affairs, Lady Beauchamp," I answered politely. "I should have thought that you had more important matters claiming your attention. But perhaps you are not part of those conversations, after all."

Lady Beauchamp flushed red with anger. "My husband and I know all the mind of the queen. And of His Majesty, the king."

"I am sure they are both most grateful for your counsel, Lady Beauchamp," I said graciously. "Please excuse me for my friends are expecting me and I must not keep them waiting." I rose and swept past her out of the chapel door. I found Nan in the dormitory and persuaded her to accompany me on a walk in the palace gardens where I poured out my fury into her sympathetic ears.

"She has always been jealous of you, Margaret," Nan consoled me. "You are much more admired than she will ever be. If she hadn't had a dowry, she would never have made a match. She has become so arrogant these days that anyone would think that she was the queen. But try to avoid a quarrel with her or she might contrive to have you sent from court. Make sure you are never alone with her and then she can't taunt you."

I followed Nan's advice but I noticed that I was rarely chosen to take part in any of the court entertainments. There was nothing I could do but accept the situation with good grace and always appear cheerful. The Seymour family were not the only power at court and the other noble families disliked them as much as the Boleyns. Lord Cromwell was particularly suspicious of their influence and urged me to report "more of matter" in their conversations.

"They don't confide in me, Lord Cromwell," I protested. "I am too humble to serve their ambitions."

He believed me. "Well, get what matter you can. I have grave doubts about their loyalty. They are too proud and greedy to be honest servants of the Crown. And they are to be found everywhere nowadays. It troubles me. I need to know their weaknesses."

"They like to be flattered, Lord Cromwell," I observed. "They have a liking for presents. And they are envious of the other noble houses. They want a great position for themselves."

"Then I shall do my best to see that they don't get one," he stated firmly. "They are puffballs of vanity and it would only cause dissent among the old nobility. After all, their only distinction is to be related to the queen. They have done the king no great service yet. I would be glad to send them to Calais or Ireland out of reach of the king's ear. But the queen says she cannot do without them. So all I can do is keep a close watch on them. Be sure that you do the same."

Queen Jane gained the respect of the court by persuading King Henry to reconcile with his eldest daughter. Lady Mary wrote a letter to the king which accepted his royal supremacy and surrendered her right to the throne. In July 1537 they went to visit Lady Mary at Hackney as a sign of unity. The king gave her a gift of a thousand crowns and the queen presented her with a diamond ring. Lord Cromwell was instructed to reassemble her household and Lady Margaret Pole was invited to return to her service. Lady Mary came back to court and was given precedence as the first lady after the queen. King Henry provided her with her own lodgings at Hampton Court and Greenwich Palace. As a result, Queen Jane gained a great reputation as a peacemaker.

However, in October 1537, a great crisis developed in the realm. A protest against the closure of the monasteries began in Lincolnshire and quickly spread to the north. The protestors called themselves pilgrims and demanded that the king restore the monasteries again. The king was furious and blamed Lord Cromwell for proceeding too fast with his religious reforms. He could not return the lands for they had already been given away or sold to his courtiers. The Pilgrimage of Grace was ruthlessly suppressed and its leaders were executed as rebels. But Queen Jane sympathised with the pilgrim's cause. She surprised us all one day when she made a public plea on her knees to the king to restore the monasteries. The courtiers held their breath at her daring intercession. Instantly, his genial look changed into one of cold anger.

"Get up, Madam," he commanded. "And do not try to meddle in affairs that you do not understand. Think on the fate of your predecessor who meddled too much."

Queen Jane turned deathly pale as the king's words reverberated around the court. I pitied her as she stood before us trembling with fear. She knew her peril only too well. I realised that he was not just warning the queen. He was warning the factions at court that he would not tolerate being manoeuvred. And reminding them that any who tried should remember the fate of his former queen. Queen Jane was visibly shaking as she made her way back to her apartments. She went straight to her chamber and threw herself down upon the bed sobbing helplessly. Her family gathered anxiously around her.

"Calm yourself, Jane," hissed Edward. "Great ladies do not weep!"

"You have acted rightly," said his wife Anne piously. "Today you showed your moral courage to everyone."

"You picked the wrong time and place to speak to the king," grumbled Thomas. "Next time you should talk to him privately in your chamber."

Queen Jane sat up and turned on them in a rage. Her face was red with blotches and streaming with tears. She had quite forgotten her queenly dignity.

"This was your fault – you persuaded me to it!" she stormed at them. "You said it was my duty. You told me that I would be like Esther interceding with King Xerxes. And now see what has happened! You have turned the king against me. I will never, ever do this again. And now, you can all leave!"

I was amazed that mild-mannered Jane had it in her to stand up for herself. Her family were equally taken aback.

"Pray don't blame us, Jane. We meant it for the best," retorted Anne in her most affronted manner.

"We are your family – and families must stick together," insisted Edward. "You would be nothing in this court if it were not for us. Your enemies would make short work of you. You need our support to remain as queen. Don't forget it!"

However, Queen Jane recognised the danger in the king's warning. She saw that she contended with him at her own peril. So she declined to serve as anyone's mouthpiece in the future. She avoided contentious topics of conversation and refused all suggestions that she should ask the king for favours. Her ambitious brothers, Edward and Thomas, were furious with her.

"We made you a queen and expect you to do your duty," insisted Edward. "You must use your position to persuade the king to promote the interests of our family and support the Church."

"Persuade him yourself," she countered sharply. "As the queen it is my duty to be loyal to the king."

"Where is your loyalty to your own family?" demanded Thomas. "All queens do their best to advance their relatives."

"I won't risk my neck for the sake of your ambition," she snapped. "You serve in the court so you can ask him yourself!"

I admired her prudence. She had the good sense not to put herself between her brother's ambitions and the king's wishes. And she was already facing his disappointment at the lack of a son. He was no longer prepared to be patient on the matter. Already she was beginning to look strained and weary under the burden of her role. She dressed with care and conducted herself with the dignity that befitted her position. She was attentive to the king and watched every word that she spoke. But it was still not enough. She knew that his favour would not last unless she bore a son. Fear began to take its toll on her. She toyed with her food and grew noticeably pale and thin. I felt sorry for her and did my best to serve her attentively. I saw that Henry would not tolerate a barren wife nor an opinionated one. He wanted submissiveness and obedience – and above all, he wanted sons. Never again would he allow himself to be dominated by a shrew. He would be master in his court and his wife would be a model of modest virtue like his mother, Elizabeth of York.

However, the dreary atmosphere at court brightened with the good news that Queen Jane was at last expecting a child. The king came in person to the queen's bedchamber with his favourite doctor. He had evidently received a cheering report for he addressed us with the greatest charm. "Good ladies, I exhort you to take the greatest care of the queen. I rely upon you to maintain her health and her spirits while we await the arrival of the little prince. Do me this service and you shall have my gratitude."

We curtsied and Mother Stoner replied on our behalf. "Your Majesty, it will be the greatest honour of our lives to attend the queen at this time. Your Grace should have no fear to leave her in our care for she will be served with our entire devotion and we shall gladly fulfil all her wishes."

"I am glad to hear it, Mrs Stoner," he stated. "She must not exert herself in any way for the sake of the child but let her eat and drink whatever she fancies."

"Yes, your Majesty," she assured him. "We shall watch over her at all times and keep her from feeling doleful while she is confined."

He gave her a gracious smile. "That is well, Mrs Stoner. I shall leave her in your charge."

The king cancelled his plans to go on a progress in order to remain close to the queen. He feared that her mind might be troubled by his absence and harm might come to the child. It was the first time that I had known him to be willing to sacrifice his own pleasure. Consequently, most of the court dispersed to their country estates during the summer months. There was little for the ladies in waiting to do and our lives settled into a dull monotony. However, the queen's pregnancy led to the arrival of a new addition in the household. Queen Jane developed a passionate longing to eat quails but there were none to be found. The anxious king sent out enquiries in every direction and the difficulty was finally solved. Lady Lisle sent quantities of them from Calais and in return she succeeded in gaining a place for her daughter as a maid of honour. Lady Anne Basset was a fair and graceful young woman who had been educated in France. She was assigned to a bed in my dormitory and soon became a good friend to myself and Nan.

"There has been such a to-do about finding me a place at court," she told us. "My mother has been trying for years. First, she wrote petitions and sent gifts to Queen Anne and then she finally succeeded after sending presents of quails to Queen Jane."

Nan and I exchanged looks. Anne Basset was not the first maid of honour to be bought a place at court. But we had never come across a case of bribing the queen with quails. It seemed that Lady Lisle was an original character.

"But then there was a dreadful fuss about my wardrobe," sighed Anne. "Queen Jane insisted that I could not wear any gowns or hoods in the French fashion. They had to be in the English style that she preferred. It was a shame because the French hoods became me so well. And unless I wore a complete set of pearl ornaments then I could not come at all. My poor mother became almost frantic."

Nan and I burst out laughing. Those ridiculous pearls again. Soon there would be a shortage of them.

"My mother says that I must do all that I can to please the queen," she said anxiously. "I hope that you will advise me what to do."

"Queen Jane is very punctilious," I warned her. "So you must be dutiful and diligent and never absent herself at meals or prayers."

"And she likes her young women to show her deference," advised Nan. "So always be the first to go to her highness's chamber and offer to bear her highness's mantle. If you are humble and obliging then you will soon gain her favour."

Lady Anne Basset proved to be a natural courtier and her French manners gave her an air of sophistication. She had pleasing manner which gained her the favour of the court. However, she was often at her wits end about her demanding mother. Lady Lisle constantly demanded that she should seek favours on behalf of her family.

"My mother sends the king boxes of quince marmalade and expects that she will receive titles and honours in return," sighed Anne as she sat on the end of Nan's bed. "She has no idea of what it is really like here at court. I wish that she would come to serve here in my place. She would soon discover how quickly self-serving courtiers fall from favour. I do not know how to answer her letters."

"Tell your mother that we have been forbidden to ask for favours on pain of dismissal," suggested the resourceful Nan.

"That would do no good for she would tell me that I must do it discreetly," said Anne gloomily. "I would gladly be an obedient daughter to her, but I cannot tell the king what he should do. I dread receiving her letters now because each one contains a new demand: I must tell the queen that my sister Catherine is a fine young girl and get her a place as a maid of honour. I must ask the king to look with favour upon her friend's suit. She has promised her that it will be an easy matter to arrange with a daughter of hers at court. I must keep my father's name before the king and queen as a loyal and worthy subject. Then they will remember him when they distribute lands and manors as rewards. I am not a member of the Privy Council. What can I do about such matters?"

"Then tell her that the king is in an ill-humour at present and is not of a mind to grant any requests," said Nan sagely.

"I fear she would tell me to pick a good moment and approach him then," said Anne picking at the counterpane in her agitation.

"Then say that the king has been ill and has withdrawn from court to recover," I proposed.

Anne Basset looked at me doubtfully. "It would only gain me a temporary stay. And she is bound to complain that I have no regard for her and that my sister would have done much better in my place."

"This is making your life here a misery," said Nan. "Why not confide in the queen about these letters?"

Anne Basset looked horrified at the idea. "I cannot. My mother would never forgive me for betraying her confidence!"

"Then explain that the king is besieged by requests all day long. He likes to be generous to those who please him, but he is liable to be offended when his servants ask him for favours," advised Nan.

Anne Basset sighed. "You do not know what my mother is like. She will ask why I have not pleased the king enough to deserve his generosity. I shall have to write back and say that he is ill at present and cannot be approached. And then he will be going away on summer progress soon and be unavailable for several months. She will be displeased to receive excuses, but it should put an end to her requests until the king returns in October. Perhaps I should not mention the progress for she may tell me to propose that the king should honour them with a visit."

Nan looked amused. "Very well. Find your pen and paper and we shall compose the perfect letter to your mother." She cleared the table beside her bed and dictated the message aloud to Anne:

"Madam, I recommend myself most humbly to the good grace of my lord my father, and yours. I am much pleased because Mrs Stoner sends to know of your welfare. We are greatly concerned for the king's health for he is confined to his apartments at present and can see none but his doctors. I have your requests very much in mind and will be sure to present them as soon as the King's Grace has returned to court again. The Queen's Majesty is in good health and I am most diligent in my service remembering your good counsel always to be sober, sad, wise, and discreet and lowly above all things. I assure you of my good health and I thank you most humbly for the lace of Flanders that it has pleased you to send me. I send this letter by way of our carrier Master John Smyth and hope that you receive it speedily. And thus I conclude, madam, praying our Lord to give you health and

a good and long life. From Greenwich this 14th of June. Your very humble and obedient daughter, Anne Basset."

"What excellent letters you write," said Anne Basset admiringly. "It makes me sound like a model of duty."

"I know what it is to have a demanding mother," said Nan "I shall probably say much the same thing to my own mother tomorrow. And now let us amuse ourselves. Let us play a game of cards. Shall it be Imperial, Primero or Pope Joan?"

Anne Basset smiled impishly. "I have my dice here in my pocket. Let us play at Hazard. And this time I will win." She took out her dice and tossed them in the air. She caught them deftly and laid them on the table.

"Oh no you won't," retorted Nan. "I am the best player of all the maids of honour." She tossed her book onto the table beside them.

Anne gazed thoughtfully at the oak table where Nan had left her copy of Cicero. A beam of sunlight eased itself through the open casement, settling on the fine gold edges of the book's pages. From somewhere in the knot gardens below the sound of a lute threaded itself into the room. She tilted her head and met Nan's challenge with a clear gaze, her eyes sparkling. "Then why not teach me how to play like a champion?"

"Your mother would say that it is a frivolous use of your time," Nan teased her.

Anne pouted and pushed her chin higher. "Not at all. She would say that it is good to practice my courtly skills and accomplishments."

"Since when is gambling an accomplishment?" Nan enquired, raising an eyebrow.

"It is the pleasure of the king and queen and so it must also be our pleasure too. It is only frivolous if you play badly and get into debt."

Anne was evidently determined to have her way. Nan paused to listen to the gentle strings below. "I see that it is your plan to make your fortune at court at dice and cards."

"It is a surer way than the favour of kings," Anne declared as she picked up the dice. "And it is a better way than marrying a weary old man for his money."

I watched as she threw the dice against Nan and reflected on her words. Was not this life at court a gamble with fortunes made or lost by the fickle turns of fate? But there was no escaping the fact that as courtiers we prospered or waned entirely by the favour of the king. Lady Lisle's marmalade was a subtle throw of the dice which might reap rewards for her family. But only if it happened to please the king's fancy. In just such a way my father had contrived to bring me to court. And all the courtiers were striving to play the same game for the same end – to catch the king's eye and gain lasting preferment.

The three of us passed a pleasant summer together until the hot days of July and August finally waned with the coming of autumn. I found that I welcomed this quiet interlude from the demanding routine of court life. In September 1537, Queen Jane retired to Hampton Court Palace to prepare for the birth of her child. The king sent her a gift of a silver-gilt bowl and flagon as a sign of his favour. It was engraved with a monogram of H and J and the scene of the death of Lucretia as a tribute to her virtue. She displayed it prominently on a table for everyone to admire. Lady Anne Beaufort was in her element giving the orders as the chief lady in waiting to the queen.

"Your Majesty shall have everything that is due to your comfort," she dictated. "Your bedchamber shall be hung with tapestries to keep out the drafts and the floor will be spread with thick carpets. You shall lie upon a great bed with a quilt of scarlet satin and curtains of crimson velvet. And only your ladies shall enter your chamber. They alone will serve you until the child is born."

The king's grandmother had laid down the regulations for the lying-in of a royal lady. She had decreed that only pleasant scenes should be displayed in the room with nothing to cause disquiet in the mind of an expectant mother. And so the chamber was hung with blameless images of The Triumph of Chastity, The City of Ladies and The Twelve Months of the Year.

Lady Anne Beaufort was also pregnant at this time which gave her an excuse to claim the queen's company and dominate the conversation with discussions about their condition and their hopes for their children's future. I noticed that she imitated the queen's attire as closely as she could while praising her exquisite taste in gold-trimmed caps and nightgowns. Fortunately, Lady Beaufort was soon obliged to withdraw into seclusion herself to the great relief of the other ladies. The queen's favourites devotedly stitched a counterpane depicting Adam and Eve in gold and silver thread. Nan and I were directed to occupy ourselves in embroidering dozens of sets of fine linen for the royal infant.

Passing the long hours in the queen's bedchamber with my needle led me to reflect upon my life as a lady in waiting. I gazed at a tapestry of a lady taming a unicorn against a background of green trees. By legend only a pure woman could capture this mythical beast. It was a gift from the king in honour of the modesty of the queen. I sighed to myself as I contemplated this virtuous scene. *I am like one of those trees in the background.* To be a courtier was to form one small detail in the great tapestry of the life of the king and queen. I rethreaded my needle with the fine silk thread. But the distracting thoughts kept coming. Queen Jane had been a lady in waiting like myself not long ago. Now she had a husband and was the mistress of her own household. Soon she would have a child. And yet she was not as fair nor accomplished nor wellborn as myself. *When would it be my turn?* I asked myself. Nan gave me a nudge to distract me from my reverie before any of the other ladies noticed my inattention. I gave her a resigned smile and resumed stitching the intertwined H and J initials upon yet another napkin. There was a plentiful stock of baby linen in the royal wardrobe but Queen Jane considered it ill-omened and refused to touch it. She insisted that the king's true-born child must have newly-made linen of the very best quality.

The queen's pains began on 9th October 1537 and the midwives were summoned to attend her. Poor Queen Jane had a bad time in labour. At first, the midwives were complacent about the delay.

"All ladies are a long time delivering their first child. Your Majesty must be patient," they assured her as the hours passed.

But as the hours turned into days, they grew increasingly anxious and began to pray aloud for the child to be born safely. The room was already stifling hot, but the nervous ladies built up the fire even more. Queen Jane grew exhausted and the king became frantic at the delay. He ordered his doctors to attend the queen. After three days, a fair-haired boy was born on 12th October 1537. The news sped through the palace that the longed-for son had arrived. The relieved king declared that it was a sign of God's favour. The birth of Prince Edward led to a time of great rejoicing in the court and in the nation. I was glad to be here at the centre of things. As soon as the news was announced in London, the church bells began to ring in celebration, bonfires were lit in the streets and free wine was distributed to the citizens. King Henry was like a man transformed.

"At last, I have a son. I have waited twenty-seven years for this day, but now my patience has been rewarded. We shall name him Edward as he was born on St Edward's day." In the days that followed, he finally got to send the letters to his fellow sovereigns announcing the birth of a prince. "Now that I have my son and heir, I say fie upon them all," he boasted. "I have no fear of any of them now that I have Edward as my true and lawful successor."

The following week a most splendid christening was arranged with all the ambassadors and nobility in attendance. All the ladies in waiting were provided with new dresses of white satin in honour of the occasion. It was not the custom for the parents to attend and I was glad for the sake of the queen. She had not yet regained her strength after the birth. Prince Edward was brought to the Chapel Royal at Hampton Court on Sunday 15th October 1537. He was carried on a cushion held by the Marchioness of Exeter under a canopy of cloth of gold. His long velvet train was carried by the earl of Arundel. The Lady Mary was appointed as his godmother and she wore a gown of cloth of silver. Archbishop Cranmer baptised the prince in a silver-gilt font and a Te Deum was sung in thanksgiving. Afterwards, the prince was taken to the queen's apartments and refreshments were served to the guests. Queen Jane looked radiant with happiness. No-one could say that she had not done her duty as the queen. Her brothers strutted around like a pair of cockerels accepting congratulations from the rest of the court. The king rewarded the queen by appointing her brother Edward as the earl of Hertford. He stuck to the king's side like a burr as if he was already a duke of the realm and his foremost adviser. Thomas Seymour contrived to lay his hands on a flagon of wine to celebrate his good fortune. He got roaring drunk and told everyone that they must show him more respect as the uncle of the next king. But Jane refused to eat anything except fruit jellies. She called for cup after cup of sweet orange water. In the atmosphere of celebration no-one realised that she was dangerously fevered.

The following day, she fell into a delirium. Her attendants covered her with furs and brought her sweets and wine to tempt her appetite. Prayers were said across the nation for her recovery. The doctors bled her, but her condition grew worse and she died on 24th October 1537. King Henry was so grief-stricken at her death that he withdrew into his private apartments and refused to see anyone. He delegated the funeral arrangements into the hands of the duke of Norfolk. The whole court went into mourning and everyone wore black for the next three months. The body of Queen Jane was covered in gold tissue and laid out in her Presence Chamber with a crown on her head and rings on her fingers. Her ladies took it in turns to maintain a perpetual vigil beside her. We wore black gowns with white head-dresses to signify that the queen had died in childbed.

When it was my turn, I knelt there in the flickering candlelight and thought how unfair life could be. Queen Jane was so young and had only been married for just over a year. And she had just made her position completely secure by giving King Henry his son and heir. He would undoubtedly have given her a coronation as queen and anything else that she wanted. But that glorious future had suddenly been snatched away from her. I prayed that she was at peace now and that her son would live. Her legacy would be to secure the Tudor succession and put an end to the discord which had surrounded it for so long. A week later, her coffin was taken to lie in the Chapel Royal which was hung with black cloth. Her funeral took place at St George's Chapel in Windsor on 12th November 1537. The Lady Mary acted as her chief mourner and twenty-nine mourners followed her procession to represent each year of her life. Afterwards, Lady Mary returned to live at Hunsdon since there was no queen at court to act as her chaperone.

After the death of Queen Jane, deep gloom enveloped the court. Her ladies were seized with trepidation. What would become of them without a mistress to serve? Sure enough, as soon as her funeral was over the king dismissed her household. But in recognition of their good service, he distributed some of her jewels among her ladies. Nan received a gold tablet portraying the Passion of Christ and I received a pair of bracelets. Lady Mary received a brooch of the history of Noah's flood set with diamonds and rubies and Lady Elizabeth received a book of gold. The rest of the collection, including her beloved pearls, he kept as a remembrance of her. I resigned myself to leaving court and returning home. My time in service to Queen Jane had been too short to arrange a match for myself. Quite unexpectedly, I had a summons from Master Cromwell. He was looking unusually gracious.

"You may thank me, Lady Margaret, for I have done you a good service," he informed me. "I have found you a post at court. In fact, it is a sinecure. The king wishes to retain the late queen's wardrobe and her favourite pearls as a remembrance of her. I have proposed you as a suitable lady to care for them. You will merely have to supervise the wardrobe staff and ensure that her gowns are properly aired and protected from the moths."

"I am most grateful for your consideration, Master Cromwell," I replied. "It will be an honour to care for Queen Jane's wardrobe."

He allowed himself a look of satisfaction. "Did I not promise that I would take care of you, Lady Margaret? I know that your court salary is important to you. And I like to see that good service is rewarded."

The departure of the ladies added to the sombre mood of the court. During the period of mourning there were no entertainments. The king was beginning to be troubled with his leg and turned from his love of outdoor sports to gambling at high stakes with his courtiers.

Soon Master Cromwell began to grumble about the state of affairs at the court. "Half of these courtiers are impecunious and the rest are consumed with greed for the spoils of the monasteries. The king has generously granted lands and houses among his nobles to reward their loyalty, but they still want more. And not content with petitioning me with their requests, they lay traps for the king. I cannot always be with him to frustrate their designs. They wait until he is overcome with wine after dinner and then try to wheedle favours from him. Or else they cunningly allow him to beat them at dice. Then they hint that they are ruined men and plead that the gift of lead from a monastery or the bells of a church would restore their fortunes. It is time that His Majesty was married again. The presence of a queen and her ladies would improve the tone of the court. There would be music and dancing and wholesome pastimes. It would cheer his mood and put a stop to all this vain practising upon him."

Fortunately, my good friends Nan and Anne Basset had both managed to remain at court, so I was not left alone. One day Nan sought me out in a state of great excitement.

"I have news for you, Margaret," confided Nan. "My brother William has found a match for me at last. Things have been so unsettled at court since the queen's death that it was impossible to make any arrangements. But it has been settled at long last."

"Who is he?" I asked in some surprise for she had not said a word about having a suitor.

"He is Sir William Herbert and he is an Esquire of the King's Body. He is thirty-seven years old and is said to be a mad fighting fellow. He has the favour of the king for his prowess in battle and he will make a fine husband for me. I am twenty-three and it is time that I was married. My older sister Catherine was already married at the age of sixteen."

"And does he share your love of the classics?" I asked.

She laughed. "No, not at all. He has never read a book in his life. But I shall see to the education of our children just like my own mother."

"I will miss you, dear Nan," I said. I felt pleased for Nan and yet saddened for myself.

"Do not be anxious," counselled Nan. "I shall return to court as a lady in waiting as soon as there is a new queen to serve. It will be just the same as before, you'll see. And I will ask my mother-in-law, Lady Herbert, to find a suitable husband for you. She has no daughters so I am sure she would be pleased to be your sponsor."

Nan was a most loyal friend. But I knew that it was too much to expect her friends to exert themselves on my behalf. I began to feel anxious about my future prospects. I had served at court under three queens and yet there was no word of a suitable match. My dear father was also becoming concerned about my situation and expressed it in his letters.

"You cannot leave it too late to marry and have children, my dear Margaret. I had hoped to see you well settled by now. It is most unfortunate that the queen is dead. But surely you have friends at court who will support you?"

I felt very doubtful that my claims would weigh with anyone. But Nan kept her promise to speak to Lady Herbert. At first, she had high hopes of finding a match as my birth, my appearance and my court service were considered to be most acceptable. I had the reputation of a loyal servant and a lady of good birth and education. A prospective father-in-law was found among her acquaintance by the name of Sir John Heveningham. He enquired about my pedigree and found it to be most satisfactory. I was elated when heard promising reports about his son Anthony who was about the same age as myself. It was a great relief to know that I was not being matched with an old man.

However, the negotiations came to a halt when Sir John wrote to my father insisting upon a great dowry. He wanted it to be paid in advance of the betrothal. My father was obliged to refuse his demand as he could barely afford to pay a modest sum. Consequently, Sir John decided that he would find a better bargain for his son. I was very downcast since I had hoped that my future was now settled. But Nan stoutly reassured me. This was commonplace in matchmaking. Even princesses could expect to be betrothed many times before a marriage was finally agreed. Our dear Lady Mary had received several proposals already, but the king had rejected them all.

At this difficult time, I received an unexpected invitation to visit my old friend Lady Maria de Eresby, who was now a widow. I requested permission for a leave of absence from the court which was readily granted. I was glad to get away from court and enjoy a change of scene. Lady Maria had sent her Master of the Horse, Master Barnaby Tresham, to escort me to her residence of Grimsthorpe Castle in Lincolnshire. When I arrived, she came to see me in my chamber straightaway. She had not changed at all from the gracious lady I had known so well.

"Do not curtsey to me, my dear," she insisted. "Come and embrace me. It is so good to see you that I really could not wait. Have you had a tiring journey?" she asked me.

"Not at all, Lady Maria. I am glad to see you again after so long," I said. The sight of her dear face and familiar smile was a great consolation to me.

"Let us sit here and enjoy a private talk together. Do have a suitor yet, my dear?"

"No, Lady Maria, I have recently had a great disappointment in that regard. The family wanted a very great dowry which my father was obliged to refuse."

She sighed. "I know that Queen Catherine regretted that she had not been able to arrange a match for you as she would have wished."

"I often think of Her Majesty and I wish that I had been able to remain in her service." The old regret resurfaced in my mind. I knew that Lady Maria understood my pain for she shared it.

"As do I, my dear," she assured me. "But at least I was with her at her death. When I received the news of her final illness, I knew that I must not hesitate. I set out for Kimbolton Castle at once and demanded that her steward admit me. As I bear the name of a great lady he did not dare to refuse. Her Majesty was so pleased to see me. She said that now she could die like a Christian rather than a brute beast. We spoke together in our native Castilian and it was a consolation to her. Poor lady, she had so little comfort in her life and hardly any of her old servants were left in her service. Even then she had not ceased to love the king in spite of everything. Before she died, she wrote him a letter to say that her eyes desired him above all things."

"It was very courageous of you to go to her, Lady Maria," I commended her. I only wished that I had had the courage to do the same.

"I felt it was my duty to my friend and mistress. I have no doubt that after such a saintly life she has gone to her heavenly reward," she asserted with her usual confidence.

"She was a great queen and it was a privilege to serve her, Lady Maria. There will never be her equal at the court again."

Lady Maria sighed. "I had a special motive for inviting you here to visit me, Margaret. Even now, I am not sure how to break it to you. But I have pondered this matter for a long time and I feel it is my duty to tell you."

I was astonished by this mystery. "What is it, Lady Maria."

"Queen Catherine was served to the end by three faithful women," she told me. "One of them was a chamberer called Margaret Pennington who was a widow like myself. As she was absolutely without means or family, I invited her to enter my service and took her into my own household. Unfortunately, the long years of service and the shock of the queen's death had undermined her health. It was not long before she took to her bed with a fever. The doctors told me that they could do nothing for her and it was only a matter of time. I thought that at least I could grant her a peaceful death. When she felt that her end was near, she asked to see me. She said that she wanted to confess the truth to me." She paused and looked uncomfortable.

"Please go on, Lady Maria."

"She told me that she was not the widow she had claimed to be, but a rejected wife. Her husband's name was Sir Thomas de la Roche and she had a daughter named Margaret. She had married far above her station and she loved her husband dearly. However, her mother-in-law refused to accept her and had turned the servants against her. After the birth of her daughter, she declared that she would ruin the chances of the child ever making a suitable alliance. She insisted that she should be sent away as a bad influence. Her life had become so miserable that she agreed to leave. She reverted to her maiden name of Margaret Pennington. She claimed to be a widow of good family and took service in the court as a humble chamberer. She was your mother, Margaret."

I sat there rooted in shock. "It cannot be true, Lady Maria. My mother is dead. It must be a falsehood."

Lady Maria shook her head sympathetically. "I fear that it is not. You were named after her. I wondered if you knew the truth about your mother and debated whether or not it would be right to tell you. But I felt that I could not keep it from you. Your dear mother left no property for she gave all her goods to support the queen in her last days."

My thoughts turned round and round in my head. Could it be true? Would my father allow his wife to be exiled from the household? There was only one way to be certain. I seized a piece of parchment and began to write.

Dear and Honoured Father,

I write to you from the household of Lady Maria de Eresby to whom our family is greatly indebted. She has given me the news of the death of my dear mother. She served the late Queen Catherine faithfully as a chamberer for many years and then continued in service to Lady Maria until her death of a fever two months ago.

It is a great sorrow to me that I missed the chance to know my mother when I came to court. I am at a loss to understand why my mother left her home and family for a life of service. And why should she have served as a chamberer rather than a lady in waiting according to her rank? These matters are a strange mystery to me. My only consolation is that she gave devoted service to the late queen of honoured memory during her time of exile from the court.

Your humble servant and obedient daughter, Margaret.

I waited anxiously for a reply from my father. I wondered if he would give me an explanation of this inexplicable affair. Perhaps it was all nonsense and he would be angry with me for believing it. It seemed much too strange to be true. Finally, after a fortnight of anxious waiting a message from Ravenseat was delivered. I recognised his handwriting on the direction and broke the seal with trembling fingers.

My dear daughter,

The news of your mother's death has caused me much grief and aroused painful memories. Her departure from home was as great a sorrow to me as your birth was a cause of great joy and consolation. Indeed, it is a sad story which I hoped you would never need to know. Your mother's name was Margaret Pennington and she came from a humble family. She came to our house to serve as my mother's chamberer and she took pleasure in improving her speech and manners. As for me, I think I fell in love with her at first sight for she was a girl of remarkable beauty and sweetness of nature. My mother had entertained hopes that I would repair the family fortunes by making a good match with an heiress in exchange for the prestige of our ancient name. My marriage to Margaret was a lasting disappointment to her. I had hoped that in time she would accept my choice of bride but she remained implacable in her opposition. She would not allow her to dine with us and she directed the servants not to wait upon her nor acknowledge her as mistress. It was an impossible state of affairs. Your mother was naturally very unhappy and my love was not enough to protect her.

When it was known that she was expecting a child my mother relented towards her in the hope of gaining an heir to the family name. At first, she was disappointed at the birth of a daughter, but soon it became clear that you were the very image of her. She treasured you as the daughter she had never had. A month after your birth she decided to claim you as her own and raise you as a noble lady. She insisted that it would ruin your future to be raised by such a low-born and common mother. The only solution was for your mother to leave the household. She wrote to a friend and arranged for her to enter royal service at the court as a widow.

I would not have agreed except that the servants assured me that your mother had no regard for me and had only married me for advantage. They claimed that she had a lover and was unfaithful. Sick at heart I agreed to my mother's plan. After her departure there was peace in the household again and you were my great solace. My mother insisted that the name of my wife should never be spoken and she should be regarded as dead. I believed my wife to be a lost cause. But after the death of my mother the servants confessed that Margaret had never been untrue. It had been a falsehood instigated by my mother to persuade me to agree. The rest of the story you know. It is a tale of sorrow and shame. It has left me heartbroken for the loss of love is something for which no worldly position can ever compensate.

Your affectionate father, Thomas de la Roche.

I crumpled up the letter in my hand in horror. I could hardly believe what I had read. I had always revered my father and grandmother and the proud history of our family. And I had hoped to be worthy of the memory of my dead mother. Now my past life was shown to be nothing but a lie. My father and grandmother were not the moral pillars that I had believed them to be. My grandmother was a jealous woman and my father was a weak man who had failed to stand up for his own wife. I wondered how he could sacrifice her to satisfy the prejudices of his mother. He was no better than King Henry! But he had never remarried. I wondered if that was to remain faithful to her memory or whether he had feared a charge of bigamy?

This was his last communication to me. A week later I received a letter from the household chaplain informing me that my father had died of a sudden decline. He was quite at a loss to explain it. The last thing he said was my name, Margaret. I alone understood that my poor father had died of heartbreak saying the name of his long-lost wife. I returned to Ravenseat for his funeral rites. But my once beloved home was no solace to me. The servants made much of me as the young lady of the house now returned to them. But I felt as cold as a stone knowing that they had conspired to drive my poor mother away. They thought me grief-stricken and left me in peace. As the chaplain delivered the funeral service in his sonorous Latin, all that I could think about was how disappointed in me my father must have been. I had fulfilled none of his hopes and ambitions. I had not found a wealthy husband to revive our family fortunes. He had never reproached me, but I felt the bitter sting of failure.

But father, you didn't know what life was really like at court, I thought. It had become a nightmare rather than a fairy tale. First, there the sad exile of Queen Catherine of Aragon, then the terrible execution of Queen Anne and finally the sudden death of Queen Jane. How could any maid of honour make a match under the constant shadow of peril? It was all that any of us could do to keep ourselves out of danger. In the end, I had survived and that was all.

What did I have to show for my years as a courtier? I could wear my clothes with style, converse most charmingly and dance every step with flair. But what sort of a person had I become? I was no longer an innocent girl and I had not become a lady of virtue. I was an intriguer and an informer who was as skilled at deception as in any of the other courtly graces. I could excuse myself by saying that I was no worse than any other attendant at the Tudor court. But my father had wanted me to be so much more. I grieved for the girl that I had been, for I could see no future for me now at court. There was no queen there to serve.

But I had to admit that my father was not the pillar of virtue that I had believed him to be. He had sent away his beloved wife and abandoned her to a solitary existence. When I looked back upon my childhood it was dominated by the figure of my grandmother Lady Agnes. What had been left for my father who was separated from his wife and excluded from his child? Why had he not tried to set things right after my grandmother's death? Perhaps he felt it was too late to make amends. Or else he feared that the scandal might mar my future at court. I would never know his true feelings now for we had never had the opportunity for a real conversation.

I shook my head. How useless such thoughts were now. It was better to accept that we each had our fate and we had to bear it. My mother had found purpose in her service to Queen Catherine and my father in planning a career for me at court. Now it was my task to find a meaningful life for myself. But it would not be among the dark shadows of the past. I was now an heiress and a woman of property. As my father's heir it was my right to stay here at Ravenseat and take over the business of the estate. But I decided that I would leave it to the steward who had managed it for years. I could not stay there among the ghosts of the past and I returned to Lady Maria in the hope of escaping my heavy burden of memories. I was certain that she would have some good advice for someone who felt as troubled as I did. As soon as I could decently take my leave I left my home and made my way back to her hospitable roof.

I told Lady Maria what had happened to my poor mother. To my surprise, she did not seem very shocked by the story. "My dear, it is the way of the world," she remarked bracingly. "You know, when I married Lord Willoughby some of his family objected to his marrying a Spaniard. But he told them that a Spanish lady had been good enough for the king and so it was good enough for him too. At that time, I enjoyed such favour with the king that no-one dared to scorn me. He gave me a dowry of a thousand gold marks and granted Lord Willoughby the castle of Grimsthorpe for us to live in. So they could not deny the advantages of the match."

"But how could my father have allowed his mother to drive his wife away?" I asked her.

"In Spain no-one of noble blood would ever be permitted to marry a commoner," she observed shrewdly. "Here too, unequal matches rarely prosper. It is best to marry within your own rank. And if you take my advice, I would not tell anyone the story of your mother. It is best – as they say here – to let sleeping dogs lie."

"I fear you are right, Lady Maria. No-one else would understand about my mother," I admitted.

"You must not dwindle into sorrow, my dear," she advised me. "You may have lost your parents, but you still have good friends. It is not good for a young woman to live alone in this world. Some scoundrel would be sure to take advantage of you. You must have a husband to support you and make you a happy wife and mother."

Lady Maria proved a staunch friend to me. Naturally she was ready to sympathise with me in my loss and to condole with the misfortune of the lack of a queen at court. But she was also extremely practical in her views.

"My dear, the life of a courtier is always very uncertain. I remember that when I first came to court to serve Princess Catherine, I had brave dreams of my future. But when Prince Arthur died, we were left bereft and penniless for eight long years. I might as well have spent my youth shut up inside a convent. We were strangers in a foreign land and far away from our kindred and countrymen. It was a weary life and we thought there was no hope for any of us. And then by a strange chance, our fortunes were restored. King Henry chose Princess Catherine as his bride and she became the queen that she was always intended to be. And in the happy years that followed I was married too. But that was not the end of our struggles. The queen and I bore daughters and lost sons. She was exiled and I was widowed. Our lives and marriages did not turn out as we had once dreamed that they would."

I sympathised with Lady Maria. My own dreams of life at court had turned out to be nothing more than a young girl's foolish fancies. She noticed my dejection and tried to encourage me.

"You may not make the great match that your family expected of you, Margaret," she comforted me. "You have no royal patron to smooth the way with a dowry and a manor-house. You should have been matched long ago but your mistresses were too preoccupied by their own troubles. However, it is not too late. I shall do my best to find a suitable gentleman for you to marry. Since you are an heiress with property to your name it will not be difficult to make a good match. I will use what influence I have with my son-in-law, Charles Brandon. He is the duke of Suffolk and has many eligible gentlemen in his household. So do not despair, but leave all to me."

Lady Maria was as good as her word. She lost no time in speaking about me to her son-in-law. And he picked out a man from his retinue who deserved a suitable wife. He was a soldier named Robert Fairley. As I was an heiress with property there was no difficulty over the matter of a dowry. He was only too pleased to have the opportunity to marry a wife with her own house and estate. Lady Maria invited him to dine so that we might meet each other. "You must marry where you have an inclination, Lady Margaret. Besides, you must enjoy having a courtship."

Lady Maria was tactful enough to extend her invitation to the friends of Robert Fairley so that he would feel at ease. She served them an excellent meal accompanied by her best wines. Since she knew me so well, she arranged an entertainment which would demonstrate my accomplishments. She was determined that the company would know I was no ordinary gentlewomen. She dismissed her minstrels and together we played on the lute and sang in Spanish and English just as we had once done for Queen Catherine. Then I played at cards with Robert as my partner which gave me a chance to study him up close. He was a man of my own age with dark hair and eyes similar to mine. He was well dressed in a new doublet and hose of tawny velvet. He turned out to be a skilled player.

"All soldiers carry a pack of cards with them," he confided. "It passes the time in the evenings when you are camped in a draughty barn."

He was the younger son of a knight and had to make his own way in the world. He had served the duke of Suffolk for fifteen years and had fought in his French campaign. I felt at ease in his company and Lady Maria was pleased with the duke's choice.

"He reports him as a capable and honest man," she told me. "And he seems to me a man of good sense. He has seen something of the world and will be able to conduct the business of the estate. And although he was trained in martial skills, he is literate and can converse in French."

Lady Maria arranged several further meetings at her house so that we could get to know each other. She sat and embroidered diligently beside the fire and we pretended to play cards while we talked together. It did not take him long to open his mind to me.

"When I was a young man, I thought the life of a soldier was one of great glory and honour," he said. "But there comes a time when a man wants more in his life than service to his lord. I have longed to take a wife and raise a family. I believe it is the path to true happiness. A fair lady like yourself should not have to fight life's battles alone. I would gladly stand beside you and be all that a man should be to his wife. We can be our own master and mistress at Ravenseat and build a strong future together. It is all that I have ever wished for."

"It is my dearest wish too," I replied eagerly. "I have been a courtier all my life. But now I want my own home and family. I would not care if I never returned to court again."

"Let us make a pledge to each other, Margaret. We will always be loyal to one another and create our own piece of heaven on earth."

He laid down his cards, took my hand and kissed it. *He is a fine man*, I thought to myself. *He is not like the spoiled young gallants of the court.* On his next visits he brought me a gold bracelet and an amber necklace. Then he brought a ring set with a fiery beryl.

"This was my mother's ring, Margaret. I hope that you will accept it as a token of our engagement."

"Yes, Robert. I will be proud to be your wife."

He put the ring on my finger and we were betrothed. I told the good news to Lady Maria and thanked her for finding me so good a husband. She smiled.

"I know these noblemen and their careless ways. And I told his lordship of Suffolk that you were no chattel to be used to settle an old debt. He was not to award you as a prize nor stake you as a bet in a game of chance. He was to find a man of sound character and good behaviour or I would reject his choice outright. I would have no frivolous ladies' man for my protege. His lordship grumbled that I should not ask a favour and then quibble at his judgement. But he knew that I meant what I said. I would never have given you to an unworthy man."

I shuddered at the thought that I might have been handed over like a prize horse or gambled away at random. But Lady Maria was more than a match for any lord and I was fortunate to have her as my patroness. She was delighted by the success of her arrangement. She sent for her clerk and instructed him to draw up the marriage contract at once. My father had hoped that I would make a prosperous match, but as Lady Maria said, fortune matches with fortune. She had found me a man of good birth, fine looks and knightly upbringing. He was not a lord, but then I was not a wealthy or well-connected lady. And it was time that I was settled in life. We married at the house of Lady Maria who was kind enough to furnish me with a new dress and a wedding feast. Then we returned to live at Ravenseat. I was tired of the constant intrigues of the court. Now I could look forward to a peaceful married life.

It was a new chapter in my life to be a married lady and no longer a courtier. I had not managed to save very much from my court salary since I had needed to pay for the upkeep of my elegant wardrobe. Now I packed away my court dresses and made myself some practical woollen clothing for life on the estate. I added my books to my father's collection and made a library in the house. One day it would become my children's schoolroom. I sewed a new set of bed hangings for our bedchamber like the ones I had seen in the palaces. Robert said that they made him feel as fine as a nobleman. I took pleasure in embroidering a set of pillows with our initials R and M and surrounding them with intertwining honeysuckles. I made his linen shirts and embellished the collar and cuffs with blackwork embroidery just as Queen Catherine had taught me. It gave me great satisfaction to use my skills to beautify my own home. In the winters to come I would work sets of table linen, cushions and quilts in coloured silks. I could not match the luxury of the royal apartments, but I intended to furnish a family household that would be tasteful and comforting.

I had feared that the servants would not welcome a stranger. But they were overjoyed to receive a new master of the house. Robert Fairley encountered no resentment from them. Perhaps they were also glad to be freed from the shadows of the past. I wished that my father had lived to know my husband. It would have pleased him to know that Robert loved the old house and estate as much as him. He had great plans for it.

"We will build it up, Margaret," he assured me. "By the time our son is grown it will be a flourishing estate."

I saw the determination in his eyes to make the estate more productive. It matched my own ambition to create a welcoming home and I felt that we were a good team. Together we would turn the manor of Ravenseat into our own haven as we had planned. But our plans did not turn out as expected. Within a year we had a child. But our firstborn was a daughter and not a son. I named her Catherine in honour of the queen. To our surprise she resembled neither one of us with her fair hair and blue eyes. But the old chaplain who christened her recognised her at once.

"She has the look of the Penningtons," he observed. "They are all as fair as angels."

I was glad to have a girl who resembled my mother. By all accounts she had been a most beautiful woman although I had no likeness of her. Now we were a family. I hoped to have many children and educate them myself. They would have the benefit of my court accomplishments and learn languages, music and dancing. But they would also learn the practical skills of how to run a household and an estate. Robert would train the boys in swordsmanship and I would teach the girls fine needlework. They would grow up to be the finest matches in the county I vowed to myself. I occupied myself in stitching little dresses for Catherine that were as dainty as those worn by the young princesses at court. The time would not be wasted for I would store them carefully for the next child. Robert redoubled his efforts to make the estate productive and spent long hours closeted with the steward. I urged him to rest but he said that he did not begrudge the work since he was his own master. The sole indulgence that he allowed himself was the purchase of a fine young stallion for riding around the estate. When the harvest was finished, he made the most of the late summer weather by going out hunting for game in the woods and fields. He said that it would provide the kitchen with fresh meat, but I knew he enjoyed the thrill of the sport. One day our sons would accompany him on these expeditions and he would teach them how to ride and use a bow. In the meantime, I insisted that he went out with the steward.

"The king would never go out alone on a hunt, Robert," I objected.

"I am not a lord, my dear," he replied. "But if it concerns you then I will take Lambert with me. I shall bring you back a fine buck for our supper."

Nothing pleased him more than dining on his own meat and he was an expert at turning a carcass into joints for the table. He had learned his skills while foraging the land as a soldier during the French wars. As summer turned into autumn, he continued his excursions despite the wet and the mud.

"I shall have all winter to pore over my account books, Margaret. There is still plenty of game to be had and why should I leave it to the kites and the foxes?"

I did not have the heart to spoil his pleasure. But one day a heavy rainstorm fell soon after he set out. I felt sure that he would cut the hunt short and became anxious as the long hours passed. Finally, I heard the welcome sound of horse's hooves clattering over the stone flags of the courtyard. I ordered a flagon of hot wine from the kitchen. But the servant returned immediately looking ashen faced.

"Beg pardon, Madam, but you must come down at once. Master has had a fall from his horse and they have carried him into the hall."

I raced downstairs and found Robert lying insensible upon the table. I shuddered to see his new riding jacket was torn and bloody. "What happened to him?" I asked the steward.

"His stallion slipped in the rain and fell upon him. I fear that he is badly injured, my lady."

I took his hand and it was icy cold. "Take off his wet clothes and cover him with blankets. And make up the fire or he will take a chill."

We waited in anguish for Robert to awaken. Master Lambert rubbed his limbs and put cold compresses on his head. His breathing grew rasping and then it became faint. Finally, it ceased altogether. My beloved husband was dead. The servants took him away to lie in the chapel. I could not believe my terrible misfortune. I sat in the chapel every day weeping for my loss. The chaplain had to take charge of the funeral arrangements and the steward had to see to the management of the house. After his burial I continued to mourn for my husband who had died in so untimely a fashion. I wondered what would become of us. My happy married life had not lasted long and I was left a widow with a child to support. That same year, my dear friend Lady Maria also died. Now I understood what it was like for Mary Carey and Jane Rochford to be left as widows without any income or friends to maintain them.

It was then that my old friend Nan came to my assistance. She urged me not to give in to despair and reminded me that her own mother, the dauntless Lady Maud, had raised three children as a widow. Nan was now Lady Herbert and had returned to court to serve as a lady in waiting to the new queen Anne of Cleves. She advised me to write at once to Master Cromwell and request a post at court. I swallowed my pride and composed a humble plea for his benevolent interest. And in due course I received an answer from my old *bete-noire*.

My dear Lady Margaret,

You cannot conceive how many requests for posts I have received. Naturally, they have all been filled months ago. However, I am pleased to inform you that I have made an exception in your case. As a deserving widow you may return to court to serve as a lady in waiting on the usual terms. I am sure that you will be ready to show your gratitude for this favour.

Lord Cromwell.

I hesitated when I read the letter and took in its implications. Did I really want to return to the dark web of the court? But I had to be practical. This was my best chance for a good future. In fact, it was considered an honour. I engaged a good nurse for my child and I repaired my wardrobe. I had not been away so long that I was behind the fashion. And at least, I would have the cheering company of Nan on my arrival. I wanted to hear more about this foreign bride.

Part 4: In the Household of Queen Anne of Cleves (1539 – 1540)

"A court without ladies is like a garden without flowers"

(King Francis I of France).

Nan was bursting to tell me all the news from the court. Lord Cromwell had persuaded the king to make a foreign marriage alliance. A number of candidates had been considered including Mary of Guise and Christina of Milan. The king's painter, Master Holbein, had been sent to paint their portraits. Finally, the king had chosen the Lady Anne of Cleves. But if he had not, it was rumoured that he might have chosen Lady Anne Basset to be his fourth wife. He had been spending a great deal of time in her company. He had given her a horse to enable her to go riding every day and invited her to go on picnics and on trips to the coast with him. However, since she was the king's cousin, he would have needed a dispensation to marry her. Now that his bride was expected she had tactfully left the court. She had gone to stay with Sir Anthony Denny and his wife at their country house.

"If you are not careful, he will choose you next," warned Nan. I grimaced at the thought. I was glad that the eye of the king had never fallen upon me. I suspected that my Spanish features reminded him too much of his first disastrous marriage. I had noticed that usually King Henry favoured women with fair colouring and agreeable natures. Queen Anne Boleyn had been the exception with her dark looks and tempestuous character, but then she had been exceptional in every way.

"I am not to His Majesty's taste," I objected. "I am too Spanish in my looks. And there will be plenty of pretty young girls at court for him to admire."

"Lord Cromwell is in need of a wife," persisted Nan. "He is a widower, you know. And he is very rich."

I made a mock courtesy. "I thank you, Lady Herbert, for your interest. But I am far too humble a lady to satisfy the ambitions of my Lord Privy Seal. He would look to take a wife of the rank of Lady Mary Howard."

"The duke of Norfolk would have an apoplexy at the very thought," said Nan. "But you are not entirely mistaken. There have been rumours that he is biding his time until he can marry the king's daughter, Lady Mary Tudor."

"What nonsense!" I declared. "She would never agree. He is only a commoner."

"The king has ennobled him. He is now the earl of Essex," said Nan. "And he has appointed him as the Lord Great Chamberlain and made him a member of the Order of the Garter."

"I wonder how the noble lords feel about that?" I remarked.

"My husband says that he is so high in the king's favour that he can do anything."

As Lord Cromwell had said, there had been intense competition for places at court from all the noble families. Most were claimed by highborn ladies including Lady Margaret Douglas, the marquess of Dorset, the duchess of Richmond and Suffolk and the countess of Rutland and Hertford. My good friends Nan and Anne Basset had both obtained places as ladies in waiting. And the duke of Norfolk had secured posts as maids of honour for his nieces Catherine Carey, Mary Norris and Catherine Howard. My role was assured for a foreign princess would need the advice of an experienced lady on the matter of her dress.

On 3rd January 1540 the Lady Anne of Cleves arrived at Greenwich for her official meeting with King Henry. The entire court were assembled upon the fields of Blackheath in their honour. The nobles had expended vast sums upon their wardrobes. But the royal couple outshone them in splendour. The Lady Anne wore a gown of cloth of gold, a round cap set with orient pearls and a necklace of glittering jewels. King Henry was dressed in a coat of purple velvet embroidered with gold and sleeves of cloth of gold set with diamonds and pearls. His cap was

Part 4: In the Household of Queen Anne of Cleves (1539 – 1540)

adorned with fine jewels and he wore a gold collar set with magnificent stones. The king escorted the queen to the palace and welcomed her to her new home and the court rejoiced to see them together. I looked forward to serving her as my mistress for the ladies in waiting reported that she was gracious, dignified and kind. She was also a capable household manager who understood how to provide comfortable rooms, a good table and spotless linen. She would have impressed any nobleman as being a worthy consort.

But the following day Lady Anthony Browne came to speak to Nan in confidence. She had been part of the advance party that had been sent ahead to meet the Lady Anne at Rochester. And she told her that all was not well with the king.

"My dear, this is such a disaster," she whispered discreetly. "The ambassadors reports and the portrait of Lady Anne were most satisfactory. But the lady is not at all what the king expected and he is in a rage about it. He says he does not know whom he should trust. I do not think he wants to proceed with the marriage. And I am not sure that it would be wise to proceed, for they are so ill-suited.

"How are they unsuited, Lady Browne?" asked Nan in astonishment at these revelations.

Lady Browne looked around the chamber cautiously. "As you know, the king's former wives were beautiful and cultured ladies. Perhaps not so much in the case of the late Queen Jane, but Queen Catherine of Aragon and Queen Anne Boleyn were highly educated and accomplished. Their dress was fashionable and their conversation was admired. They could speak foreign languages and play musical instruments. Perhaps the king took it for granted that a foreign princess would have an informed mind and the courtly graces. But it seems that at the court of Cleves they take a different view. It would have been better if the king had made a visit there in person. But it is too late to think of it now."

"How are things different in Cleves, Lady Browne?" enquired Nan as she poured out the wine. "I have never been abroad."

"Well, they do not pride themselves upon the sophistication of their court," explained Lady Browne as she took a cup. "I do not say that there is any fault in her character for she is a kind and amiable lady. But she has no language in common with His Majesty for she can only speak German. She has only been trained in domestic skills and knows nothing of literature, music or dancing. The Admiral tried to teach her how to play card games on the voyage over for she had no knowledge of them. And her style of dress is most unbecoming. As soon as I saw I her I realised that a great mistake had been made. She is not at all the type of lady to suit the king's tastes."

"But surely she can learn to speak English and in time she will become familiar with the ways of the English court," said Nan.

"I am afraid it is too late," said Lady Browne shaking her head. "The king has already taken a bad impression. He says that he does not like her. Their first meeting was a shambles. But indeed, it was not the fault of any of the courtiers."

"What happened, Lady Browne?" asked Nan. It seemed inconceivable that the king should have taken a dislike to his bride after such a long search for a fourth wife.

"Well, you know how much the king likes his disguisings," she sighed. "He thought that it would be a romantic idea to ride out and meet his new bride on New Year's Day. None of us were expecting his arrival. It was a complete surprise to everyone. He came in wearing a cloak and tried to embrace Lady Anne. But she was shocked and turned away from him. He had to go out and return wearing his royal garments. She greeted him politely and he gave her a gift of sable furs. But he was sadly disappointed that his courtly gesture had fallen so flat. He had imagined that she would recognise him as her true love."

"She can hardly be blamed if he chose to make an informal visit," protested Nan. But she knew that if the king had been humiliated then he would never forgive nor forget the matter.

"Someone is going to take the blame for it, my dear," observed Lady Browne perceptively. "My husband told me that the king sent for Master Holbein and berated him for making him think that Lady Anne was a beauty. He even accused him of taking bribes from the duke of Cleves. Master Holbein confessed that Master Cromwell had told him that His Majesty had received pleasing reports of Lady Anne and he would expect to see a portrait that was equally pleasing. The king declared that she is nothing so fair as she has been reported and he is ashamed that men have praised her as they have done. But he can hardly refuse to marry the lady now. It would cause a tremendous scandal!"

On 6th January 1540 King Henry and the Lady Anne were married in the King's Chamber. The king wore a gown of cloth of gold embossed with silver flowers and trimmed with black fur. His coat was of crimson satin embroidered with gold and fastened with diamond buttons and he had a richly jewelled collar around his neck. The Lady Anne entered the chamber dressed in a gown of cloth of gold adorned with a design of flowers made of pearls. Around her neck was a border of fine pearls, gold and diamonds. Her long blonde hair hung loose about her shoulders. On her head she wore a coronet of gold and gems set with sprigs of rosemary. They were married by the archbishop of Canterbury and upon her wedding ring was engraved the motto: "*God Send Me Well to Keep.*" In the evening they changed their dress and celebrated with a banquet and a masque. To all the courtiers it appeared a most impressive occasion. But over the following days I heard rumours that the wedding night had not gone well.

I awaited the inevitable summons from my patron Master Cromwell. When it came, I was shocked by the visible change in his demeanour. Gone was the calm and confident statesman. He was in a pitiable state of distress.

"Lady Margaret, I implore you to speak urgently to your mistress. Advise her how to make herself more agreeable to the king. Otherwise, the consequences will be disastrous for us all!" He mopped his brow with his sleeve leaving a stain on the fine tawny velvet.

I wondered at his lack of composure. "The new queen is most content in her station and her servants find her a very agreeable mistress," I assured him.

"Aye, but the king does not," he snapped. "And it is imperative that she should change his opinion of her while she still can."

"Queen Anne is only too willing to be instructed on all English customs, Master Cromwell," I reported. "She is diligent in practising English conversation and she has asked us to tell her the king's favourite pastimes and dishes so that she may adopt them herself."

"It is not enough, Lady Margaret," he retorted sharply. "The king feels no sense of attraction to the queen. In fact, he has complained that her body has unpleasant smells which spoil their times of intimacy together. You must ensure that the queen takes a bath every day. And send for the perfumer and make sure that the queen uses the scents which the king likes best. Her hair and her clothes must be dressed in the best English style. All these points should have been addressed before the king ever met her. I fear that he has taken a lasting aversion to her."

My heart sank at this litany of disaster. What would become of the queen? "Surely not, Master Cromwell," I protested. "She is a most kind and gracious lady and is already popular with the court." It was true. The royal household were only too pleased to serve a genuine princess rather than a presumptuous maid of honour.

His eyes narrowed and his mouth twitched. "I tell you it is so. And it is the duty of you ladies to smooth the matter with whatever feminine devices are necessary to engage the king's appetite. You must create a sense of romance to feed his fantasy. Attire her alluringly, place scented candles in her rooms and prepare soft speeches for his ears. Or else he will repudiate her. He is already speaking of it."

I could hardly believe it since they were so lately married. Queen Anne of Cleves was as fair as any of his previous wives. It is true that she lacked the sensuous attraction of Queen Anne Boleyn, but so did the demure Queen Catherine and Queen Jane. "We will do all that is possible to make the queen more attractive and pleasing to His Majesty, Master Cromwell."

"You must do more than try, Lady Margaret," he insisted. "You must succeed in transforming her into the lady of his dreams. Nothing else will satisfy him."

Queen Anne was only too willing to change her appearance to please the king. On 11th January 1540 solemn jousts were held in honour of the new queen and the guests from Cleves. On this occasion, Queen Anne dressed herself in the English fashion with a stylish French hood. It was so much more becoming to her that I regretted that she had not changed her dress before. The courtiers were pleased that she had conformed so readily. But it was not enough to satisfy the king. His growing distaste made her even more nervous in his company. She was quite unable to play the part of an alluring damsel. She forgot her carefully prepared phrases, she fumbled at her cards and she often seemed on the verge of tears. The king could not abide the sight of ladies in distress and took his leave of her as soon as he could. He sent her no gifts and made no more visits to her bedchamber.

Any woman would have struggled to overcome such a calamity, but Queen Anne of Cleves had no beguiling charms to win him back. Queen Anne Boleyn would have rallied with an entertainment, a poetry contest or a picnic expedition to pique the king's interest. But Queen Anne of Cleves had no knowledge of such things. And the court being the court, there were those who were ready to take advantage of the king's grievance. The duke of Norfolk and Bishop Gardiner staged a series of elegant supper parties for the king. When he attended there were a number of attractive ladies who were ready to catch his eye. Among them was Lady Catherine Howard who was young, pretty and charming. The dowager duchess of Norfolk boasted that the king fell in love with her at first sight. He delighted in making her extravagant gifts of landed estates, fine clothes and costly jewels to demonstrate his pleasure. One day she received a girdle of diamonds and pearls and the next day she received a brooch in the form of ship set with diamonds, rubies and pearls. Soon the report that the king had a new favourite was all around court. It was the old story of Queen Catherine of Aragon and Lady Anne Boleyn all over again.

We were all at a loss and the burden of the situation fell upon Lord Cromwell. The king had no scruples about repudiating his new wife to satisfy his desire for a maid of honour. Lord Cromwell tried in vain to convince him that he could not insult the duke of Cleves by rejecting his sister. Henry insisted that some pretext could be found. But Lord Cromwell had drawn up the marriage contact himself. There were no reasonable grounds for annulment. The king's frustration over his marriage boded as ill for Lord Cromwell as it had for Cardinal Wolsey. And he was only too well aware of his danger. "What remedy?" demanded the king. But

Part 4: In the Household of Queen Anne of Cleves (1539 – 1540) | 188

there was no remedy. The king grumbled that he was ill served and ill-used. Lord Cromwell's enemies seized the opportunity to take their revenge. The dukes of Norfolk and Suffolk reminded the king that he was an over-ambitious man and not to be trusted. Soon Cromwell was in the Tower for treason and there was no coming back.

On 24th June 1540 Queen Anne was sent to Richmond Palace for the sake of her health. A deputation of noblemen then informed her that her marriage was invalid due to a pre-contract with the Duke of Lorraine. But if she would agree to an annulment then the king would make her a generous settlement and esteem her as his own dear sister. I admired the fortitude of Queen Anne as she endured her shameful rejection. In one stroke she was deprived of her queenship and marriage and any hope of children. But I saluted her wisdom in accepting the king's offer instead of contesting it like Queen Catherine had done. In return for her compliance, she gained the king's friendship and was given her own household to rule as a great noblewoman. Her Flemish ladies went with her, but most of her English servants were summoned back to court. And then it became quite clear to everyone why the king had been so determined to end his marriage. His affections had become engaged by another lady in waiting, the young and fair Catherine Howard who was everything that Queen Anne was not.

Part 5: In the Household of Queen Catherine Howard (1540 – 1542)

"Nobility, however great, is worth nothing if it is not adorned with virtue"

(Anne de Beaujeu, Lessons for my Daughter, 1497).

On the same day that the king married his charming lady-love at Oatlands Palace, he sent Lord Cromwell to the block to pay the penalty for his incompetence. Some lamented his fall, but many others rejoiced. At the demise of my ruthless patron, I felt nothing but relief. He had cast a dark shadow across my life, but at last I was free. I was now an experienced courtier and I was determined to serve the new Queen Catherine honourably. I resolved that I would keep myself free from any further court intrigues. In future I would follow the counsel of Queen Anne de Beaujeu who advised that ladies should have eyes to notice everything and yet see nothing. I would make myself indispensable to my mistress, but I would not seek intimacy. I would be agreeable with the other ladies, but I would not share confidences. If anyone asked me for information, I simply would not know.

The court looked on in fascination as the king presented Queen Catherine as his fifth wife. She was well-born and pretty and he was convinced he was the envy of every man at court. She was barely educated but loved fine clothes and dancing. And she suited the king to perfection. *She has all the charm of her cousin Anne Boleyn, but not her fiery nature,* I thought. King Henry gave his new queen rich presents of fine dresses and costly jewels. They included a splendid necklace with a pointed diamond, eight large rubies and a large pearl pendant, a brooch containing the image of king and queen with a crown of diamonds and a gold tablet with a rose of rubies and their initials set in diamonds. She had never worn such finery and was openly delighted. She had none of the sophistication of Queen Anne Boleyn who had received the king's gifts with pretended indifference. The duke of Norfolk was bursting with pride at the triumph of his house. All the members of the Howard family had gathered at court in the expectation that positions and honours would soon be theirs for the asking. The foreign ambassadors swallowed their astonishment and made their compliments to the second queen of that year. Afterwards, ambassador Chapuys took the opportunity to pay his respects to me.

"It is well known that the late Lord Cromwell offended the king by arranging the unfortunate match to the Lady Anne of Cleves, whom he so disliked," he confided to me. "But I heard that he also displeased the king by meddling too far in matters that pertained to the king. And it was rumoured that he aspired to marry the Lady Mary and make himself the king. Of course, he had some powerful enemies who grudged that a man of low birth should wield such influence in the realm. The same thing happened to Cardinal Wolsey in his time. It is said in the court that the king never made a man but he destroyed him again. He would have done better to have served my master."

King Henry later regretted the loss of Lord Cromwell, for he found no-one capable of replacing him. He accused his councillors of persuading him to put to death the most faithful servant he ever had. If the king had the power to unbehead his victims, I wondered whom else he might restore? Cardinal Wolsey and Thomas More perhaps? But what of Anne Boleyn? Did he ever regret her death? I doubted it, since he now had his son and heir Prince Edward. And he had his new wife whom he praised as a perfect jewel of womanhood. Queen Catherine had become a wealthy woman. She had extensive lands and manors and a wardrobe and a jewel collection to rival any of his former wives.

King Henry was flattered by her childish pleasure at his gifts and showed his favour by sending more every day. Soon she fancied that she was a great lady and became spoiled and demanding. I saw the distaste on the face of Lady Mary at her indecorous behaviour. She was appalled at having such a foolish young girl as her stepmother. She spoke to the queen as little as possible and her ladies made a point of ignoring her. Queen Catherine took offence and complained to the king.

"Your daughter shows me no respect at all," she pouted. "She hardly replies whenever I speak to her. And her ladies are extremely rude. They completely disregard me instead of paying homage to me as the queen."

His forehead creased into a frown. "Which ladies do you mean, my dear?"

"The ones who always stand next to her with disapproving looks and are forever whispering in her ear."

"Well, they will not bother you again," he said decisively. "They are clearly a bad influence upon my daughter and I shall see that they take their disapproving looks away from court."

Lady Mary was grieved by the dismissal of her ladies. But ambassador Chapuys advised her to reconcile her differences with the queen. She gave some presents of jewellery to Queen Catherine and she was placated. The rest of the court hid their feelings and treated the queen with deference. Soon she was as imperious as Queen Anne Boleyn had once been. But in the eyes of King Henry, she was his rose without a thorn. She took as her motto: *"No Other Will Than His."*

Lady Anne Basset had returned from the countryside in time to witness the king's headlong courtship of Catherine Howard. She still had her fine horse in the stables as a sign of the king's regard, but he no longer had any interest in going out riding with her. She knew that he never returned to his former favourites and I wondered how she felt about being set aside.

"You would have made a far better queen than her," I commiserated. It was true. Lady Anne Basset not only had beauty but learning and culture. I wondered how the king could prefer to have the empty-headed Catherine Howard as his wife.

"Any one of us would," she assured me. "All she does is dance and dress up. She is just like a child. But I don't want to be a queen. It is far too dangerous. There is constant scheming in the court and no queen is safe from it. I would be satisfied with a respectable match and the chance to get away from it all."

It did not occur to Queen Catherine to make moral speeches to her ladies in waiting nor to encourage us to sew garments for the poor. She was far more interested in setting the fashion at court. She dressed herself in the most flamboyant French style with gold decoration on her sleeves and jewelled borders around her neck. She surrounded herself with a set of attendants drawn from her family and friends and they spent their days in dancing and merriment. The king was quite besotted with her. The following month he took her on a honeymoon progress. He adopted a new rule of life in the country and his health improved considerably.

The Christmas revels of that year were particularly magnificent. The king was in such a mellow mood that he invited Lady Anne of Cleves to come to court at New Year. She sent the king a gift of two fine horses with trappings of purple velvet. On her arrival at Hampton Court, she fell to her knees before the queen in homage. When the king entered, he embraced her and kissed her. They sat down and dined and then they conversed together. They all looked as composed as if there had never been any previous relationship between them. The king gave Queen Catherine a present of a ring and two spaniels which she promptly gave to Lady Anne. Then the queen and Lady Anne spent the evening dancing together like the greatest of friends.

I admired the fortitude of Lady Anne and wondered what she was thinking. Was she remembering the previous New Year and wishing that things had gone differently? Or had she made peace with the past? She had conquered her feelings to the extent of paying her respects to her usurper. And yet she was of far nobler birth than Catherine Howard. It was something which Queen Catherine of Aragon would never have contemplated. *Which one of them was right?* I wondered to myself. They had both lost their rightful position as queen and been forced into exile. But Queen Catherine of Aragon had fought for her rights and died in poverty whereas Lady Anne of Cleves had accepted the king's will and enjoyed a comfortable life. Had Queen Catherine's sense of justice compensated for the years of suffering she endured? But perhaps as a princess of Spain she felt she had no other choice. And the battle was not only for herself but for her daughter. *This king has a great deal for which to answer*, I thought. *Although he can be generous, it is the generosity of a tyrant.*

In February 1541 King Henry fell so ill from the ulcer on his leg that his face turned black. His doctors were forced to lance the swelling which caused him great pain. He gradually recovered but became ill-humoured with everyone. He refused to attend court entertainments or listen to music, but remained shut away in his apartments. Not even the queen was allowed to see him. Many members of his household were sent home and those who remained had nothing to do. The trials of our life in service were compounded by the fact that Nan had family troubles at this time.

"My brother William has had such misfortune in his married life," she confided to me. "My mother spent all that was left of our family fortune to make a match for him with Anne Bourchier. She was one of the wealthiest heiresses in England. But she has proved altogether unworthy of him. She has run away to be with her lover and says she will live as she pleases. Poor William does not deserve such treatment. He is a fine man and has worked so hard to restore our family's honour. And now his wife has brought disgrace upon us all. I do not know how we will be able to hold our heads up."

"Perhaps it will not be known if she lives in the country, Nan."

"William says that he must get an annulment on the grounds of her adultery. If he does not then her illegitimate children will become his heirs. There is no hope of hushing it up. I think her guardians were much to blame. She was brought up to take pride in her wealth but her education was badly neglected. When she came to court, she was dismayed to find that she lacked the culture and learning of a great lady. So she fled back to the countryside and said that she preferred to live there. It caused a breach in her marriage for William had a post at court. I wish that you could have married my brother. He would have suited you so well for he loves poetry and music."

The unfortunate Sir William did not seem too distressed by his wife's desertion. He consoled himself by a romance with Lady Dorothy Bray who was a maid of honour to Queen Catherine. He obtained a legal separation from his wife and married Lady Elizabeth Brooke. His former wife was left languishing in poverty at the manor of Little Wakering. Her Bourchier titles and estates were awarded to her former husband who became the earl of Essex. She could have been one of the proud ladies of the court but instead she was living an obscure life with the man for whom she had given up everything. I wondered if she was satisfied with the life of her choice.

Part 5: In the Household of Queen Catherine Howard (1540 – 1542)

By the summer of 1541, the king had recovered his health and made plans for a great progress to the North. But before he left, he took the precaution of executing several of the prisoners of royal blood in the Tower of London. This included the elderly Lady Margaret Pole. She had been arrested with her entire family on suspicion of treason. She protested that she was no traitor and had committed no crime. However, the king would tolerate no rivals around his young son. The only surviving members of the Plantagenet line were two young boys named Henry Pole and Edward Courtenay. Not even King Henry was ruthless enough to put innocent children to death, but they were kept in the confines of the Tower.

As fortune would have it, I was not one of the ladies chosen to accompany Queen Catherine on progress. She preferred to be served by her lively young friends with whom she liked to dance and feast after the king had retired to bed. I was relieved to be left behind at the palace when the great retinue departed from Greenwich at the end of June. The weather was particularly bad that summer and the roads were washed out so the carts and baggage could not proceed without great difficulty. It seemed that I had escaped the trials of a long and unpleasant journey to Lincoln, Pontefract and York. I reflected that with the passing of Lord Cromwell I was now without a patron. In the future I would have to rely on my wits to survive at court. It was a cause for anxiety since competition for places at court was always intense. Queen Catherine had not only appointed many of her Howard relatives to attend her, but she had also found posts for many of her friends from the household of the Dowager Duchess of Norfolk. I regretted that the Lady Anne of Cleves had not found favour with the king for she the reputation of being a fine mistress.

At the end of October, the king and queen returned to Hampton Court Palace. King Henry was so contented that he ordered a service of thanksgiving for his marriage to be held in the Chapel Royal. But the next day, his happiness was shattered. Archbishop Cranmer reported that allegations had been made about the past life of the queen. The king was convinced it was a case of slander, but told the archbishop to enquire into the matter. Queen Catherine was confined to her apartments at Hampton Court until her name was cleared. The king's secretaries, Thomas Wriothesley and Ralph Sadler, led the investigation. All the queen's ladies were questioned, but I had nothing to tell the officials. They reminded me of Lord

Cromwell and his sly methods of getting the answers he wanted.

"You mean to tell us that you saw nothing amiss? How can that be possible, Lady Margaret?" asked Wriothesley with a sneer on his face. I remembered when he was just a gangly young clerk in the service of Lord Cromwell.

"Do you mean to question my loyalty to the king? I have served all five of his wives without reproach," I replied calmly. I was determined not to let him unnerve me.

"All the other ladies have confessed their suspicions of the queen. How is that you had none?" he persisted. Sadler looked bored and fidgeted with his dagger. *I bet he wishes he was out hunting in the forest instead of cross-examining ladies in waiting*, I thought.

"I do not deal in gossip or scandalmongering," I asserted. "And I am not engaged to spy upon the queen but to serve her faithfully. I attend to my duties with the greatest diligence and there has never been any complaint about my service. I am most grieved to hear these accusations about the queen."

"You still maintain that you saw and heard nothing in the course of your duties? The queen has been accused of treason. Her accomplices will share her fate. We advise you to think again, Lady Margaret. Think most carefully." The miserable creature leered at my discomfort. *He is enjoying this role*, I thought.

"I assure you gentlemen that I saw and heard no treason against the king," I firmly declared. "If I had, then I would have reported it at once."

He picked up his quill pen and looked at me in exasperation. "And you heard no rumours concerning the queen's virtue or her past life?"

"I know nothing of the queen's past life other than she was raised in the household of the Howards of Norfolk. I suggest that you take your enquiries there."

He twisted the quill between his fingers. "Oh, we will, Lady Margaret. And if it comes to light that you had any knowledge or involvement in the queen's disgrace then you will suffer the extreme penalty. Your only hope of mercy is to confess everything to us now."

"I can only repeat that I have nothing to confess," I insisted.

"Then you have wilfully cast away your only chance of salvation," he taunted me. "All those who concealed the queen's treasonable behaviour will find themselves in the Tower. And they will have only themselves to blame for whatever happens to them there."

"All traitors deserve to be sent to the Tower," I declared. "I am innocent of any guilt in regard to the queen and I am a true servant to His Majesty."

"That we will test, Lady Margaret. You may leave us." He threw down his quill in disgust.

I rose and left the interview as a model of outraged dignity. But inwardly I was terrified. I collapsed upon my bed with trembling limbs and felt too sickened to eat. Now I could only wait in silence to discover my fate. But nobody denounced me and I was glad of my resolution to remain clear of intrigues. At first the enquiries had focussed upon the past life of the queen. Her former companions Mary Hall and Joan Bulmer revealed her misconduct with Henry Manox and Francis Dereham in the household of the Dowager Duchess. It was said that the queen's marriage would be annulled for unchastity. But then matters took a more serious turn. Dereham testified that he had been succeeded in the queen's affections by Thomas Culpeper. He was the king's favourite male courtier. The queen's maids Katherine Tylney and Margaret Morton admitted that on the progress Queen Catherine had arranged secret meetings with Culpeper in her stool chamber. The queen now stood accused of committing adultery. When these rumours began to spread throughout the court, I thanked my stars that I had not been on the progress. Whatever had taken place there, I could not be blamed for it. Queen Catherine's apartments were searched and her papers were confiscated. Among them was found a letter addressed to Thomas Culpeper.

> *"Master Culpeper, I heartily recommend me unto you. It makes my heart die to think what fortune I have that I cannot always be in your company. My trust is always in you that you will be as you have promised me, praying you that you will come when my Lady Rochford is here for then I shall be best at leisure to be at your commandment. Yours as long as life endures, Catherine."*

This foolish letter which sealed her fate – and that of the unfortunate Lady Rochford. It proved that she despised her marriage and that Lady Rochford had assisted her misconduct. When the evidence was disclosed to the king he broke down and called for a sword to slay the queen. Then he lamented his misfortune in meeting with such ill-conditioned wives. The distraught king immediately left Hampton Court for Whitehall Palace.

I heard that Lady Rochford became hysterical in her interviews. She insisted that she had in no way encouraged the misconduct of the queen. But she did not dare to speak against her and she could not afford to give up her post and leave court. She complained that she was being unfairly blamed by the two guilty parties. She was no accomplice but only an innocent bystander. "But you knew, Lady Rochford. You knew, did you not?" She could not deny it. That was enough to condemn her for treason along with the queen.

Thomas Wriothesley summoned the queen's household to a meeting in the Presence Chamber. He announced that our mistress had forfeited her honour and no longer bore the title of Queen of England. Henceforth, she would be known as Lady Catherine Howard. Consequently, every member of her household was discharged. The only exception was Lady Anne Basset as the king had promised to find her a match. The queen's attendants and servants were indignant and sorrowful at this great disaster. They had expected to spend their careers in the service of the young queen. Nan and I said nothing as we were accustomed to the sudden reversals of fortune at the court. However, a further surprise awaited us both. Wriothesley informed us that we had been selected to accompany Lady Catherine Howard to Syon Abbey the following day. She was permitted to have a few attendants in her confinement. But they were not to include her relatives nor any of the ladies who had accompanied her on the ill-fated summer progress. We were instructed to bring a wardrobe of six dresses and hoods for her, but they were not to be too fine. In fact, he rather thought that black would be the best colour.

Lady Catherine did not have the fortitude of her cousin Anne Boleyn. She cried all the way to Syon Abbey. Nan did her best to comfort her. "Do not grieve, Lady Catherine. Syon Abbey is a pleasant place to stay. You will be peaceful there."

"Nay, it is a place of penance. The king shut up his niece there and now he is doing the same to me. What if he never lets me out again?"

It was true. Lady Margaret Douglas had engaged in a secret romance with the queen's brother, Charles Howard. The king had sent her to Syon Abbey until she had learned her duty. She had been confined there for a year. I wished that we had not been chosen for this service. When we arrived at Syon Abbey, Lady Catherine was assigned three chambers to live in. They were adequately furnished but the wall-hangings were poor quality. It reminded me of the dormitory of the maids of honour.

Lady Catherine lamented her dismal situation. "I always thought it was too good to be true. I never looked to be queen or imagined that I was worthy. But how could I refuse the honour? I don't know why the other girls denounced me. I was good to them and let them have a place at court. I wish I had never done so. They are jealous cats. They have ruined everything!"

At other times she would be more hopeful. "I am sure that my uncle Norfolk will speak for me for he told me that I was his favourite niece. And the king loves me too much to be parted from me for long. I am sure he is missing me. If only they would let me see him then I know that he would forgive me." Even now, she would not admit her guilt. But at night we heard her crying for her beloved Thomas.

Archbishop Cranmer came to visit to hear her confession looking unusually stern. But when he emerged from the interview he appeared visibly shaken. "Good ladies, go and give some comfort to your mistress. I found her in such lamentation and heaviness that it would have pitied any man's heart to have looked upon her."

Lady Catherine was weeping bitterly. "I told my lord archbishop that the king was so good and kind to me that it grieves me to remember it. I was so anxious to be taken into his favour that I did not consider how wrong it was for me to conceal my former faults. Do you think that the archbishop will persuade the king to forgive me?"

It was hard to know how to comfort her. When we were alone in our chamber, we discussed her likely fate together. It was extremely dangerous to talk about such matters but we were bursting to share our thoughts.

"I feel sorry for her," I confided to Nan. "She had no parents to protect her and she was only a pawn to her relatives."

"Yes, she was suddenly raised from obscurity to eminence and it all fell apart," she said. "Queen Jane managed to gain the respect of the court with her modest dignity, but Catherine was just a foolish child. Only the king's regard upheld her."

"Queen Jane was renowned for her virtue. How could Catherine think that her past would not come to light?" I wondered.

"I don't think she dared to admit it," observed Nan. "Her family would have cast her off. She took the chance but her past caught up with her in the end."

"But if there has been no misconduct since the marriage then she cannot die for what was done before," I insisted.

"I wouldn't be so sure," said Nan. "Queen Anne was executed without any proof at all."

"That was different," I protested. "The king was desperate to end the marriage and he wanted an excuse."

"He will want to end this marriage too. She has brought shame upon him and he will not forgive it."

"He may annul the marriage for the sake of his honour, but I cannot believe he will execute her. It isn't a crime for an unmarried girl to take a lover. It is only fornication, not adultery."

"It won't make any difference in his eyes," said Nan soberly. "She is no longer the pure young girl he adored. She is a wicked deceiver and he will punish her for betraying him."

"Surely, he won't want to make a scandal," I declared. "Do you think there is any chance of a pardon? He could decide to annul the marriage and send her away."

Nan shook her head. "It will be the same as with Queen Anne. She was accused of adultery and the king refused to see her. She was taken to the Tower and executed. And the accused men died with her. Her household was dismissed and her family disgraced. He is a vengeful king and it touches his pride."

Nan was proved right in her predictions. The only difference from the downfall of Queen Anne was that this time one of her ladies was charged. It could have been myself or Nan if we had been singled out for the queen's favour. Thomas Culpeper and Francis Dereham were arrested for high treason and taken to the Tower. On 10th December 1541 they were both executed at Tyburn. Several members of the Howard family were sent to Tower as a sign of the king's displeasure. Parliament made it a capital offense for a queen consort to commit adultery and for an unchaste woman to marry the king. Lady Catherine Howard was doomed. She was charged with leading an "abominable, base, carnal, voluptuous and vicious life like a common harlot."

On 10th February 1542, a party of armed guards arrived at Syon Abbey to escort Lady Catherine to the Tower of London. As soon as she heard their commission, she knew it was the end of her. She became hysterical and had to be dragged to the waiting barge. On her journey to the Tower she passed under London Bridge, where the rotting heads of Thomas Culpeper and Francis Dereham were still on display. In her apartments at the Tower, Lady Catherine resigned herself to her fate. She asked for a block to be brought to her chamber so that she could practice how to lay her head upon it. Three days later she was executed. Her last words were, "I die a queen, but I would rather have died the wife of Culpeper." Lady Jane Rochford was executed afterwards as her accomplice. It was said that she had lost her reason under the strain of repeated interrogations, but there was no mercy for her. They were both buried in the chapel of St Peter ad Vincula.

When Nan and I returned to court, we were tasked with the duties of caring for the late queen's valuables. Nan was entrusted with the queen's jewels and I took charge of her wardrobe. There were scarcely any ladies to be seen at the court. Only Lady Anne Basset remained from the late queen's household. She was greatly relieved to see us again. "The king is determined that he will only have virtuous ladies serving in his court in the future," she told us. I had come out of the affair blameless and so I was invited to remain and serve the king's daughter, Lady Mary, in the absence of a queen.

Later that year, Lady Anne Basset came to me in great distress. "My sister Catherine has been arrested and has been sent to the Tower! What shall I do?"

"What has happened?" I asked.

"You must promise not to tell anyone," insisted Anne.

"I won't say a word," I promised.

"Well, my sister serves the Lady Anne of Cleves. She is a good mistress. And when the late queen Catherine was condemned one of the ladies said to her, "Is God working his own work to make the Lady Anne of Cleves queen again?" And then my sister said, "What a man is the king! How many wives will he have?" But somebody overheard their conversation and reported them. And they were both arrested and taken to the Tower. What will become of them?"

My heart plummeted. It was a reminder of how vulnerable those in royal service were. There were spies everywhere and people could be denounced at any time. I was sure than many courtiers had talked about what might happen next. Her sister had simply been unfortunate.

"Do you think my sister will be executed? Should I go and plead to the king for her?" asked Anne.

"Nobody can see the king at the moment. He has shut himself away from everyone. I am sure that your sister won't be executed. They are just making an example of her and then they will let her go."

My stepfather, Lord Lisle, was sent to the Tower," she confided. "He was the governor of Calais and he was accused of plotting to betray the town to the French. He was completely innocent but he was imprisoned and we feared that he would be executed for treason. In the end, the king decided to release him. But the shock was so great that he died on the spot. My poor mother has not been the same since. She says that we are an unlucky family and she does not know what will become of us. I cannot imagine what this news will do to her."

"Perhaps you could write a petition to the king," I suggested. "The Privy Council read all the petitions now and they will make a recommendation to the king. They will think this is a small matter."

And so Lady Anne Basset wrote a petition and in due course her sister was released and resumed her service. It turned out that the Lady Anne of Cleves did cherish hopes that the king might return to her after the disappointment of Catherine Howard. Her brother, the duke of Cleves, even sent a proposal to the king. But the king firmly declined the suggestion. Soon the question of Catherine Basset was on everyone's lips. Would the king marry again and who would it be?

Part 6: In the Household of Queen Catherine Parr (1543-1547)

"Gentlemen, I desire company, but I have had more than enough of taking young wives, and I am now resolved to marry a widow"

(*The Spanish Chronicle*).

In January 1543 Nan told me that her sister Catherine was coming to court for a visit. Her elderly husband, Lord Latimer, had been ill for a long time and she had been nursing him herself. But she was so exhausted that Nan had told her to hand over her responsibilities to the servants and come to see her brother and sister at court. Finally, she had agreed.

When Lady Latimer arrived at court, I could see the resemblance to her sister Nan at once. She was a lively and elegant woman with red-gold hair and hazel eyes. She wore fashionable clothes and enjoyed the pastimes of dancing, music and good conversation. She was also a scholar who read Petrarch and Erasmus for pleasure. I was certain that Lady Latimer would flourish at court just like her capable mother Maud. After the death of her husband, she joined the household of Lady Mary. Nan was pleased to have the company of her sister at court.

"Will she marry again, do you think?" I asked her.

"Yes, I hope that she will when she has finished her time of mourning," said Nan. "After all, she is only thirty and looks younger than her age."

Soon, the widowed Lady Latimer had a suitor. She was seen dancing, walking and conversing with Sir Thomas Seymour. And it was evident that she welcomed his attentions. Sir Thomas was considered one of the most eligible men at the court and Lady Latimer was a wealthy widow. It seemed an ideal match in the eyes of the court. However, Sir Thomas was not the only man to have noticed the superior qualities of Lady Latimer. Nan came to find me one day in consternation.

"Margaret, the king has sent my sister Catherine a gift of pleats and sleeves."

"Well, why should he not show her a sign of favour?" I said as I stitched a loose spangle onto a hood more securely. It was set with a pearl so I could not afford to lose it.

"I do not think it is just a token gift," she fretted. "He has started visiting his daughter, Lady Mary, more often. And every time he visits, he singles out Catherine for attention. He invites her to come and sit next to him for conversation or a game of cards. The other ladies are beginning to talk."

It was unlike Nan to be uneasy over a trifle. She was always so level headed. I set my sewing aside and gave her my complete attention. "What are they saying?"

She hesitated a moment before answering. "That the king is looking for a sixth wife. And he is seriously considering Catherine for the role."

I could hardly believe it. It was such a change from his previous wife. "What does she think?"

"She thinks it would be better to be the king's mistress than his wife," she confided. "Besides, Catherine has had two arranged marriages already and this time she is resolved to choose her own husband."

However, Lady Latimer was not given the opportunity to marry where she pleased. The king appointed Thomas Seymour as the ambassador to the court of the Netherlands. He was ordered to leave immediately. Lady Latimer was deeply grieved at the news.

"I am sure that the king has sent him away because he will not brook a rival," she told Nan. "He wanted to defy him and remain in England but I persuaded him to accept the post. I could not bear any harm to come to him."

"And what about you?" said Nan. "What will you do when he asks you to marry him?"

"I do not know," she admitted. "I have thought about it a great deal. It may be that this is a chance to do God's work by inclining the king towards Protestantism."

"Don't agree to it, Catherine," Nan warned her. "You know how the king treats his wives."

"I do not think that I can refuse," she replied. "He will consider it a great honour and if I turn it down then he is bound take offense."

"Well, if you do become the queen then I hope that you will make me your chief lady-in-waiting."

"Of course I will, Nan. You will be right beside me."

Shortly afterwards, the king sent for her. He was splendidly dressed in a crimson doublet and hose embroidered with gold thread and a gown of russet velvet lined with lynx fur and looking very affable. She sensed that he intended to make his proposal.

"Lady Latimer, I am pleased that you have joined my daughter's household. She could have no better example of a virtuous and accomplished lady than yourself," he complimented her.

"Your Majesty is most gracious to say so," she responded. "It is my pleasure to serve the Lady Mary."

"Lady Latimer, I esteem you above all the other ladies at my court, he assured her. "I wish you to be my wife." He looked at her expectantly.

Catherine knew what was expected of her. She fell to her knees and replied, "Your Majesty is my master, I have but to obey you."

Their wedding took place in the Queen's Closet at Hampton Court on 12th July 1543. Bishop Stephen Gardiner, the Bishop of Winchester, presided at the ceremony. Queen Catherine wore a robe of cloth of gold with a train that was two yards long. The sleeves were lined with crimson satin and trimmed with crimson velvet. She had a jewelled head-dress and wore a gold cross around her neck. The court considered that the king had made a sensible choice this time. It was said that the Lady Anne of Cleves was bitterly disappointed and complained that Queen Catherine was less beautiful than herself. She had hoped that the disgrace of Catherine Howard would encourage Henry to reconsider her qualities as a wife. She had always been praised for her queenly bearing and modesty. And now she was entirely English in her dress and customs. But the king showed no inclination to regard her in any other way than his dearest sister.

Queen Catherine was determined to show herself worthy of the position of queen. She dressed the part in a regal gown of scarlet damask banded with cloth of gold, a necklace with a jewelled cross and a gold girdle with large pendants. She provided herself with a wardrobe of French gowns in her favourite colours of crimson, black and violet which set off her auburn hair and pale complexion to advantage. And she ordered shoes trimmed with gold and fine perfumes of lavender and rose. The king gave her the magnificent collection of queen's jewels to wear and gifts of songbirds for her apartments. She wrote to tell her brother William that being the king's wife was the greatest comfort that could happen to her. The foreign ambassadors reported that Queen Catherine was quieter than any of the young wives the king had, and as she knew more of the world, she always got along pleasantly with the king and had no caprices. She persuaded the king to allow all three of his children to attend the court. She established close relationships with them and selected the best tutors for Prince Edward and Lady Elizabeth. Her serene common sense was just what was needed to set the king and the court at ease again.

Only Nan and I knew of her constant endeavour to keep the king contented. His temper had grown increasingly uncertain with age and it took all of her resolve to maintain her composure both in public and in private. She admitted that sometimes she feared that he would tire of her as he had done of his previous wives.

"He likes you just as well as Queen Jane," Nan assured her. "So do not worry."

"But they were not married long enough for his attention to wander elsewhere," she observed. "And she gave him a son which I am not likely to do."

"You are still young enough, sister," said Nan. "And the king is not too old. Is he?"

Her cheeks flushed pink and she looked down at her hands. "I cannot speak of that, Nan, not even to you. The king is satisfied with me for now. But who knows if he will always be so? If it were not for the consolation of my faith, I do not think that I could sustain my peace of mind."

Nan's rise to the position of chief lady in waiting made her one of the success stories of court. Her family had made steady progress until the sudden good fortune of her sister's marriage to the king. Then every mark of favour was shown to them just as it had been to the Boleyn's, the Seymour's and the Howard's before them. Her brother William Parr and her brother-in-law William Herbert were granted titles, manors, grants of land. As a close friend of Nan, I was drawn into the inner circle of ladies around the queen. But my state could not have been more different from the affluent Parrs. I was a humble widow like Mary Boleyn and Jane Rochford. I was neither young enough nor wealthy enough to expect to marry again. And I had a daughter to support.

Fortunately, Nan was a steadfast friend. She proposed that my daughter Catherine should join her household and be educated together with her children. Since the Parr family were renowned for educating their daughters, I accepted her offer with alacrity. The king showered Queen Catherine with presents and she shared this abundance with her sister. I would often be called to Nan's chamber to view the latest array of gifts. And Nan would persuade me to accept bolts of silk, fashionable hoods and painted fans. I used this finery to refurbish my wardrobe so that I could appear at court in the proper style of a lady in waiting.

Queen Catherine appointed several members of her close friends and family to her household including Nan, Elizabeth Tyrwhitt, Maud Lane and Mary Parr. Her circle of ladies included many who shared her interest in the New Learning including Mary Howard, the duchess of Richmond and Somerset; Catherine Willoughby, the duchess of Suffolk; Anne Seymour, the Countess of Hertford; Elizabeth Brooke and Jane Champernowne. They spent much of their time in theological discussion and study. They set a fashion of dressing themselves in gowns of black velvet lined with black sarcenet to present a virtuous appearance. I was glad to have the opportunity to know Catherine Willoughby at last. She shared the beauty and fearless spirit of her mother, Lady Maria de Eresby. But unlike her, she was a convinced Protestant. She preferred her life at court to life at home with her husband, the duke of Suffolk.

"He is an old man and we have nothing in common," she declared forthrightly. "He lives for sports and warfare which bore me to death. And I like to study the New Learning which he detests. We never should have married but he thought my youth and wealth were a good match for his high rank. I was fourteen and he was forty-nine. Such unequal matches should not be made but since I was his ward, I had no choice. But now that I am older and wiser, I said that he should go his way and I would go mine. I have given him two sons so he can have no complaint."

I was astonished to find a young wife to be so outspoken. "But doesn't the duke object to living separately?"

"Not at all," she said dispassionately. "He married me for my fortune, so he is quite content. And we both lead busy lives in service to the king and queen. He is the king's favourite courtier so he is very much in demand. Of course, we always appear together at great state occasions. He is the father of my sons so naturally it is important for us to remain on good terms. But I have no wish to hang upon his sleeve. He has a mistress to keep him company, but he has agreed not to bring her to court."

It seemed a sad state of affairs for such a beautiful young woman. But Catherine Willoughby was not the sort to feel sorry for herself. She had the strength and wisdom of her mother to rise above misfortune. She viewed life at court as an amusing game and was noted for her witty tongue. She was high in favour with both the king and queen and a popular member of the court. When the duke of Suffolk died in 1545, the king paid the costs of his funeral as a tribute to their long friendship. Catherine was left as a wealthy young widow of twenty-six. But she disdained to be anyone's matrimonial prize for a second time. Instead, she defied public opinion to marry her gentleman usher Richard Bertie. He managed her households and estates and they had two children together. I admired her determination to live her own life according to her own values. She was another Anne Bourchier, but she was nobody's fool and had made the most of her situation.

My life in service to the sixth wife of the king was happier than it had been since I had first come to court. Only one thing caused me disquiet. Both Queen Catherine and her sister Nan were ardent followers of the Reformed faith. The queen encouraged her ladies to read the Bible in English and discuss its meaning. Soon the whole court knew about the queen's reading group. And that meant that the king knew too. I thought that parading our interest in theology in the queen's own apartments was a reckless pursuit. There were sure to be informers who would report on who was present and what was said. Many of the ladies were of high rank and had no concern for such things. But I knew better and feared for the queen and for us all. One night I went secretly to Nan's room to express my foreboding.

"I am becoming uneasy about these gatherings, Nan," I told her. "The ladies are sharing forbidden books with each other. It could lead to a charge of heresy."

Nan dismissed my fears. "The times are more open now. These books are circulating throughout the whole court and everyone knows it. My sister is the queen. Who would presume to tell her what she can and cannot read?"

"There is Bishop Gardiner for one," I pointed out. "He is openly against any Protestant reform. And he is very influential with the king. For women even to read the English Bible is contentious. But she makes no secret of encouraging it."

"Queen Anne Boleyn did the same thing with her ladies," said Nan defensively.

"Yes, and you know what happened to her."

She shuddered at the thought. "I know that you are not as fervent in your faith as the rest of us. My sister stands high in the king's favour. He approves of her piety."

"I am just as sincere as you, Nan," I asserted. "But I prefer the ways of the old faith and I think the king does too. You know that a law has been passed which forbids women and serving men from reading the Bible in English."

"The law was amended to allow women of good birth to read it in private," she argued.

"But the queen is not reading it privately," I persisted. "She is reading it with her ladies and discussing it with them. And she is inviting reformers to come and preach evangelical sermons."

"It is only in her private apartments. It is not being done in public."

"If the court knows about it then it is not a private matter. People are talking about it. They are starting to take sides."

"There is always gossip in the court," said Nan, quite unconcerned. "And there are always factions. There is no scandal surrounding my sister's name as there was with Queen Anne and Queen Catherine Howard."

I wondered how to convince her of the peril. "What the queen says and does sets an example. She is far too open in her views and it will do her no good. You must talk to her and advise her to be more circumspect. It would be safer to provide her ladies with prayer books rather than Bibles. And it would be wiser to invite conservative chaplains to preach in her closet. It would reassure the Catholic faction that the queen is not opposed to them."

But Nan would not be persuaded. "I know my sister and she would never agree. She would think it hypocritical for one thing. And for another she feels it is her bounden duty as the queen to promote the gospel. She is certain that she can convince the king that the church should adopt the Reformed faith."

I remembered when Queen Jane had tried to sway the king's opinion. "No-one convinces the king. He is sure that he is divinely guided and that his opinion is always right. And he decides what his people should believe. She must take care not to offend him."

"Why should he take offense if his wife discusses the scriptures with her ladies?" she protested. "He should commend her for her virtue."

"It all depends on how it is perceived," I explained. "It could be seen as heresy."

Nan refused to acknowledge it. "I don't believe it. No-one would dare to make accusations about the queen. The king would never permit it."

As it happened, she was wrong. She had never been the unwilling pupil of Cromwell and she did not see the danger signs. My suspicions were confirmed when I received a summons to meet with Bishop Gardiner.

"Come in, Lady Margaret," he said, regarding me benignly. "I wish for your assistance as a lady-in-waiting to the queen. It has been reported to me that you are a faithful Catholic. You are not one of the corrupted Lutherans who surround Her Majesty."

His cold eyes and thin lips belied his benevolent air. I sensed the danger and I knew what was coming next. *Will this never end?* I wondered.

"I wish to know about the Reformist talk in the queen's apartments," he continued smoothly. "In particular, what books are being read and discussed, who comes to preach and what errors they proclaim and which ladies are heretical in their opinions and what they say to the queen. And what the queen is saying to them."

I felt sick at heart to hear his words. And then I felt a burning anger. First Queen Anne Boleyn, then Queen Catherine Howard and now Queen Catherine Parr. I took a deep breath and composed myself. This was the court. What else did I expect?

"Your Grace, I only attend to my duties," I assured him. "I can tell you nothing about other people's conversations and opinions."

He was displeased and his eyebrows drew together sharply. "Come, come, Lady Margaret. Do not trifle with me. This is the Lord's work and it is your duty to assist me."

"I regret that I know nothing of these matters, your Grace," I replied tonelessly.

"I am the chief advisor to the king, Lady Margaret" he said with quiet menace. "I caution you not to refuse me or I will have you sent from court." I saw the flash of anger in his eyes and felt the power of his will exerting itself against me.

He is another Cromwell, I thought. But I did not quail. "I do not listen to gossip, your Grace. So I regret that I would be of no use to you." I curtsied and fled from the room leaving him fuming. I waited for my letter of dismissal to come from the king. But none came. It was all a bluff on his part and faced with such a determined display of ignorance, he could not compel me to serve his designs. *Why does the king keep such creatures about him?* But I knew why. It was in order to keep his own hands from getting dirty. *Lady Maria was right*, I reflected. I only needed to stand firm to resist the wiles of these devious men. It seemed to me that life at court was becoming ever more precarious. People were being reported and imprisoned for heresy on the basis of mere suspicion. I was glad of my resolution to avoid all intrigue. I warned Nan that Bishop Gardiner was gathering information about the queen but she still refused to take the situation seriously. She was convinced that her family enjoyed the complete protection and favour of the king. Katherine Willoughby went further and named her pet spaniel Gardiner in mockery of the Bishop of Winchester. As the duchess of Suffolk, she did not feel in any awe of him.

The next sign of danger came with the arrest of Mistress Anne Askew. The news of her arrest struck the company like a thunderbolt. She had visited the queen at court and discussed her Reformist beliefs with her circle of ladies. When we gathered in the queen's apartments that day it was not to discuss the Bible but to consider what might be done for her. They were indignant that a gentlewoman should be accused of heresy. But they did not realise that it was the first attempt to implicate and destroy the queen. She was imprisoned in the Tower and questioned to reveal her associates.

"I shall appeal to the king to release her," said Queen Catherine resolutely. She has done nothing wrong. It is outrageous to arrest her."

"These men care nothing for that," I said. "They have only arrested her as a pretext for attacking you. If you try to intervene, they will denounce you. It is a trap."

"But we must do something! What can we do?" asked the queen.

"We can only pray for her and hope that they do not force her to testify against you," said Nan.

"Anne would never betray us. She is faithful and courageous. She would rather die first."

"But they have taken her to the Tower. And who knows what they might do to make her speak."

"They would not dare to use force. She is a gentlewoman and it is against the king's laws to torture a woman. They will question her and then they will let her go," insisted the queen.

"I hope you are right. I never dreamt that they would go this far," said Lady Anne Seymour.

"I fear this is part of a deadly plot," said Nan. "We must protect ourselves. We must remove all the books and papers from our apartments and send them into safekeeping. Our Bibles too. And we must give up our prayer meetings until this affair has blown over. There must be no grounds for any suspicion of the queen."

"They surely would not dare to search the queen's own apartments!" said Lady Anne Seymour indignantly.

"It has been done before," I reminded them. "When Queen Catherine Howard was investigated, they searched her rooms, they read her letters and they interrogated her ladies and her servants. If they force a confession from Mistress Askew then they will come here looking for evidence. I fear that we should prepare ourselves for the worst."

"You are right," said Queen Catherine. "These are dangerous and determined men. And we must take precautions. We should pack our books and papers into locked chests without delay. And then we must send them far from here with a trusted servant. The safest place is the house of my uncle William Parr. He lives far enough from court not to be troubled."

"And what about Mistress Askew? We must help her in some way. We cannot forsake her," declared Nan.

"Leave that to me," said Lady Anne Seymour decisively. "I shall send my maid Joan to the Tower with money for her needs. She will say that it is from an anonymous friend. She will know that she has not been forgotten."

"It is an excellent idea, Lady Anne," said Queen Catherine. "Let it be done. I hope that this is a false alarm. But I fear that our enemies are plotting our downfall. They must not succeed."

Nan personally supervised the packing of the chests and the loading of the cart. She sent a trusted family servant to her uncle's house in the dead of night. He was to tell him to hide the chests in his attic and keep the entire matter secret. Her husband, Lord Herbert, wanted her to leave court but she refused to abandon the queen. Lady Anne Seymour sent her maid with a gift of eight shillings to the Constable of the Tower. She said that it was alms from a friend of Mistress Anne Askew. The maid was recognised. However, the Catholic faction were not prepared to attack the powerful Seymour family.

We waited anxiously for news. When it came it shocked us all. Mistress Anne Askew had been put on the rack by Chancellor Wriothesley and Sir Richard Rich. Sir Anthony Kingston, the Constable of the Tower, had objected to their violence and made a personal visit to report their actions to the king. But she had refused to give them any names. She was in such a bad condition that they were obliged to give up their questioning. She had to be carried into the courtroom on a chair for she could no longer stand or walk. At her trial she spoke out boldly against her accusers and refused to recant her beliefs. She was condemned to be burned at the stake as an impenitent heretic. That was the only satisfaction that Bishop Gardiner and his supporters gained from their investigation. They had to give up the idea of proceeding against the queen and her court circle. On the day of her execution, Lady Anne Seymour sent her maid with a handsome bribe for the executioner. He agreed to hang a bag of gunpowder around her neck so that her sufferings might be cut short. She died a martyr to the Reformed belief.

Queen Catherine took warning and no more evangelicals were invited to her apartments to preach. Yet I feared that she was still in danger from powerful enemies. Nan told me not to dwell upon it. All queens were the subject of intrigues, but that should not mean that we should live in fear. I hoped that the danger had passed. But the conservatives bided their time for another opportunity.

One fatal day, Queen Catherine displeased the king by expressing her views on religion much too decidedly for his liking. He was offended that he should be challenged in public by his own wife.

"Things have gone too far when women become such clerks," he complained. "It is little comfort to me in my old age to be taught by my wife."

Bishop Gardiner saw his opportunity. "Your Majesty, it is unbecoming for a wife to contradict her husband. And it is even more improper for a subject to presume to know better than the king. I feel it is my duty to enquire further into the queen's opinions. May I have your Majesty's permission to proceed?"

The king agreed that the bishop should conduct an investigation into the conduct of the queen. It signalled the beginning of the downfall of the queen just as surely as with Queen Anne Boleyn and Queen Catherine Howard. However, Queen Catherine Parr was more fortunate than her predecessors had been. By a strange chance I happened to find a document lying in the corridor outside the queen's apartments. When I picked it up, I saw that it was an arrest warrant made out in in the name of the queen. I took it at once to Nan.

"You must show this to the queen at once," I urged her. "And counsel her, for you are her sister. She will listen to you."

"Lord save us! It is the end! she exclaimed in horror. "They will come for my sister and for all the rest of us as well. What can we do?"

"You must act quickly. Tell her to throw herself on the mercy of the king at once. He will not be able to resist her pleas and she will save herself."

"Come with me, Nan. We must tell the queen at once."

When Nan showed the warrant to Queen Catherine, she turned pale with fear and collapsed into her chair. "And so it has happened. I have been waiting for this day ever since the arrest of Anne Askew."

"Take heart, sister. You must do something to save yourself!" urged Nan.

"What can I do? She lamented. "The king has made up his mind. It is because of that foolish conversation the other day. Bishop Gardiner was there and he has turned the king against me."

"It is not too late, your Majesty. Go to the king and plead for his forgiveness," I advised.

"I feel faint. I must rest awhile. Take me to my bed." It was clear that the queen was in no state to persuade the king. Nan and I were both at a loss what to do.

"This is a court intrigue, Nan. This is just how the other wives were brought down. Neither Queen Anne Boleyn nor Queen Catherine Howard had the chance to speak with the king before their arrest and afterwards it was too late."

"Someone must speak to the king. But who does he trust?"

I had an inspiration. "He trusts his doctors. Send for Dr Wendy and say that the queen has been taken ill. When he comes you must show him the warrant and ask him what to do. The king has a high regard for him and I am sure he will help us."

"Yes, he is a good man," she agreed. "I will send for him at once."

When Dr Wendy arrived, Nan took him into her confidence. "These are terrible times, Lady Herbert. People are being denounced over trifles. But I am convinced that the king has a true regard for the queen. I will inform His Majesty that the queen is unwell and has asked to see him. When he comes she must do her best to touch his heart. And put that document back where you found it. There must be no suspicion that you are aware of the plot. That is all I can do for you."

"We are most grateful, Dr Wendy."

I hurried to return the warrant while Nan rallied the queen.

"Your Majesty, you must gather your courage and make yourself ready to speak to the king."

"No indeed, Nan," she protested. "I could not see him now. I am feeling much too ill."

"It is your only chance," Nan insisted. "You must try to gain his sympathy. If you do not then it is the end for all of us. Drink this glass of wine quickly."

A page knocked on the door to announce the arrival of the king. He entered breathing heavily for he found it a struggle to walk very far. We dropped in low curtsies before him.

"Rise ladies and take me to the queen," he instructed us. "Dr Wendy is most concerned for her. He tells me that she is unwell and only my presence can give her the comfort she needs. We grudge no effort for the benefit of the queen and so we have come here in person."

"We are most grateful to your Majesty," said Nan. "I know that the queen will be glad to see you."

Queen Catherine was lying on her pillows looking as pale as death. Tears were glistening upon her cheeks.

"What is the matter, my dear? he asked. "What is it that trouble you?"

"Your Majesty is so good to come," she replied. "I have been so afraid that it was more than I could bear. It is such a comfort to see you here."

"We would see you well again," he said firmly. "What is this anxiety that oppresses you?"

"It is the fear that I have lost your regard entirely," she wept. "I would not wish to live if I felt that you no longer cared for me."

"You are our beloved wife and we care for you dearly," he assured her. "Why should you think otherwise?"

"The other day I spoke to you unadvisedly," she confessed. "I feared that I had offended you and lost your affection. I have not known a moment of peace ever since. I beg you to forgive me for displeasing you."

The king pursed his lips. "Well, Kate, it is true that we were grieved by your insistence. As the Head of the Church, it is my constant care to guide my people in the way of truth. And yet you would claim to have superior knowledge to instruct myself and my bishops." If we had needed confirmation, it was there. Bishop Gardiner saw the queen as a threat and he had turned the king against her.

"Alas, my lord, I had no such intention," she pleaded. "I only wished to distract you from the pain in your leg. I thought that a discussion on theology might entertain your Majesty and I am deeply grieved to have caused offence."

"Is that so Kate?" he mused. "And did you make your argument for no other reason?"

"It is true that I hoped that I might benefit from your Majesty's great learning."

"Then we are perfect friends again, sweetheart," he declared. "Put away these fears and weep no more. We shall think no more of it. And now I will bid you a good night."

The king rose clumsily to his feet and shuffled away. But his face wore an expression of great satisfaction. I was sure that the danger had been averted.

"You answered wonderfully well, your Majesty," exclaimed Nan in relief.

"God must have inspired me for I was so afraid that I hardly knew what to say."

"It was certainly a great deliverance, your Majesty."

The next day the king sent the queen an invitation to join him in the palace garden. He was sure that the fresh air would do her good. And so they sat outdoors and talked together amiably. Queen Catherine had quite recovered her assurance and looked every inch the dignified queen. She wore a dress of crimson satin, her brooch in the shape of a crown with three pendant pearls and a pair of diamond and ruby bracelets. Suddenly Chancellor Wriothesley appeared with a detachment of yeomen guards. He brandished a document in the face of the queen. "Madam, I arrest you on a charge of heresy and treason. I must ask you to accompany me to the Tower."

I wondered if the king had deceived us all last night. But he rose with a menacing frown to confront his Chancellor. "What do you mean by this intrusion, you knave? How dare you show such disrespect to the queen? Begone at once, varlet, or it will be the worse for you!"

"But your Majesty!" protested the astounded Chancellor.

"Did you hear me? Begone, I say! Never let me hear such nonsense again."

In the face of the king's wrath, the Chancellor and his guards made a hasty departure. Queen Catherine was deeply shaken and realised how close she had come to calamity. But she pretended not to have recognised the plot.

"I hope that your Majesty will pardon the Chancellor for his mistake," she told the simmering king.

"He is a knave and a fool, Kate," he declared. "You do not realise how little he deserves to receive such grace from your hands."

Soon the new of the scandal was all around the court and Queen Catherine was admired for her adroitness in handling the king. After their humiliation, Chancellor Wriothesley and Bishop Gardiner made no more attempts to accuse her. And Queen Catherine took care never to risk the king's displeasure again. Nan was convinced that I had saved the queen's life. I remembered how Queen Anne Boleyn had been brought down when she lost the favour of the king. And how Queen Jane was almost ruined by her family trying to use her to intercede on behalf of the monasteries. And how Queen Catherine Howard was denounced by the evangelical faction under Cranmer who brought the Howard faction into disfavour. The court was seething with religious tensions and the rival factions feared the influence of the queen upon the king. But Henry was a devious man and a consummate actor. I could not be certain whether he had really intended to bring down the queen or if he had staged the scene as a warning to her.

The king's health declined to the point where he could no longer walk and had to be carried around in a special chair. In his final illness he would see no-one but his gentlemen and his doctors. Queen Catherine was beside herself with anxiety. "He has been ill like this before and recovered," she said wringing her hands together. "We must not lose hope." But this time, it was the end.

Queen Catherine spent Christmas and New Year quietly at Greenwich with the royal children. She awaited news of the king's recovery, but none came. After New Year, the king's children returned to their own households. On 31st January 1547 a messenger arrived from Windsor. It was Sir Anthony Denny, the Groom of the Privy Stool.

"Your Majesty, I regret that I have grave news to report. His Majesty has departed from this life to the great sorrow of us all."

"Poor Henry!" lamented Queen Catherine. "If only I could have been with him to give him comfort. I had hoped that it was just another one of his episodes and that he would make a good recovery and come to join us here. Did he suffer much, Denny?"

"His Majesty was constantly attended," he replied evasively. "Archbishop Cranmer was with him in his final hours and reported that he made a most edifying end."

"This will come as a great shock to His Majesty's children," exclaimed the queen. "I must go to them and break the news."

"That will not be necessary," he demurred. "King Edward and Lady Elizabeth have already been informed of their father's death. They have been brought to the Tower of London for safekeeping and in preparation for His late Majesty's funeral and the coronation of the new king. Indeed, the proclamation of King Edward has been made today."

"How can that be?" asked Queen Catherine. "When did His Majesty die?"

"His Majesty's demise occurred three days ago, your Majesty," he admitted looking rather uncomfortable.

"Why was I not informed at once?" demanded the queen.

"It was necessary to keep the matter secret until the safety of the young king was assured," he explained. "Archbishop Cranmer would have liked to have come and offered you his consolation for your loss. But he is preoccupied with making the arrangements for the coronation of King Edward. There is much work to be done. But it will all be completed by the Regency Council."

"What is this Regency Council?" enquired the queen. "I had expected that His Majesty would appoint me as the Regent during the minority of his son. He is only nine years old and I have been like a mother to him."

"His late Majesty in his will appointed a Regency Council of sixteen members to govern on behalf of King Edward."

"And who is on this Council, Denny?" she enquired. "Am I not one of its members?"

"I regret to inform you that you are not," he stated. "But His late Majesty has endowed you most handsomely in his will in recognition of your great love, obedience and chastity of life. You shall be styled as the Queen Dowager and ranked as the first lady in the realm. You will continue to be honoured in the same way as if his late Majesty was still alive. You shall receive a thousand pounds and retain the use of your royal wardrobe and the queen's jewels. Naturally, there will be no more ladies present at court until King Edward takes a wife. But you may maintain your household at your manors of Hanworth and Chelsea."

"And what arrangements have been made concerning the Lady Elizabeth?" asked the queen.

"You may act as her guardian and continue to supervise her education. If you so wish, she may reside with you and your household. For any other matters you may enquire of the duke of Somerset who is the Head of the Regency Council and will be known as the Lord Protector."

"I am not familiar with the title of the duke of Somerset. To whom does it belong?" said the queen.

"It belongs to the king's uncle, Lord Edward Seymour who was formerly the earl of Hertford. But according to the wishes of His late Majesty he has now been created a duke."

"Is that so? Have any other members of the Council been rewarded with titles?"

"Yes, Madam. Your brother, Lord William Parr has been created the Marquis of Northampton. Sir John Dudley has become the earl of Warwick and Chancellor Wriothesley has become the earl of Southampton. Sir Thomas Seymour is now Lord Seymour of Sudeley and High Admiral of England."

"And this was all set down in His Majesty's will?" she enquired.

"Not exactly, Madam. But his closest attendants recollected that these were his wishes before his death. As a reward for their loyalty and good service to him."

"And were you one of these witnesses, Denny?" she asked.

"Indeed, Madam," he admitted. "But I should not detain your Majesty any longer. I am sure you will need to rest. You have my sincerest condolences for your loss." He bowed and withdrew.

I admired the queen's clarity of mind at such a time. I wondered who was rewarding whom. And what Sir Anthony Denny was getting out of it. And I suspected that the king's attendants had persuaded him not to include the queen in the Regency Council. She would certainly have objected to this sudden round of promotions.

"It seems that the Councillors have been busy in ensuring their own rewards," said Nan indignantly. "And you have been excluded from governance for no good reason."

"I am deeply hurt that the king did not name me as Regent for his son," admitted the queen. "I would have cared for him and defended his interests. Now these self-serving courtiers have taken over. But there is nothing that I can do. It is clear that the Seymours are now the pre-eminent family in the land and they wish me to go into retirement."

The queen put on black mourning dress and the entire court did the same. The king's body was placed in the Presence Chamber of Whitehall and surrounded with burning tapers. Then it was moved into the Chapel Royal to be watched over by the household chaplains. On 14th February 1547, the cortege began its journey to Windsor. The king's coffin was covered with drapes of blue velvet and cloth of gold. It lay upon a chariot drawn by black-caparisoned horses and was followed by a solemn procession of a thousand horsemen stretching for four miles. The cortege rested overnight at Syon Abbey. The next day it arrived at St George's Chapel in Windsor in readiness for the funeral service the following day. The Dowager Queen Catherine watched the proceedings from the Queen's Closet above the choir. Sixteen members of the Yeomen of the Guard bore the coffin into the church and lowered it into the vault to lie next to the body of Queen Jane Seymour, the mother of the new king. A solemn Requiem Mass in Latin was conducted by Bishop Gardiner. At the end of the service, the chief officers of the household broke their white staves of office and cast them into the vault.

After the funeral the Dowager Queen Catherine withdrew to her manor of Chelsea. Most of the court ladies dispersed to their homes for there was now no queen for them to serve at court. Nan went to join her sister's household at Chelsea and the Dowager Queen Catherine invited me to serve her too. She had not forgotten my loyalty to her during the intrigue with Bishop Gardiner. I was glad to find such a pleasant and congenial company in which to live. There would be no more need of any ladies-in-waiting at the court for many years. My daughter Catherine Fairley joined the household of Sir William Herbert and his son Henry at Wilton House to be educated with him. Nan and I secretly hoped to make a match between our children when they were older.

On Saturday 19th February the young king led a procession from the Tower of London through the city of London. He was dressed in a gown of cloth of silver embroidered with gold and a cape trimmed with sable. On his head he wore a cap of white velvet garnished with rubies, diamonds and pearls. His horse was trapped in crimson satin embroidered with gold and pearls. His uncle, the Lord Protector, rode at his left side and six knights bore his canopy of crimson silk and cloth of gold topped by silver bells. They were followed by the clergy and nobility of the realm in order of precedence. At Cheap cross King Edward was met by the city aldermen who presented him with a purse of a thousand gold marks. The young king could barely hold it in his hands. "Why do they give me this?" he asked. His uncle told him that it was the custom of the city and he gave the purse to the captain of the guard. In the course of his progress, he was greeted by a number of pageants depicting Edward the Confessor, St George and "Truth", a child representing the New Religion. When he reached St Paul's churchyard, he paused to watch the performance of a tightrope walker from Spain who balanced along a cable to the delight of the crowds. Finally, the procession arrived at Westminster Palace where the young king remained overnight.

The following morning, King Edward travelled by barge from Westminster to Whitehall. There he dressed in a robe of crimson velvet trimmed with ermine in readiness for the coronation service. He walked to Westminster Abbey under a canopy of state carried by the four Lords of the Cinque Ports. The duke of Somerset carried the crown, the duke of Suffolk held the orb and the earl of Dorset bore the sceptre. Behind them came a procession of the Gentlemen of the Privy Chamber, the nobility, the guards and the court servants. The Dowager Queen Catherine felt all the pride of a mother when she saw him at the coronation. He listened attentively as Archbishop Cranmer preached a sermon which proclaimed him as "a new Josiah." Then the rituals of anointing and crowning were performed and he was presented with the orb and sceptre. The young king sat on a throne with two cushions to raise him up to receive the homage of the nobility. Then the whole assembly walked from the Abbey to Westminster Hall for the coronation banquet. All along the street were spread fine cloths and as soon the king had gone past, they were cut to pieces by the crowd and taken away as souvenirs. At the banquet the Lord Mayor of London served the king with a gold cup of wine and after he had drunk it, the Lord Mayor took the cup as his prerogative. The new king insisted on wearing his crown throughout the banquet. "How proud his father would have been," the Dowager Queen confided wistfully to Nan. After the feast, the king rode to Westminster Palace but we returned to Chelsea with the Dowager Queen. Our time as royal courtiers was at an end.

Part 7: The Household of Dowager Queen Catherine Parr (1547 – 1548)

"As truly as God is God, my mind was fully bent to marry you before any man I know"

(Letter of Catherine Parr to Thomas Seymour, February 1547).

I should not have been surprised when Admiral Thomas Seymour became a frequent visitor to Chelsea. The Dowager Queen Catherine was now the wealthiest widow in the land and a prize for any aspiring nobleman. He was a tall man with blue eyes and a long red beard. He had an easy charm of manner which concealed the depths of his ambition. He exerted his magnetism upon all the ladies of the household so that he became a general favourite. I noticed that he went on long walks in the garden with Catherine and when she returned to the house she looked as enraptured as a young girl. One day, Nan confided to me that she believed that her sister intended to get married again to the Admiral.

"But she can't!" I objected. "The court is required to observe a year of mourning for the late King. Catherine would need to have permission from the Regency Council to remarry. And they would certainly refuse to give it."

"Sir Thomas has thought of that already," Nan assured me. "He is going to get the permission of King Edward. After all, he is his uncle."

"But it would look disrespectful for her to marry again so soon," I protested. "It would cause a scandal. Why doesn't she wait a while if she is determined to take another husband?"

"She does not want to wait," replied Nan. "She has had three marriages already which were not of her choice. This time she says it will be different."

Catherine was captivated by him. She admired his good looks, praised his witty jests and treasured his courtly compliments. *What does she see in him?* I wondered. He was an amusing companion, but hardly a sensible choice for a husband. He lacked any gravity of mind or maturity of character. In fact, there were rumours that the late King Henry had not wanted to include him in the Regency Council but had been persuaded into it. I reminded myself that Catherine had experienced little romance in her previous marriages. She was touched by his protestations of eternal fidelity.

"There was never any woman but you, dear Catherine," he assured her. "I could not think of marrying anyone else. I have waited these five years and more for you to be free, but I would have waited forever."

"It was you that I wanted to wed before the king asked for me," she admitted. "I am so happy that you waited for me, Thomas. But I will need the permission of the Council to marry again. Do you think your brother would support us?"

"He is the very last person who would help us, my dear," he replied. "But do not be concerned. I intend to ask permission of the king instead. We will marry in secret. By the time they find out about our marriage there will be nothing they can do. After all, it is not a political matter." It was plain that he thought that being the uncle of the king meant that he deserved the highest honours.

Admiral Seymour had bribed one of the king's attendants to pass his letters to him. He asked his permission to marry his dear stepmother. King Edward thought that it was a splendid idea and readily agreed. However, when the news of the marriage broke it caused a considerable scandal. The duke of Somerset was outraged that his younger brother should presume to make such a match without seeking the permission of the Council. Admiral Seymour countered smugly that as he had the permission of the king, he did not need to enquire elsewhere. He thought it was a great joke to have outwitted his brother and the rest of the councillors. But he did not consider the effect upon the reputation and standing of his wife. Lady Mary was deeply hurt and shocked that her stepmother should have remarried so soon after the death of her father. She thought that she ought to have waited for at least a year out of respect to his memory. And when Catherine returned to court, she found that the duke and duchess of Somerset had no intention of according her precedence.

"I am the wife of the Lord Protector," the duchess informed her. "And so that makes me the first lady in the realm."

"Not at all. The king wished me to be treated as if he were still living," protested Catherine.

"The late king married you in his doting days when no lady of honour would go near him," she retorted spitefully. "Those days are over now."

"His late Majesty's will clearly states that I am to be honoured as the Dowager Queen," insisted Catherine.

"Doubtless His late Majesty never envisaged that you would remarry," she replied coldly. "That changes everything. You are now the wife of the Lord Admiral and he is my husband's younger brother."

Catherine was trembling with suppressed fury when she told the Admiral of her humiliation. "That woman is a veritable hell. Her pride knows no bounds. She fancies that she is now the queen and her husband is the king. Poor young Edward is no more than their puppet. And they have no respect for us whatsoever."

Worse was to come. The Lord Protector and his wife began to treat the late king's possessions as their own property. He opened the king's wardrobe at Whitehall Palace and removed his best furs to trim his own robes. The duchess took the royal counterpanes and pillows embroidered with silk and gold to embellish their bed and the monogrammed royal napery to furnish her own table. She had even had the effrontery to bring a great bedsheet and fill it with quantities of silks and satins from the royal storehouse which she carried triumphantly away. She then set her heart on wearing the queen's jewels. And as she was a forceful character, her opinion prevailed. Catherine protested that this was her right, but no-one was going to argue with the Lord Protector. And in any case, he kept the key to the

Jewel House where they were stored. The Admiral was furious at this slight to his wife's prestige, but he could not prevail upon his brother. Their relationship had degenerated into a bitter rivalry. Consequently, Catherine increasingly withdrew from public life and focussed upon her own household.

"I shall not attend the court if I am to be treated in this disgraceful manner," declared Catherine. "I shall stay here in Chelsea where I am far happier than I ever was at court. My only regret is my separation from young King Edward. If His late Majesty had known how his wishes would be disregarded, he would have been furious. I have no doubt that he would have taken the Lord Protector's head for his presumption. Some of those jewels are my own personal property. There is a diamond cross which my dear mother gave to me. I only kept them with the queen's jewels for safety."

"If only His Majesty had made you the Regent for his son, then you and I would be in their places," observed the Admiral. "Aye, and we would make a far better showing than long-faced Ned and his hell-cat of a wife! By Jupiter, we would! It maddens me to see them scorn you, Catherine. If only the young king were older then he could pick his own advisers. I have no doubt that he would choose us above all others!"

"Let them squabble over their rank and status. I am content just as I am," Catherine told him. Now she was at liberty to study the New Learning as much as she wished for the Council members were predominantly Reformers. She wrote a series of reflections called "*The Lamentation of a Sinner*" which encouraged people to read the Bible in English for themselves. In her pleasant household at Chelsea, I felt that I had found a place where I could settle down in peace. I was surrounded by the company of good friends and freed from the tension of the court. And Catherine was overflowing with happiness at her marriage to the affable Admiral Seymour. I was pleased for her until I discovered that under the genial charm lay an experienced predator.

One day, when I was exploring in the extensive library, I felt an arm slide around my waist and tighten. I turned to see him smiling into my eyes with easy confidence. "Lady Margaret, you need not resign yourself to the life of a lonely widow. I promise you a warm welcome whenever you feel the need for some lively company."

I felt stunned. The scoundrel had not yet been married for a month. "My Lord Admiral, I have no taste for these sorts of flirtations," I protested. "I would remind you that the court is still in morning for the death of His late Majesty and this kind of talk is out of place."

"My dear Lady Margaret, what are you saying?" he replied affably. "It is merely a little fun, but I fear you have no sense of humour. I see it as my duty to cheer all you ladies after the sadness of the king's death and the breakup of the court. I like to keep a merry house and so does my dear wife."

I realised that the rogue was far too plausible and slippery for me to call to account. I dared not complain to the Dowager Queen for it would be my word against his. In her eyes, he was a veritable angel. I did not even know if I could risk confiding in Nan. To Lady Herbert he was always a model of gentlemanly propriety. I suspected that he did not care to cross swords with Lord Herbert. No, I would not be believed. I reminded myself of the counsel of Christian de Pisan that if your reputation was at risk, it was better to find a quiet excuse to leave than to make an open scandal. But I did not wish to leave this comfortable house or my dear friends. All that I could do was contrive never to be alone in a room with him. I took the precaution of always keeping a pair of scissors handy at my waist. The next time he accosted me I threatened to cut his manhood short. His good humour was replaced with a scowl and a jibe that women such as I belonged in a nunnery. But it proved to be an effective method. After that encounter he directed his attentions elsewhere.

In the following weeks and months, I made it my business to keep a watchful eye upon his doings. I saw that he prided himself upon his ability to charm every lady in the household with his courtly compliments. To my dismay, most of them were taken in by his ready tongue and rough humour. Soon he allowed himself the freedom of indulging in hearty smacks and kisses which were excused as, "one of my Lord Admiral's jests." He did not even bother to hide it from his wife who smiled and called him "a naughty man" with the pride of a fond mother. *How can she be so blind?* I wondered. But then, she had been married three times in succession to men who had been chosen for their wealth and status. No wonder she was revelling in the freedom of married life with the man of her choice. And if she was tied to a blatant philanderer, she was more to be pitied than blamed.

Catherine had asked permission for the Lady Elizabeth to join her household which had been granted. She had supervised her education ever since she married the king and they had developed a deep family feeling for one another. Lady Mary wrote to her sister advising her to leave the queen's household for the sake of her reputation. She invited her to come and live with her instead. But Lady Elizabeth politely declined the offer. She was then aged thirteen with a sharp intelligence and the reputation of a scholar. She bore the promise of growing into a striking beauty with auburn red hair and a fair complexion. I did not miss the avid look of desire whenever the Admiral laid eyes on her. But he prepared his campaign with the greatest subtlety. He behaved towards her like a favourite uncle. He indulged her taste for fine things with gifts of ribbons and expensive sweets. He entertained her with clever riddles and stories of adventure on the high seas. At the same time, he courted the goodwill of her governess Mistress Kat Ashley with his flattering attentions. The foolish woman was easily won over by his jokes and compliments. Soon she was condoning his horseplay with her young charge as good pastime. *Before long he will have wormed his way into her bed*, I thought. I decided it was my duty to try to warn her.

"Mistress Ashley, it troubles me to see the Admiral handle the Lady Elizabeth in so familiar a way," I said firmly. "She is the late king's daughter and he should show her due respect."

The worthless lady bristled at once. "Are you accusing the Admiral of misconduct, Lady Margaret? I fear that the Dowager Queen will not take kindly to idle gossip about her husband."

"There should be no cause for gossip about the Lady Elizabeth," I reminded her. "She is just a young girl and I advise you to keep her out of his way."

"I have always done my duty by my young lady," she replied stoutly. "I brought her up myself from a child and I will not tolerate any doubt as to her virtue."

"Mistress Ashley, you must not let him touch and kiss her. It is no jest for a grown man to fondle a young girl as he pleases."

"This is stuff and nonsense! The Admiral is a fine man and he would not dream of besmirching my lady's reputation. It is you who lack respect by imagining such vile things. If you ever speak in this way again then I will report your insolence to Her Majesty."

The clever schemer not only turned the governess into his accomplice but his doting wife too. He persuaded Mistress Ashley that he was quite at liberty to visit the girl's chamber in the mornings. He pretended it was a merry game to spank her for lying so long abed. He teased his wife that the young lady was acting presumptuously in dressing herself in matronly black. Then he encouraged her to hold her arms while he cut the dress off and feasted his eyes upon her youthful body. He won the young girl's confidence with his humour and charm and accustomed her to being tickled and pinched at his pleasure. And he grew bolder and bolder as he found his attentions were met with compliance. Soon he thought nothing of taking her on his knee in full view of the company and making her squeal aloud as his fingers pressed into her sleeves and her bodice.

"So you think you are a grown woman to dress yourself in such frippery?" he bellowed. "I'll teach you to wear such French fashions, you minx!"

His wife laughed heartily. "For shame, Sir Thomas. There is nothing amiss with the cut of her sleeves. I wear them like that myself!"

"I tell you that she shall not wear them," he gloated. "The next time I will cut the laces and tear them off completely."

The servants witnessed the Admiral's unseemly displays and the Dowager Queen's indulgence of them. The household officers began to exhibit disapproving looks. Tongues began to wag. The gossip began to spread when visitors came to the house. Their servants heard that the Dowager Queen allowed Sir Thomas to frequent the young lady's bedchamber. It was said that she was already his concubine and that he intended to discard his wife and marry her when she came of age. Things finally came to a head when the Dowager Queen walked into a room and found the Admiral locked in a passionate embrace with the Lady Elizabeth.

"Do not make a fuss, Catherine. I was just teasing our young lady. It was all a jest!" he blustered.

"That was no jest!" she snapped. "I know what I saw. Does our marriage mean so little in your eyes?"

"You are the only woman for me, I swear," he pleaded." You have no need to be jealous over one little kiss. It was merely a play."

"You have gone too far, Thomas," she asserted. "I will not have such carryings-on under my roof. What a fool I have been!"

"I tell you it was nothing, Catherine. It was only a boyish prank. Let me give you a hearty kiss and we will forget the matter."

"Not this time, Thomas. I intend to put things to rights in this house for once and for all."

She swept out of the room and sent for Lady Herbert and Mistress Ashley to come to her chamber. Before the end of the day, she had arranged for Lady Elizabeth to stay with Sir Anthony Denny and his wife at Cheshunt in Hertfordshire. At the same time, she announced that the rest of the household would be moving to Sudeley Castle in Gloucestershire. She had effectively placed her out of his reach.

Admiral Seymour was visibly dejected that his designs had been frustrated by his wife. He protested that she had taken a foolish fancy into her head. She was the one who had made a scandal by sending Lady Elizabeth away. But the Dowager Queen's eyes were well and truly opened and her pleasant fantasy world was shattered. She saw her husband for what he was: a shallow, deceitful and ambitious man. And what was worse, she was expecting his child. It should have been a source of joy to her, but she was too heartbroken to rejoice. Her health began to decline along with her spirits. Three months later she died after giving birth to a daughter. She confided to Nan that her husband had never loved her. I thought it was a tragedy that she should have survived the deadly perils of her marriage to King Henry only to have succumbed to the wiles of a practiced seducer.

After the death of the Dowager Queen Catherine, her household was obliged to disperse. Her income had ended with her death and Admiral Seymour found himself with nothing to show for his ambitious marriage. He distributed his late wife's gowns among her ladies according to their rank as was customary. I received a gown of russet satin and a pair of green velvet French sleeves embroidered with gold flowers. Nan received a gown of blue velvet lined with sarcenet and a pair of white satin sleeves garnished with pearls. And Lady Mary received a gown of purple cloth of gold with sleeves of purple velvet and a fan of black ostrich feathers with gold sticks.

The Dowager Queen had been a moderating influence upon the Admiral. Now that she was gone, he became increasingly resentful that his brother effectively ruled in place of King Edward. He felt that he ought to share the role of the Lord Protector. "I am just as much his uncle," he openly complained. "In fact, I know that my nephew prefers me." He became increasingly reckless in his actions. He boldly asked permission to marry Lady Elizabeth. When the Council refused and rebuked him for his presumption, he was furious. He concluded his follies by attempting to kidnap King Edward while his brother was away on campaign in Scotland. His attempt to seize the young king failed when his pet dog began to bark and raised the alarm. The Admiral shot it dead and then fled into the night. When he was arrested, he lamely protested that he was merely testing the security of the king's apartments. But the Lord Protector had lost patience with his wayward younger brother. He was putting his position in jeopardy with his constant hare-brained schemes to grab power. Admiral Seymour was attained and found guilty of attempting to kidnap the king, conspiring to marry the Lady Elizabeth and plotting a rebellion. On 20th March 1549 he was executed for treason on Tower Hill. And so died a man of great wit but very little judgement.

Part 8: The Household of Lady Mary Tudor (1548 – 1553)

"Lord, give us grace to forget this wayfaring journey, and to remember our proper and true country. And if thou do add a weight of adversity, add thereunto strength, that we shall not be overcome with that burden."

(A Meditation on Adversity by Lady Mary, 1549).

The sad death of the Dowager Queen Catherine had left me without a mistress to serve. But I was fortunate. Lady Mary invited Nan, Lady Catherine Willoughby and myself to join her household. On our arrival at Hunsdon she received us most warmly. She was now thirty years old and still took pleasure in fine clothing and jewels. She wore a dress of black velvet with a gold-edged French hood and a gold brooch depicting the story of Abraham. I was pleased to have the opportunity to serve the daughter of my beloved first mistress, Queen Catherine of Aragon. By the terms of her late father's will she had been left an income of three thousand pounds a year and the residences of Hunsdon, Beaulieu and Kenninghall. I felt at home in the household of Lady Mary for she had kept to the old ways of her mother as much as possible. She had chosen her servants for their commitment to the Catholic faith. Mistress Susan Clarencius was her chief lady in waiting and had been with her for many years.

Following the accession of her brother Edward, Lady Mary had looked forward to a more congenial life than under her turbulent father. However, it was not to be. The Protestant councillors were set upon introducing religious reforms in the king's name. It was announced that the use of rosary beads, the ringing of bells and the lighting of candles on the altar were forbidden. Furthermore, all images in churches were banned which meant that statues were abolished, wall paintings were whitewashed and stained-glass windows were destroyed. All the rood-screens had to come down and the altars were replaced with communion tables. The churches were left looking plain and bare. It was ordered that a copy of the English Bible was to be provided in every church and a new Book of Common Prayer in English replaced the Latin mass. Even in our country manor the news of the reforms still reached us. Lady Mary was aghast at the changes. She remained constant to her Catholic faith and celebrated the traditional Latin mass three times a day in her own chapel.

"We will not be disturbed by any changes here," she insisted. "I have written to the Lord Protector objecting to these newfangled ideas. My father left the realm in godly order and quietness and no changes should be made to his religious settlement until King Edward has come of age."

Lord Protector blandly replied that King Henry had died before he had done all that he had intended to do in religion. So Lady Mary appealed to the emperor Charles to intervene on her behalf. His ambassador demanded a guarantee of her freedom of worship from the Lord Protector. He promised not to enquire into her household until the young king came of age. Lady Mary was not the only one to object to the changes. Bishop Bonner of London and Bishop Gardiner of Winchester were both imprisoned in the Tower for protesting against the Protestant reforms. And the people of Devon and Cornwall rebelled against the new Prayer Book which they called "a Christmas game." They declared that they would have the mass in Latin and the images set up again in the churches. The Lord Protector suppressed the revolt ruthlessly with the loss of five thousand lives. Then there was a rebellion led by Robert Kett against the enclosure of common land in Norfolk. The rebels succeeded in taking the city of Norwich before the rebellion was quashed. This time, the councillors accused the Lord Protector of weak governance and deposed him in favour of John Dudley, the earl of Warwick. He took the title of Lord President of the Council and was soon raised to the rank of duke of Northumberland.

Lady Mary was gladdened by the news of the fall of the Lord Protector whom she regarded as a godless man who had misled the young king. However, John

Dudley was an even more ardent reformer. He proclaimed that the government would do whatever might serve to the glory of God and the advancement of his holy word. This soon became a cause of tension. The Council and the young king did their best to persuade her to give up the celebration of the mass. She protested that the Council had no right to change the religious policy of her father during the minority of her brother. But it did no good. When the Council began to make threats, she appealed to her cousin Charles V for support. He wrote to the Council insisting that the Lady Mary should be permitted religious freedom in her household:

"It is unthinkable that a member of my family, a royal Hapsburg lady, would ever become a heretic. She would sooner die as a martyr of the faith."

The Council backed down for fear of provoking conflict with Spain. But it caused a serious breach between King Edward and his sister. This was a cause of great grief to Lady Mary. "We used to be so close," she confided wistfully to me. "He used to love me more than anyone else. These heretics have taken advantage of his youth to deceive him. And they are appropriating lands from the royal estates. He is surrounded by rogues and thieves while honest men lie in the Tower." I did not regard Bishop Gardiner as being in any way more honest than the rest of the Council. But Lady Mary had a right to feel aggrieved. She was the heir to the throne, but she was being persecuted by the Council. However, she was determined not to give in. For most of her brother's reign she remained on her own estates and rarely attended court. She tried to maintain her relationship with her sister Elizabeth, but she found that she preferred to take the side of King Edward. "It is not her fault," sighed Lady Mary. "She was educated by Reformers just like my poor brother."

In the summer of 1550, the pressure was so great that Lady Mary considered fleeing the realm and taking refuge in Spain for her own safety. Her life had become as mired in controversy and strain as it had been at the time of Queen Anne Boleyn. She asked the Spanish ambassador to visit her at her estate of Woodham Walter in Essex. "I need your assistance to escape from my current danger," she pleaded. "Those around the king are wily in their actions and malevolent towards me. I must not wait till the blow falls."

The emperor Charles devised a plan for Lady Mary to be rescued from the coast of Essex by boat and taken to an Imperial warship. His envoy, Johan Dubois, was entrusted to transport her to safety in the Netherlands. She intended to leave with four trusted ladies and two gentlemen and bring only her jewels with her. In July 1550, the warship arrived at Maldon. Master Dubois sent a message to Lady Mary bidding her to come that night and escape from England. Her household officials were aghast at the news that she might leave. What would become of them? Her comptroller, Master Robert Rochester, undertook to change her mind.

"I beg you not to go, my Lady," he pleaded. "It is far too dangerous an exploit to consider. Suppose you were caught escaping by the town watch? You would risk imprisonment or even death at the hands of the Lord President."

"But I must leave, Master Rochester," she protested. "I have been petitioning the emperor for the past year to send a ship to my rescue. He will surely be offended if I send his envoy away."

"It can be managed very easily, my Lady," he assured her. "We will delay your departure. Send word to the envoy to come and meet you here. Then I will warn him that his ship is in danger of being impounded by the watch. He will be forced to leave at once and report that it was impossible to fulfil his mission."

"But how can I stay in England?" she declared as she wrung her hands in distress. "You see how I am persecuted by my brother's council. I have no freedom to worship as a Catholic here."

"Stay strong and be prudent, my Lady," he advised her. "If you leave England and go abroad you will lose the houses and lands your father left to you in his will. You will be dependent on the emperor's charity and end up married to a minor royal at best. Here you are a wealthy landowner and the rightful heir to the throne. Do you want to give that up?"

"I can always return sometime in the future when the situation is more propitious," she contended.

"You will never be able to return, my Lady," he insisted, shaking his head. "Your goods will be confiscated and your sister Elizabeth will become the next heir to the throne. I beg you to reconsider."

"I cannot think what to do for the best, Master Rochester," she pleaded. "There is peril in going and peril in staying. I must pray on the matter before I decide."

"Of course, my Lady," he agreed. "But if you decide not to go then I will arrange the whole affair so that you are not blamed. You can leave everything to me."

And so it fell out. The envoy was rowed from the warships to the shore disguised as a grain merchant. He called upon Lady Mary and urged her to depart at once. But she announced that she could not possibly leave that night. She would need at least two days to pack her things and get ready. He insisted that there was no more time. He feared that the plot was already known. Master Rochester warned him that the watch had been doubled that night and his ship was in grave danger of discovery. The frustrated envoy returned to the warships under the cover of darkness and sailed away. As soon as he had gone, Lady Mary reproached herself that she had lost her best chance for escape.

"I could have been on my way to the court of the Netherlands and lived there in peace and safety," she lamented.

"But you would never have returned to this realm, my Lady," said Master Rochester. "Be patient and wait for better times to come."

"I have spent my whole life in waiting, good Master Rochester," sighed Lady Mary. "How long must I live in hope of a better future?"

"We are all waiting for that future, my Lady," he assured her. "You are the hope of all the true believers. If you endure this time of trial patiently, then one day you can restore the mass and rebuild the monasteries for the good of the whole nation. But if you leave then you will undoubtedly lose your claim to the throne. And the true faith will never be restored."

So Lady Mary persevered in the face of great opposition, but it took its toll upon her health and spirits. In January 1551 the Council wrote to tell her that the mass must no longer be heard in her household. Lady Mary was appalled by this demand, but stood firm. She replied to the Council expressing her objections.

"My faith and my religion are those held by the whole of Christendom and formerly confessed by this kingdom under the late king my father until you altered them with your laws. This is my final answer to any letters you might write to me on matters of religion. My health is more unstable than that of any creature and I have all the greater need to rejoice in the testimony of a pure conscience."

The Council then became more subtle in their tactics. Sir Richard Rich came to visit Lady Mary bringing instructions for her household. His eyes shone with triumph as he gave his orders.

"None of Lady Mary's household are permitted to attend mass in her private chapel on pain of instant dismissal." He smiled slyly at her. "I do not think the emperor will go to war for the sake of your ladies."

She was incensed at his insolence. "More shame upon you, Sir Richard, for persecuting the lowly."

"Your Grace, I am charged to purge this realm of error from the highest to the lowest in the name of the king," he replied with great satisfaction. "I could arrest these ladies now for I know they are guilty."

"You may cease your threats and go," she demanded. "Do you think that I endured a youth of such taunts that I should be moved by them now? If you have a commission to arrest me, then fulfil it now and be done with it."

"Not this time, Lady Mary," he said unperturbed. "But who can tell what the future may hold if you continue to defy His gracious Majesty? I bid you farewell – for now." He gave a slight bow and departed.

"This is intolerable," said Lady Mary. "Things have gone too far. I shall write to my brother. He needs to remember that I am not just a subject but his own sister."

But King Edward remained implacable. "If we were to give you license to break our laws and set them aside, would it not be an encouragement to others to do likewise? Sister, consider that if an exception has been made in your favour this long time past, it was to incline you to obey and not to harden you in your resistance."

Lady Mary assured him of her steadfast allegiance. "I am the most loyal of your subjects and would be willing to die in order to prove it. I will nowise enter into disputation but in the humblest manner possible beseech you to suffer me to live as in the past."

"I do not doubt your loyalty, sister," conceded the young king.

Lady Mary had made her point that she was prepared to die for the sake of her faith and the king did not wish to push the matter that far. There were no more visitations and we hoped that we would be left to live in peace.

On 20th February 1552 my dear Nan died at the age of thirty-six. She had been a steadfast friend to me throughout all turns of fortune. I knew that I would miss her dreadfully. I expected that I would have to bring my daughter Catherine to live with me. But her husband, the earl of Pembroke, wrote to say that he would allow her to complete her education in his household out of consideration for his late wife's wishes. However, he made it clear that there could be no thought of making a match with either of his sons. They were both of too high a rank to marry her. I wrote to Catherine to say that I missed Lady Herbert just as much as she did. And she must honour her memory by making the most of her education in order to become the lady she intended her to be. Nan had sent me regular reports of Catherine's progress and I was encouraged that she would become as accomplished as my friend had been. She had also written that Catherine was so good tempered that she was called the sunshine of the house. *Just like my mother*, I thought.

Catherine wrote a dutiful letter back to me in her fine Italian handwriting. She promised to fulfil all of Lady Herbert's plans for her education. I wished that I could have her with me. But I reminded myself that this arrangement was for the best and Queen Catherine of Aragon had made the same sacrifice for the sake of her daughter's future. One day we would be together again. I could not help resenting Lord Herbert's snub to my daughter who was the last descendant of one of the oldest houses in the land. But we were a poor family now and that was what counted. The fortunes of the Parrs and Herberts had risen together while mine had fallen. And now I had lost both of my dearest friends and my mistress was in continual danger. It seemed that I was destined never to know prosperity or safety and I was deeply anxious about my daughter's future. Nan would have found her a good match but now I feared that she would end up being married to one of Lord Herbert's retainers. And I would share the fate of Lady Mary for good or for ill.

On 4th July 1553 a messenger arrived at Hunsdon with an urgent letter from the Lord President. He advised Lady Mary that King Edward was gravely ill and she must set out at once to visit him at court in Greenwich. Lady Mary showed the letter to Master Rochester.

"What do you say, Master Rochester? Should I go to London?" she asked him.

"We have no other news from court, my Lady," he replied. "You will have to make your own decision in this matter."

"Then I will go to my brother," she decided. "It may be the last opportunity I have to speak with him. Please make the necessary arrangements and I will set out tomorrow. I will write to the Lord President advising him that I will arrive as soon as possible."

The following day, Lady Mary set out with her retinue for London. It was a sombre journey for we feared that the king must be seriously ill. We arrived at her house in Hoddeston and rested from the journey. But the next day, events took an unexpected turn. Lady Mary was playing a game of cards with Susan Clarencius and I was embroidering one of her gloves with gold thread in her Privy Chamber. Master Rochester came to speak to Lady Mary. His face looked grave.

"My Lady, a messenger has come from London on urgent business. And he insists that he can only give his message to you."

"Then let him come here," said Lady Mary. "But you will accompany him Master Rochester."

"Certainly, my Lady."

The messenger looked exhausted and his garments were soaked through. "Goodness, my man. Why did you not change your garments before entering? You will catch a dreadful chill. Susan, bring him a blanket and a hot drink."

He shook his head. "My message is of the utmost urgency, my Lady. I have been sent by a well-wisher at court to bring you warning. The Council have sent you a message to say that the king is very ill and you should come to attend him at Greenwich. But you must not go. I regret to have to tell you that it is believed that King Edward is already dead. And the Council wish to have you in their hands. Indeed, you are in the utmost peril and must flee to safety at once. On no account must you be found here."

Lady Mary turned pale and made the sign of the cross. Her ladies did the same. "I can hardly believe these tidings. What is your name? Who has sent you to me?"

"Forgive me, my Lady, but I cannot say," he replied. "You have friends at court who are also in great peril. But above all they fear for you lest the Council take you captive and imprison you in the Tower."

"What are these rumours about the king?" she demanded. "I had heard that he was seriously ill, but not that he was dead."

"The Lord President has allowed no-one but his doctors and a few close attendants to see the king for weeks," he revealed. "But my master has been reliably informed by an attendant that he died three days ago. The news has been kept a closely guarded secret for the Council intend to summon you unawares."

"I am grateful for your message," she said resolutely. "It was a brave venture to bring me warning. You may tell your master that I will take good heed of it. And you shall be well rewarded for your courage. But first you must go down to the kitchens and take something to eat." The messenger was ushered out.

Lady Mary summoned her household to assemble in the Great Hall. She had put on a regal gown of purple cloth of gold lined with silver. "I wish to share with you the news which has just been brought to me. By the providence of God, my brother Edward is dead and the right to the crown of England has descended to me by divine and human law. And I desire to begin my reign with the aid of my most faithful servants as partners in my fortune."

At these rousing words the whole household cheered her to the rafters and hailed her as Queen of England. She smiled graciously as they pressed forward to kiss her hands and call her their dearest princess. When the excitement had subsided, she dismissed them to speak with her advisers.

"That was well done, your Majesty," said Master Rochester approvingly. "I am glad to see that you intend to assert your claim."

"Of course I do, Master Rochester. But I wish to hear your counsel on the matter," said Queen Mary.

"It is incredible news, your Majesty. But I advise you not to go to court until the situation becomes clearer. If there is the slightest risk of danger to yourself, then we should take action. I advise that we leave here at once and ride through the night to a place of safety. Your baggage can follow after you."

"Very well, Master Rochester. I shall travel with yourself, Edward Waldegrave and two of your most trusted officers," she decided. Her eyes scanned the room. Some of her ladies looked fearful, but I held her gaze steadfastly. She nodded at me. "Lady Margaret and Mistress Susan will accompany me. We will change into our riding gear and set out as soon as it is dark."

We rode north from Hoddesdon avoiding the main roads lest we should encounter a company of troops sent from London. It was a dreadful journey through the night. We were forced to make our way along narrow rutted trackways by moonlight. We arrived at the home of Sir John Huddleston at Sawston Hall in the dead of night. The family and servants awoke to the shock of discovering the new Queen of England at their door. However, they treated us most hospitably and soon we were sitting in front of a roaring fire clasping goblets of hot spiced wine. We dared not linger there in spite of our fatigue, but set out again the following morning for Hengrave Hall. The gallant Sir John escorted us by the safest route but he was to pay a high price for his loyalty. The Lord President's men were already hunting for us and when they realised that the bird had flown, they burned

Sawston Hall to the ground. When the news reached us, Queen Mary realised how narrowly she had escaped.

"I grieve for your loss, good Sir John. You must send word to your family to join us. And when I am crowned, I vow that I shall rebuild your hall so that it is finer than ever."

We travelled on again to the home of Lady Burgh at Euston Hall and finally arrived at Kenninghall in Norfolk. We were quite exhausted by the long journey, but Queen Mary was indefatigable. She could hardly be persuaded to rest. She knew that we were all in deadly peril and she would need to act decisively. Soon Master Rochester brought a messenger from Euston Hall to see her. He looked quite overwhelmed by his mission and made an ungainly bow.

"Lady Burgh sent me urgently with this letter, your Grace," he blurted out. "She told me that I should give it into your hands or else destroy it."

"I thank you for your trouble, my good man. Let me see her message." She broke the seal and scanned it quickly. "This is ill news, Master Rochester. It says that my brother is dead and Lady Jane Grey has already been proclaimed as queen in London."

Master Rochester fell to his knees. "Your Majesty is the true queen as all honest folk know. This is black treachery on the part of the Council and you are in great danger."

"Lady Jane is my father's niece but she is a Protestant," said Queen Mary scornfully. "And she is married to Guildford Dudley, the son of the Lord President."

"The duke of Northumberland seeks to be the power behind the throne," warned Master Rochester. "And he has won over the rest of the Council. They will seek to arrest you."

"Indeed, there is no time to lose, Master Rochester," announced Queen Mary. "I shall write to the Council at once and assert my right to the throne according to the will of my father, King Henry. I will instruct them to display their loyalty to my just and right cause by proclaiming my title in the city of London. And I will promise to pardon them in order to avoid bloodshed and civil war. I shall sign it as Queen Mary. You must find a trustworthy messenger to deliver my words."

"Of course, your Majesty," agreed Master Rochester. "But you realise that if you challenge them, they will undoubtedly send an army against you."

"Then I must raise an army of my own," said Queen Mary resolutely. "I shall write letters to all the local knights and gentry. I will tell them that I defy the duke of Northumberland as a traitor to God and the realm. And I will call upon them to support my cause by gathering their tenants and coming to my aid."

I greatly admired her courage and clarity of mind in facing this crisis. She did not fear to fight for the crown in the face of treachery. And her judgement was sound for the honest men of East Anglia did not let her down. They did not hesitate to face death for the sake of the true queen and rallied to support her. The first gentlemen to arrive at Kenninghall were Sir Henry Bedingfield, Sir John Shelton, and Sir Richard Southwell. Queen Mary was greatly heartened by their readiness to defend her cause. Then, Henry Radcliffe, earl of Sussex, came bringing money, provisions and armed men. Master Rochester advised her to move to her stronghold of Framlingham Castle in Suffolk which would be easier to defend.

And so Queen Mary set out for Framlingham where a great crowd of supporters had gathered in the deer park to welcome her. She urged them to try the hazard of death if need be. They declared that she should have her right as queen or else there would be the bloodiest day that ever was in England. She unfurled her standard and boldly displayed it over the gate tower for all to see. Over the following days, more gentlemen declared for the queen including John Bourchier, earl of Bath, Sir Thomas Cornwallis, Sir John Sulyard and Sir William Drury. However, one prominent nobleman by the name of Lord Wentworth remained aloof from the campaign. Queen Mary sent two of her officials to his home at Nettlestead. She warned him that forsaking her cause would lead to the perpetual dishonour of his house. He agreed to support her and brought a large military force to Framlingham. And every day the countryfolk of Norfolk and Suffolk flocked to the support of their rightful queen.

A report reached us that the duke of Northumberland and his army had set out from London and was on his way to Bury St. Edmunds. But Queen Mary remained undaunted for she was convinced of the justice of her cause. She summoned a household council and appointed Lord Henry, Earl of Sussex, as the Lieutenant General of her forces. On 20th July 1553 she rode out on a white horse to inspect her troops. The soldiers threw their helmets into the air and shouted, "*Long live good Queen Mary!*" and "*Death to the traitors!*" Queen Mary prepared to do battle for her crown just as her grandfather Henry VII had done at Bosworth. But merciful providence decreed that no battle would be fought. As soon as the Lord President had departed from London, his fellow councillors changed their minds about supporting a usurper against the rightful heir to the throne. They sent Arundel and Paget to swear loyalty to Queen Mary at Framlingham and seek pardon on behalf of the Council. The heralds proclaimed that Mary was queen and the people of London rejoiced crying, "*God save Queen Mary.*" The church bells were rung in celebration and bonfires were lit in the streets. When the news of the proclamation reached the duke of Northumberland at Cambridge, he admitted defeat. The earl of Arundel was sent to arrest him in the name of the queen and he was executed for treason. Lady Jane Grey and her husband Guildford Dudley were both imprisoned in the Tower for the queen would not agree to have them put to death.

On 3rd August 1553 Queen Mary entered London accompanied by ten thousand men. She was dressed in royal purple velvet with gold embroidered sleeves and rode upon a horse covered with cloth of gold. She was followed by Lady Elizabeth, the duchess of Norfolk and the Marchioness of Exeter. It crossed my mind that Lady Elizabeth always took care to place herself on the right side. She had avoided the summons of the Council by pretending to be ill. But Queen Mary was delighted to see her and gave her a necklace of coral beads and a ruby brooch as a sign of her affection. She rode at the head of her procession to Aldgate where she was met by the Lord Mayor of London and his aldermen. They welcomed her into the city and all along the route the crowds thronged the streets and hailed the queen with shouts of "*God save her grace!*" Queen Mary was greatly moved by this demonstration of the loyalty of her people.

I thought how unfairly Queen Mary had been treated during her life. She had been deprived of her mother's guidance and support at an early age. After her father had married Anne Boleyn, he no longer treated her as his heir. She had spent her youth in danger and loneliness being deprived of her rank and title as a legitimate princess. Her father had negotiated numerous matches but had never allowed her to marry. And then the Regency Council of her brother Edward had tried to exclude her in favour of Lady Jane Grey. If she had wavered in her resolve, she would probably have ended up imprisoned or executed. It was greatly to her credit that she had not given way to despair. Now she had her reward. She was the Queen of England just as her mother had always said she would be. She had inspired her troops in readiness for battle in a way that her father had not believed possible for a woman.

When we arrived at the Tower of London, Queen Mary lost no time in ordering the release of the prisoners. She saw them as her persecuted fellow Catholics. They included Bishops Bonner and Gardiner, the old Duke of Norfolk and Edward Courtenay who had been in prison since the age of nine. The bishops were restored to their sees and the lords to their estates. She was determined that her reign would be just and righteous and this was the first proof of her intentions. Her first duty as the queen was to arrange the funeral service of her late brother King Edward. She intended to bury him according to the traditional rites of the Catholic church. However, her advisers persuaded her that this might alienate the goodwill of her subjects. And so Queen Mary agreed to a compromise. She allowed Archbishop Cranmer to conduct a Protestant service at Westminster Abbey while she attended a solemn Requiem Mass for his soul in a private chapel with her ladies.

Part 9: In the Household of Queen Mary I (1553 – 1554)

"What I am loving subjects, ye know your Queen, to whom, at my coronation, ye promised allegiance and obedience, I was then wedded to the realm, and to the laws of the same, the spousal ring whereof I wear here on my finger, and it never has and never shall be left off."

(Queen Mary I's speech at the Guildhall, Holinshed's Chronicle, 1554).

The coronation of Queen Mary took place at Westminster Abbey on 1st October 1553. The queen wore the traditional state robes of crimson velvet and she was followed by Lady Anne of Cleves, Lady Elizabeth and the royal attendants dressed in the Tudor colours of green and white. And the highest noblemen in the land carried her regalia before her. The duke of Norfolk bore the crown, the marquess of Winchester the orb, and the earl of Arundel the sceptre. The ceremony was conducted by Bishop Stephen Gardiner in the form of a full Catholic mass. Four days later, Queen Mary opened her first Parliament. As one of its first acts, it asserted that the marriage of her parents, Catherine of Aragon and Henry VIII, was valid and that she was legitimate. In addition, the religious reforms of King Edward VI were repealed. This restored the Church to its former state at the end of King Henry's reign. The pendulum of religious opinion had shifted once again. However, the queen was disappointed that due to the greed of her nobles she could not reverse the effects of the dissolution by re-establishing the monasteries. The nobles had grown wealthy from the confiscation of the monastic lands and refused to give them up. She felt her Catholic supporters at home and her allies in Spain did not understand the extent of the difficulties she faced in restoring the nation to the Catholic faith.

Part 9: In the Household of Queen Mary I (1553 – 1554)

Queen Mary especially valued the ladies who had been the faithful attendants of her mother. For the first time in my service at court I felt at ease. Queen Mary was so loyal in her affections that there was no danger of her being influenced by jealous gossip. She was like her mother that way. But the role of a queen regnant was far more demanding than that of a queen consort. She often felt frustrated that the lords of the Privy Council did not show her the respect that she was due. She told them that if her father were still alive, they would not dare to speak in the way they did. Her chief adviser was the Spanish ambassador, Simon Renard. He made secret visits to the queen in her Privy Chambers at night to discuss the affairs of state.

The next important matter to be settled was the question of the queen's marriage. Queen Mary was now thirty-seven and needed to marry soon in order to provide a Catholic heir to the throne. I felt that it was selfish of her father not to have allowed her to marry in her youth. And now she faced difficult challenges as the first queen regnant. I hoped that her husband would prove worthy of her affection and provide the support she so greatly deserved. Any suitable candidate would have to be of royal blood and a loyal Catholic.

Bishop Gardiner requested an audience with the queen to discuss the matter. "Your Majesty, I urge you to consider Edward Courtenay as a suitable husband. He is a descendant of King Edward IV and is the highest-ranking English lord in the kingdom."

Queen Mary thought that it was an absurd notion. "My dear bishop, that is quite out the question. The unfortunate young man has spent most of his life imprisoned in the Tower. He not only lacks the usual knightly and courtly skills belonging to one of his rank, but he is a complete innocent in matters of politics. It would be impossible for him to govern as a royal consort."

Bishop Gardiner looked affronted. "Your Majesty, I beg you to reconsider. I came to know this young man well during our imprisonment and I can assure you that he is a most worthy gentleman. The people would look kindly upon your union with an Englishman. It would be an ideal match!"

Queen Mary was displeased by his persistence. "You must not press me in this matter, my lord bishop. It is far too personal a question to be decided by others. I can hardly be expected to marry a man simply because you befriended him in the Tower. I have restored Edward Courtenay to his title and estates. But I have no intention of marrying any of my subjects."

The bishop's face fell. "Your Majesty, may I ask whom you consider to be worthy of this great honour."

"There are a number of possible candidates including Don Luis of Portugal and Maximilian of Spain," replied the queen with dignity. "They are both mature men of royal blood who would be strong and capable partners. And most importantly they are committed to upholding the Catholic faith. That is most necessary, my lord bishop, for you know that it is my intention to restore the realm to the true Church."

The question of a choice of husband was resolved when the emperor Charles proposed his son Prince Philip of Spain. When Queen Mary saw a portrait of the handsome young prince, she declared that it was a match far greater than her deserts. At the end of October 1553, she announced their betrothal. But her intention to marry a Spaniard was not at all popular with the Privy Council, the Commons or the people. The ill-feeling that it generated led to the crisis of the Wyatt rebellion.

The leader of the conspiracy was the son of the famous poet Thomas Wyatt and shared his name. The conspirators planned to depose the queen and replace her with Lady Elizabeth and Edward Courtenay. In January 1554 Wyatt brought a force of three thousand men to Maidstone. He urged the townsfolk to join then in a march on London and preserve their liberty against the Spaniards. The news of the rebellion soon reached the palace. Some of the ladies were frightened by the reports of an approaching army and pleaded with the queen to leave at once.

"What will become of us?" they cried in distress. "We must escape while there is still time!"

But the queen remained undaunted by the threat. "We will not yield the city to a pack of rebels. I do not fear this traitor, Wyatt. There is an army of men in the city and I will call on them to rise to its defence. I do not doubt that they will do their duty as loyal citizens."

Queen Mary kept her nerve better than anyone. She rode to the Guildhall and gave a stirring speech to rally the people of London to her cause:

"I am come in mine own person to tell you of the traitorous assembling of the Kentish rebels against us and you. If subjects may be loved as a mother doth her child, then assure yourselves that I, your sovereign lady and your Queen, do earnestly love and favour you. I cannot but think you love me in return; and thus, bound in concord, we shall be able to give these rebels a speedy overthrow. Good and faithful subjects, pluck up your hearts, and like true men stand fast with your lawful prince against these rebels and fear them not, for I assure you that I fear them nothing at all."

The crowds cheered and cried out, "*God save Queen Mary and the prince of Spain!*" The queen's speech inspired the citizens of London to resist the rebels. When Wyatt and his force arrived at Southwark they found London Bridge was closed against them. They were forced to lay down their arms. Their leader Thomas Wyatt was captured and taken to the Tower. Lord Henry Grey, the father of Lady Jane Grey was also arrested for taking part in the rebellion. His persistent treachery caused the deaths of his unfortunate daughter Lady Jane and her husband Guildford Dudley. Queen Mary was forced to accept that they represented too great a danger to remain as prisoners in the Tower.

I felt that Queen Catherine of Aragon would have been proud of her daughter. She had not only resisted the demands of the Regency Council to abandon her Catholic faith but she had restored that faith to the nation as its queen. She had not hesitated to assert her claim to the throne despite her lack of an army. And now she had rallied her troops to defeat the Wyatt rebellion when those around her were shrinking with fear. She had the courage of her mother and grandmother to handle an emergency. I was glad that she now had the opportunity to marry a husband of her own choice.

Wyatt was tried for treason and admitted that he had written a letter to Lady Elizabeth warning her to get away from London. This brought the loyalty of Lady Elizabeth into question. Simon Renard was convinced that Lady Elizabeth represented just as great a danger to Queen Mary as Lady Jane Grey.

"Your Majesty, you have four enemies to your rule: the heretics, the rebels, the king of France and the Lady Elizabeth," he warned her.

Queen Mary admitted that she was disappointed in her sister. She courted public attention and made a play of her Protestant sympathies at every opportunity.

"I have treated her too generously," she declared. "I allowed her to enter London with me when I was proclaimed as queen and to ride in my coronation procession. And now she presumes upon it to style herself as my heir. No heretic shall ever succeed me, but only my own true-born child and a faithful Catholic. My father would have executed her merely for being proclaimed by a rebellion. However, I am not my father. She shall go into close confinement beyond the reach of traitors who would tempt her to usurp me."

The life of an heir-apparent was invariably fraught with peril. I recalled how the name of Lady Mary had once been called by the rebel forces of the Pilgrimage of Grace. They had demanded that she should be reinstated in the succession. King Henry had lived for years in secret dread of a rebellion or an invasion in support of Queen Catherine and Princess Mary. Yet he had refrained from sending either of them to the Tower or the block in spite of the urgings of Anne Boleyn. Was it on account of his feelings for them or his fear of Spain? I wondered how Queen Mary really felt about her father. They had seemed to take a certain pride in each other while suffering the burdens of mutual fear and doubt. But Queen Mary wanted to be merciful to her sister. She did not care to have her death on her conscience together with her cousin, Lady Jane Grey. And she would not abandon her to perpetual imprisonment in the Tower as many of her advisers urged her to do. It was agreed that she would be sent to the palace of Woodstock under the charge of Sir Henry Bedingfield.

However, Lady Elizabeth was angry and ungrateful. She wrote numerous letters from Woodstock protesting her loyalty until Queen Mary grew weary of reading them. She ordered Sir Henry Bedingfield to trouble her with no more of them.

"When I am married, I shall find her a suitable husband in Europe and that will put an end to these conspiracies," she pronounced. "Lady Elizabeth should be grateful to me for allowing her to marry while she is still young. She will not have to suffer the misery that I endured in my youth."

But Lady Elizabeth was strangely unwilling to be married. When Queen Mary proposed a match with Emmanuel Philibert, the Duke of Savoy she pleaded with her not to force her to marry against her wishes. She said that did not think that she would ever marry. Queen Mary was nonplussed by her refusal.

"It is her best chance for a happy future," she asserted. "She is fortunate to receive such an offer since she is no legitimate princess. I can see nothing of my father in her, but only her deplorable mother. I am quite certain that she is Mark Smeaton's child."

However, it was quite plain to everyone else that Lady Elizabeth was a true Tudor with the characteristic red hair, quick intelligence and fiery temper.

"I cannot think why a young woman should be so fearful of the married state," she wondered. "She has not been well raised, that is certain. Mistress Ashley was no suitable guardian for her."

For my part I was not surprised by Lady Elizabeth's objection to marriage. Her mother and her stepmother Queen Catherine Howard had both been executed by King Henry. And Queen Jane and Dowager Queen Catherine Parr had both died soon after childbirth. It was no wonder that marriage spelled death in her mind. However, princesses did not have much choice in the matter. Sooner or later, she would marry like every other noblewoman.

On 19th July 1554 Prince Philip of Spain landed at Southampton where the earl of Arundel presented him with the Order of the Garter. Queen Mary travelled to Winchester to meet him in the garden of the Bishop's Palace with her ladies in waiting. She was dressed in a gown of black velvet adorned with splendid jewels and he wore a gold-embroidered suit and a coat of cloth of gold. They spoke together in private for half an hour and Queen Mary was most impressed with her bridegroom.

"I was not deceived at all by his portrait," she confided to us. "He is just as handsome in person. In fact, I do not think it does him justice for he has a great charm of manner which no artist could express."

I was relieved that the arrival of Prince Philip had gone so well and there were no protests or disturbances. The queen deserved a peaceful reign and after her marriage I hoped that she would have the support she needed to curb any further rebellions. She deserved a measure of happiness after the many disappointments of her early life. As her husband was one of her own relatives, I was certain that he would treat her well. And an alliance with Spain would bring protection to the realm.

On 25th July 1554 Queen Mary and Prince Philip of Spain were married. Winchester Cathedral was splendidly decorated for the occasion with banners and standards that displayed Spanish emblems. Prince Philip wore a doublet and hose of white satin decorated with jewels which Queen Mary had given to him. Queen Mary wore a matching dress of white satin and a mantle of cloth of gold which glittered with jewels. Her wedding ring was a plain gold hoop for she wished to be married as maidens were in the old time. The ceremony was a traditional Latin mass conducted by Bishop Gardiner. The form of the service was based upon Catherine of Aragon's marriage to Prince Arthur. I thought how happy Queen Catherine would have been to see her daughter married to one of her own Spanish relatives.

After the service the royal couple walked hand in hand to the queen's palace for the wedding feast. They sat at a raised table in the presence of the assembled English and Spanish nobility. Following the banquet, the company celebrated with an evening of dancing and entertainment. The evening ended with the blessing of the marriage bed. We all hoped earnestly that this marriage would provide an heir to the throne. Ten days later the royal couple set out for London to begin their married life. Prince Philip was always most courteous and attentive to the queen. They attended mass, they went out riding and they dined together. Queen Mary declared that they were the happiest couple in the world.

Now that my daughter Catherine had turned fourteen, I asked Queen Mary's permission to bring her to court. She readily agreed to accept her as one of her maids of honour. When I saw the beauty of my daughter, I understood why my father had defied his mother's expectations to marry my mother. She was extraordinary lovely with deep blue eyes and long golden hair. Truly, as fair as an angel, as the old chaplain had said. And able to turn any man's head for she had the grace and vivacity of the young Bessie Blount. But who remembered her charms now? I was thankful that my daughter did not have to serve in the reign of the lascivious King Henry. And I was determined that no rogue would trifle with her affections. I need not have worried. Queen Mary was just as charmed by her as Queen Catherine of Aragon had been by me. She could not do without her company. Young Catherine soon became her favourite maid of honour. She rose so high in her favour that she carved her meat at dinner and slept in her bedchamber at night. With the queen's protection I knew that I need have no fear, for no courtier would risk offending the queen for the sake of a mere dalliance.

Queen Mary sent for me one day. She wore a flamboyant gown of purple velvet which sparkled with jewelled spangles and gold thread embroidery. Her hands were a mass of rings set with large coloured stones. But she did not wear the great ruby thumb-ring of her father. She considered it sacrilegious to do so since it had been taken from the shrine of St Thomas Becket at Canterbury. Instead, she had it set in the lid of a reliquary containing a fragment of the True Cross. The royal apartments looked different from the time of King Henry. She had refurbished the privy chamber to suit the taste of a reigning queen. Her father's great collection of clocks and armaments had been cleared away. There were new Turkish carpets on the floor and the wall hangings featured devout images of the Beatitudes and the Seven Virtues instead of battle scenes of the Trojan Wars and the Siege of Jerusalem. In pride of place was a tapestry of Aeneus and Dido which was flanked by the portraits of Prince Philip and the queen. She sat on a chair of crimson velvet beneath a gold canopy of state and received me graciously. To my great surprise, she proposed making a Spanish match for Catherine.

"Lady Margaret, you are one of the few that are left from my mother's household," she said earnestly. "I know that you are a true believer who has suffered and endured just as I have done. My mother could not reward your service as she would have wished. But I would see you and yours well provided for. Lady Catherine is of good lineage and a faithful Catholic. I shall provide a good dowry for her and find a husband who is worthy of her. I wish to show you that your loyalty is not forgotten. I shall discuss the matter with my husband. He has many fine gentlemen in his retinue. Stand here beside me in case any points arise that you can answer as her mother."

As soon as Prince Philip was announced, the queen rose to meet him and escort him to his seat beside hers under the royal canopy. It displayed her coat of arms portraying the eagle of Spain opposite the lion of England. She was anxious to show him every sign of honour since Parliament had refused to grant him the title of king which he felt was his due.

"I hope that you slept well, my dear," she asked. "It is beginning to get chilly at night."

"I do not notice the cold," he asserted. "I sleep with my windows open in every season. It is good training for a soldier."

"Would you care for a cup of wine?" she enquired.

"I thank you, no."

"Husband, I have a young maid of honour in mind whom I wish to see well married to a suitable gentleman," she said clasping her hands on her skirts anxiously. "Whom would you recommend from among your attendants?"

"Who is the lady in question, my dear?" he enquired in a non-committal manner.

"It is Lady Catherine Fairley who stands beside my chair and carves for me." I held my breath wondering if he would scorn the proposal.

"I know whom you mean," he nodded in approval. "She is fair by name and fair by nature. But what is her lineage?"

"She is descended from an old aristocratic family," said the queen smoothing down her skirts. "Indeed, she is the sole heiress to the estate. And I myself intend to give her a dowry."

"Is she of the true faith?" he asked sharply.

"She is most devout," she assured him. "And moreover, her mother was in the service of my own mother."

"Since you recommend her so highly, I shall have no hesitation in making the proposal," he agreed. "I am certain that a good match can be found for her. However, she will have to be willing to learn Spanish and to make her home in Spain."

"There is no obstacle there," she affirmed. Her face looked more relaxed now that the conversation was progressing so well. I wondered if she had also feared a refusal.

"And how large a dowry did you intend to provide?" he asked.

"A thousand gold marks," she said proudly. "And in addition, there is her family manor and estate."

"Do they have jewels or horses to add to her fortune?" He seemed determined to make the best bargain possible for his candidate.

"Is that so necessary?" asked the queen in surprise.

"It is expected of a noble Spanish bride," he insisted.

"I can provide jewels, weapons and armour from the royal treasury," she said decisively.

"Then I think that I can promise you a favourable answer," he assented. The pact was made and he seemed well satisfied with the terms.

"But he must be a landed nobleman and not a younger son," she specified. Such a rich dowry warranted nothing less than the best man in his retinue.

"That is more difficult," he mused. "But I think that it may be done. I have some gentlemen in mind and I will discuss the matter with them. It is our duty to make such arrangements. I commend you for your concern for your household."

"I would have all my servants as well matched as we are ourselves, dear Philip."

"Quite so, my dear." He scrutinised the clock on the mantelpiece. "And now I must leave for I am expected to ride out and hunt with my gentlemen. I will see you this evening and we will show the court how well we can dance together."

"I shall look forward to it, husband."

"Adieu, until then," he saluted her hand and departed.

Queen Mary's eyes followed him as he left the chamber and she sighed. "Our lives are not our own as you see, Lady Margaret. But all is well. He will do as he has promised for he is ever a man of his word. Now we must display Lady Catherine to her best advantage. She must wear her best clothes and I shall provide a set of jewels so that she will appear to prospective suitors as a young lady of substance. We cannot have her looking inferior in the eyes of the Spaniards."

"I am so grateful to your Majesty," I said. "I do not have the words to express my thankfulness."

"I think of Lady Catherine almost as my own daughter, Lady Margaret," she said warmly. "I am determined to see her well married. You need have no fears on that score." I was delighted at the good fortune of my daughter. *This is what it means to gain the favour of a queen*, I thought. It had only taken one conversation to arrange a good future for her. I felt a pang of regret that none of the wives of the old king had taken the same trouble on my account. I had spent my entire youth at court waiting for my opportunity to make a match. But at least my daughter would be spared that trial.

The queen wasted no time in selecting a new gown and several costly pieces of jewellery for Catherine to wear. Her ladies dressed her in a gown of blue satin with a collar of pearls set with a fine sapphire to complement her fair colouring. Young Catherine was delighted by her new finery.

"The queen is so good to me, mother," she exclaimed. "These jewels are even more splendid than yours."

"The queen wishes her maids of honour to do her justice," I explained. "She wants her English ladies to represent the dignity and glory of her court."

"I shall feel as grand as a princess when I am wearing them," she said as she practiced the steps of a cinque pas.

"You can best show your gratitude by acting as the gracious lady she wants you to be," I reminded her. I hoped that her new dress would give her confidence and bring her to the notice of potential suitors. That evening she outshone the rest of the court and I felt the pride that only a mother can feel. The old saying that fine feathers make fine birds was perfectly true. Her natural beauty was arresting but when it was matched with a splendid dress it was quite overwhelming. I might have feared that her success would provoke jealousy were it not for the evident satisfaction of the queen. She could not resist introducing her to Prince Philip.

"This is Lady Catherine Fairley who is the youngest of my maids of honour."

"She is quite enchanting, my dear," he said as he studied her appearance. "I am sure there will be no lack of partners wishing to lead her out."

The following day, Prince Philip brought good news to the queen. "You may thank me, my dear. I have found you a most eligible suitor. It is Don Pedro Dávila y Córdoba who is the Marquis of Las Navas. And he is a brave, loyal and gallant gentleman. He could naturally take his pick of brides, but we are fortunate that he much admires the golden English beauty of Lady Catherine. And he greatly desires to have his own suit of armour for the jousts. I have promised him the best that may be found. So he is ready to marry the lady as soon as you please."

"That is excellent news, dear Philip," exclaimed the queen.

"I am glad that you are pleased," he said as he inclined his head. "But I hope that it will not set a precedent. I cannot have all my gentlemen expecting suits of armour with their dowries."

"Certainly not," said the queen. "This is a special case. It is symbolic of the union between our households and our countries. They may marry in the Chapel Royal so that the whole court may share in their happiness. Our good Bishop Gardiner will perform the office."

"Well, I have done my part in providing the groom," he remarked with satisfaction. "So I will leave all the details of the celebration to you and your ladies. I know that there is nothing you like better, my dear."

"It is true that I take much pleasure in weddings," she replied. "It was a dream fulfilled for me to plan our wedding day and it will give me great joy to plan those of my ladies. I hope there will be many happy marriages in our households in the future. You must present this young man to me so that I may give him my good wishes."

"Certainly, my dear. We are riding out tomorrow, are we not? I will bid him accompany us so that you may assure yourself that he is worthy in every way."

"I have no doubt of it, my dear. And I shall invite Lady Margaret and Lady Catherine to attend me. It will give the young people an opportunity to speak together and develop a regard for each other."

"That is a radical English notion, my dear Mary. As you know, it is the custom in Spain for a highborn lady to be veiled in the presence of her future husband."

"It is not quite so strict here. But nothing has yet been announced, so there can be no objection. There is no reason why they should not dance together in the evenings. It would please me to see them partner together."

"Let it be as you wish, my dear. I see you would hasten the marriage day."

"And if they agree together, then why not? I do not approve of long engagements."

"Quite so. Ladies should marry young and have many children. And men of means should consider it their Christian duty to take a wife and bring up a family in the service of God and their sovereign."

"That is an excellent sentiment, dear Philip. I wish you would mention it to the palace chaplains so they may give homilies on it to the court. That is just how I would have my courtiers understand Christian marriage. It is not about worldly advantage and profit, but a holy estate to the glory of God."

"I fancy that we set just such a godly example ourselves, dear Mary. But I shall be sure to tell my secretary to take a memorandum to the chaplains. I shall say that we look forward to hearing their sermons to the court at the earliest opportunity."

"Thank you, dear Philip. I thank God every day for the blessing of such a good husband as you. It is in this way that we shall restore England to the true Catholic faith again."

"We shall build a godly nation here together. My father, the emperor Charles, expects no less of us. And now I must leave. It is time for my morning ride with my gentlemen."

Queen Mary was delighted by the success of her plan. "Did I not say that he was to be depended on? Naturally, to a Spaniard true piety and a good lineage are paramount considerations. And I shall provide her a dowry of a thousand marks to mend her lack of fortune. It will mean that Lady Catherine would make her home in Spain one day and naturally you would accompany her household. Do you think that she would consent to such a match?"

"She would be only too grateful for your kind consideration and generosity to her, your Majesty," I said fervently. "It is good of your Majesty to spare us both." I was overwhelmed at the great honour being shown to Catherine. She had achieved the good match which I had failed to make at her age. True, she was young and merry and her looks were much admired at court. But this was far beyond my expectations. It was an even better match than the sons of Lord Herbert. I felt proud that after being rejected by them, she had made a far superior alliance. I wondered what Lady Maria de Eresby would have thought. My daughter would make her journey in reverse by setting out from England for a new life in Spain. I preferred that Catherine should marry young and escape from the temptations and dangers of the court.

I was most relieved that my daughter had succeeded in making a good match so soon after coming to court. Unlike me she would not have to brave the frustrations and betrayals that were part and parcel of life in royal service. She could live the respected and dignified life of a noblewoman in charge of her own household.

She was fortunate to have served at a virtuous court where young women were not in danger of drawing the eye of a lustful king. Catherine could have ended up like Bessie Blount or Mary Boleyn in the days of old King Henry. But Queen Mary was vigilant concerning the welfare of her ladies. She did not want a court where young girls were encouraged to become mistresses rather than wives. She considered it her duty to arrange good matches for her ladies in waiting. I know that her mother would have done the same for me under normal circumstances. I hastened to inform Catherine of the good news.

"Are you willing to accept this offer?" I asked her.

"Yes, mother," she replied. "Don Pedro is a most courteous man and I believe that he will make a good husband. The queen has told me of your troubles as a lady in waiting at court. And she said that a marriage would provide a better life for me. As a duchess I will be respected and have the opportunity to do much good. And you will be able to leave your life of service at long last." It was true. At last, I would be able to share a household with my daughter. I regretted that I had spent so time with her in the past. But I reminded myself that I had done my duty as a mother. She had been educated in a noble household and she had been offered a splendid match. She would be spared the dangers of life at court and the hardships of poverty. Even if she was widowed, she would still have a jointure.

It was arranged that Don Pedro would make his official proposal to Catherine the next day in the presence of their Majesties. The situation seemed absurdly formal to me, but Queen Mary assured me that the Spanish were a very ceremonial people. The queen was as excited as Catherine by the romance of the occasion. Of course, as the sovereign she had been obliged to make the proposal to Prince Philip. And so the following morning, Don Pedro appeared wearing a splendid dark blue doublet and a scarlet sash. He was accompanied by his young page who was looking extremely solemn. He made a sweeping bow to their Majesties and made an eloquent speech to them in Spanish. Then he turned to address me.

"Madam, I request the honour of paying my address to your noble daughter," he said with a charming smile.

"My daughter would be honoured to receive it, my lord," I replied.

Finally, Don Pedro turned his attention to Catherine who had succeeded in maintaining a calm demeanour. The queen must have forewarned him that she did not speak Spanish so he switched to Latin to address her.

"Lady Catherine, it is an honour and a joy to ask for your hand in marriage," he solemnly declared. "I hope that you will make me the happiest of men by accepting my proposal."

Catherine blushed, but replied just as fluently. "My lord, I am greatly honoured by your proposal which I accept with all my heart."

Don Pedro was undoubtedly ready to commence upon a further speech to mark the occasion, but he was forestalled by Prince Philip.

"I congratulate you on an excellent morning's work, Don Pedro!" he announced. "I can assure you that you are the envy of the court for obtaining so fair a bride as Lady Catherine."

"I am deeply grateful to your Majesty for giving me the opportunity to make so excellent a match," he replied.

I could see that Queen Mary looked rather disappointed that Prince Philip's interruption had cut the proposal short. But the resourceful Don Pedro was not deterred in the least. He signalled to his page who approached Catherine and presented her with a large diamond ring.

"Lady Catherine, I hope that you will accept this token of my deep affection," he said proudly. "It is an heirloom of my house which was given to me by my mother on the day of my departure for England. I know that it will make her immeasurably happy to see you wearing it when I return home with you as my bride."

"Thank you for your precious gift, my lord," replied Catherine. "Shall I put it on now or wait until the day of our wedding?"

"It would please me to see you wear it now, Lady Catherine," he answered graciously. "I would like the whole world to know that your heart has been claimed by the one whose ring you wear."

Catherine put on the ring and curtsied to Don Pedro, who bowed in return. Queen Mary looked delighted by the chivalrous gesture.

"Most gallant, Don Pedro!" she declared. "I know that you will make the perfect husband for my dear Catherine. She is such a treasure that I could only part with her for the sake of such a good marriage."

"Did I not tell you that Don Pedro was the best candidate, my dear?" said Prince Philip. "Let us drink a toast to the happy couple."

I sensed that Don Pedro had prepared another speech, but he diplomatically deferred to the prince. He was clearly impatient to conclude the formalities. After making the toast he claimed the company of Don Pedro to ride out with him on his morning exercise. Since such an invitation was considered an honour, Don Pedro was obliged to leave Catherine without the opportunity for any further conversation. Queen Mary looked rather chagrined by the gauche behaviour of her husband.

"Spanish gentlemen are quite devoted to their morning rides, my dear," she explained to Catherine. "Let me see your ring. Indeed, it is quite a beauty. You must take care not to lose when you are dancing."

"Yes, your Majesty. I will treasure it," said Catherine.

"I have spoken to the bishop and we will arrange the wedding ceremony for next month," she continued. "That will give you time to prepare your wedding dress and trousseau. And Don Pedro is sure to need time to meet with his tailor. He has asked permission to take you back to Spain after the wedding to meet his family and Prince Philip says that we can hardly refuse his request. In the meantime, you must make every effort to learn some Spanish so that you can converse with Don Pedro and his family. One of the Spanish chaplains will practice speaking with you every morning. And your afternoons will be taken up by ordering your wardrobe."

The next month proved to be just as busy as the queen had foretold. Fortunately, Catherine had been well instructed in languages and soon became proficient in conversational Spanish. There was a great deal else to arrange since we also needed to pack up our belongings to travel to Spain. Fortunately, the royal servants gave us every assistance for the enterprise. The news that one of the queen's ladies was marrying a Spanish nobleman caused quite a stir at court. Catherine received a number of poems in praise of her beauty and the other maids of honour told her that she was most courageous to set out for an unknown land.

Don Pedro and Catherine were duly married in the Chapel Royal. Queen Mary and I were overcome with pride and joy at the sight of them making their vows. Prince Philip graciously consented to give the bride away as she had no father. He boasted that he had made this match and surely everyone could see that it was a good one. The queen generously provided the wedding feast and the celebrations continued until midnight when I brought Catherine to the apartments of the Marquis. The priest blessed the marriage bed and then we departed. We were due to set out on the long journey to Spain in a few days' time so the queen took the opportunity to speak to me privately.

"Lady Catherine is a beautiful bride," she said. "I hope that she sets a fashion for weddings here at court. I would have all my ladies well married like myself. I will write to tell the emperor of your coming to Spain and he is sure to invite you to court. Please give him my best wishes and tell him how well we are faring here. I will ask him to show favour to Don Pedro for my sake."

"I do not know how to thank your Majesty for all your kindness to us," I said wholeheartedly. This match was the fulfilment of my dreams. I felt that my many years at court had finally been rewarded.

"It is hard for me to spare you," she admitted. "But Lady Catherine is much too young to go to a foreign land on her own. She will need you there. I know that if my own dear mother had lived then she would have stood beside me and helped me in a thousand ways. She was only fifty when she died and yet my great-grandmother Lady Margaret Beaufort lived to be sixty-six and outlived her own son Henry VII."

"She was a strong woman. Just as you are, your Majesty," I affirmed.

"My father thought that a woman could not bear rule in England," she remarked.

"But I have proved him wrong. I am the first Queen Regnant of England. I have defeated usurpers and rebels to prove my right to the throne just as my grandfather King Henry VII did before me. And now I hope to reign in peace. I intend to return the nation to the true faith. And I pray that I shall enjoy the blessings of a Christian marriage and be the mother of children who will reign after me. I have waited many years but now my time has come at last."

"Your mother would have been proud to see you married and a queen, your Majesty," I replied. "I named my daughter Catherine after her. But if I have a granddaughter then she will be called Mary. Then we will always remember and treasure the bond between our families."

Queen Mary's eyes grew bright with tears. "That is well. Of course, in Spain her name will be Maria. You must help your daughter to learn the language quickly."

"I have nearly forgotten my Spanish after so long, your Majesty. But I can still remember the words of your mother's favourite ballads. I will teach them to Catherine."

"I shall have the Queen's players sing them for us tomorrow evening. I know that Prince Philip will enjoy hearing them too. A wife should always be mindful of her husband's pleasure."

Epilogue

"Noble and good women are honoured by everyone for their virtuous patience, their humility and their great constancy"

(Anne de Beaujeu, Lessons for my Daughter, 1497).

I have packed up my belongings for the last time and said my final farewell to the queen. She gave me a ring from her finger as a remembrance. It is set with a ruby and I shall wear it always. Now I await the summons of the Master of the Horse to depart for Spain. My life over there will be very different to my life in service here. Yesterday, Don Pedro said to me, "You shall be my mother's companion and tell her of your life here at the English court." So I am glad that I learned the language and customs of the Spanish nobility in my youth. When I look back upon my life, I realise that there is much that I can tell. I have served under seven Tudor queens which is something that few others can claim to have done. I see how well my arduous court training prepared me for the unexpected twists and turns in life. And how the example of great ladies like Queen Catherine of Aragon and Lady Maria showed me the best way to conduct myself. I did not make my fortune at court, but I did not experience disaster either. I did not have any powerful relatives to assist me, but then I did not have any foolish ones to bring me harm. I learned the importance of integrity, friendship and striving to do one's best in any situation, even the very worst. And I discovered that fortune can be fleeting and misfortune can be endured. Thanks to the teaching of my good friends, I feel that I am well prepared to meet whatever challenges may lie ahead. I am sure that they will not be as testing as my turbulent years in the English court.

I was brought up with demanding expectations which came to little in the end. And like Queen Catherine of Aragon and Lady Maria, I am now a lone woman with a daughter. But I have the satisfaction to know that I brought up Catherine without the burden of having to restore the fortune and prestige of our De Roche forebears. I wanted her to live a more normal life than mine. The life of a courtier was privileged but hazardous. My life was shaped by the dramas and crises of the six wives of the king. But I would have preferred to have run my own household and brought up my own children. I have witnessed the dangers of vaulting ambition at court. After all, four of my fellow maids of honour were matched with a king, but it brought little good to them in the end. It is preferable to seek an equal match, a moderate fortune and a life free from the vanities of the court. Lady Margaret Pole was raised up to the rank of a Countess but then brought down in ignominy to the block. It was better to have the fate of my dear friend Lady Anne Herbert. She married a gentleman who was more suited for the field of battle than politics and they raised a family of three children.

In the end, I was neither the firm oak of Queen Catherine of Aragon nor the pliable willow of Sir William Paulet. Perhaps I was just a feeble reed, but I survived my time at court where others did not. The chapel of St Peter ad Vincula was paved with the bones of those who had been executed by King Henry. Some were only guilty of failing to please him. Others were the victims of court rivalries. Lord Cromwell contrived the downfall of Queen Anne Boleyn. And later, the dukes of Norfolk and Suffolk had settled the score by bringing him down. Fortunately, I was not important enough for anyone to bother denouncing me. When I look back on my life at court, I find little profit there except in the true friendships I made and the lessons I learned from experience. If I were to imitate Queen Anne de Beaujeu, I would say these things to my daughter: Integrity is not found in blind obedience. Nor does it ever take the form of revenge on behalf of another. It is not found in seeking to emulate the proud, the ambitious or the self-serving. It lies in heeding the voice of one's conscience.

One final adventure remains for me. My daughter is the same age as Princess Catherine of Aragon and Lady Maria de Salinas when they set out from Spain for a new life at the English court. I pray that my daughter will be happy in her life as the wife and chatelaine of a Spanish grandee. I am saddened to relinquish our ancestral home at Ravenseat, but my daughter and grandchildren will never know want in the household of a Marquis. And so I bid the court adieu and turn towards my unknown future.

THE END

Bibliography

Primary Sources

Muriel St Clare Byrne ed, *The Lisle Letters* (Penguin Books, 1985).

Henry Clifford, *The Life of Jane Dormer, Duchess of Feria* (Nabu Press, 2010).

John Foxe, *Narratives of the Days of the Reformation* (Hard Press Classics Series, 2019).

Martin Andrew Sharp Hume ed, *Chronicle of King Henry VIII of England* (George Bell and Sons, 1889).

David Starkey ed, *The Inventory of King Henry VIII, Volume I, The Transcript* (Harvey Miller Publishers, 1998).

Sharon L. Jansen, *Anne of France, Lessons for my Daughter* (Boydell and Brewer, 2004).

Emrys Jones, *The New Oxford Book of Sixteenth Century Verse* (Oxford University Press, 1992).

William Latymer's Chronicklle of Anne Bulleyne, Camden Miscellany XXX, Camden Fourth Series Volume 39 (Royal Historical Society, 1990).

Sarah Lawson, Christian de Pisan, *The Treasure of the City of Ladies: Or the Book of the Three Virtues (Penguin Classics, 2003)*.

Nicholas Harris Nicholas, 2021, *The Privy Purse Expenses of King Henry the Eighth, from November 1529 to December 1532* (Alpha Editions, 2021).

R. A. Rebholz ed, *Sir Thomas Wyatt: The Complete Poems* (Penguin, 1988).

David Starkey ed, *The Inventory of Henry VIII: The Transcript* (Harvey Miller Publishers, 1998).

David Starkey ed, *The Inventory of Henry VIII: Textiles and Dress* (Harvey Miller Publishers, 2012).

Charles Wriothesley and William Douglas Hamilton, *A Chronicle of England during the reigns of the Tudors from AD 1485 to 1559, Vol 1* (Leopold Classic library, 1874-1875).

Mary Anne Everett Wood, *Letters of Royal and Illustrious Ladies of Great Britain, Vols 1 and 2* (Forgotten books, 1846).

Secondary Sources

Dulcie M. Ashdown, *Ladies In Waiting* (Arthur Barker Limited, 1976).

Tracy Borman, *Henry VIII And The Men Who Made Him* (Hodder and Stoughton, 2018).

Tracy Borman, *The Private Lives of the Tudors* (Hodder and Stoughton, 2016).

Tracy Borman, *Thomas Cromwell: The untold story of Henry VIII's most faithful servant* (Hodder and Stoughton, 2014).

Susan Brigden, *Thomas Wyatt: The Heart's Forest* (Faber, 2012).

Elizabeth Cleland and Adam Eaker, *The Tudors: Art and Majesty in Renaissance England* (Yale University Press, 2022)

Simon Courtauld, Lady of Spain: *A Life of Jane Dormer, Duchess of Feria* (Mount Orleans Press, 2021).

Carolly Erikson, *Great Harry: The Extravagant Life of Henry VIII* (Robson Books, 1998).

Victoria Sylvia Evans, *Ladies In Waiting: Women Who served at the Tudor Court* (2014).

Julia Fox, *Jane Boleyn: The Infamous Lady Rochford* (Orion Books, 2007).

Natalie Grueninger, *The Final Year of Anne Boleyn* (Pen and Sword Books, 2022).

Kelly Hart, *The Mistresses of Henry VIII* (The History Press, 2009).

Eric Ives, *The Life and Death of Anne Boleyn* (Blackwell, 2005).

Amy Licence, *Catherine of Aragon* (Amberley, 2017).

David Loades, *The Seymours of Wolf Hall: A Tudor Family Story* (Amberley, 2015).

Lauren Mackay, *Inside the Tudor Court: Henry VIII and His Six Wives Through the Writings of the Spanish Ambassador Eustace Chapuys* (Amberley, 2014).

Maria Hayward, *Dress at the Court of King Henry VIII* (Routledge, 2007).

John Jenkins, *The King's Chamberlain: William Sandys of the Vyne, Chamberlain to Henry VIII* (Amberley, 2021).

Eleri Lynn, *Tudor Fashion* (Yale University Press, 2017).

J. L. McIntosh, *From Heads of Household to Heads of State: The Pre-accession Households of Mary and Elizabeth Tudor, 1516 – 1558* (Columbia University Press, 2010).

Franny Moyle, *The King's Painter: The Life and Times of Hans Holbein* (Apollo, 2021).

Elizabeth Norton, *The Anne Boleyn Papers* (Amberley, 2013).

Joanne Paul, *The House of Dudley: A New History of Tudor England* (Penguin Random House UK, 2022).

Margaret Scand, *Tudor Survivor: The Life and Times of William Paulet* (The History Press, 2011).

Anne Somerset, *Ladies In Waiting from the Tudors to the Present Day* (Weidenfield and Nicholson, 2020).

Sylvia Barbara Soberton, *Ladies In Waiting: Women Who Served Anne Boleyn* (Golden Age Publishing, 2022).

Lacey Baldwin Smith, *Henry VIII: The Mask of Royalty* (Amberley, 2012).

Nicola Tallis, *All The Queen's Jewels 1445-1548: Power, Majesty and Display* (Routledge, 2023).

Alison Weir, *The Six Wives of Henry VIII* (Penguin Random House, 1991).

Alison Weir, *Henry VIII: King and Court* (Vintage, 2001).

Tudor Sources

There are a range of sources of evidence for events at the Tudor court. There are the chronicles written by Polydore Vergil, Edmund Hall, Raphael Holinshed, Thomas Wriothesley and the wonderfully gossipy anonymous Spanish Chronicle. There are the biographies of Cardinal Wolsey by his servant George Cavendish, Sir Thomas More by his son-in-law William Roper and Archbishop Cranmer by his secretary Ralph Morice. There are also two biographies of Queen Anne Boleyn which were written by her chaplain, William Latymer and George Wyatt, the grandson of the poet Thomas Wyatt. John Foxe's Book of Martyrs (1563) is highly complementary about the early Protestant reformers including Queen Anne Boleyn, Thomas Cromwell and Queen Catherine Parr. There is the revealing correspondence of the ambassadors of Spain, France and Venice to their masters which combines their first-hand experience with the reports of well-placed informants at the Tudor court.

Most notable is the correspondence of Eustace Chapuys to Charles V, the doughty supporter of Queen Catherine of Aragon and Princess Mary. His letters can be read in the order of their date in the Letters and Papers of Henry VIII on British History Online. Chapuys had a number of informants at court including Elizabeth Stafford, Duchess of Norfolk; Gertrude Courtenay, Marchioness of Exeter and Sir Nicholas Carew, Master of the Horse. The Letters and Papers of Henry VIII also include fascinating details about the itineraries (or giests) of the summer progresses of the king and his court in England (1511, 1519, 1526, 1528, 1535, 1541) and the surviving New Year's Day gift rolls (1528, 1532, 1534, 1539). In addition, there are the Privy Purse Expenses of Henry VIII (1529-1532), the Last Will and Testament of Henry VIII (1546) and the Inventory of Henry VIII (1547). There are also the love-letters of Henry to Anne Boleyn, the letters of the widowed Mary Carey and Jane Rochford to Thomas Cromwell, and the Lisle letters between Lady Lisle and her factor John Husee which reveal the culture of gift-giving among the Tudor elite. There is also the courtly poetry of Henry VIII, Sir Thomas Wyatt and Henry Howard, Earl of Surrey.

To understand how Tudor courtiers thought and behaved it is useful to consult *The Book of Three Virtues* by Christian de Pisan (1405), *Letters To My Daughter* by Anne de Beaujeu (1505), *The Book of the Courtier* by Baldassare Castiglione (1528) and *The Prince* by Niccolo Machievelli (1531). The children of Henry VIII were educated to read and translate the moral precepts of the Greek and Roman philosophers Plato, Cicero and Seneca.

Christian de Pisan offers the following moral advice to married ladies on how to show loyalty to one's husband: *"No greater honour can be said of a lady than she is true and loyal to her husband ... She will love not only the relatives of her husband but also those whom she knows that he loves ... If a husband strays into a love affair she must pretend that she does not notice it and does not know anything about it. You must live and die with him whatever he is like."*

Queen Catherine of Aragon's famous speech to Henry VIII at Blackfriars on 21st June 1529 is a fascinating summary of this advice: *"I take God and all the world to witness, that I have been to you a true and humble wife, ever conformable to your will and pleasure, that never said or did anything to the contrary thereof, being always well pleased and contented with all things wherein ye had any delight or dalliance, whether it were in little or much, I never grudged in word or countenance, or showed a visage or spark of discontentation. I loved all those whom ye loved only for your sake, whether I had cause or no; and whether they were my friends or my enemies."*

Similarly, Christian de Pisan offers the following advice to ladies on how to protect their reputations at court: *"We say to respectable women that they must not be too flirtatious and that no good can come of using unchecked language and receiving too many men friends ... It is not at all seemly for her to speak or confer privately with men and they should never be in her chamber. For such things can cause her character to be besmirched and fall into disrepute."*

Ambassador Chapuys reported the case against Queen Anne Boleyn to Charles

V on 19th May 1536: "*What she was principally charged with was having cohabited with her brother and other accomplices; that there was a promise between her and Norris to marry after the king's death, which it thus appeared they hoped for; and that she had received and given to Norris certain medals … She confessed she had given money to Weston, as she had often done to other young gentlemen. Her brother was charged with having cohabited with her by presumption, because he had once been found a long time with her, and with certain other little follies. She was also charged, and her brother likewise, with having laughed at the king and his dress, and that she showed in various ways she did not love the king, but was tired of him. I must not omit that among other things charged against him as a crime was, that his sister had told his wife that the king was impotent. He was likewise charged with having spread the rumour or expressed a doubt as to Anne's daughter (Elizabeth) being the Kings.*"

Ambassador Chapuys also reported that Cromwell had admitted to him that he was responsible for the downfall of Queen Anne Boleyn: *"He, himself had been authorised and commissioned by the King to prosecute and bring to an end the mistress's trial, to do which he had taken considerable trouble. It was he who, in consequence of the disappointment and anger he had felt on hearing the King's answer to me on the third day of Easter, had planned and brought about the whole affair."* (Calendar of State Papers Spain, June 1536 no. 61)

Alexander Alesius wrote a letter to Elizabeth I about her mother in September 1559: "*These spies [Cromwell and Wriothesley], (because they greatly feared the Queen) watch her private apartments [cubiculum] night and day. They tempt her porter and serving man with bribes; there is nothing which they do not promise the ladies of her bedchamber.… Not long after this the persons returned who had been charged with the investigation of the rumours which had been circulated, everything having been arranged according to their entire satisfaction. They assure the King that the affair is beyond doubt; that they had seen the Queen dancing with the gentlemen of the King's chamber, that they can produce witnesses who will vouch to the Queen having kissed her own brother, and that they have in their possession letters in which she informs him that she is pregnant. Thereupon it was decided and concluded that the Queen was an adulteress, and deserved to be burnt alive.*"

Printed in Great Britain
by Amazon